Red Like Wine

Red Like Wine

The North Fork Harbor
Vineyard Murders

Joseph Finora

Rev. date: 03/21/2014

To order additional copies of this book, contact:
Xlibris LLC
1-888-795-4274
www.Xlibris.com
Orders@Xlibris.com
601108

ACKNOWLEDGEMENTS

Writers are trained to be brief. Generally this is a good thing but in some cases length is warranted. This is one of those cases.

Most books rarely represent the labors of one individual. This is no exception. There are many people to thank. The fertile North Fork wine community allowed my imagination to thrive like a merlot vine in the sun. Friends like Ellen and Henry Santacroce, Bev Wowak, and Mary and Al Krupski expressed ongoing enthusiasm and encouragement for the project from the first time I shared the idea for it with them. My writer-editor friends Richard Koreto, Ted Hoyt, Georgeann Packard and Troy Gustavson helped to keep the dream alive with their professional criticisms combined with generous servings of support.

My three children, Joseph, James and Gabrielle, are a steady source of inspiration. They regularly asked: "Dad, how's the book coming?" Their persistence helped me to keep my focus on the finish line. It is Gabrielle in fact, who deserves full credit for the title. They're great kids and I could not imagine my life without them.

There is one more person whose presence, if omitted here would be a great error. Some time ago I met a beautiful young woman at a college pub. For some unknown reason it was not long before I confessed to her my desire to write, a feeling I did not widely share at the time. Her immediate response was one of excitement and enthusiasm, a feeling which she has never stopped sharing.

Some time later I began to unravel the mysterious relationship between muse and writer. For some 30 years after that accidental yet fateful encounter, Mary Grace has steadily provided the support, imagination, enthusiasm, sense of humor and unvarnished criticism that impulsive, creative types like myself need in order to thrive. Unlike the mystery you now hold in your hands, our story is still being written. While we are far from the final chapter, with the characters involved I'm sure it will have a happy ending.

This book is for her.

CHAPTER 1

The Whine List

"Stop ringing. Please stop," pleaded Vin Gusto as he rolled over in his bed to reach for the telephone. "This better be good." It was 7:15 a.m. on a Tuesday.

"Hello," Vin hoarsely said into the receiver.

"Is that you Vin?"

"I think so."

"It's Patricia."

He paused as he tried to think of who Patricia might be. Vin hated when people he barely knew called without warning and acted like he should instantly recognize their voice and be ready to talk.

"Patricia Goode, now with Travel & Pleasure magazine." Vin's eyes began to open.

"Oh, hi Patricia. You caught me off guard. I'm on a deadline. You know how that is. I was so . . . focused." Vin rubbed his forehead to encourage blood circulation to his brain in an attempt to quickly become more alert while rising from the bed.

"You sound a little out of it. Been out late again?"

"No, just in the zone. Go ahead. I'm listening now."

"I've just come from the gym. I'm on my way to the office and calling on sort of an emergency. I'm in a bit of a bind and thought you know, since the layoffs, you might be available. Our writer who regularly covers these things suddenly became inaccessible, detained writing a story in Romania I think and the schedule's creeping up on us very quickly. We've really got to move."

Just then an envelope was pushed under the door of his studio. It was the second notice for that month's rent.

"No problem," he said, smelling an assignment. "Whatever it is I can handle it."

Vin needed the meal ticket but didn't want Patricia to know he was hungry. Assignments had been few and far between since The New York Tattler layoffs, where he had worked for four years and nine months—just three months short of vesting for retirement when the paper had been taken over by international media giant SNN. Known in journalism circles as the "Stingy News Network," Vin, along with numerous other writers, editors, illustrators, photographers, receptionists, accountants, managers, administrators, messengers and mailroom clerks was unceremoniously "let go," his career at the paper he loved suddenly derailed by someone he'd never met, who'd flown in from the "new home office" specifically to give employees the bad news on an otherwise pleasant Friday afternoon.

"It's not so bad," Vin recalled the hatchet man telling him.

"I grew up with this paper," he said. "Every morning it was on my kitchen table."

"It still can be. In times like these we need our loyal readers more than ever."

Vin looked straight at him.

"You're young. You're talented," he continued.

"Then why are you eliminating my job?" Vin asked.

"You reporters never stop asking questions? It must be something in your DNA. It's not me. It's the company. I'm not doing anything. I'm just the messenger, one of the good guys. Not in the plans of the higher-ups, unfortunately for you. Company's consolidating. You'll be back on your feet in no time," he said with a smile while handing Vin his last Tattler paycheck plus a thick envelope explaining benefits but not before he signed a waiver promising not to sue the company, discuss his job in public or disclose any "trade secrets" or other information that may prove damaging or detrimental to his former employer.

"What about my retirement?"

"You've got a long time to go before you need to worry about that."

"How about my rent? I don't have too long for that."

"Let's not panic. Anyway, to your first question, according to what I have here you're three months shy of qualifying for retirement. I wouldn't worry about the health coverage either. You appear to be healthy enough. Being a reporter's not a high-risk occupation. It's not like you're laying subway track or digging tunnels. Sorry."

Vin stared into the stranger's cold, shallow brown eyes and studied his facade of a smile. The last two comments proved he knew very little about the realities of the job he was helping to eliminate. But that wasn't his responsibility. His job was to deliver the bad news and alert company personnel to anyone exhibiting signs of potentially dangerous or threatening behavior.

"There's a professional counselor waiting for you in the next office," he continued. "I urge you to visit with her and seriously look into the services the company's offering for those of you being dismissed. The company's paying the bill for a limited time. It's a very good offer. I've heard the service can be very helpful for those in your situation."

"I don't need counseling," Vin said, rising from the chair. "I need a paycheck," he said, slamming the door on his way out before going straight to his now former cubicle. Once there a security guard watched over him and a few others as they quietly cleared their desks, loaded personal things into company-supplied shopping bags and were then escorted to the building lobby where their belongings were searched by another security guard before their ID badges were taken from them for the last time.

Vin hadn't found another staff job and it had taken some time for him to adjust to life as a fulltime freelance writer/reporter. He learned to survive through erratic assignments, unpredictable editors and pay that was not what he'd been earning at the paper. He also lost his other benefits like the health and retirement plans as part of the layoff. Vin's savings were rapidly being depleted despite the fact that he was doing his best to delay the slide. Plus there was the regular rejection that comes with most job searches. Vin could survive but he could not thrive. Patricia's call was a welcome one, whether he wanted her to know it or not.

"What do you know about the North Fork of Long Island?" Patricia asked.

"Plenty," he lied. "Often summered there as a child."

"I know you're used to writing the hard stuff, crime news and all that, but we need a 'puff piece,' on the North Fork, quaint farm stands, cozy inns, friendly locals fishing on the docks. And we need it by the end of next week. Eleven days from today to be exact. About five thousand words plus photos. Can you change gears and write a happy piece?"

Vin's mind was starting to percolate. He did know something about the North Fork. Shanin Blanc, a photographer he worked with at The Tattler and with whom he had more than a professional relationship had moved there before the layoffs to take a job with a local newspaper and possibly to get away from Vin.

"How's freelancing?" Patricia asked.

"Pretty exciting. I'd never go back to a staff job," he again lied.

"Lots of writers try it. Very few can make a go of it."

"It's only been a few months for me," said Vin. "But I think I have the right temperament for it. I've gotten used to the phone ringing in the middle of the night or early in the morning. How's working at Travel & Pleasure? Sounds like it's better suited for you than the paper."

"I love it here. Cappuccino machine down the hall. Fresh flowers in the reception area. I'd take this assignment myself but I don't have much experience with the North Fork. I was mostly on the South Fork, you know summers in the Hamptons, Amagansett, those towns."

Vin knew those towns, he spent one summer helping a friend park cars at a Southampton country club for tips, most of which he used to help repay his City College loan. To minimize expenses he had mostly slept in his car which he discreetly parked behind the club's dumpster.

"We were definitely North Forkers," Vin mused. "Sometimes we'd bring Hildred, our nanny for the entire summer to the beach house. She never could get all of the sand out of the carpet."

"Glad you haven't lost your sense of humor," she cut in.

"Let me check my calendar. The chauffeur's just about to bring the car round front," he said buying time. He didn't want Patricia to think he was desperate for work. "Can I put you on hold for a minute?" Vin's phone did not have a "hold" button. He slipped it under a pillow before she could answer.

Vin checked his schedule for the week. He had a few small assignments but nothing approaching the payday Patricia would offer. There was a pet store specializing in snakes to profile for a trade magazine, a few hard-sell postcards to write for the local car dealer and a technical manual to edit for a software company—just another week in the life of a freelance writer. The three of them would probably cover his rent for the month but a week on eastern Long Island was something he could certainly use. It had been a while since he'd been able to get out of the city. He'd push the other assignments aside to visit wineries and restaurants, maybe squeeze in a fishing trip. He wondered if Shanin would come back on assignment with him. It had been some time since he'd spoken with her. They had a rocky break-up. Would she want to work with him again? Would she talk to him? Maybe like him, she was struggling a bit.

"Hello, hello. Are you there?" It was Patricia's voice vibrating from under the pillow. Her tone of urgency had returned and he decided to roll the dice.

"You landed on your feet pretty quickly after the layoffs," Vin remarked, buying a bit more time as he continued thinking up his negotiating strategy.

"Yeah, got lucky I guess."

Vin had heard that Patricia was part of an "old money" New England family with an interest in the Travel & Pleasure Publishing company. It was frequently part of office gossip that an uncle, a well-known industrialist with a seat on the Travel & Pleasure board "found" the opening just when the Tattler was trimming staff. Otherwise, he was certain, she'd be scrambling for assignments like he was. But now was not the time for the hardscrabble boy from the Bronx to show resentment.

"I'll blow off my other editors. I'll make you top priority but . . ." he stopped
"But what?"

"You haven't said what you'd pay me."

"I can go as high as $2,500 but nothing more, including travel expenses."

"Patricia, you made me think you were serious."

"I am."

"That's less than 50 cents a word once you include travel . . . and my time. Sorry, I can't blow off other good-paying assignments and deliver in a little over a week for that kind of money. Make it $5,000 plus travel and use my photographer."

"You've got a photog out there? That may speed things up a bit. Can you send me some samples of his work?"

"Her work," Vin corrected. "And no, I can't send samples. It's about 7:30 on a Tuesday morning. You want a reporter, photo samples and an award-winning story in a little better than a week. That's a bit demanding even for Travel & Pleasure, don't you think?"

There was a pause. Vin wondered if he had pushed Patricia too far. It was now up to her to decide whether the negotiations would move forward.

"Look Vin, if you're too busy I can look for someone else. It's just that I know you're good and was hoping you'd be able to jump right in and help. You never know, if this works out it could lead to future assignments. But if you're too busy . . .

"I didn't say that. I'm happy to help. I just want to be treated fairly." He'd heard the promise of "future assignments" from anxious editors more times than he cared to remember.

"We treat you like family."

"That's what they used to say at The Tattler too. When can you send my advance to cover expenses?"

"We've got a room booked at The Crashing Seagull Inn. I'll overnight you a check. Shouldn't be a problem cashing or depositing it there."

"You're overnighting a check to an inn? I've got to be there tomorrow?"

"Yes, there's a big up-and-coming winemaker or grape grower, a Dr. Frank Lamborghini or something. He's a bit of a recluse but close to being very famous in the wine world. We absolutely want him as a major part of the story. You're meeting with him tomorrow morning. It's all set. He's expecting you seven-thirty sharp at the winery. Speaks a few languages, with an accent I imagine. Sounds like a charming, old-school European gentleman. Get everything you can out of him. Like I said, I'm going to have my assistant overnight a package to the hotel with an agenda, contacts, an assignment letter and anything else I can think of for the story in addition to the winemaker interview."

"And don't forget the check," said Vin.

"Yes, of course," said Patricia. "Are you always this apprehensive? And while you've got some time, do a little internet-research on this winemaker before you get out there but I'm sure he'll have plenty to talk about. They're typically a chatty group. He runs the North Fork Harbor Vineyards. The vineyard's name is the same as the town's so it should be easy for you to remember."

"The interview's already set up? At seven-thirty in the morning?!" Vin was not a morning person.

"Grape growers are early risers. Besides, he's leaving the country soon. Going to Argentina or some far-away place to attend a boring agricultural conference. Be gone about three weeks. This is the only time he's available. Now, I'm paying your fee and using your photographer, the least you can do is get there when I need you to do so. If you leave now you can be there in time for lunch. I hear The Crashing Seagull's lobster *fra diavolo* is very good. Besides, you freelancers are supposed to be fast and cheap."

"Fast yes. Cheap no. Not the good ones."

"You're driving right? Because you'll need a car to get around out there."

Vin no longer had a car. To reduce expenses he sold his second-hand Ford Tempo with the dented fender, torn upholstery and missing hubcaps. He thought he'd recently seen his quasi-reliable, four-door sedan transformed into a gypsy cab working the city's rougher neighborhoods.

"No problem," he said.

"Vin, if someone told me there was a room waiting for me at The Crashing Seagull I'd have my bags packed and would be there in no time. Have you seen the pictures of this place?

"I've never even heard of it."

"Absolutely gorgeous. Rolling surf. Colorful boats in the harbor. Lots of pretty girls. I certainly wouldn't be arguing."

"I'm not arguing Patricia. I appreciate you thinking of me. I just want to be sure everything is clear before I take this on. Ever since the paper let me go I've been a little gun shy."

"Forget the paper Vin. It was just a job. Now's time to move forward! I'm putting a letter of assignment in with the overnight. It'll spell out all the terms. Just sign and mail it back."

"Okay. So you're sending me a twenty-five percent advance on a $5,000 story."

"I never said twenty-five percent and I'll only cover reasonable expenses—transportation, basic meals, hotel bill, nothing elaborate."

"If you want a 'happy' piece then the writer's got to be happy too."

"Don't push it," she said. "And you're delivering ten days from now with photos."

"Yes, but you're paying the photographer separately for the photos."

"Okay, but you're sure she'll do a good job."

"Of course. And you'll send the advance?"

"What's her name anyway?"

"You remember Shanin Blanc from the paper. We did the street-gang series together."

"Sure, I know Shanin. I didn't realize you two were still in touch. What's a nice girl like her doing out in the sticks?"

"She got tired of photographing dead bodies."

"If you can get her to shoot orange sunsets over vineyards and children eating ice cream on the docks then she's got herself an assignment. Tell her to call me. You're sure she's available, right?"

"Absolutely. And we want a cover."

"Let's see what you come back with. And don't forget, pictures and story with the winemaker or grape grower or whoever he is or the deal's off."

Vin had no way to get a car and couldn't rent one with his fragile credit status. And it had been some time since he talked to Shanin. He had no idea if she'd be available, if she was still on eastern Long Island or if she'd return his phone call. He'd work out the details later.

"No problem," he said. "Consider it a done deal."

"Why don't you give me her number so I can be sure she's available?"

The only information Vin had on Shanin was the address of the newspaper for which he hoped she was still shooting, The North Fork Harbor Reporter. He had to scramble.

"I'll call you from the road Patricia with that information. It's in my other computer. If you want this masterpiece by your deadline then I've got to get going. The sooner I clear the decks here the sooner I can hit the road and start your story."

"Thanks for taking this on Vin."

"Sure thing."

"And one more thing, when you interview this Dr. Frank, the winemaker dig deep."

"What?"

"Find out what makes him tick. Get inside his head."

"Sure and when I'm back I'll come to the office. We can have lunch."

"Totally. Bring me a few bottles of Long Island wine. I love white zin."

"Let me grab a cup of coffee and I'll get moving."

"Remember what Emerson said about coffee and writers."

Early in the morning Vin had no idea what Emerson or anyone else ever said about nearly anything.

"It's been a while since I've read any Emerson," said Vin. "You'll have to refresh my memory."

"*Talent writes with coffee but genius writes with wine.*"

"I'll keep that in mind Patricia and thanks."

Vin hung up the phone. Nothing would make him sicker than lunch with Patricia but he suggested it because he wanted her to like him. He wanted the job. He wanted more Travel & Pleasure assignments. With its loyal and lucrative subscriber base Travel & Pleasure was one of the few survivors in the incredibly shrinking magazine-publishing industry. But now he had other things to think about—transportation, finding Shanin, maybe even a substitute photographer if he couldn't reach her. This assignment was going to be more challenging than usual and he hadn't even started writing, hardly taken a note. He was barely awake. But he knew how good it would feel when the check arrived. And a few days out of the city would be nice too. But there were questions that needed to be answered—where is The Crashing Sea Gull Inn? How could he get to North Fork Harbor? What did she want the story on, this Dr. Frank or North Fork Harbor? Why was Patricia Goode, who he never recalled working very hard, calling at 7:15 on a Tuesday morning with a rush assignment? And what's "white zin"?

Vin banged the keys on his ancient laptop. He'd found a telephone number to the hotel but no website. It rang for what seemed like an eternity before a gravelly voice answered. The first thing he did was confirm that a reservation had been made in the name of the magazine.

"How do I get out there from, New York City?

"Long Island Expressway, last exit, I think 73 and keep driving east on 25 'til you can't go no more. You'll see our sign."

"I'm not driving. I don't have a car."

"Then why don't you take the train?"

"Which one?"

"There's only one."

"Would you know which one it is?" Vin could feel his blood pressure rising.

"Long Island Rail Road."

"Long Island Rail Road operates hundreds of trains. Could you be more specific?"

"There's only one. If you're comin' from the city, it leaves from Pennsylvania Station."

"All Long Island Rail Road trains leave from Penn Station."

"Then that's what you gotta do. Get over to Pennsylvania Station and get on the train to North Fork Harbor. This ain't no travel agency."

"Thanks," Vin said hanging up the phone. He'd try his luck with the railroad.

Not having enough patience to wait for his dial-up connection, Vin tried the phone. After about 15 minutes of waiting he learned there was just one train per day leaving Penn Station for North Fork Harbor—the 5:41 arriving at 8:40 pm—a three-hour ride with one transfer. Lunch at The Crashing Sea Gull was out for today. He then brought up the website for The North Fork Harbor Reporter, searching for Shanin's name. He found it in the archives from about three months back on a photo credit. It was a shot of a child in a swimsuit standing next to a large beach ball. The caption beneath it read: *Having a Ball at the Beach.* He could barely make the small photo credit out on the grainy computer screen. She'd come a long way from photographing gang victims for the crime page—about as far away as any photographer could get. Was she happy taking shots of smiling children on a beach? Patricia wanted photos of "people with happy faces, colorful boats in the harbor," plus 5,000 words in about a week. It looked like Shanin would know how to deliver. Now if he could just deliver Shanin.

He wondered if Shanin missed the action of city reporting—the confusion, police officers keeping onlookers away, the bands of yellow tape isolating crime scenes, the cool-headedness of the emergency-medical workers, the rush to meet the morning-edition deadline. As he began packing he realized that in a short while he might find out. Vin began packing faster—laptop, note pad, pens, socks, toothbrush, shave cream, razor, a few spare shirts, his old swimsuit (he hoped it still fit) and he was ready. And just in case Shanin was not available—his camera—an ancient 35 millimeter with autofocus, one lens, a few old rolls of film and a weak flash—each of which he'd inherited from his father with the exception of the film. In the digital age it had become a relic but it would work in a pinch as it had many times for him when assignments offered no budget for a photographer. Besides the three spotted bananas he had on the kitchen counter, which went into the same worn duffle bag, there was no other food to worry about spoiling. It was going to be a long ride. He downed some leftover coffee that was on the counter from yesterday, still in its light blue take-out paper cup decorated in classic white Greek lettering. He had about $45 in his pocket. That would have to hold him until he could cash the advance Patricia had promised which he expected to be about $1,000. In the corner of his apartment was a stack of old journalism textbooks he salvaged from the basement of his mother's house to sell at a secondhand bookstore for extra cash. There was a concept he thought, "extra cash." He had never had extra cash in his life. Maybe this new assignment was a sign that his finances and career were about to improve.

Vin then phoned his mother to tell her about his sudden job and to ask her to pick up his mail—he was, as always, expecting a check. Gloria lived only a few blocks from him, still in the same, small house in which Vin was raised. She had a key to his tight, third-floor walk-up. He'd gotten her answering machine. Gloria did not use e-mail. She did not own or care to learn about computers and felt the same way about cellular telephones. Fortunately, she was able to operate a basic telephone-answering machine. But Tuesday was her "Bridge day" and she couldn't be disturbed as she prepared for the arrival of her card-game partners. Knowing his mother most likely wouldn't get his trip particulars straight over the phone, he left her only a brief message that he'd be away for a few days on a sudden assignment. On his subway ride to Penn Station however, he'd write a detailed note including where he'd be staying, how he'd be traveling, when he was due back and for whom he was writing and mail it to her. This was a habit he developed from his days covering gangs and other inhabitants of the city's underside—always leave a trail. In the case of an emergency it was sometimes his only form of insurance and one which had helped him in the past. He usually kept a few stamps in his wallet. But he had to hurry. He didn't want to miss the day's only train to North Fork Harbor.

CHAPTER 2

Heading to the Harbor

After packing ever-so-lightly Vin briefly searched one more time on the internet for anything he could find on North Fork Harbor winemakers and finally stumbled upon a few useful words about Dr. Frank Lambrusco. While there was a lot of information on his winery there was actually very little on the man himself but enough to whet Vin's appetite. Vin uncovered that Dr. Frank had been a leading botanical researcher specializing in plant genetics with a major agricultural corporation but left his position several years ago to pursue winemaking, his "passion" according to an obscure wine-industry website. But several other searches had turned up scraps of information about Dr. Frank working on a new strain of grape—a so-called "super grape" one that was designed to be resistant to many diseases as well as drought and temperature extremes—scourges which could ravage an entire crop and subsequently an agricultural community. While the fruit from the new vines could be used to make a decent wine he learned, more importantly, it could serve as a food crop in "agriculturally challenged" areas, especially those in arid climates where raising any fruit on a large scale was nearly impossible. If this new strain showed such promise why was it given minimal attention by the press? Perhaps the wine establishment doubted its potential thought Vin.

While others were critical of the potential of this discovery, "pioneer vines" had been secretly and successfully planted in Central America and North Africa, according to a few scattered news reports but nothing more in-depth was available. Vin hunched that the international agricultural community was quietly starting to pay attention. In one photo Dr. Frank was holding a monstrous bunch of grapes said to have been produced from his experimental vines. But there was a hitch. It was noted in another obscure industry report that he would only reveal the formula to companies that "pledged to share his vision." As part of any commercial negotiation, Dr. Frank would insist that for every vine purchased, another would be donated to the international charity Farmers Without Fences, to help those in developing countries grow more food and cultivate a commercial crop. So far no company had come forward to accept the deal, most saying they wanted to wait for more results before committing. Vin theorized that the upcoming trip to the agricultural summit might turn out to be a turning point in Dr. Frank's career. But how did Patricia find out about him? Why would a travel magazine editor be interested in an agricultural scientist dabbling in genetic engineering? Why wasn't more media on to this? Maybe he'd find out the next morning.

Vin took the Number Two subway train directly through the South Bronx, underneath West Harlem, the upper West Side, Midtown Manhattan and ultimately into New York's massive Pennsylvania Station. He immediately bought a round-trip ticket while he still had enough cash to do so and sauntered to one of the newsstands as he waited for the North Fork Harbor train announcement. Regularly visiting newsstands had become a habit of his since he became a fulltime freelance writer as he needed to develop new markets in which to sell articles. He'd once read in a writers' magazine about the value of selling the same article, maybe slightly altered, to different news outlets. This was a trick he had yet to master but estimated that maybe more than one publication would be interested in a story on Dr. Frank. Or maybe another travel magazine would want something on eastern Long Island. Patricia said nothing about exclusivity in their conversation although that might be coming in the agreement she promised to send.

Vin looked at a few covers but decided not to make any purchases—save some money and try to remember the other titles after Patricia's advance arrived. Then a new publication had caught his eye. Travelzonia promised an "avant-garde" look at the world of travel. Vin thought it might also promise a new outlet for articles so he bought a copy for "train reading." He then proceeded to the Penn Station ticket-holders waiting room, also a good spot to find reading material as passengers often left behind near-pristine copies of newspapers once their trains were announced. Vin found a seat in a not-too repulsive area and sat on the hard bench. Knowing there'd be lots of time during the long ride east made it difficult for him to concentrate on his new assignment. He spent his time thumbing through Travelzonia and looking up from his seat when train departures were announced to see if he could score a newspaper when he thought he heard a female voice talking to him.

"How do you like that magazine?" she asked.

"Me?" he asked, caught off guard. "Yeah, it's nice. Actually, I just started with it. I haven't read much. Do you know it?"

"It's mine."

"It can't be. I just bought it at the newsstand. I have the receipt."

"I mean I'm its editor," she said with a smile.

"Then you must like it. Nice job," Vin said flipping pages between his thumb and forefinger. "Very professional. I'm Vin Gusto." He stood to shake her hand.

"I'm Nadia Rivera . . . editor."

"I'm a freelance writer . . . formerly with the Tattler." Vin had heard of Nadia. She had a reputation of being tough on reporters but didn't look so at the moment in her cream-colored pants, striped shirt and oversized straw sunhat.

Nadia had short-cropped dark hair brushed back over her forehead, minimal make-up and a bright blue necklace with matching bracelet and earrings. She could have easily been covering fashion instead of travel. Nadia exuded confidence which also had the effect of making Vin feel self-conscious about his own appearance, to which until then he had barely given any thought. Was he dressing the part of someone down on his luck? Probably. Would it turn Shanin away if he got the chance to see her again? He didn't want to think about that.

"Too bad about the Tattler cuts."

Vin nodded.

"Are you on assignment now?" she asked.

"Yes. Going to North Fork Harbor."

"Nothing's happened in North Fork Harbor for about 200 years. I didn't think the train still ran there."

"Once a day," Vin said trying to smile but still feeling uncomfortable. "Heard there's been a big revival at the hotel, The Crashing Sea Gull or something. I'm looking forward to checking it out."

"Weren't you the 'City Streets' reporter at the Tattler? The guy who they said had blood on his copy?"

"Yeah that was me," Vin said with a smile.

"Thought you'd be off to some war zone or mobster shootout scene, not some soft hotel story," Nadia said with a bright smile of her own.

"It's good to change gears once in a while," said Vin. "You never know, something may actually happen while I'm there."

"I hope something does," she said, her smile vanishing. "If you're going all the way there to write a review of the revived hotel in that sleepy town I'll bet it will be one of your dullest assignments."

"Right now 'dull' doesn't sound so bad. I'll find something to write about," Vin offered. While his hardnosed reporter's instincts began to sting in response to Nadia's comments Vin did not offer anything on the winery.

"Well, you never know," she said. Just then the 4:15 to Westhampton was announced. "That's my train," she said.

"I heard the lobster's very good at the hotel. I'm looking forward to it," Vin said.

"Who told you that?"

"It's just something I've heard."

"Let me know about the lobster and the hotel too. Maybe there has been a revival there. I'll be in Westhampton Beach for a few days, about an hour's drive from where you're staying," said Nadia who smiled as if she knew something that Vin didn't. She then looked up at the schedule board to check her departure track.

"Gotta run. Who are you writing for?" asked Nadia, reaching into her bag.

"Travel & Pleasure, Pat Goode."

"That explains it," she said with a grin.

"Explains what?"

"Pat's a vegan. How would she know about lobster?"

Vin looked at Nadia.

"If anything happens call me on my cell phone. It's on the card," she said. "Good meeting you and good luck with the story. I mean it," Nadia said, firmly putting her card into Vin's hand. He quickly shook her hand a second time and said good-bye. Nadia then turned and in a few seconds disappeared into the seemingly endless sea of commuters.

Was Nadia serious when she said to call her should something happen in North Fork Harbor? Could anything worth calling about happen there? Vin retuned to his seat and thought about the look in Nadia's eye as he tapped the sharp edge of her card into his shirt pocket. How could she have known that Pat was a vegan? Vin didn't know that. On the seat she left her copy of that day's New York Tattler. He flipped through it while eating his first banana. It would be a few more minutes before the train to North Fork Harbor would be announced.

He checked the Police Blotter page to see what had washed up from the city's notorious underside. There were a couple of unrelated shootings scattered across the boroughs and one non-fatal stabbing. He didn't recognize the names of any of the victims and there were no photos of them but he was familiar with each of the hospitals. In one case he knew the arresting officer. No one's going to work too hard to solve these crimes thought Vin. It was generally only the truly outrageous crimes—those concerning a public figure or some ultra-violent and morally reprehensible act that made it to the front pages of the paper. These were the ones that were outrageous enough to be considered "real news" and were frequently accompanied by gruesome photographs of the victim or grieving relatives. Vin often felt that the sheer publicity level of these crimes put pressure on the police force to try to solve them. But at that point, Vin suddenly wasn't sure if he missed covering the crime beat. Maybe it was the prospect of breathing in the fresh sea air outside The Crashing Sea Gull while sipping a glass of locally pressed wine as the sun set over the bay or maybe it was something else.

Vin's thoughts then drifted to memories of Shanin. He hurried back to the newsstand and bought a phone card to call her. He no longer had a cell phone. His previous one had belonged to the Tattler and service had been stopped within 24 hours after he'd been laid off. He never got a new one—another expense he had to put on hold. His apartment phone and secondhand answering machine he got from his mother had been able to handle the low volume of calls he'd been getting.

He dialed the number at the newspaper where he hoped she was still working.

"North Fork Harbor Reporter," a receptionist answered.

"Shanin Blanc please."

"May I ask who's calling?"

"Vin Gusto."

"May I ask what this is in reference to?"

Vin hated stonewalling receptionists. Why did they have to ask so many questions? They're not the reporters.

"Personal call," he blurted.

"I'm sorry, Shanin's not in the office. Would you like to leave a message?"

Vin again felt his pressure rising. Couldn't she have told him that before? Why ask who was calling and what you wanted before saying that the person you needed to speak with was not in the office?

"Sure," he said, trying to sound calm but realizing he had no phone number to leave.

"Can you tell me when she'll be back?"

"I don't really know. She's one of our stringers. They keep irregular hours but we do take messages for her."

"Do you have her home or cell phone number?"

"Not allowed to give that out."

"Does she have a voice mailbox there?"

"You're talking to it." Just then he heard his train being announced.

"I'm about to leave for a train," he shouted into the receiver. "Can you please ask her to call Vin Gusto tomorrow? I'll be at The Crashing Sea Gull in North Fork Harbor."

"Very good. Have a nice day."

"Vin Gusto, Crashing Sea Gull," he repeated before hanging up the phone and hurrying to get in step as best he could with the hordes of commuters heading to "points East" on the 5:41, all the while wondering if the receptionist actually took his message. Not dressed in a shirt and tie—the commuter's uniform—Vin felt out of place but no one seemed to notice. On board he got a tight window seat next to a tired-looking middle-aged man who quickly opened a beer can he removed from his briefcase and then passed out with The Wall Street Journal unopened across his lap, splashes of beer blurring the front page.

Vin was never very good at sleeping on trains and spent most of the time looking out the window. He thought about whether he'd be able to revitalize his career with this assignment or should he try to find a nondescript office job like some of the people around him had. Right now he had no benefits, no health insurance or retirement plan. There was no regular paycheck or girlfriend any longer—nor was there a prospect for either. Was he happier now then when he was a staff reporter? The list of negatives had grown long. While he was scraping for assignments every day he was his own boss. Things would get better he told himself, especially if Shanin called him but even if she didn't he was now a man on a new mission. And he liked his odds.

In between writing the note to his mother, Vin would glance out the train window, watching how the landscape changed from ultra-urban in Manhattan and

Jamaica, Queens to the suburbs of Nassau and western Suffolk counties. Things got more and more spread out the further east the train plodded. Shopping malls, office buildings and housing developments were placed further apart. High-rise apartments and gray commercial buildings gave way to ranch-style homes with swing sets in the yards and bicycles on neat lawns. He saw children playing on soccer fields and moms talking on the sidelines as gray yielded to green in greater scale. Eventually, the train lunged into Ronkonkoma Station, the line's last suburban rail stop. As seemingly thousands of commuters scurried from the train platform to the nearly endless parking lot, Vin made his connection to the North Fork Scoot. A relatively new, double-decker train with wide, comfortable seats and bright lights, Vin settled in with a handful of other travelers—none of whom looked like members of the nine-to-five Manhattan crowd and continued heading east.

According to the schedule he had about 90 more minutes of travel time before reaching North Fork Harbor. He saw his first farm as he handed his ticket to the conductor. Horse farms and vineyards began appearing on the landscape in greater numbers. He watched a flock of geese in V-pattern disappear on the horizon and then saw men in baseball caps and flannel shirts drinking beer from cans while leaning on the hood of a pick-up truck. He looked at his own hands, soft and clean from desk work. He tried to imagine what a rugged life would be like—how it was making a living with your back and hands as opposed to a pounding a keyboard, waiting for the telephone to ring, racing to meet a deadline. His schedule was set by the clock, not the calendar. What was the farmer's deadline? When the sun gave way to the moon? When seed had to be sewn into the earth or when Mother Nature signaled that crops had to be harvested?

As darkness descended he thought he saw a few deer dart into the woods as the train continued its eastward lurch. North Fork Harbor was the last stop on the line. Since there was no chance of missing it, Vin tried taking a nap. He let his pen fall onto his note pad as his thoughts drifted to that day's events. Was there more to Pat's sudden and stringent demands? Why was it so urgent to interview Dr. Lambrusco? Why did she call him? And what about Nadia's comments in the train station? Was any of this important? He'd do his job, collect his check and then hope for future assignments he told himself, trying to relax on the long train ride east. Once again his anxieties began drifting from his mind as he realized there was the possibility that he might soon see Shanin for the first time since their break-up. Had she gotten his message? Would she return the call? Agree to meet him? Was it really over? Or was Pat Goode right? Maybe it was time to forget the paper and everything associated with it and "move forward"—whatever that meant.

CHAPTER 3

Meet the Night Crawlers

When Shanin Blanc was done taking a set of industrial-grade photographs for Simkowitz & Sons Undersea Salvage Company she phoned The North Fork Harbor Reporter office to see if there were any assignments waiting for her. She'd never received a fulltime job from the paper and had been working for it strictly as a freelance photographer on an "as needed" basis. During the rest of the time Shanin did her best to find work as a photographer in the erratic economy of Long Island's East End. As part of her "deal" with the paper, she received a free classified ad marketing her photography services—occasionally it brought her a phone call. In between assignments she often found work as baby sitter and mother's helper. Each call came from a classified ad in The North Fork Harbor Reporter.

The undersea-salvage company needed its new equipment photographed for an ad that was to appear in a trade magazine and of course it was on a tight budget. Shanin understood and spent the day shooting dredges, pumps and cranes from every conceivable angle as if she had been doing so her entire life and when done wondered from where her next job would come. This had become standard procedure after cutting her ties in New York and making a one-way move to Long Island's North Fork, a place she had actually spent summers as a child. Had she taken a step back in her career with her move or was this merely a detour? She was becoming increasingly concerned it was the former and when, between assignments, almost steadily wondered how a once promising biology student wound up spending her days as a country photographer. When would her career take a positive turn? Relocating to North Fork Harbor had removed her from the pressure of working for a big-city daily but at the same time severely limited her career options. As she looked out across sparkling Peconic Bay, the sun's last rays of the day glimmering on the horizon, she wondered from where her next opportunity might come.

Not only was her career at a standstill but she was seriously out of circulation. Shanin's social life had also taken a turn for the worse by moving to the "Far East," as she liked to call it. A single girl in a city has nearly endless choices on the social scene but in farm country suitable entertainment was hard to find. What few bars and restaurants there were often had parking lots full of pick-up trucks, especially on NASCAR race nights. Shanin never succeeded in getting her social life percolating on the North Fork. As she didn't spend her days in the office and mostly worked solo she was beginning to wonder if she had fooled herself with the romance of living alone in a place she had previously only spent childhood summers. While she still carried warm memories of North Fork Harbor summers, in this chapter of her life she'd not met one person she considered a close friend. She usually spent nights working on her photo portfolio or scouring help-wanted ads on the internet for photography assignments. In the absence of new friends she regularly felt the urge to be with someone who knew her from the "old days."

Shanin's father had been a successful sales representative for an international chemical company. He had been with the same firm for nearly his entire career, rising to the rank of vice president for global sales. And while her father spent much of the year traveling for business, each summer until she was 16, her family vacationed at the same beach house on the shores of fabled Peconic Bay. When her parents divorced, the summers at the beach house also ended but the memories for Shanin never did. It was the time she spent on the beaches that fostered her love for science and photography. It was her father who pointed out things like the sand-colored grasshoppers that jumped ahead of them when they explored the dunes or how the moon helped to direct the tides. Long afternoons at the beach gave way to bright orange sunsets. The earlier the sun set the sooner she knew they'd be leaving to return to their private school in a leafy New York City suburb. As a teenager she began taking pictures of her father and older brother Eric on the small sailboat they'd sometimes rent. On each excursion, as if it were the first time they'd sailed together, her father would explain to Shanin and her only sibling, how the rudder "steered" the boat through the currents and how to manipulate the sail to "catch" the wind. Occasionally she'd operate the tiller, her father always close by. The bright sun at the beach helped to fill her photos with color as the family's smiling faces created the memories she captured on film and would take with her into adulthood.

One afternoon Shanin had actually tried to find the beach house she and her family used to rent. After spending nearly an afternoon driving east and west along Peconic Bay Blvd., she thought she found the spot. The house was gone. In its place was a tidy row of nearly identical beachfront condominiums. She got out, removed her shoes and walked along the cool white sand while staring across the sparkling bay. It was impossible to recapture the feeling of what now seemed like a magic childhood but it was still good to feel the sand beneath her bare feet—a confirmation of her fading memories.

At college Shanin joined the school newspaper as a photographer and occasional writer. She photographed nearly everything and anything about campus life, from sideline shots at football games to professors giving lectures. But while she was in the protective cocoon of college, life outside the university walls changed. During her sophomore year her father suddenly suffered a heart attack in his office and died in the ambulance on the way to the hospital. A little more than a year later her brother had married and shortly after that her mother announced that a new man had entered her life.

"I've moved on," her mother told her by telephone one night from the new one-bedroom apartment she now shared in Los Angeles. "It's time you do the same."

The camaraderie on the campus helped fill the void that was created by the new stage her family had entered. While her family had previously operated as a unit, now each member, for better or worse, went in a separate direction. After graduation it was time for a new beginning. While teaching science in the inner city had at first seemed promising, after two years she was certain it was not how she wanted to spend the rest of her career. Good science, like photography, was deliberate and depended on commitment, focus and dedication. Her personality was not suited to the often unpredictable demands of the classroom but as she had used most of the money she received from her share of her father's life insurance policy to pay her college costs the need for a steady job was imminent.

Fortunately, the same combination of precision and patience that attracted Shanin to science also made her a good photographer. She could capture the smile of a child holding a pumpkin as easily as she could a sailboat tacking around a buoy. She had a "fast eye" as they would later say in the newsroom and instinctively knew how to "score a shot." Once she decided to leave teaching, Shanin began sending resumes with copies of her work to editors at different publications and New York City-based news agencies but got no return calls. Then one day she saw the byline of a former college professor in a local magazine. She called him. They met for coffee late one afternoon and Shanin told him of her desire to work as a photographer for a big-city newspaper. He sent copies of her work with a short note to Charlie Stine, the Tattler's photo editor and another of his former students. About one month later Stine invited Shanin to an "introductory meeting." A few weeks after that Shanin started her new career as a photographer in The New York Tattler's features department.

"Handling the lens is enough to worry about," Stine told her in no uncertain terms when she also expressed an interest in writing for the Tattler. "Leave the writing to the journalists. You'll earn your pay if you just shoot the pictures and get 'em to me by deadline."

At the Tattler Shanin was first given the "soft" assignments. Similar to what she would later be doing at The North Fork Harbor Reporter, Shanin was usually called when they needed someone to photograph things like children on the first day of school, the mayor's wife at tea or the opening of the dog show. She'd heard newsroom coworkers talking about reporters who kept irregular hours and covered the things that wound up on the "Police Blotter" or "crime page" as the newspaper insiders jokingly called it. Occasionally their stories wound up on the paper's front page. One morning she asked Stine if she could try the overnight shift. "I could bring a new look to the page," she said. What she was really hoping for was a chance to find her way. Teaching science was not for her. She had also grown tired of taking the paper's "happy" photos. Maybe feeling the edge of working the overnight shift, covering New York's underbelly, was the change she needed.

Stine, the managing editor and grizzled veteran of the city's "newspaper wars" laughed when she first made the request to be moved from features to crime. He had the reputation of being a hard drinker who liked to spend time at New York's horse-racing tracks. Stine did little to dispute the reputation. Photographs of famous race horses hung from cheap frames on his office walls and Shanin thought she often detected a hint of bourbon in the air when in his company.

"You're from the dog-and-cat page. Do you have any idea what it's like working nights in this city? It's the worst shift in the business. Do you know what sort of characters you'll come up against? After a few weeks you'll feel like something on the bottom of a shoe," he told her. "The only reason a guy like Gusto does it is because no one else will take it and it's the only way we'll take him." While she'd seen Vin's byline it was the first time she'd heard Stine mention a fellow staff member during one of their discussions and was struck by the seriousness of his expression when he told her.

"You want to know the night crew's standing orders?" he asked. Before she could answer he told her: "Graphic photos. Extra blood. And don't get shot."

Thinking he had pushed Shanin far enough Stine then turned his attention to some files on his desk. After a few seconds he noticed she had not left his office.

"I can shoot blood," Shanin said, not sure of what Stine's reaction would be.

"If we move you to overnight, who's going to shoot the Thanksgiving Day parade?" Stine retorted, trying to hold back a grin. "It's no place for a . . .

"What? A girl like me?" she said, finishing the sentence he did not want to complete.

"It isn't a place for you," Stine said. "It isn't a place for anyone. You can't build a career there. All you'll get is blood on your lens and the nightmares that go with it." He then returned his attention to the files he'd been holding as if to signal that the conversation had ended.

Again there was a pause as Shanin collected her thoughts. Stine had been expecting her to leave his office. She sensed for some reason he was shielding her and at the same time holding her back. Maybe it was because Shanin was overwhelmed by the frustration in her life or was simply too tired of being told what to do she played her last hand with the grizzled editor.

"You're a gambling man," Shanin said.

The remark caught him off guard and Stine looked up from his desk.

"What's that supposed to mean?"

Shanin then gestured towards the racehorse photos and Stine nodded in response.

"Yeah. So what?" he said.

"I'll bet you I'll shoot so well you'll go to sleep with the lights on," said Shanin, with only a slight hint of tremble in her voice. At this point she wasn't interested in the money, the hours or even the blood, which she hoped was an exaggeration meant to scare her from taking the job. She was scrambling to fill a void in her life—searching for the direction that had eluded her since finishing college. "If I don't, you can fire me after three months."

Her estimation of his character was correct as Stine the gambler, couldn't resist calling her bluff. "Look," he said, assertively poking a stubby, tobacco-stained middle fingertip at the files on his desk as if to emphasize the importance of the point he was about to make. "If you're serious, go to Human Resources. Tell someone there you want to change shifts. Complete the forms. Once they're sent to me, I'll sign 'em and you'll be on the night shift as soon as an opening comes up, which is about one every other month. There's a reason the night shift has high turnover but I guess you're not interested in hearing it."

"No, I'm not, but thanks," said Shanin who had heard enough. She was afraid if she listened any further to Stine she might actually change her mind. Instead she nodded her head and gritted her teeth as she slowly realized that her transfer request might actually become a reality in the not-too-distant future. Without another word Stine then turned his attention back to the files as Shanin walked backwards out of his office.

To make the move to nights she had to formally submit her request in writing before Stine could do anything about it. Once the paperwork was put forward it was just a few weeks when another photographer abruptly left to take a job in Australia and Shanin received the transfer to the night shift.

"There's no turning back," Stine told her as her first night was about to start. "Don't come to me in three weeks and say you want to go back to photographing Baby Animal Day at the zoo. It's not happening. We've already got some new kid to take your old spot. He's easy to recognize. He's the one who just started shaving. He's going to use his first paycheck to buy some fake I.D. From here on in for you it's the night shift or it's nothing."

Shanin nodded as she wondered if she made the right decision by pushing for the job. Separately Stine made a point to warn Vin about the new photographer with whom he'd be working. Following his editorial instincts, he sensed the two of them would get along and without directly saying so, felt Vin would look out for Shanin.

"Don't take any chances with this kid," Stine later told Vin. "I don't think she knows what she's getting into. There's no place for risks in reporting." The last line was one of Stine's favorites and he used it often, especially around Vin, who wondered if he dispensed it as a way to help clear his conscience after giving out the rougher assignments.

"Can she shoot?" was all Vin asked.

"I don't know. She comes from the dog-and-cat page."

"Then why'd you put her on nights?"

"She asked me to."

"When did you start doing what photographers ask?"

"I don't know," said Stine. "I guess I just wanted to get her the hell out of my office. Those society kids always get under my skin."

There then was a pause in the conversation. The only people who asked to work the night shifts were younger reporters looking to break into the business or married people who wanted the overnight desk jobs and the extra money they paid. Stine rarely did what staffers asked. He liked to put the best people he could find on the job and rarely worried about hurting feelings or office politics. He preferred spending his spare time at the race track without worrying about what was taking place at the office or at home.

"Just be careful with her. I don't want to hear later from upper management that I shouldn't have put her on the beat," Stine said rising to leave for the train that would take him to his suburban Long Island home but not first without a stop at Aqueduct Race Track. "Make sure she doesn't unravel. I can't afford a psycho-babe on the staff."

Stine the editor and Vin the reporter shared a relationship that was both cold and warm. Vin's major flaw as a reporter was his over-aggressiveness which became apparent to everyone but him when he was on the trail of a story. While many admired the passion he displayed for his work there was such a thing as moving too quickly in the news business. If Vin had any journalistic weakness this was it. Journalists who could not wait for all of the facts to come to the surface before filing ran the risk of providing an incomplete story and would rightly be labeled irresponsible for their carelessness if something was found to be wrong. While it was often the deadline pressure that compelled reporters to take such risks very few could survive the fallout of such a consistent habit. Vin had generally managed to avoid this but there were times when he came very close to erring on the side of irresponsibility only to be bailed out by a wary editor whose deep list of contacts and experience enabled him to reliably check the facts or sufficiently alter the story before it went to press.

"There's a reason we proofread stories before they go to press and not after," Stine once bellowed at Vin, loud enough for whoever else was in the newsroom to hear. "If it's not fact it's fiction," Stine would regularly emphasize. "Novelists write fiction. Reporters write facts."

While Vin would occasionally retreat to his cubicle with his head down after one of Stine's lectures the editor never succeeded in dampening Vin's enthusiasm for being first with a story. While Stine, a former reporter, was periodically angry with Vin, he did not want to crush the young reporter's spirit. Stine knew Vin had a thick skin and this was invaluable when it came to dealing with the criticism that regularly came with being a reporter. The two of them shared a relationship that was inexplicably amiable one day and hostile the next.

When things were relatively calm Vin and Stine would occasionally leave the newsroom for a drink at a nearby bar. His favorite was one that broadcast highlights from the previous night's racetrack action. These meetings would often start with Stine peppering Vin about what had happened that week on the streets in between peeks at the race results as they flashed on the television screen. Stine always wanted to know who was with which local politician and which competing reporters were at the same scenes as Vin. But their conversations would often evolve into more subjective matters with Stine lecturing Vin on newsroom dynamics and journalistic nuances.

"A good editor can make or break a writer," Stine habitually said. "He can give you the good assignments or the dirty details. Bury your stuff deep in the paper or place you near the front. Match you with a sharp photographer or put you with some klutz."

Vin often wondered if this was true or if Stine was trying to promote his own importance. Writers needed editors but editors needed writers more Vin always believed. Vin generally would politely nod during these talks as Stine had a habit of telling the same story more than once and Vin could see no good in arguing with the person who gave the assignments. Periodically however, Stine would reveal something about himself, things he usually did not share with the other reporters. While many of the reporters envied the relationship between Vin and Stine, Vin sometimes sensed that Stine envied the life Vin lived. A former reporter, Vin felt Stine probably missed the action of being on the street but not enough to give up the pay and benefits he was receiving as an editor to return to it. In his eyes, it probably wasn't worth it. After all, Stine had a family and a gambling habit to support.

/ / /

While at first it seemed odd to Shanin to be coming into the office when most of the staffers were leaving she soon got used to waiting in the "bullpen" with the other night crawlers for the assignments to be issued. Editors would log on to the police channels on a scanner to learn about accidents, crimes and other police activity and then assign writers and photographers to comb out to wherever the action had occurred. Sometimes they went in a van supplied by the paper. Other times they'd use their own transportation. Sometimes they took the subway. During those rare times when the city was actually quiet and the evening assignments had been submitted the photographers and reporters would congregate in the all-night diner down the street, sharing stories or griping about life. Shanin had little to gripe about but liked listening to the others. She felt it was part of her education as a city newspaper photographer.

In the loose society of city journalism, the night-shift crowd enjoyed a certain degree of notoriety. Its members were usually excused from the daytime meetings covering policies and procedures, an informal agreement the paper's management had struck with its rank and file. They came to work wearing sneakers and baseball caps. They drank lots of coffee and smoked cigarettes at their desk. There was an edge to what they did and she soon found herself attracted to it. The night crew bent the rules and thrived on the chaos. In return they took the assignments when most of their coworkers were putting their children to bed and getting their suits ready for the next day.

"To the daytime staff we're like shadows," Vin explained to Shanin one night in the diner. "They know we exist but don't acknowledge us. They don't like to admit we get the stories they read on their way to the office."

The night crawlers came to like Shanin. While very few of the daytime staffers acknowledged the contributions made by the perpetually short-staffed overnight crew, Shanin almost effortlessly began to "run with the pack." She volunteered for assignments in the city's rougher neighborhoods. Raced past ambulances to get to hospitals for a shot at workers delivering wounded gang members and found ways to sneak into private clubs, camera hidden, to shoot New York's glamorous in compromising positions. It was a far cry from photographing the circus when it came to town.

Working the night shift exposed Shanin to a new lifestyle and an education unlike the formal one she received from behind the university's ivy-covered walls. She got to see the city's soft, white underbelly through a lens before showing it to the rest of the world in the morning edition. For a young woman who had at one time seriously considered no other future for herself than that in the sterile setting of a laboratory, chasing the pulsing beat of the city after dark, recording images of its chaos and violence, proved to be more exciting than she ever imagined. At times she felt that each night was a new surprise waiting to be uncovered and was a vital part of the discovery, capturing the images that enhanced the stories supplied by other night crawlers like Vin Gusto.

"Gusto goes too far," one of the other reporters complained during a slow night in the diner to whichever staffers would listen. "One night he's going to find himself on the wrong end of a pistol."

"Stine would be okay with that," another reporter chimed in. "It would sell a lot of papers. Here's the headline—'Tatter Reporter Shot, Exclusive Pix Inside'." Vin was no stranger to trouble. An undercover series he wrote on gang violence had nearly gotten him killed. Although he had an unlisted phone number and address, standard procedure for most big-city reporters, someone he'd been covering had learned where he lived. Early one morning after a night of tailing gang members he was awoken by a pounding taking place in his apartment hallway. The gang members had gotten into the right building but were hammering at the wrong door. Vin could hear his next door neighbor, a single, middle-aged woman, screaming as the sledge hammer crashed through her door, loosening it from its hinges. Dogs were barking. He phoned the local police station, called the superintendent and then turned on his burglar alarm. The gang scattered before entering the apartment but the police apprehended one of the members while he was running out the building's service entrance. At the advice of a police officer he'd gotten to know, Vin quickly finished the series and then spent the next few night's sleeping at his mother's house. A few days later police had gotten a confession from the apprehended gang member, other suspects were then taken into custody, the pressure eased and Vin was able to move back into his apartment.

Another time, earlier in his career, he'd been sent to West Virginia to cover a landslide. Driving across a washed-out road that had been closed, a mudslide hit his car, knocking it to the edge of a ravine. He survived by kicking out one of the car windows and crawling through the mud to safety. He was picked up a day later by a search-and-rescue crew, camera and notebook in hand. While neither of these episodes had helped Vin climb up the editorial ladder, events like these had given him a certain reputation in the newsroom. Some said he was crazy. Others said he was lucky to be alive. It was not a cozy relationship Vin shared with his fellow reporters. While many reporters complained that Vin's stories usually received prime placement in the newspaper, few wanted to take the assignments he'd regularly pursue. Either way, he'd become known as the one who was not afraid to chase the "dangerous story" and when police activity was broadcast over the newsroom's scanner, Vin was usually first out the door.

"Guys like Stine say I'm only here because I take the assignments no one else wants," Vin told Shanin on one of the first nights they were assigned together. It was a relatively mild assignment, they were to camp outside a police station and wait for a local politician to be brought in after charges of corruption had been filed earlier that day. The assignment was simple. Get the statement. Get the photo. Get back to the office. As it often was in this business, the waiting was the most difficult part but it was especially tough this time as it was an extremely humid night in the city. Clothing stuck to skin and nearly everyone who did not have the luxury of being in an air-conditioned room seemed to be on edge and uncomfortable. Waiting on the concrete steps outside the police station both Shanin and Vin were draped in sweat-filled clothes. They kept their press badges hidden in their shirt pockets. It was hardly a glamorous night and Shanin was starting to understand what Stine had meant when he told her the overnight was the worst shift in the business. She could not help but wonder if she did the right thing by asking to leave the day shift. She'd heard the photographer who replaced her spent the day covering the opening of a new French restaurant owned by a Hollywood movie director. The only interesting part for Shanin was that the assignment gave her a chance to get to know Vin Gusto—to see if the person actually lived up to the reputation.

"Is it true?" Shanin asked.

"What?"

"That no one wants these assignments?"

"I do," answered Vin. "A lot of guys are 'wannabees'," he continued. "They say they want to be reporters but as soon as it hits the fan or they get offered a little more money they hide behind the desk. I wish they'd just be honest. They make a big deal when they fiddle with our headlines or correct some grammar. They're just in it for the paycheck. They'd be better off selling used cars or life insurance." There was a pause in the conversation as the thick night air hung like a veil between them. Shanin broke the silence with a remark that was friendly advice disguised as a joke.

"Some of them say you need life insurance," said Shanin with a smile.

"You only need life insurance when you have kids," answered Vin. "And guys with kids don't work the crime shift."

"Then what are you in it for? She then asked, her deep brown eyes opened wide with curiosity.

"I'm not sure," Vin answered after a pause. "I think it's the pace, the not knowing."

"Not knowing what?"

"Not knowing what's going to happen when I get to work. Not knowing where they're going to send me or what's going to happen when I get there. Who am I going to see? Will I get the story in by deadline? I don't move too fast without a deadline hanging over me."

While Vin may not have understood the reason behind his own intensity, to Shanin it was obvious that he hungered for the story. There was no questioning that. He gave no indication that he was in it for the money. Nor was he after recognition like so many other reporters who had their eyes set on climbing the editorial ladder. What drove him to regularly hit the streets when nearly everyone else in the city was sleeping? Was it the rush of being first? Was it the chase? Did he relish being something of an outsider in his own town?

"Is that it?" she asked.

"It's part of it."

"What's the other part?"

"When I was a boy, I used to deliver papers. The money helped my mom but that wasn't why I did it. There was always this excitement to be one of the first to see that front page—to know what was happening before anyone else in the neighborhood did. This was before the internet and 24-hour cable. Sometimes, when I get home after being out all night, I lie in bed and think of the expressions on the readers' faces when that morning's edition hits kitchen tables across the city and people see what took place while they were sleeping. I wonder what people are talking about in the break rooms, while they're getting their hair cut or standing on line at the supermarket. Other times I think of that little boy and how happy he was delivering the news. People were always happy to see me when I put that newspaper in their hands. It was like delivering a little present each day."

By the time the politician arrived it was too late to get the story for the morning edition. Shanin tried taking several shots of him when he emerged from his car. But with a coat draped over his face and limited light there was no way anyone could say for sure it was who they wanted it to be. Inside however, Vin got a brief statement.

"I'm sure his media guy made him wait before turning himself in so he wouldn't make tomorrow's headlines," Vin complained on their way back to the office.

"Stine's not going to like us not getting the story in time," said Shanin.

"Doesn't matter," said Vin. "Stine's butt's not roasting in this humidity. I'd like to have him wait for three hours in the heat to see an elected guy on the take. He probably went home, knocked back a few bourbons and fell asleep in his easy chair watching OTB highlights."

The two of them drove back to the office in Vin's battered Ford Tempo, bouncing across potholes and steering clear of vagrants approaching the car for handouts whenever they stopped for a light. In a city where a parking space was a rare commodity, Vin chose not to put "press plates" on his car although as a working journalist he was entitled to do so. The special license plates would enable him to park almost anywhere without penalty but they'd also identify his car as belonging to a member of the press. For a reporter who liked to slip undetected into the shadows this could be a liability. And unlike most of his fellow reporters who clipped their press pass to their shirt pocket or draped them around their neck like a badge, Vin only revealed his pass when he absolutely needed to do so. Similarly, he never took out his pad and pencil or miniature tape recorder until it was necessary.

"Tense people don't talk," he said. "Or they don't tell you what you need to hear. They don't like to have their picture taken either. When you want someone to talk keep them relaxed. First get their trust. The guys behind the desks don't understand this. They think you just shove a microphone under a guy's nose and he starts talking."

Shanin nodded. It was one of her first lessons in street reporting, or as Vin called it, "Guerrilla Journalism."

"And you might try being a little more discreet with the camera," he continued. "We might've gotten something better than a crook with a coat pulled over his face if you hadn't run up to his car with that Moby Dick lens pointing at him."

Shanin had not been expecting the abrupt criticism but it came with the territory. She'd thought waiting on the police station steps all night in the 90-degree heat and humidity would have earned her some respect in the guerrilla journalist's eyes.

While Shanin could not be sure of Vin's motivation she did know that whenever she worked with him for some reason her pulse beat a bit faster. She accepted the criticism he leveled at her and promised herself that when she returned to the editorial offices she'd request to be sent out again in the near future with Vin Gusto.

Later that day, after she'd finished photographing the undersea-salvage equipment Shanin phoned the North Fork Harbor Reporter offices to check for messages. Emma, the receptionist read her the following: Vin Gusto, Crashing Seagull.

Shanin's pulse skipped a beat.

CHAPTER 4

The Rush of the Crush

The sun was starting to set when Dr. Frank Lambrusco, North Fork Harbor Vineyards winemaker and world-renown botanist took what would be his last walk of the day through the fields. The grapes were beginning to form into heavy, purple-black clusters. As the last rays of that day's sun shined on them the thick skins glistened—just beginning to hint at their full potential which he hoped would be realized later that fall. Occasionally he'd reach down and cut a bunch loose from the vine with his hook-knife to analyze later in the converted potato barn which served as his office, laboratory and fermentation area. It would be a good crush this fall he thought. It would mark the first full crush with his experimental vines that were now reaching maturity after only three years in the sandy Long Island soil.

If Dr. Frank was happy with his crop's outlook he kept his emotions secret. Remain professional he reminded himself as he stepped out from the row and continued quickly walking to the barn. He put a handful of the grapes he picked into a small plastic bag and then put the package into the outer pocket of his field coat. A paper label was on each bag to identify from which vine he made the cutting as well as the date and time. Updated reports on the grapes' water, sugar and acid levels would help him to further refine his forecast before he left the next day for the International Viticulture Expo and Conference in Buenos Aires, Argentina, where he would be one of the speakers.

Outside of the wine world, very few knew or cared that the conference was taking place. An annual event, it attracted some of the best scientific and technical minds the world of viniculture had to offer. It also attracted a large contingent of business people, each eager to find the next big thing in the world of wine for commercial exploitation.

So far, Dr. Frank had managed to release very little information on his "super strain" of grape. What he had released to the trade was precisely controlled drips of information, enough to interest his scientific peers and intrigue some commercial producers but not enough to reveal crucial parts of his progress. Dr. Frank's botanical-cloning experiment was beginning to bear fruit and hint at its potential as he had bred several varieties into one "super grape." The plants were kept in a secret location. Surrounded by other "regular" vines, only Dr. Frank knew exactly which ones held the genetic keys to the future of grape growing. He deliberately grew a wide variety of grapes in his field to confuse anyone trying to take samples of his secret crop. Not even the vineyard workers knew which vines were marked for experimentation. A small "map" was encoded in his handheld computer, listing each experimental vine's exact location and even Dr. Frank himself could only access this information after entering a special code and password. The handheld rarely left his jacket pocket.

This new variety, Dr. Frank was sure, would not only be a good eating and reliable winemaking grape but highly drought and insect resistant, as well as fast-growing, able to withstand temperature extremes and could be cultivated with a minimum of fertilizer and pesticides. More importantly, Dr. Frank envisioned the super grape becoming an important food source for impoverished people around the world. In some very preliminary meetings with representatives from select international agriculture companies Dr. Frank had made these intentions known early in the negotiations. Some of the companies were not shy when putting forward their interest in propagating the grape on a commercial scale. Dr. Frank insisted that for every vine sold for commercial purposes one must be donated to the international charity group Farmers Without Fences. Most companies were not very enthusiastic about that part of the deal but were nevertheless anxious to gain access to his genetic formula. During one speech before a small industry group Dr. Frank compared the international agricultural conglomerates to Europe's former aristocratic elite, noting how they lived thanks to the sweat of the common people. It was a spontaneous yet ill-timed comment and he wondered if it made him enemies.

While the potential conflict had remained confined to industry circles Dr. Frank often wondered how much longer he would be able to keep his progress secret and when he'd get a company to do business on his terms. "Food," he told one industry executive who had unexpectedly arrived at his vineyard, "is not to be hoarded by a few but enjoyed by the many." He refused to compromise his idea of sharing with the world's poor. "Sustainable agriculture will help solve many of the world's problems," he said. He wanted his pioneering work in agricultural science to benefit the masses as much as it could help the conglomerates. It was clear that most of the executives he met with in his earlier meetings did not share this vision. Dr. Frank, as he did so many times in his career, forged ahead hoping his chance to articulate his dream at the conference would enable him to meet with a corporate partner willing to share in his vision. But even Dr. Frank, a nearly endless optimist, knew if he did not find a partner at the conference his ability to grow and distribute the vines as generously as he'd like would be severely limited.

But while walking back to the barn with the warm afternoon sun on his back and a few thick bunches of grapes in his pocket Dr. Frank's thoughts drifted to his childhood. As a young boy in Italy he knew what it was like to be hungry. After the Second World War, when his family and country had lost nearly everything in what was perversely described as a victory Dr. Frank remembered the few families that had their farms and businesses intact. The war that was to end all wars left an immeasurable wake of destruction from which some said the world would never recover. He also remembered who shared with their neighbors and who didn't.

Dr. Frank descended from a long line of professional winemakers and grape growers. While they had technical skill they were not titled. They had no estate to their name and at the end were little more than sharecroppers in the eyes of the aristocracy. Dr. Frank's father, who spent most of the war imprisoned in Germany, sensed there might finally be a change in the world order and that with education, bright young people like his son Francisco might be able to shape futures that were better than those of their parents and grandparents. Like the promise delivered with every spring planting season, he hoped that the future would be better.

Dr. Frank, the youngest of five children attended Italy's Agricultural School in Ostuni. Earning an advanced degree in viticulture, with a concentration in plant genetics, he first went to work for the Italian government, helping to restore vineyards and get Italy's ravaged wine business back on its feet. Later he did similar work in Latin America, helping to modernize vineyards in Argentina and Chile until political instability forced him to look for a new place to work. Always fascinated by pioneering projects, Dr. Frank became very interested when he read about the first quality wines being produced on the North Fork of Long Island. An old agricultural area better known for growing potatoes and giant pumpkins, like others, Dr. Frank theorized wine grapes would fare well in the sandy soil and temperate climate. While on a visit to the area he had the opportunity to purchase an old potato farm which he converted to a vineyard, never once forgetting what it was like to feel hungry.

Later on a visit to a remote Central American village he left several vines with a local farmer. He gave the farmer virtually no instructions on raising the vines because he wanted to see how they would fare with minimal assistance. While they were not the same strain as the ones he was now hoping to propagate around the world they were very similar. A few years later he quietly returned to the village at what he approximated would be harvest time. The vines had produced as he had anticipated and the villagers had a new crop that they were selling and trading with their neighbors. He repeated this secret experiment in remote locations on three continents. When he had similar results in each experimental site Dr. Frank was confident he was on the verge of making a great contribution to world agriculture. But he knew he would need a partner to help him fully realize his plans and finding the right one would be difficult.

/ / /

That afternoon as Dr. Frank approached the barn a few of the field workers were lingering around the vineyard, waiting for the ride that would take them back to the house they shared. Dr. Frank would always say a few words to them in Spanish, admiring them for their willingness to sacrifice everything they knew for a better life in the north. A lot of them had spent time in California before heading north and as a result, were good with pruning and managing vines. Dr. Frank paid them fairly, giving them extra if they worked overtime, helping them find medical care and loaning them money when they needed it. He also appreciated the fact that their inability to speak English and the natural sense of apprehension many immigrants have helped his operation maintain its low profile. Anyone who happened by the vineyard would have a difficult time getting information from the field workers.

While his tasting room was not open to the public, people did come by despite "No Trespassing" and "Not Open to the Public" signs posted at the head of the driveway which was a simple gravel-covered road lined on each side by large maple trees. Some were innocent tourists who either ignored or missed the signs and assumed all wineries maintained an open tasting room with free-flowing samples. Other times they'd park their car and walk through the vineyard. When this happened he'd send one of the workers out to chase them. Maybe the fact that he kept a low profile was what actually attracted some onlookers he sometimes wondered. Did people actually care about what took place at this unnamed, unmarked vineyard? Were they corporate spies sent from agricultural or wine companies pretending to be tourists and seeking information?

While other wineries were in the business of entertaining passersby as this practice often resulted in sales, Dr. Frank built his winery strictly for the trade. He made sure it did not appear on tourist maps and did no advertising. In addition to relying on his own savings, to help fund his operation Dr. Frank took orders from the most discriminating collectors, sommeliers and restaurateurs. They paid in advance banking on his reputation, ability and trustworthiness. The wines were shipped in plain bottles and unmarked cases. The only distinguishing mark was his simple signature and production date, each of which appeared on an otherwise plain white label set across the bottle's midsection. He knew some collectors frequently sold his wines in a secondary market at a profit but accepted that as a cost of doing business. Occasionally he'd donate a bottle or two to a charity auction. This practice also heightened awareness of his ability among the wine cognoscenti and accordingly the myth that surrounded him grew. Dr. Frank intentionally kept his annual production low—just enough to keep the farm operating and to pay for his other business expenses as he had his sights set on a more meaningful goal.

On the few occasions when an intrepid wine writer would call asking for an interview or tasting samples Dr. Frank would have Cindy Murphy, his secretary and office manager respectfully decline, saying neither he nor his wines were ready to meet the press. Occasionally, local well-heeled collectors seeking to build their own reputation would entertain a wine writer and in such conversations word would often leak out about Long Island's secretive winemaker, thus perpetuating the mystery which many found hard to resist.

Inside the barn were the tasting room, lab, offices, bottling facility and fermentation area. When Dr. Frank entered, assistant winemaker Andy LaBroom was talking with Scott Larson, an independent mechanic who often repaired and maintained the vineyard equipment. A farm-equipment mechanic by trade, Larson taught himself how to fix vineyard machinery once it became apparent that the industry was going to permanently take root on eastern Long Island. Starting with tractors and combines, Larson had become an expert on repairing bottling machines, conveyor belts, sprayers, crushers, destemmers and fermentation-tank hardware. Larson was very short-tempered, making it difficult for him to keep an assistant, most of whom quickly tired of his sudden tirades and empty threats. Assistants never lasted more than a few months with Larson and he often came to the vineyard solo. While Dr. Frank had never seen Larson get violent he sensed he was a very smart but frustrated man, a position he well understood. Larson was also a very large man. Well over six feet tall, he was lanky with thick wrists and heavy hands, the result of a lifetime of swinging wrenches and carrying various machinery parts. Dr. Frank had occasionally heard his workers joke that Larson had "arms like legs" but only when he was beyond listening distance. Others simply referred to him as "the monster." But his arguments with Dr. Frank never lasted beyond a few minutes and with very few exceptions, Larson reliably repaired the vineyard equipment.

Talented, not good at taking orders and sorely lacking in social skills, Larson was able to make a living because he was the last mechanic in the area who'd fix equipment that had broken down in the field. Each of the other mechanics insisted equipment be towed to their facility or at least a barn. It was not always possible or feasible to move heavy, broken-down equipment long distances across often muddy fields or up and down vine-covered hillsides. Larson was the only area mechanic who would repair equipment wherever it had become incapacitated—giving his business a competitive advantage. He also gave a fair price if customers paid in cash. But he had a terrible independent streak and no qualms about sharing his limited opinions with others, whether they cared to hear them or not.

"Hey Doc," Larson hollered when he saw Dr. Frank walking through the tasting area.

"Yes, Scott," Dr. Frank replied.

"When are you gonna do something about all them freeloaders out front?"

"I see only hardworking men."

"All they do is hang around and wait for handouts. I ain't never seen a lazier bunch of people than that crew you got."

"Those men are up at dawn and work all day without complaint."

"Whenever I see 'em they're standin' around talkin' Spanish. They think we don't understand what they're sayin'."

"What are they saying?" asked Dr. Frank.

"They think I don't know but I do."

"What is it then?"

"They're talkin' about how they're gonna take over this country. That's their plan."

"Is it?"

"Their plan is to get as many of their Spanish-speakin' cousins over the border down in Texas and Arizona and places like that and eventually they're gonna be the majority here. One day we'll be workin' for them."

"They're just trying to feed their families," said Dr. Frank, trying to suppress a grin. "The same as your ancestors. Your people came from somewhere too."

"Don't start with that. My ancestors built this country. We built roads and cities. We didn't go sendin' every dollar we made back across some border. We learned to speak English. Fought in wars. I ever see one of them near my truck I'm lettin' a wrench fly in his face. I'm just tellin' ya. When I was a kid you never seen a Mexican around here."

"These men are not Mexican. They're from Chile and Argentina. They're each here legally and they each pay tax, unlike a certain mechanic I know who insists on being paid in cash."

"Ain't this the 'land of the free,' Doc?"

"These men understand grapes. That's why they're here."

"They understand grapes but they don't' understand English. Ain't much to understand about a grape. That don't make no sense. Grapes don't talk. Why don't they go back to wherever they came from?"

"This is my business," said Dr. Frank who knew what it was like to be a refugee. "I handle the workers."

"I'm just lettin' you know. You should keep your eyes open."

"My eyes are open and you know what I see? A tractor out back that someone promised me last winter he'd have running by spring. I'm still waiting."

"That thing's a dinosaur. I can't get no parts for it ever since the Chinese took over the company. They stopped makin' parts so you gotta spend fifty-thousand every couple a years on a new tractor. What do the Chinese know about buildin' tractors? They don't use no tractors in a rice paddy."

"Tell Andy what you need," he said before turning to face the always dependable LaBroom. "Or get a list of the parts and leave it on Cindy's desk. We'll make it happen because if I have to buy a new tractor," Dr. Frank stopped without finishing the sentence.

"Yeah, what?" asked Larson.

"Then I wouldn't need a repairman, would I?"

Larson shrugged and headed towards his truck. "I don't care. I got plenty of work. I'll see you at The Apple Tree later," he said, nodding towards his friend, the quiet LaBroom.

Andy LaBroom was a North Fork native. He was born and raised within walking distance of Dr. Frank's vineyard. His family farmed potatoes for generations on the very soil that was now bearing world-class wine grapes. While LaBroom knew every inch of the soil and had quickly learned the basics of professional winemaking he never fully explained to Dr. Frank how his family had come to leave the farming business. LaBroom and Larson were opposites. As tall and muscular as Larson was, LaBroom was short and slight of build, barely five feet, six inches tall with a very quiet, pensive demeanor. Dr. Frank wondered what attracted LaBroom to the vineyard and even more so, what enabled him to remain friends with the obnoxious Larson. But before he could get too lost in his thoughts he remembered the grapes in his pocket. He excused himself and went to unlock his office.

"I'll be in the office. Lock the barn when you leave," he told Andy, whose girlfriend Cindy had called in sick that day.

A confidential computer code was needed to gain admittance to Dr. Frank's office and once the heavy steel door closed behind him it automatically locked. There were no windows in the office which was further protected by an electronic surveillance system that signaled when the entranceway was locked and when it was open. The sparse apartment where he slept was above the office and protected by a compatible security system. While he abhorred all forms of violence and cruelty, Dr. Frank's experiences growing up in war-torn Italy never allowed him to fully trust or depend on others—especially when it came to his personal security.

Inside his office was a large, fireproof file cabinet with combination lock, a desk, lamp, chair and laptop computer. A closed-circuit camera system let him view what was taking place in and around the barn and at key points of the vineyard, such as the entranceway. On the desk was a photo of his small family, his late wife Antoinette and only child Maria. A grainy, sepia-tone print of his parents who'd died while he was still a young man hung on the wall. His brothers and sisters were also gone. The only other ornamentation was a wooden crucifix he'd brought with him from Italy. It was hand-carved from the wood of an ancient olive tree.

Once inside the closed office he'd sit at the desk and feed information from his handheld computer into the laptop and wait for the data to be analyzed. After his workers had left for the day and he could see from the monitor that he was alone in the winery he'd exit his office, go to the lab and analyze the grapes he'd brought in from the field. Once he had the lab data he needed he'd repeat the process to double-check the results, return to the office and transmit the second round of data to the laptop which was secured to the desk with a special lock to which only he had the key. Once the data was transmitted into the laptop he cleared it from the handheld and then e-mailed it to his daughter Maria, his only remaining close family member and the one person he truly trusted after his wife died. If there was something he'd need to remember, he'd scribble the briefest of notes onto a scrap of paper, usually in Italian but sometimes in Spanish and occasionally in English. Once he no longer needed the data he'd be sure to destroy the paper, usually tearing it to shreds and letting the pieces randomly fall through his fingers as he walked across the field. It was an overly elaborate process and probably unnecessary but it was a part of him, very much like the wine grape DNA he was studying.

Before he'd fall asleep he'd pray for the harvest and for his daughter to find a "good man." According to the preliminary data, the harvest looked like it would be a promising one but he did not send this information to Maria. He would wait to tell her in person once he returned home. Nor would he mention much of it at the conference.

"The human race could be very beautiful," he added in the e-mail to Maria who was studying agricultural economics at a California university. "But it can also be very dangerous. Be careful who you trust. Will call before leaving. *Baccione*, Papa."

Once the monitor light flashed green Dr. Frank double-checked the security codes, set the locks and began his exit. It had been a long day. Cindy had left him a note detailing his schedule for the next few days. He thought about the long flight ahead of him and more importantly, how his talk would be received at the conference. Dr. Frank did not like being away from the vineyard, especially so close to harvest time. One of the things he needed to be completely sure about before he left was that his data was secure. He waited until his screen indicated that Maria's computer had received his e-mail before deleting the message from his own hard drive. Only then did he prepare to exit.

As he did each evening, Dr. Frank returned the handheld to his jacket pocket. He then went from his office, through the lab and towards the barn door, checking locks and security codes along the way. On one of the panels a previously green light was now flashing red. Dr. Frank went to check the code. It was the barn entrance. Probably a family of raccoons scavenging for dinner, this frequently was the case. He double-checked the code on the monitor and re-set the system. The green light returned. Dr. Frank entered the "exit code." He had 17 seconds to leave the barn/office before the system would re-lock itself and a second code would need to be entered in order to exit. He tried the barn door but it would not open. Dr. Frank then felt a sharp pull on his coat collar from behind. He wildly flung his arms in a desperate attempt to regain balance. As he fell backward Dr. Frank suddenly felt a piercing pain in his chest. His breathing got heavy. In a few seconds the chest pain grew worse and spread to his throat and arms. He tried pulling himself from the floor only to fall backwards again and roll onto his side. Dr. Frank tried to rise one more time but became dizzy and could not see in the dark barn. Falling back again in the darkness his head hit the cement floor. His eyes shut. His breathing stopped. The monitor flashed red.

CHAPTER 5

Last Stop, First Impressions

"North Fork Harbor! Last stop! North Fork Harbor!"

Vin was awakened by the conductor's sharp barking. He didn't remember when he had fallen asleep. The bright lights inside the train hurt his eyes and were in sharp contrast to the near total darkness he experienced when he exited. Bag in hand he surveyed what was less than a lively summer town.

Happy scenes of a few husbands reuniting with families quickly gave way to an empty street. One bar with a neon beer sign flashing in the window and a single taxi filled out the landscape. A lone street light and a full moon provided the rest of the illumination. From where he stood Vin could hear country music from the bar's juke box.

"Taxi?" called the lone driver, arm dangling from the open window as Vin stood there, taking in his first impression of North Fork Harbor. Since he hadn't yet received his advance Vin thought it might be best to continue rationing his funds but wanted to get an idea of how far his destination was.

"How far is the Crashing Seagull?

"Down the road."

"Can I walk it?"

"Don't know," said the cabbie who sensing no forthcoming transaction, started the car and drove into the darkness.

Vin headed down the same road as the cab. Was this a harbinger of things to come. What happened to the lively seaside village Pat told him he'd be covering? Maybe he arrived on a slow night, a very slow night.

After about 30 minutes of walking he found the Crashing Seagull. He entered the front door under the lit "Vacancy" sign and headed towards the counter.

Since it was late and North Fork Harbor's main street was not well lit Vin could not get a good look at the hotel's outside. Inside however, was a far cry from the "absolutely gorgeous" description Pat Goode had mentioned that morning.

The lobby was in desperate need of a facelift. A fake leather couch, holes patched with electrical tape was the lobby's predominant feature. Paint was chipped and peeling off the walls and counter. A couple of lawn chairs filled in the corners and old copies of American Commercial Fisherman and Potato Farmer magazines were scattered across a coffee table that had one broken leg supported with a stack of three bricks. A free-standing lamp provided the only interior illumination. He could see a few moths orbiting the light bulb beneath a faded lampshade. Vin wondered if he was in the right place and went back outside to double-check the sign. According to the sign he was definitely in the Crashing Seagull. Preparing to check-in he reentered the lobby and noticed a sniff of diesel fuel in the air when he approached the counter to ring the bell for the night clerk.

He let his bag fall to the floor and then hit the bell one time. On a counter an old police scanner was buzzing static. He waited as the bell faded and the silence resumed. He then hit the bell harder, forcing its ring to rise above the scanner's buzz.

"I'm comin'. Don't worry. I'm comin'," a voice bellowed from somewhere deep inside the bowels of the hotel office. Vin thought he recognized the gravelly tone in the clerk's voice from that morning's telephone conversation.

"Everyone's always in such a darn hurry." After a few more seconds a tall, bald man emerged, his arms tangled in what appeared to be a fish net.

"Can I help ya?" the man asked, pulling the nets from his arms and letting them fall onto the counter. The police scanner crackled throughout their conversation.

Vin wondered if it was the same person who had attempted to give him directions to North Fork Harbor earlier that day but after some five hours of traveling he did not want to ask.

"Checking-in," Vin said.

"Were you the fella who called earlier today? The one who needed directions?"

"Yeah. That was me."

"Did you do like I said?"

Since this appeared to be the only operating hotel in the vicinity Vin did not think it would be wise to let the clerk know his attempt to provide directions was useless.

"Yes, I did," said Vin. "Took the train. Just like you said. No problem at all."

"You got a credit card?"

Vin had no working credit card. His credit was in tatters. The last time he tried to use his card in a restaurant the waitress returned with it cut into two slices on a cake plate. Paying back the credit card company and repairing his credit were things he'd been trying to manage but from that night in the restaurant he'd been a cash-only customer.

"I was told the room was reserved by Travel & Pleasure magazine," Vin said.

"They reserved it but I ain't got no credit card should something go wrong," the clerk said. "You ain't got a credit card?" he repeated.

"The magazine's sending me a check tomorrow. I was planning on paying you from that," said Vin.

"That ain't no good if you want a room for tonight," said the clerk, staring straight into Vin's eyes as if he was trying to ascertain something from them.

"The magazine was supposed to have the reservation taken care of."

"Like I said, they made a reservation but ain't sent no payment."

"They're a big company," said Vin. "They told me it was paid for."

"And I'm a small company. I don't let no rooms without nobody payin'? You ain't got no credit card you ain't got no room."

Vin thought of Pat Goode, her abrupt offer earlier that morning and haggling to get him to quickly take the assignment. To buy some time Vin dug into his wallet. Despite his horrendous credit history, Vin had actually recently received a credit card in the mail from an online bookseller from which he'd managed to purchase a used directory of literary agents some time ago, when his fragile credit was intact enough to do so. Not giving into the temptation to activate the card and take advantage of its promises of easy money, he nonetheless slipped it into his wallet on a just-in-case basis.

"Of course I have a credit card," said Vin, handing the clerk the yet-to-be activated card.

"Okay," he said, taking the card in his hand and sliding it through the machine. "I ain't gettin' no readin' on it," said the clerk with just the slightest tone of frustration.

"You sure it's okay?"

"Let me check it," asked Vin.

The clerk handed it back to Vin.

"I didn't sign it," he said. "Let me take care of this." He began fumbling through his bag seemingly searching for a pen but actually stalling for time.

"Never mind," said the clerk. "It's late. I gotta get these fish nets sorted and you're with that magazine. I'll run this through in the mornin'. This thing ain't never worked right. You ain't goin' nowhere else tonight and I gotta get to the dock or we'll miss the tide."

"And the fish. I understand," said Vin.

"Suppose you never did much fishin' down in New York City."

"Actually as a kid I did a lot," said Vin. "My Dad used to take me under the Throggs Neck Bridge for bluefish and mackerel. It was a lot of fun but I haven't gone for years."

"We're getting' ready to fix a midnight bass run. The full moon should be makin' 'em run wild in the race tonight. I ain't got no time to be messin' around with plastic," said the clerk. "Just give me two pieces of I.D."

Vin handed over his driver's license and writers union card as he put the plastic back in his wallet.

"You a writer?"

"Yes. I'm here on assignment. Writing a review of North Fork Harbor."

"So that's what you meant by that magazine stuff. I didn't know you was the writer. And you're in a union too?"

"It's more like a club. We get together each month to talk about all the people who try to take advantage of writers. And we throw a few good parties."

The clerk stared at Vin's cards.

"Is that a problem?"

"My gran' daddy was a union man, railroad workers, back in the '30's. That's why we got a train runnin' out here today. 'Cause them guys laid the track back then. In them days they was shippin' fish and potatoes to the city. Everything went by the train then. Kicked this town into the 20th century."

"For a minute there, I was just thinking . . ." Vin fumbled.

"No. No. I mean it's just that, you look so . . . never mind."

"Never mind what?" asked Vin, sensing a controversy.

"Aw nuts. It's just you ain't what a writer looks like."

"You mean like a guy with thick glasses and a tweed blazer."

"Yeah sometin' like that I guess."

"Well haven't you ever heard of surprise endings? Good writers surprise people."

"That's what you did!" the clerk bellowed with a hearty laugh. "Listen. Since I ain't got time to be checkin' your credit card and we're union guys and all, you be sure to say sometin' nice about this hotel when you write whatever it is you're fixin' to write. Like how friendly the staff is and how cute this place is . . . understand."

"Or maybe the cozy lobby," Vin countered.

"Yeah. Sometin' like that.

He handed Vin back his license and union card. He had dodged yet another bullet and gotten his lodging for the night. "You gonna be here for the Potato Festival?"

"When's that?"

"In a couple a weeks."

"I don't think so. They didn't mention that in the assignment."

"No problem. We got plenty of people comin' anyway. Whole place'll be full. Here's your key. Room number's on it."

"No problem," said Vin, taking the key. He was assigned room 13 and did not feel lucky about it.

"Hey, one more thing," called the clerk to Vin.

"Yes."

"Which magazine is it again you said you write for?"

"Travel & Pleasure."

"That ain't the one with them nudie pictures in it? You know, with them women in the jungle with no tops. 'Cause we don't want to be in no magazine like that. This is a family operation. You know what I'm sayin'."

"No. That's not it at all," said Vin. "We're strictly upscale vacations. No jungle expeditions. I'm surprised you're not familiar with it, being in the travel business," said Vin.

"Runnin' this place and keepin' the boat don't give me no time for readin'. But see if you can get me a couple of issues. I'll keep 'em in the lobby."

"No problem," said Vin. "I'll ask my editor tomorrow to put some in the mail. By the way, I'm expecting a package tomorrow. Could you hold it for me at the desk?"

"Sure and if you ain't got no credit card that goes through by then it'll be out on the street with your bags. So anyway, we got a deal?"

"Yeah. Sure," said Vin. "Does the hotel serve breakfast in the morning?"

"No, but there's coffee and tea bags in the room and a good café down the street. Or you can get some snacks at the IGA."

"How far is North Fork Harbor Vineyards from here?

"A few miles down the Main Road."

"I have a meeting there in the morning. Will I be able to call a taxi?"

"Sure." The clerk handed Vin a business card with the telephone number for Lefty's Taxi Service. *"Arrive alive, let Lefty drive,"* was the slogan across the bottom of the card. It offered 24-hour service.

"Payphone's down the hall near the arcade room."

"You know anything about it?"

"The payphone? I just told you, it's down the hall."

"No I meant the vineyard."

"Not North Fork. They're pretty quiet. That's the one that don't go in for no festivals or nuthin'. Their wine's pretty expensive. I hear they sell mostly to snobs."

Reaching into his jacket pocket Vin removed a small white envelope. "And would you be good enough to drop this in the mail for me?" It was the letter to his mother that he'd forgotten to mail from New York.

"As long as it's got a stamp on it."

"Of course," said Vin. He opened his wallet again, took out a worn stamp and stuck it onto the envelope.

"Okay then," obliged the clerk, tossing the letter into an old cardboard shoebox on the end of the counter with the faded words 'U.S. Mail' scrawled in crayon across its end.

"They pick up the mail here every day?" Vin asked.

"Usually. 'Cept when they forget. Why, you movin' in?"

"No. Just passing through," Vin said as he turned and headed towards his room. It then occurred to him that there was one more question he needed to ask.

"Did I get any messages?" called Vin to the clerk who was gathering up his net and preparing to leave the night desk.

"You just checked in. How the heck you gonna have any messages?"

"Slipped my mind. Sorry," said Vin. "Been on the road practically all day. By the way, when do you serve the lobster *fra diavolo?*"

"The what?"

"Never mind."

Vin turned and with slumping shoulders, resumed the walk to his room when he heard a police call come over the scanner. He stopped and listened to the grainy broadcast and unmistakably heard that an officer was being sent to North Fork Harbor Vineyards.

Dropping his bag Vin directly went to the payphone and dialed Lefty's Taxi Service. To his surprise, the dispatcher answered the phone on the first ring. After ordering to be picked up at the hotel, he then called the Travel & Pleasure office. In a voice mail for Pat Goode he let her know that he arrived at the hotel while reminding her to be sure the contract and advance had been sent. Vin did not let her know that the room was not paid for as she had promised, that something unexpected had happened at the vineyard or that he was going there earlier than planned. He was acting on instinct. And his instinct was telling him that there was the possibility of a surprise ending to his assignment.

CHAPTER 6

A Crushing Discovery

It was North Fork Harbor Police Officer Nicholas Krupcheski who had gotten the assignment from the dispatcher to check the vineyard. When he got there, he had to stop the patrol car at the head of the long, dark, gravel driveway. While he could not get his vehicle through the gate without an access code, he saw nothing amiss from his vantage point. Although he'd never before been to the property, there was nothing he could see that appeared to be disturbed. Leaving the patrol car outside the gate with the headlights on and walking down the driveway and around the barn he reported that all entrances were secure and there were no signs of disturbance. He reported this by radio to his commanding officer for the evening, Sgt. Henry St. Charles.

When St. Charles later conveyed this information by telephone to Maria Lambrusco, who had phoned the police station when she had not heard back from her father after leaving two messages, she explained to him how unusual this behavior was. St. Charles, a 15+ year police veteran and amateur wine aficionado, had heard of Dr. Lambrusco's fabled wines and promised to personally investigate. As very little appeared to be happening that night in the sleepy village and there was enough back-up in the police station St. Charles thought it would be worthwhile to personally visit the winery and perhaps make the acquaintance of the famous but talented recluse. Once Maria had provided him with the code he'd need to enter the winery, St. Charles ordered Officer Krupcheski to wait at the gate as he would soon be joining him—news Krupcheski did not welcome.

Krupcheski generally had too casual an attitude for St. Charles' liking. His laid-back mannerisms often irritated St. Charles who preferred a police officer who was more alert than indifferent. But in this case, that would probably not be an issue thought St. Charles, who at the very least was hoping to get a glimpse inside the exclusive winery, possibly a chance to meet the legendary winemaker and maybe receive a bottle of wine for his trouble which he would take home and share with his wife Ellen rather than bring back to the station where it would certainly not be appreciated by his fellow officers. Calls such as these, when adult children were concerned for their parents were referred to by the police officers as "well-being calls" and they were made frequently in North Fork Harbor which had a growing senior population.

Maria Lambrusco would not allow herself to sleep until she heard back from Sgt. St. Charles or of course her father. She paced back and forth across the floor of her tiny apartment on the fringes of California's Napa Valley as she waited for the call. Her room was lined with books on chemistry, viticulture and the history of wine. Stuffed in between the hardcover volumes were notebooks crammed with tasting notes and records on growing conditions from the various vineyards at which she worked. Maria tried hard to be her father's daughter. Understanding from an early age she would inherit the job of carrying on the family legacy she pursued the male-dominated world of wine with a relentless passion. Maria picked grapes in Piedmont, served as an assistant winemaker in Spain's La Rioja region and helped plant vines in Chile and South Africa. One fall was spent learning how to master the elusive French champagne-making technique known as *methode champenoise*. This was followed by a season distilling brandy in Germany. Her resume was unparalleled and in the tight fraternity of professional winemaking, Maria was widely acknowledged to be a rising star. But while she learned how to navigate the risks and uncertainty Mother Nature annually heaped on winemakers around the world, she could not withstand any irregularity from her father's behavior.

If her father said he would telephone at a certain time, she'd dutifully hold her phone at the appointed time as it was all but certain that the call would come. As the last two survivors of their family, they shared a common destiny and a special bond that transported them beyond the world of winemaking. So when Dr. Frank Lambrusco failed to call or return two messages from his daughter the evening before he was to leave for a very important trip, Maria did not hesitate to ask Sgt. St. Charles to personally investigate, giving him the winery's access codes. Vin Gusto was not the only one who knew the importance of "leaving a trail."

Sgt. Henry St. Charles was actually a bit excited by the prospect of investigating the winery and did not hesitate when it came to complying with Maria's request for him to personally check into it. The winery's secretive status had intrigued him as it had others ever since word leaked to the community that there was a world-famous winemaker quietly working in their midst. While police officers in rural communities often have a great deal of knowledge about many of the residents they serve, Dr. Frank and his work had remained largely a secret. Having the access code in his possession put St. Charles in an exclusive club in the village of North Fork Harbor, one in which his fellow police officers would certainly envy. Speaking directly with Maria Lambrusco had been a mild thrill for St. Charles. He considered himself a bit of a wine aficionado and read a brief newspaper article about her father when he first launched his vineyard. It was not without a touch of excitement that he drove alone to the winery to assist Krupcheski.

When St. Charles reached the winery he used the code Maria had given him to open the gate and unlike Officer Krupcheski who had been waiting in the patrol car at the front end of the driveway as directed, St. Charles drove straight to the barn passing the "No Visitors" signs with the junior officer following. He stopped about halfway through and using a searchlight surveyed the barn from a moderate distance. Satisfied that nothing seemed out of place he continued straight to the barn entrance.

St. Charles approached the front door. It was a heavy steel door and frame to match. Above the steel doorknob was an intricate electronic locking system. He first knocked loudly on the steel frame with his night stick, hoping not to set off an alarm. He received no response. He then knocked again before yelling, "This is the North Fork Harbor Police! If anyone's inside, please open the door!" There was no response as his commands faded into the silence.

St. Charles knocked once more with the night stick, then took a step back from the door before he began walking around the barn to directly examine the obvious entry points—double-checking Krupcheski's work. The main building was surrounded on three sides by a vineyard. Directly behind it was an outdoor work area filled with tanks, crushers, de-stemmers and other various pieces of equipment such as shovels, rakes, a maze of hoses and pumps plus stacks of the plastic yellow boxes or lugs used to cart freshly picked grapes from the field to the work area.

Like the junior officer, St. Charles found no signs of forced entry and nothing appeared out of place. The pair then returned to the front door. Without making any further announcements St. Charles ordered Krupcheski to turn away as he directed his flashlight on to the computer key pad and methodically punched in the entry code Maria had given him. Once the digits had been entered the heavy door easily gave way. Sgt. Charles was first to enter. He took one step into the doorway and stopped to inhale the slightly pungent aroma of fermenting wine which was everywhere.

"Smell that?" St. Charles asked the junior officer who followed him into the building.

"That's fermenting wine."

"People pay money to drink that?" asked Krupcheski.

"You've got a lot to learn," said St. Charles. "Keep your flashlight on and your eyes open."

St. Charles and Krupcheski observed the dark barn as best they could without turning on any of the interior lights. St. Charles took one more deep breath and then took another long step forward across the cement floor. Instead of searching for the light switches, they carefully panned the winery interior with their flashlights—golden beams shining on worn, wooden walls decorated with various antique farm artifacts—a common touch on the rustic North Fork. The sturdy tools, signs from a seemingly ancient era, looked alarmingly out of place amidst the security system's blinking lights.

"St. Charles yelled again. "North Fork Police! Anyone home?!" They received no response. "Seems like it's just us chickens," St. Charles said to Krupcheski.

"Yes Sarge," he replied.

"Let's keep walking. And don't touch anything." Not having total confidence in his partner, St. Charles felt he had to regularly point out rudimentary police procedure to Krupcheski.

"Yes Sarge," the junior officer repeated.

To St. Charles the old potato barn did not appear to be the type of facility that would be home to a pioneering agricultural-research facility. But despite its appearance, St. Charles, ever the professional, sensed he was in a special place and treated it as such. He understood that appearances could be deceiving and that Maria Lambrusco's father, a well-known figure in his industry, might be missing. If this were true it would mean that he and Krupcheski could be at a crime scene, which is why it was imperative that they disturb as little as possible until they could be sure of what, if anything had happened there that night.

The two officers walked forward, single file in the darkness, St. Charles in the lead with head back and eyes wide open like a tourist visiting a famous museum for the first time. Krupcheski was dutifully tailing his superior officer, clutching his flashlight in one hand and notepad in the other, expecting nothing more than to file a routine search. But unlike Krupcheski, St. Charles was experiencing a slight rush due to the excitement he personally felt from being in a place not many others got to see.

Still relying on their flashlights, they went through the entranceway, past the secretary's office and lab, the only noise being the soft tap of their rubber-soled uniform shoes on the cement floor. Passing through the foyer they entered the fermentation room. Above the doorway was a printed sign of bold red letters on a white background: Authorized Personnel Only. The door was slightly opened. St. Charles nudged the bottom with his shoe to further open it. The odor of fermenting wine grew stronger the further they walked into the room. "Someone could get drunk just breathin' in here," remarked Krupcheski who stopped at the entranceway and used his notebook to swipe a few gnats from his face. St. Charles then turned his attention to the center of the room where there was a large, uncovered cement tank that was partially buried into the earth beneath the floor.

Knowing that no modern winemakers used cement tanks St. Charles was intrigued by the discovery. All fermentation was now done in either stainless steel tanks or oak barrels. Did the cement, a material used by winemakers from another era help the legendary Dr. Frank in creating his distinct wines or was it there for another reason? Perhaps due to instinct or years of experience, St. Charles's demeanor changed at that moment.

"It really stinks in here," said Krupcheski.

"Anyone ever tell you that you have a great ability to point out the obvious?" replied St. Charles. "What's that?" St. Charles then asked. He directed Krupcheski to move the flashlight back. Beyond their reach was a small slightly white and purplish object protruding from the must.

"Looks like a piece of paper," said Krupcheski.

It was nearly in the center of the tank, too far for either officer to reach.

"Go out to my patrol car and get the tape measure," ordered St. Charles who was no longer the excited visitor but instead the sanguine investigator as he stopped to put on a pair of latex gloves he carried in the pouch attached to his gun belt.

While Krupcheski was out St. Charles continued examining the room. He could notice nothing amiss. He walked around the perimeter of the tank looking at its contents. Countless crushed grape skins had floated to the surface forming a hard cap across the top of the fermenting juice or must. St. Charles was growing inpatient waiting for Krupcheski who returned after only a few minutes.

"Where'd you go for the tape measure, the hardware store?"

"We got company," said the junior officer. "A limo driver's out front. Says he's here to take the winemaker to the airport."

"Did you get his info?"

"No but I told him to wait right there."

"That's generally what a limo driver does, waits for the passenger," sighed St. Charles.

"So we got a driver with no passenger. Wine and no winemaker," continued St. Charles as the two officers watched the flashlight beam dance across the must's surface.

"And you don't think anything may be wrong?"

"I ain't said nuthin'," replied Krupcheski.

"I'm not interested in what you're saying or not saying," said the senior officer. "I'm interested in what you're thinking," said St. Charles who tapped the side of his head with his index finger for emphasis. "Now let's check this out," he said as he extended the tape measure in an attempt to secure the white object. When he poked it with the tip of the tape measure it slipped beneath the surface.

"Damn, it went under," said Krupcheski.

"Stand by," said St. Charles.

He again felt around with the tip of the tape measure but could not relocate the object. St. Charles then grabbed a long wooden pole that was leaning against a wall behind them. One end of the pole was square while the other had a spoon shape. St. Charles carefully grabbed the square end and with the spoon end tried to find the object that had become lost in a sea of grape skins and fermenting juice.

"Step back," ordered St. Charles.

"We ain't supposed to touch nuthin'," said Krupcheski.

"Sometimes you've got to break the rules," said St. Charles. "But in your case you've got to learn the rules." With the spoon end he stirred the indigo-colored liquid.

"What do you think you are a winemaker?"

"Smell that?" asked St Charles, ignoring the last comment. His stirring action had freed odors that had been lingering beneath the cap of grape skins.

"Hell yeah" said Krupcheski. "Smells like sulphur."

"There must be 200 gallons of wine in here," said St. Charles.

"More like 200 gallons of manure," said Krupcheski. "Probably makes good compost."

Dark grape skins and light-colored pits stirred across the surface in response to the tiny whirlpool he made. The still-active fermentation provided a light show of effervescence as the freshly crushed juice was stirred. He touched the end of the spoon with the tip of his index finger. Fermentation in the tank had only recently begun and this was reflected in the early wine's harsh taste and relatively warm temperature.

"You tasted that?" asked Krupcheski in apparent disgust as he waved away a bunch of gnats circling his face.

"Just indulging in an impromptu barrel tasting," answered St. Charles. "Could be evidence. Want a taste?"

"No thanks."

"Sorry, I forgot," said St. Charles. "You're too young to be served alcohol."

"I'm into vodka," said Krupcheski. "Vodka don't have no odor. The fumes alone in here are enough to make someone drunk."

"Don't worry, I won't tell anyone that you're getting drunk on the job."

"Let's get going. This stink is making me sick," complained Krupcheski.

"What's your hurry? You're going on your first date?" asked St. Charles.

"If you ask me it looks like a case of another old geezer who forgot to call his kids. Happens every year when the snowbirds start flyin' south," said Krupcheski. "He's probably already at the airport. Happens all the time. Just 'cause some guy forgets to call home don't mean no catastrophe took place."

"And what about the limo driver?" asked St. Charles who then paused to further study the tank. "Like a good wine, good police work can take time. When are you going to learn that?"

"You doin' police work or you tastin' wine?"

"Do you have any idea how many people want to taste this guy's wine?" said St. Charles, getting annoyed with Krupcheski.

"Maybe a friend came by and drove him to the airport and the old guy forgot to tell anyone. Things like that happen every day," complained the younger officer. "Just 'cause some worried woman calls and a limo driver makes a mistake with his pick-up don't mean we got to spend the night here, free wine or not."

"If he was distilling vodka would you be more inclined to hang around?"

"You might be able to talk me into it."

"Listen," said St. Charles clearly turning serious. "If a daughter's concerned about her father's whereabouts and a driver's waiting for the same man we may have to check out a few things. It doesn't hurt. Put yourself in the daughter's shoes. It's what you call building good community relations." He often wondered if Krupcheski actually valued anything he said to him or was the younger officer simply nodding his head—either out of politeness, boredom or both.

"I'm going to try one more time to find that paper or whatever it is," said St. Charles who then reinserted the pole into the tank. "If I don't find anything we'll look in the old man's apartment and if everything's okay, we'll go. Scout's honor," he said, turning to give Krupcheski the two-finger, boy-scout salute. He then again stirred the must, seemingly fascinated by the whirlpool of spinning skins and seeds while he searched for the elusive white object when the tip of the pole hit a heavy object on the bottom of the tank. He poked at it again. It was soft and hard to move.

"Come here," he called to Krupcheski. "Shine your light in there," he said motioning to where the end of the pole disappeared into the pool of fermenting wine.

"What is it?" asked Krupcheski.

"I don't know."

"Probably just a mess of grapes."

"No grapes are this heavy."

St. Charles was leaning over the tank as he carefully manipulated the pole. He did not want to lose track of the heavy object he had on the other end or risk breaking the pole. St. Charles continued struggling with the pole and what it encountered on the other end. Krupcheski held the flashlight with one hand and with his other grabbed St. Charles by the back of his belt to steady him as he worked. Using the pole as a lever and gripping it with each hand, St. Charles felt something rising to the surface on the other end. The white object had resurfaced.

"There it is again," said Krupcheski.

"I'm going to keep working this pole," said St. Charles.

After about one strenuous minute of pulling downward, from the other end of the pole emerged a heavy, motionless, wine-soaked hand inside and a purple-stained sleeve.

"Holy crap," muttered the rookie Krupcheski, shining the light across the purple-colored hand.

"Stop shaking. Hold that light," St. Charles automatically said as he bent down on one knee. Years of police work had made such reactions common for St. Charles, under nearly any circumstance. The baby-faced Krupcheski silently followed the order, trying to direct an unsteady beam with his still shaking free hand. St. Charles turned and handed the pole to Krupcheski before leaning over the tank to grab the thick wrist that was protruding from it.

"No pulse," was all he said. With two hands St. Charles then grabbed the wrist and pulled the body towards the tank wall. A forearm then broke through the surface, followed by the elbow, upper arm and shoulder as the back of a skull pierced the surface. Krupcheski then dropped the pole and reaching into the tank, grabbed hold of the coat collar. Together they pulled the body towards the surface.

"Get him out! Get him out!" yelled St. Charles.

The two officers pulled the wine-soaked body over the tank wall and onto the cement floor. This time it was St. Charles who was nearly stunned.

"It's the winemaker," gasped St. Charles.

Dr. Frank's face was purple and swollen. Wine freely dripped from his gray hair and bushy white eyebrows. A heavy, barrel-chested man, they placed him on his back, turning his head to the left. Deep purple streams poured down his face and across his neck and chest, forming a puddle as they splattered violently against the cement floor.

"Oh my god," said St. Charles, peering at Lambrusco's swollen face.

"What is it?" asked Krupcheski.

St. Charles pointed at Dr. Frank's face. His mouth had been stuffed with grapes.

CHAPTER 7

Pressing for Evidence

St. Charles opened Dr. Frank's shirt and placed a hand on his chest.

"Anything?" asked Krupcheski.

"No. Nothing," he said. He then put his ear against Dr. Frank's chest. "Still nothing."

"Looks like he fell into a vat of grape soup," said Krupcheski. "And you tasted it."

"Grow up," said St. Charles. "We got a dead winemaker on our hands. A famous dead winemaker."

"How long you think he's been dead?"

"Probably a couple of hours."

The two officers stared down at the purplish and swollen corpse. St. Charles then felt the back of Dr. Frank's neck. It was cold and hard. Moving up he felt something protruding from the base of Dr. Frank's skull.

"Serious bump on the middle-back of his head," said. St. Charles. "I'd say about an inch in diameter." Krupcheski jotted down the observation. St. Charles then withdrew his hand and looked at his own fingers that were pressing through the thin latex gloves. As he rubbed his finger tips together most of the residue fell away but purple stains were starting to appear. St. Charles smelled his gloved fingertips. "Smells like half-fermented grape juice. Can't detect any blood. Probably too much wine."

"How come stiffs don't bother you Sarge?"

"My father was a mortician," he lied.

"So it's in the genes," nodded Krupcheski as if he'd just been let in on a family secret. "What about the grapes?" he then asked. "How'd they get in his mouth? asked Krupcheski.

"I don't know how they got in there but we're not touching them. I want a detective to see this," said St. Charles. "Whoever did this is sending a signal," said St. Charles.

"You about ready for me to call it in?" asked Krupcheski.

"Absolutely. Tell them to get a homicide detective and medical examiner over here. We're going to have to take all kinds of measurements. Then go outside and make sure that limo driver doesn't go anywhere until we talk to him."

"Yes Sarge."

"Nicely ask for his license and while you're running a check on it ask him to wait in your car," St. Charles continued. "Then get the keys and lock his car. Run the plates too. Find out who he works for and who owns the car. Then tell him he's got to wait in the squad car until you, me or the detective talks to him. He may want to leave or call his dispatcher. I don't want him talking to other drivers and having this broadcast over some cheap car-service radio. News like this could be all over the Island in a few minutes. You don't know who'll hear it or why he showed up. If he's got a cell phone take that too. Be nice at first but if he argues tell him you're going to arrest him for interfering with an investigation. If he won't cooperate cuff him. He's not to leave the premises until he gets permission from us to do so. That's an order. And do not under any circumstances even hint at what occurred in here."

"Then what Sarge?"

"Get the camera from my car and bring it to me. Also tell the Station House we need a pump and a sieve. You're going to pump that vat dry. Check the premises for some spare barrels."

"Yes Sir. You want me to seal off the driveway with tape too?"

"No. For now I want to keep a low profile. Just be sure the gate's locked. We don't need any more company until a detective and the ME get here."

"Yes Sarge," said Krupcheski who then turned and exited.

St. Charles then reopened his pouch and removed a small, eye-dropper bottle. Unscrewing the top he dipped the end into the purplish fluid on the floor. After drawing a few drops he placed them into the bottle. It was probably going to be some time before a detective arrived. As the Greenport Harbor Police Dept. did not have detectives of its own, one would be dispatched from the county's police headquarters in Hauppauge. Unless a detective happened to be in the area, which was unlikely, it would probably take about one hour for a homicide detective to arrive. Knowing how fragile some evidence can be, St. Charles did not want to wait for the detective to arrive before starting to collect it.

But St. Charles found it difficult to take his eyes from the body lying before him. The victim's clothing was disheveled—a sign that he had probably been involved in a struggle but he could not be sure having moved the body while it was submerged in the vat. He then lightly touched Dr. Frank's half-opened eyes with his fingertips. A few tiny flies buzzed from the victim's face. He could see no lacerations or serious amounts of blood and no other signs of a disturbance on the premises. As the grape juice began to dry, purplish blotches were appearing on Dr. Frank's face which had creases in it both from age and from spending a lot of time in the sun.

St. Charles then began trying to mentally reconstruct what may have occurred. Because he found the victim under some 200 gallons of wine St. Charles had no idea of the position of the victim's body at the time of death. The facial muscles were visibly rigid, the first to stiffen as rigor mortis sets in but the purplish blotches could have come from almost anything—bruises from an impact, the effects of lividity—a pooling of the blood in certain parts of the recently deceased, or the effect of wine and grape skins on his flesh. St. Charles' gloves already had purplish stains on them. This was not what he expected to find when he told Maria Lambrusco that he'd check on her father.

There were two basic rules that St. Charles' years of police work had taught him. The first was that no matter how certain one may feel never disturb the body or any other element of an accident or crime scene. Unfortunately, he had broken that rule. When the hand first emerged from the tank St. Charles thought there was still a chance the victim may have been able to have been saved. This was not the first time that a police officer's efforts to save someone could become an impediment to an investigation.

The second was that even in sleepy North Fork Harbor, it was possible that things may not be what they at first glance appeared to be. St. Charles therefore firmly believed that it was imperative to regularly follow basic police investigative procedures as over time this patient practice generally uncovered more evidence than nearly anything else. Whether that would be the case here he did not yet know but St. Charles regularly preferred erring on the side of caution. However he could not wait for the Medical Examiner's confirmation before phoning Maria Lambrusco.

St. Charles went through Dr. Frank's pockets, recording what he found in his log: an unopened pocketknife, wallet, handkerchief and some loose wine grapes—they appeared to be the same variety as the ones that were stuffed into the victim's mouth. A religious medal dangled from Dr. Frank's neck on a gold chain. He slipped each item with the exception of the medal which he did not touch into a separate plastic evidence bag, leaving it on the floor beside the body. St. Charles then gazed across the immediate area, drawing an imaginary circle that grew wider and wider, he scanned the room for clues or evidence. As he stared at the cold corpse of Dr. Frank Lambrusco while waiting for the medical examiner and detective to arrive, he tried to imagine possible scenarios that may have led to the winemaker's death. What exactly had happened? How did it happen? Who would do this? And why?

This was the work of someone who clearly knew their way around the winery as the access codes were not disturbed and they knew Dr. Frank's habits. Nothing appeared to be stolen or broken. And why stuff his mouth with grapes? What sort of signal was someone trying to send? Good officers used tried-and-true investigative methods combined with experience and a bit of imagination to unravel crimes. St. Charles was sure this was the work of a very determined murderer. He tried to imagine what may have taken place in the barn that evening. It was a highly unusual crime and the usual investigative techniques would most likely, not lead to the murderer. But he would start with the basics, dust for fingerprints, photograph the scene, take measurements of the room, examine telephone and e-mail records, test for footprints and tire tracks and interview anyone who may have anything to offer. It was going to be a challenging case and he wondered if the North Fork Harbor Police Dept. had the resources to see it through.

CHAPTER 8

Coming Uncorked

Krupcheski returned to the crime scene as St. Charles was about to start measuring the circular cement tank.

"What did you get from the driver?"

"He knew the Doc. Said he's taken him to the airport before," said Krupcheski. "Spoke with an accent."

"From where?"

"Said he's from Croatia. Wherever that is. English is pretty broken but understandable. Name's Franjo Kovic. I frisked him. He was clean. Showed me a Green Card. His driver's license was legit. The car's owned by some company in Middle Island. I locked the doors to his car with the cell phone in it and took the keys. Says he drove the Doc to the airport a few times. Sounds like they were kinda friendly. He's waitin' in my car."

"Let him wait," said St. Charles. "I've got to call the daughter."

This was the part of his job St. Charles dreaded. The task of telling someone that a close family member was dead was something with which he could never be comfortable. While St. Charles never shied from performing his duties, if he could have someone else do this part of his job he would have done so. But she'd waited long enough.

St. Charles knew that he could only give Maria the briefest of information. Understandably, this almost never satisfied the surviving family members. He knew Maria Lambrusco was waiting to hear from him and he had promised he'd call but could he tell a young woman on the other side of the country that her father was the victim of a fatal assault, probably committed by someone who was determined not just to kill him but to send a warning. As he prepared to exit the room and leave Krupcheski alone with the corpse St. Charles took a deep breath and then walked outside to dial Maria Lambrusco's number.

She answered the phone before the first ring had finished.

"Hello," answered Maria. Even the grizzled St. Charles was struck by the level of anxiety in her voice.

"Ms. Lambrusco, this is Sgt. St. Charles, North Fork Harbor."

"Yes. How is my father?"

"I'm sorry to tell you that your father has passed away," said Sgt. Charles.

The phone went silent. St. Charles thought he heard weeping on the other end.

"Ms. Lambrusco, are you there?"

"Yes. I'm sorry Sergeant. What else?"

"That's all we have right now."

He could hear Maria breaking down.

"Ms. Lambrusco, I want you to know your father was a widely respected person here."

There was more silence on the line.

"What happened?"

"I'm sorry. That's all I can say at this point."

"What's happened to my father Sergeant?"

"We'll know more once the medical examiner gets here."

There was a pause in the staccato-style conversation.

"I need to know what's happened to my father."

"I'm very sorry Ms. Lambrusco. I wish I had more information for you. Your father was a highly respected man. I realize you're on the West Coast. Is there anyone in the area you wish to notify? Anyone at the winery? A family friend? A caretaker? His physician?"

"No, not at the moment Sergeant. I appreciate the call."

"You're welcome Miss. If there's anything else, please let me know."

"Yes, of course," said Maria.

"Ms. Lambrusco, before you go there's one thing I must ask you."

There was another pause.

"What is it?"

"Did your father have any enemies?"

"None that I know of," answered Maria between sobs. "Can I go now?" she asked.

"Yes of course. Once again, I'm very sorry and if there's anything I can . . ."

The line went dead. On the other side of the country Maria Lambrusco was weeping and St. Charles was feeling very badly for the second time that night. Despite his years on the force, he never liked having to give bad news, especially to the family members of crime victims. During the conversation neither had given much information to the other. Maria and St. Charles were each trained to listen more than to talk. St. Charles became that way after years of police work and Maria after a lifetime of her father's nearly daily warnings.

Maria would be on the first available plane. In fact she was already at San Francisco International Airport. Perhaps it was because she was in a mild state of shock or maybe it was the sense of apprehension she inherited from her father but while Maria was appreciative of St. Charles' efforts she was not comfortable telling him anything more than she absolutely had to, at least not until she could be certain of what actually had happened to her father.

Outside of her father, Maria was the only person who knew the true potential of the nearly completed grape-cloning project and her father's global-expansion plans. She also knew rivals had been trying to gain information on the project. While Maria told St. Charles she did not know of any enemies her father may have had, she did not tell him that there were many business competitors who were anxious to get their hands on his genetic formula. Some were fearful that a new, widely productive, high-yielding grape strain would flood the market with fruit and lower prices. Others wanted access to the formula to apply it to other crops. Still others wanted it to sell to agricultural companies, farmers and maybe even governments. Her father had trained her well.

Later from her first-class seat Maria ordered a glass of wine to help calm her nerves. She then arranged for a car to meet her at New York's LaGuardia Airport and take her directly to the winery. Maria would have the grim task of identifying her father's body. She tried to rest during the flight but even with the wine her mind was racing. Although her father sent daily reports Maria had not been to the vineyard in some time. What else would she find when she got there? Maria knew her father had staff at the winery that would help with the day-to-day affairs but how much could they be trusted? From her father's office would she be able to keep the vineyard operating, maintain her own work and cooperate with an investigation? And what about the talk her father was to give at the international agricultural conference? Why did she spend so much time away from her father when she knew he needed her?

If a crime had been committed, who was behind it and why did they do it? How did her father actually die? Did he suffer? Was there more than one murderer? And if the murderer did not get what he was after would he return? And what about St. Charles' last question? In light of everything else she was thinking about this was the one question that kept recurring in her mind? "Did your father have any enemies?"

A veteran police officer like St. Charles apparently knew something deliberate and malicious had occurred. But personalities such as her father's were not formed without good reason. Growing up in war-torn Italy had made Maria's father naturally suspicious of outsiders from a young age, perhaps even a touch paranoid. While his obsession with security and the lengths he took to hide his experimental vines may have seemed extraordinary to some, he felt it was warranted because he was well aware of the potential of his work. So were others. How far would outsiders go to learn his secrets, things he spent a lifetime learning from the days when he took some of the very first plant-genetics courses offered in Europe? Similarly Dr. Frank often wondered if some of the so-called visitors who spontaneously appeared at his vineyard were just curious tourists or spies sent by competing agricultural companies intent on learning the secrets held within his new breed of vines?

Deciding that there was too much to think about she then closed her eyes and waited for the plane to land.

///

After St. Charles finished speaking with Maria Lambrusco he returned to the fermentation room and began calling measurements to the now visibly shaken Krupcheski.

"I hate being alone with stiffs Sarge."

"Then you may be in the wrong line of work."

"I ain't from the city. This type of stuff ain't supposed to happen here."

"It's not supposed to happen in the city either but it does."

St. Charles had Krupcheski note that the tank rose exactly three feet from the floor's surface. Its inner diameter was ten feet and the cement walls were about four inches thick. While Krupcheski did as he was told, shaking his head from side-to-side, St. Charles inserted the tape measure into the tank. Removing it, he noted the level. "Add that it goes down six inches past the floor," he told Krupcheski who duly entered the recording. Overall, the wine came up to the tank's two-foot mark, leaving 12 inches between the surface of the wine and rim of the tank.

"I can take the rest of the measurements myself," St. Charles told Krupcheski. "Go back outside and start looking around for possible tire tracks, footprints and anything else that might look like a clue. Then get ready to start pumping."

"Yes Sir," said Krupcheski.

"Allow me to let you in on a little secret," said St. Charles, leaning close to Krupcheski's baby face and for the first time during the investigation, revealing a bit of his temper. "It wasn't a heart attack," he said. "You don't need to know anything else except that you're here to assist in this investigation. Need I say anything more?"

"No Sir," said Krupcheski, who from that point on dutifully helped and said little else.

"One more thing," said St. Charles. "I want to be out of here before the employees start arriving. We've got about four hours."

"Yes Sir."

"Nothing gets by us," commanded St. Charles. "Not a thread of clothing, a piece of hair. Anything that doesn't look like it belongs in a wine vat gets pulled. I'm gambling that the missing piece to this puzzle is in this vat."

When an officer arrived with the pump, Krupcheski met him at the gate. He brought the equipment alone to the crime scene, thinking St. Charles would be pleased with his efforts to minimize the amount of officers who were exposed to the crime scene. He assembled the pump and hose apparatus himself, found an available electrical outlet and began directing wine from the vat, through the sieve and into the various buckets and barrels he had scavenged on the property. Like a prospector mining for gold, he would stop the pumping action every few minutes to examine the contents left behind in the sieve. Not sure what he was looking for, it marked the first time the senior officer saw him take part in serious police work in a meaningful way. Mostly he found what appeared to be logical contents, grape skins, seeds and yeast residue. He wore rubber gloves and carefully sifted through the remains with his fingers, examining the contents as he did so. St. Charles knew it would be painstaking and meticulous work but he had no intention of stopping until the vat was empty.

Unlike the veteran St. Charles, for Krupcheski, a North Fork native, the methodical work suited him well as he was not yet comfortable when it came to reacting to the unexpected. Over the course of his 21 years he rarely strayed beyond the boundaries of Suffolk County. Occasional family vacations took him to Florida and Washington DC. There were class trips to Radio City Music Hall and the Statue of Liberty in New York City and a few baseball games at Yankee Stadium in the Bronx but nearly all of his life had been spent within the relatively safe confines of North Fork Harbor. After graduating high school a relative well-connected in local politics had helped him gain admittance to the "Force." It was expected that he'd very likely remain there until retirement, compiling the benefits and relative security that come with such a position. He was the first in a new "class" of officers to join after a scandal had forced several senior officers to resign, creating a relatively large amount of openings for the positions which were highly coveted for their salary and security. But Krupcheski's upbringing was not unusual in the area that had been virtually self-sufficient since Colonial Days and had an unspoken tradition of "taking care of its own." His background and approach to law enforcement were in sharp contrast to that of the seasoned St. Charles, especially when it came to coming face-to-face with dead bodies.

St. Charles also entered the North Fork Harbor Police Force as a result of the same scandal that created the opening for Krupcheski. It was during this time that it was deemed necessary by a state-authorized watch-dog group that an experienced officer with no connections to the local community be enlisted to help it move forward in a new, more honorable direction. A New York City native who spent five years serving around the world for the US Coast Guard followed by a career with the New York City Police Dept., before taking a job with the relatively tiny North Fork Harbor Police Dept., St. Charles was actually a bit like the late Dr. Frank as he remained something of an outsider within the very community he served. And while St. Charles generally enjoyed the relaxed pace of being part of a small-town police department, there were times when he missed the rush of city work. While assigning police-coverage details to such events as the annual horse show or arranging traffic control at the potato festival was not without need in the village, there were times when he wished for something a bit more urgent, which was why he took it upon himself to personally respond to Maria Lambrusco's request. On his way to the winery he used the privacy of the patrol car to phone his wife Ellen. Understanding the stress that comes with being the wife of a police officer, even a small-town one, he liked to let his wife know where he was going. The more information they shared and the more times they talked the less each of them worried.

While St. Charles was generally pleased with his decision to leave the city in which he had been raised, there were other times when he questioned whether or not he had made the right move. In North Fork Harbor St. Charles was always the last officer to be invited to police-based social events. Other times he'd hear of get-togethers at officer's homes to which he was the sole member who was not invited. Mild and subtle affronts such as these made him wonder if his fellow officers would ever truly treat him as one of their own or would he forever hold the role of outsider. While he had had similarly alienating experiences in the New York City Police Dept., it was for far different reasons and played at least a partial role in his decision to take the North Fork Harbor job. But retirement, the Holy Grail, was not too far off for St. Charles and when the time would come for him to "hang up his badge," as he frequently told his wife, also a native New Yorker, they'd consider moving to a more gentrified location—one where they could go for lively walks at night or play chess in the park, where newsstands carried magazines from around the world and every café served a good cappuccino. Ellen St. Charles was a dyed-in-the-wool city girl who like her husband, also occasionally had difficulty adjusting to country life. While New York City certainly had a dark side, it also had a very beautiful one. Often the couple missed the deep ethnic diversity, the vast displays of culture and the nearly endless diversions, from professional sports to world-class restaurants and theatre. But everything had its price he'd often tell Ellen. He could not remember the last time he had to stand on a line, wait in traffic or lock his door.

It was usually while he was alone at the desk or driving down a dark road when he most missed the pulse of the city in which he was born—the city that never sleeps. It was also usually during these times that he'd remember the promise he made to Ellen about moving. But staring at the corpse of Dr. Frank, St. Charles, for a few seconds, actually felt as he did when he was in New York City.

After measuring the tank, St. Charles began photographing the crime scene. Working methodically and without emotion, it was easy to see how St. Charles' business-like style served him well in the often unpredictable New York City precincts. He was thorough, did not take chances and did not work long with those officers who did. St. Charles was daring and aggressive when he had to be and took his share of dangerous assignments but more often than not he methodically followed procedure. He submitted his reports when they were due, cooperated with detectives during investigations and consistently paid his union dues. His daily and private goal was to get home to his wife Ellen and their two daughters at the end of each shift—to achieve that he had to regularly be careful.

His plan worked. There were no citizen complaints against him, his reviews were consistently satisfactory and he was on schedule to make the move to detective when the North Fork Harbor opening became available. Sensing one day his luck may run out in New York City and the relative safety a community like North Fork Harbor offered, he and Ellen made the decision to relocate to Long Island's east end. Wineries, fishing, good schools, maybe even an occasional homicide or murder, what more could a big-city police officer with retirement on the horizon desire?

///

Dr. Damian Dionasis, the county medical examiner arrived at the winery alone and approximately one-half hour after Krupcheski phoned for him. In his long black coat, wingtip shoes and trilby hat he was an impressive figure to nearly everyone he'd met. Dr. Damian Dionasis, or "Dr. D.," as many of the police officers referred to him, was almost never without his large black leather bag which he always carried in his left hand. As his territory covered the entire county, over the years he and St. Charles had collaborated on several cases. There was an implicit understanding between the two professionals as each knew they needed the other's expertise and cooperation to solve cases.

"If I wasn't expecting the ME I would've thought a door-to-door suit salesman had come calling," said St. Charles as he opened the winery door and extended his hand to greet the well-dressed doctor. The two shook hands warmly. Dionasis, who always exuded a touch of old-European formality, greeted St. Charles with his usual firm grip. It had been some time since they'd worked together.

"I was astonished when your man called me," said Dr. Dionasis. "I didn't think anything could ever happen when St. Charles was on guard."

"Every rule's got its exception," said St. Charles, turning to guide Dionasis towards the fermentation room and to the body of Dr. Frank Lambrusco.

"You don't need to show me. I know my way around," said Dionasis.

"You've been here before?"

"Yes. Lambrusco and I have or had a mutual friend in Europe," said Dionasis. "With that introduction I was able to arrange a private tour and tasting."

"You were one of the privileged few," said St. Charles. "You'd better brace yourself. This isn't a garden-variety case." St. Charles then stepped ahead of Dionasis who continued talking as they walked.

"He was actually a very humble man," said Dionasis as the two continued towards the fermentation room. "There were two things about him that especially impressed me. He had a great intellect yet when you considered his accomplishments you realized he was extraordinarily modest. I never spent so much on wine in one day as I did then. Great stuff. I may still have a few bottles in my cellar."

St. Charles just shook his head as the two entered the room.

"Oh my god," said Dionasis when he first saw the body. "Who would do a thing like that?"

"I told you to brace yourself," said St. Charles.

"You pulled him from the vat like that?"

"Had to. Found him while I was poking around in this tank," said St. Charles pointing to the fermentation vat.

"What prompted you to search the tank?"

"We noticed a small white object poking through the surface. I wasn't sure what it was. It turned out to be his shirt sleeve," said St. Charles, motioning towards Dr. Frank as Dionasis put on a pair of latex gloves. "I tried to grab it with my tape measure. When it went under I tried finding it with a pole. That's when I found the body. It was lying on the bottom. With Krupcheski I pulled him out. Thought I might've been able to save him 'til I saw the grapes in his mouth."

Dionasis stood and studied the body. "Apparently there was some sort of struggle?" he asked, flexing his fingers in the examination gloves.

"We got a torn shirt sleeve, a bump on the back of the victim's head and a mouthful of grapes," said St. Charles.

"Any medical conditions?

"I spoke with his daughter. She said he was in reasonably good health," said St. Charles. "She's in California. I'm not sure when she'll be here. No family nearby."

Dionasis sighed.

"It's early in the game but the fact that there was very likely a struggle, probably rules out the chance of a heart attack or the sudden onset of any debilitating illness," said St. Charles.

"I'm inclined to agree," said Dionasis.

St. Charles and Dionasis had confidence in each other. Each was a consummate professional that took no chances in their work and handled every case with the utmost thoroughness. Dionasis knelt besides the corpse. He looked into Dr. Frank's eyes with a tiny light and for the record searched his chest with his stethoscope. "What a way for such a great man to go," he said while turning to St. Charles.

"How long do you think he's been dead?" asked St. Charles.

"I can't exactly tell, probably three to four hours," answered Dionasis who then felt the back of Dr. Frank's head. "It's a small bump. Most likely inconsequential. It's probably from hitting his head on the floor or on the side of the tank. I doubt it's the cause of death."

Dionasis then took one of Dr. Frank's hands. It was already getting stiff. He reached into his bag for a small syringe. He used it to inject water into Dr. Frank's thumb and index finger to make them more pliable for fingerprinting.

"What's the temperature in the room and what's the temperature in the vat?" he asked while taking the fingerprints.

"The room's 65 degrees. I haven't yet checked the temperature in the vat," said St. Charles.

Reaching again into his bag Dionasis then removed a device that resembled a food thermometer and dropped it into the vat. St. Charles watched it float across the top as Dionasis looked at his wristwatch. After ten seconds he withdrew it.

"Seventy-three degrees," Dionasis said, jotting the temperature data into his notebook. "Ideal fermentation temperature. You know he was famous don't you?"

"Sure," said St. Charles. "In the wine world anyway. Around here he was sort of a recluse."

"Find any medications on him?"

"None."

"Anything else?"

"Nothing unusual. I've got a wallet, an unopened pocketknife and these," St. Charles said holding the evidence bag containing the grapes.

"He had grapes in his pocket?" asked Dionasis.

The two men stared at the grapes for a moment.

"I guess that's not unusual for a winemaker," said St. Charles.

Dionasis looked over at the grapes and then again at Dr. Lambrusco.

"Where's the detective?"

"On his way," said St. Charles.

As Dionasis began filing his preliminary report, St. Charles began the tedious task of searching the crime scene as well as swabbing, lifting with tape, photographing, dusting, collecting with forceps and plastic bags while searching for anything that might resemble a clue such as a footprint, clothing fiber or human hair. When he was done he'd have Krupcheski filter-vacuum the area. St. Charles regularly believed that no matter how perfect a crime may appear the perpetrator always left something behind. For St. Charles, it was just a matter of finding it and the clock was ticking—in his world it was always ticking. A voice then could be heard from the corridor.

"Anybody home?"

St. Charles and Dionasis looked up and then looked back at each other. It was Suffolk County Homicide Detective Conrad Thorsen.

"What do we have here?" continued Thorsen, stepping between the two men before stopping to look at the corpse. "My oh my," he said as he stared down at the body of Dr. Frank Lambrusco. A senior detective, Thorsen had the reputation for being smart but irritating with the briefest of attention spans. "I guess this guy's got a mouthful."

"How we doing Sergeant?" he then asked turning to St. Charles.

"We're gathering the evidence Detective."

"And Dr. D., so nice to see you," he then said turning to Dionasis. "What have we got so far?"

"So far, all we've got is a lot of work to do," said the ME.

"Nice suit," he said, fingering the lapel. "You Europeans always carry yourselves with such style. Dressed for death. Where'd you pick this up? Milan? London?"

"Astoria. If you're interested I'll send you to my tailor," said Dionasis returning the volley of subtle sarcasm.

"That won't be necessary. I could never afford to dress like you on what they pay me. I'm only a detective. Listen, I see you've detained someone. I'm going to go outside for a cigarette and talk to the guy in the car," he said turning back to St. Charles while he removed a slim pack of foreign cigarettes from his shirt pocket, firmly tapping the box on the heel of his right hand. Try to have everything all tidied up by the time I get back so I can have a clean look around. You and your boy," he said referring to Krupcheski. "Should be able to do that for me? *S'il vous plait*," he added, turning to Dionasis.

"That's French," he said glancing back to St. Charles.

"*Oui capitaine*," answered the Sergeant.

"We're all so *mucho* continental tonight. It must be because we're in the presence of this great man here," said Thorsen, looking down at the victim. "*Ciao vino bambino*," he said, still looking at the corpse. He had already removed a cigarette from its box. "Be back after just one. Promise."

St. Charles and Dionasis again looked at each other as Thorsen exited.

"*Vino bambino*," Dionasis repeated. "What a disgrace," he said, staring in the direction of Thorsen's exit. "When I was in the army, he was the type of man who'd have been shot by his own men."

"Talk about a flare for the dramatic," sighed St. Charles. "Finish up. Then Thorsen will have his look around and we'll be able to get the body to the morgue."

"*Oui, oui*," answered Dionasis with a sardonic grin. "The ambulance should be here shortly." Dionasis then reached into his bag and removed a narrow tongue depressor to scrape the inner linings of Dr. Frank's nose. The scrapings were put into a vial which went into his bag. Dionasis then pressed around Dr. Frank's chest and felt his throat.

"Anything Doc?"

"Nothing."

They then placed a paper bag over Dr. Frank's hands, sealing them with tape to prevent contamination and/or loss of any evidence that may have accumulated around his hands or fingernails.

"Going to order an autopsy?" asked St. Charles.

"I think this calls for one," said Dionasis.

After a few minutes Thorsen returned as promised.

"I talked to the limo driver," said the detective. "He didn't know anything and had an appointment to be here. Showed me the work order. Doesn't know what happened. He had a clean record so I sent him on his way. But it was good of you to detain him Sergeant, you never know, right?"

"Right," answered St. Charles. "What do you think we've got here?"

"A guy who died while eating grapes," he said, barely able to suppress a grin.

"I was thinking beyond the obvious."

"I know you were. I was playing with you. Teasing subordinates is the only way I can get through my day. You should know that about me by now," said Thorsen. "If it wasn't for the mouth filled with grapes," he said, his tone returning to a serious one, "I might've dismissed it as an old guy who got drunk and had a little accident. Hit his head and maybe drowned. Everyone's got to go one day."

"Not likely," said Dionasis. "He was a professional winemaker, a real pro. That type rarely drinks to excess."

"Maybe then a sudden heart attack, a hemorrhage," countered Thorsen. "Did he have any medical conditions?"

"None that we know of," said St. Charles. "What about the grapes?"

"That's what throws off the equation," said Thorsen.

"You think someone's trying to send a message?" asked St. Charles. Thorsen had a background in criminal anthropology. He was particularly adept at identifying personalities and uncovering the motivations behind the crimes they'd commit. He also had a warped sense of humor and was self-centered enough not to care about who and who did not appreciate it.

"Yeah. I'll tell you what the message is. Be careful when you're eating grapes," said Thorsen. "I don't want to speculate until I've had a chance to look this place over. Examine the evidence. Read your notes. And wait for the autopsy report. But if you want my early forecast," continued Thorsen.

"Sure," said St. Charles.

Thorsen leaned close to St. Charles and prepared as if to tell him a secret. "It's a crazed loner," whispered Thorsen. "A psycho killer."

"A psycho?" repeated St. Charles.

"Sure. Someone with a fruit fetish," said Thorsen.

St. Charles stepped back and looked at Thorsen. "Dead grapes tell no tales," he continued in a sadistic whisper loud enough for the two other men to hear. "It's just my initial theory. Besides, ultimately, crazed loners and psycho killers want to be caught," said Thorsen. "I believe that. That's why they commit spectacular crimes. They usually want to send some weird message but they also want to be caught. They secretly want to be seen. They want the attention. Which means we'll catch the sick genius who did this."

"Is that what you think?" asked St. Charles.

"Actually, I'm not sure," said Thorsen. "I'm thinking aloud. Fantasizing a bit. And of course, still playing with you. How long have you known me?"

"Too long."

"Wrong. Not long enough. We should have dinner one night, just the three of us," Thorsen countered. "Now, regarding this grapey fellow," he said, turning the focus back to Lambrusco. "It's just too damn early to tell. Right now it's all speculation. Tomorrow we start gathering persons-of-interest for questioning. Let's start with the winery employees and anyone else who was here the day of the crime. Any family around? Where's the wife?"

"Daughter's flying in from California. Not sure when she'll get here," said St. Charles. "She's all he's got."

"No wife?"

"Widowed some time ago. He only had the one daughter. She's not married."

"Got his physician?"

"We're working on that."

"Did he have any business partners who might be angry? Some financial disagreements? Business competitor?"

"None that we know of."

"Who are the nearest neighbors?"

"Krupcheski will work on that," said St. Charles.

"Any security tape? Registry of visitors to the premises? Phone, e-mail records?"

"We're in the process of gathering those things, Sir," said St. Charles.

"How about any history of prior threats? Any suspicious employee behavior? Did he keep personnel files?"

"Nothing on any of those things yet," said St. Charles to Thorsen who had the natural ability to create a seemingly endless stream of questions without warning. He sometimes asked follow-up questions without waiting for answers to prior ones.

"Bad associates of any sort? Did he play around with the ladies? A jealous husband's always a possibility. You know the Europeans. They always have someone on the side. Right Doc?" he said, looking towards Dionasis after his last comment.

"He wasn't the type," said Dionasis, who had been quiet for some time as he finished his examination. "And I don't think you'll find much on the phone or e-mail records. He played it very close to the vest."

"Wouldn't seem likely," agreed St. Charles.

"Kept a very low profile," added Dionasis.

"Maybe a slight touch of paranoia?" asked Thorsen.

"He did survive the War," said Dionasis. "Trauma has a way of changing people."

"True, but that doesn't mean he he's got no motivated enemies, whether Doc Vino knew it or not," countered Thorsen. "I have one more question for you Doctor," he said to Dionasis.

"Yes Sir."

"What's the number-one motivation behind murder?"

"I'm not really sure but if I had to say," he paused.

"Yes," said Thorsen. "Let's hear it."

"I can't prove it, but from my experience, I'd say humiliation or revenge."

"Correct," said Thorsen. "I'd hand you a cigar, a nice Dominican-made Macanudo, if I had one, for enlightening us with that answer."

The three then looked at each other, none of them saying anything further. At this point, any theory held possibility. The sudden glare from the headlights of a newly arrived vehicle then passed through a window.

"The ambulance is here," said Dionasis. "Excuse me."

"Wait a minute Doc," called Thorsen.

"Yes Detective," he said, stopping by the door.

"Let's keep this one quiet."

"Absolutely," said the doctor who then exited. "You don't need to tell me that."

"You've got to watch these Europeans," said Thorsen to St. Charles after the doctor had left the room. "They love to talk and they've always got that superior attitude. Make sure he knows who's running this investigation," he said winking at St. Charles. "I doubt if Dr. D. would ever say anything negative about one of his esteemed counterparts from the Continent," Thorsen continued before pausing and resting his chin on his right palm while folding his left arm across his chest. "Maybe," the detective continued, "talking too much to the wrong person may be how our little *amico* here got a mouthful of grapes."

St. Charles, who was rarely satisfied with initial theories patiently waited for an opportunity and then spoke. "What do you really think we have here Detective?"

"No signs of a break-in, right?" Thorsen asked.

"None so far."

"Telephone wires intact?"

"Yes."

"Anything else?"

"A pretty good bump on the back of his head and disheveled clothing."

"Well . . . it could be," said Thorsen, who then abruptly stopped in mid-sentence. "Whoever did this spoiled the soup, or in this case we should say the wine by stuffing this sucker's mouth with grapes. Otherwise, it might've been dismissed as an accident but sounds like some struggle took place. The perp was probably familiar with the premises or had a layout supplied to him. Also knew his way around the security system. Looks like someone had prior knowledge so it's pre-meditated. Let's see what comes back from the morgue and what we can learn from talking to people tomorrow. When's the daughter getting here?

"Not sure."

"Is she good-looking?"

"I don't know."

"Probably is if she's Italian," said Thorsen with a slight grin of anticipation. "Make sure she's on the top of my interview list. Maybe she's free for dinner. Otherwise, I've seen enough for one night. Make a list of whatever else you find and if it's anything worth my time let me know first thing in the morning."

Thorsen extended his hand and St. Charles shook it. Thorsen always delivered a firm grip and St. Charles enjoyed responding in kind.

"Nice to see you again," said Thorsen.

"You too," lied St. Charles. "I'm going to finish up and then get started on my report."

"And I mean it," said Thorsen.

"Mean what?" asked St. Charles.

"Dinner one night. You, me and the Greek," he said with a half grin. "Maybe after we crack this case. We can go out, compare notes and knock back a few ouzos with Dr. Death. I'll bet he knows which Greek restaurants have the best belly dancers. That would put a smile on his wrinkly face."

"You got it Detective," said St. Charles.

"*Merci*," said Thorsen who had already turned to exit.

"*Au revoir*," answered St. Charles who just then thought he may have seen the glow from a different set of headlights near top of the driveway. But since he was not sure did not mention it to Thorsen.

CHAPTER 9

Squeezing the Grapes

As Lefty's taxi approached North Fork Harbor Vineyards Vin could make out the silhouette of an ambulance heading down the roadway. It was a scene not unfamiliar to him but not one Vin expected to see on this assignment.

He told the driver to stop the car and shut the headlights when they were about 100 feet from the winery driveway. "Don't tell anyone you took me here," Vin said after paying him and taking a receipt. "Turn around and don't put on the headlights for a while."

Not used to such instructions from passengers the surprised driver shook his head but promised to do as directed while Vin, not wanting to arouse any suspicion, walked the rest of the way in the relative darkness on the edge of the road, close to the tree line. He stopped near the top of the driveway, wondering what had happened at the same spot where he was scheduled to interview the famous winemaker early the next morning.

From where Vin stood he could see police vehicles in the driveway. He chose to remain exactly where he was. It was not wise to walk onto a crime scene in unfamiliar territory as his city press pass would probably not be honored here and the reaction from law-enforcement personnel could be unpredictable. From where he stood he watched Det. Thorsen enter what appeared to be an unmarked car, write some notes onto a small pad and then make a call on the car radio. A detective's presence meant a serious crime took place, something more than someone suffering a sudden illness or having an accident.

The isolated feeling that comes with being on stakeout was starting to return to Vin. While he was nearly 100 miles from New York City, beyond the patrol car's radio static the only other sound were chirping crickets. Nevertheless, Vin was becoming overwhelmed with anticipation. It was something with which he was more than familiar. Vin made it a point to stay out of the glare of the headlights from two passing pick-up trucks, whose drivers slowed to take a look at the scene as the rays from the full moon that had so excited the hotel clerk/fisherman could barely penetrate the broad leaves from the old maple trees that lined the driveway, nearly forming a perfect canopy over it.

Sgt. St. Charles then emerged from the winery. Closing the door behind him he spoke directly to Krupcheski. Vin wondered if the superior officer would stay at the barn or if another patrol officer was coming to relieve him. Any officers being called to the area would be charged with making sure that the scene would remain uncompromised until it could be proven that no crime was committed on the premises. If so, business would effectively stop at the winery until the police finished their work.

Vin was familiar with such police procedure but still wanted to know what had happened. Ducking behind a thick maple he watched Thorsen leave down the same dark, empty road. Vin saw the car's bright red taillights grow smaller and eventually vanish into the blackness of an otherwise quiet country night. Sgt. Henry St. Charles then walked towards one of the patrol cars. He was unaware that Vin was standing in the darkness. Vin watched St. Charles as he approached the patrol car. As he drew closer Vin thought there might be something familiar about the officer but he could not be sure. He carried himself differently from the other officers on the scene. Vin saw St. Charles sit in the driver's seat of the patrol car, open his police book and begin entering notes. St. Charles then picked up the police radio but Vin could not hear what he was saying. The anxiety of not knowing what had happened combined with the fact that he was supposed to come to this very same winery later that morning was too much for Vin to bear. Plus, he'd need a ride back to his hotel and without a cell phone did not know how he'd call for a taxi. He decided to make his move. He'd ask the officer if he could call a taxi for him and try to gain some information in the process. As he approached the patrol car from the rear he heard the window roll down.

"Who's there?" called St. Charles, tilting his head back.

"Reporter," said Vin standing one step behind the window. St. Charles had yet to turn around.

"Reporter?" repeated St. Charles, who did not turn around to face Vin. "Don't you have enough to report without coming out so late?" He rolled the window back up.

This sort of behavior, a question disguised as a warning and an abrupt signal that there would be no conversation was nothing new to Vin. There were members of certain occupations that generally did not like being involved with reporters for understandable reasons, such as police officers, criminals and basically anyone with something to hide, which meant almost everyone at one point or another. Vin sensed the relationship between the local press and the North Fork Harbor Police Force was probably not very warm—a familiar dynamic. Police officers were private figures trained to deal with the public. Most of them never cared for dealing with reporters as well, which is why police departments had spokespeople who gave "official responses." Unfortunately, reporters with deadlines usually could not afford to wait. This made a "no comment" response never much of a deterrent in the face of a pressured reporter.

Vin tapped on the glass and the window reopened.

"Was it the winemaker?" he asked, moving a bit closer. St. Charles responded by again closing the patrol car window. Vin waited a minute, planning his strategy. Should he try one more time to make contact with the officer or should he try finding his own way back to the hotel? Vin knocked very slightly on the window which the officer rolled down. This time the officer turned to face Vin and before he could say anything St. Charles stated: "I already told you, no comment. Ain't you got ears?"

"You haven't told me anything," said Vin, desperately trying to keep the communication alive.

"That's right. And I'm not going to."

"Can you call me a taxi?" asked Vin. St. Charles stared at him. "I don't have a car. I'm not a local reporter," continued Vin, reaching into his shirt pocket to show St. Charles his New York City Police Dept.-sanctioned press pass. St. Charles continued alternately staring at him and then at the pass. Vin stared back, looking directly into St. Charles' eyes.

"You from the city?" St. Charles asked him studying the pass.

"Yes. Vin Gusto, former crime reporter for the New York Tattler, now on my first assignment for Travel & Pleasure."

"Where you from?"

"I told you. New York."

"Yeah."

"That's it."

"I'm supposed to believe you're just out for a stroll? What do you want?"

"I need a taxi to take me back to my hotel. Since I'm stuck out here I was wondering if you could call one for me."

The officer continued to stare at Vin.

"Was it the winemaker?" he asked.

"What do you think?"

"I don't' know," Vin shrugged.

"That's enough questions. I've already told you too much."

"You haven't told me anything," said Vin.

"It's not my job to talk," said St. Charles. "Where are you going?"

"The Crashing Sea Gull. I have a room there. At least for tonight."

"When my relief shows up I'll take you there. If I call a taxi it'll be dawn by the time he gets here. We have one taxi and one driver in this town. He's got to sleep too. Might want to put that in your article under 'Helpful Hints.' The Gull's not too far out of the way for me."

"That's very nice of you," said Vin entering the patrol car from the passenger side. He was already thinking about how to use the extra time in the patrol car to try to learn if he'd have a subject to interview.

A few minutes later another officer arrived. St. Charles stepped out of the car and talked well out of earshot for Vin who quickly glanced around the inside of the patrol car for any clues as to what may have happened. When St. Charles returned without saying a word he started the motor and left on the same road the ambulance and other officer had taken a few minutes earlier, only traveling in the opposite direction.

"You never told me what happened," said Vin, attempting to break the silence.

"Got to be very careful on these roads at night," responded St. Charles. "Deer's a real nuisance. They can dart out at any moment. Cause lots of damage."

"I appreciate the ride," said Vin, understanding that St. Charles did not want to talk. It was very likely that he should not even be giving him a ride thought Vin who then decided it was probably better to remain quiet and not risk aggravating the officer and possibly getting left on a dark road in a place he knew very little about.

"Pretty much only two ways you can go on Long Island," said St. Charles without warning. "East or west. You head north or south and before long you'll find yourself in the water."

"I see," said Vin, wondering if St. Charles' last comment was another warning disguised as unsolicited information. "So which way are we headed?"

"East. You get to the Gull, almost the end of the North Fork and the next stop's Europe."

Vin nodded and the silence resumed until St. Charles again spoke without warning.

"Where there's blood there's Vin Gusto. Now I remember," he said.

"You knew that?!"

"All the cops read the crime page."

"So you were a New York City cop."

St. Charles nodded.

"Where'd you work?"

"Midtown South mostly. Not too much violent stuff there. A lot of hotel room break-ins, some street crime, a couple of drug hustlers."

"I didn't get much into that neighborhood," said Vin. "I was mostly on the fringes, the outer boroughs."

"That's where most of the wild stuff usually took place," said St. Charles.

"The only times I got to Manhattan was when we tried to photograph celebrities in clubs or if a few gang members traveled in and things got out of hand," said Vin.

"I was never involved with any headline crime. Not the stuff that would make your old page," said St. Charles. "Too bad the Tattler whacked you. That hurts. So that's how you got out here, new assignment."

"Yeah, pretty much," said Vin. "I've just got to find out if my main interview's alive. I'm supposed to be back at the winery in a few hours to interview Dr. Frank."

If Vin was trying to bait him, St. Charles was unmoved by the last remark.

"So why are you here in the middle of the night?" St. Charles asked.

"I heard over the Crashing Sea Gull's scanner that there was some sort of disturbance. I thought it might pay to check it out for my story."

"I'll be damned," was all St. Charles said.

"So," said Vin, deciding to take his chances. "Was it Dr. Frank who went down?"

"Look," said St. Charles. "I know you got a job to do but so do I. I can't comment. Sorry."

"Is it an open-shut case, just some old guy having a heart attack?"

"You feel like walkin' back to the Gull?"

"Otherwise my assignment's over," said Vin.

"There's still lots to write about in North Fork," offered St. Charles.

"The winemaker's a key to the story according to my editor. It would help if I knew whether he's dead or alive," said Vin.

"I ain't sayin' he's involved."

"If he's not alive, I mean available, they'll probably revoke the assignment," said Vin.

"Ain't you got a contract?" asked St. Charles.

"Not yet," said Vin. "It's in the mail."

"I see," said St. Charles who then briefly paused. "So what's the story supposed to be about, some winemaker or our quaint seaside village?" he then asked with a nearly undetectable touch of sarcasm in his tone.

"A little of each," countered Vin.

"That won't be so bad," said St. Charles. "Maybe you can kick back a bit if you don't have nuthin' to write. Take a little vacation. Fishin's pretty good this time of year. That's just what I hear. Being an old city boy I don't have much experience on the water."

"I'm not too bad on the water," said Vin, trying to win St. Charles' over with friendly conversation on common ground. "Growing up my friends and I sailed a lot of boats in the waters around the Bronx, mostly under the bridges and around City Island."

"Sounds nice."

"You've got to know where the rocks are in those waters," said Vin. "And the currents could get pretty rough. Not to mention the commercial traffic."

"Still sounds nice," said St. Charles. "Being on a boat's a nice way to beat the summer heat."

"It was nice. Unfortunately the boats usually didn't belong to us."

"Get caught?"

"Not by the police," said Vin. "Usually by someone who worked in the marina. They'd come out chasing us once they'd see someone's boat was missing."

"Boys will be boys," said St. Charles.

The patrol car slowed to a halt and stopped outside the entrance to The Crashing Sea Gull.

"I appreciate the ride," said Vin. "But if you could tell me the status of whoever it was that went to the hospital I'd be very grateful. You'd save me a lot of trouble."

"Let me ask you an off-the-record question," said St. Charles. "Hypothetically speaking, what if it was the guy you're supposed to meet in a few hours?"

"I don't follow."

"If he's dead or sick and I ain't sayin' if he is, I'm just speculating," St. Charles continued. "Then you ain't got a big part of your story. Am I correct?"

"Correct," answered Vin.

"Maybe I'm just playin' with you. Since you ain't got a car, why don't you take the ferry to the South Fork. A lot more action for a guy like you over there. And don't go sticking your nose where it don't belong," warned St. Charles. "This ain't the city. We don't give out all-access passes."

"Thanks again for the ride," said Vin, slamming the car door. He'd been thwarted by police officers too many times during his career to be detoured by St. Charles' refusal to cooperate. The sergeant knew he did not have to discuss the case and therefore didn't. But why be so courteous as to drive him to his hotel? Perhaps, Vin thought, the sergeant was doing a bit of investigating of his own, trying to learn why a New York City crime reporter suddenly appeared at the scene of what might be one of the most outrageous crimes in the history of North Fork Harbor—if a crime had actually been committed.

Vin had seen enough police behavior during his career. He theorized St. Charles was "sizing him up," trying to learn details of his assignment as well as what kind of person Vin was while at the same time making sure he was removed from the crime scene. Vin sensed he'd tipped too much of his hand when he told St. Charles how important Dr. Lambrusco was to the story. But Vin was sure he saw a detective. That would indicate that at the minimum, a homicide had occurred. The evasive maneuvers from the friendly and then tightlipped and nearly threatening St. Charles made Vin almost certain that there was something the sergeant felt was worth hiding.

In reality police officers and journalists generally did not mix well. While on the surface it appeared that they cooperated with each other, the only times there were exceptions to this was when police were baffled and out of desperation felt publicity might help them crack a case. Sometimes it worked. The other time when they "worked together" was when a police spokesperson would "feed" the media a story. This was usually done when the police department or mayor's office wanted the public to know how hard its officers were working by publicizing accounts of their efforts. The release of such stories was approved well in advance by high-ranking members of the department. This phenomenon usually took place around election season or before budget votes but no serious journalists participated and the involved officers were thoroughly briefed on how to respond to reporters' questions which were often submitted in advance. Editors would generally send a junior reporter and provide some space for the story and photo in order to keep relations cordial between the two institutions. Right now, the North Fork Harbor police, most notably Sgt. Henry St. Charles wanted neither assistance nor publicity, which is why after he learned what he needed from Vin, chose to try to scare him off the case. Vin would almost certainly have to find another way to learn what may have taken place at the vineyard.

Vin wondered if he should call Pat Goode to tell her that Dr. Frank may be sick or dead. He liked to follow his instincts and did not trust Pat. Vin was suspicious as to why she suddenly called him for this assignment and also thought there'd be too big a risk that she might cancel it if there was bad news about Dr. Frank. He decided he would not speak further with Pat until he knew exactly what had taken place. Vin could wait until morning and try his luck again at the winery or he could find out where the victim was and learn something concrete, possibly even before St. Charles would know he was following through with the story.

As Vin entered the Crashing Sea Gull lobby on the way to his room he turned to see St. Charles drive into the same darkness from which they'd arrived. The sergeant now not only knew what Vin was writing about but also where he was staying. On one of the walls was a cartoon-style map of the local area. On it Vin could see where the hospital was. He was actually closer to the hospital when he was at the winery then he was now. These thoughts made Vin more than a bit uncomfortable. But his attention was drawn from St. Charles' moves by the payphone that was ringing at the end of the hallway. It was the same phone he'd used earlier to call the taxi service and he had to pass it on his way to his room. As he passed the phone he instinctively picked up the receiver.

"Crashing Sea Gull," Vin said.

There was a silence on the other end. After a few seconds came a request:

"I'm trying to reach a guest, Vin Gusto," said the caller.

Vin thought what he heard was the sound of a familiar voice.

"Shanin?"

CHAPTER 10

Breaking the Seal

"Vin? Is that you?"

"Yes."

"Why are you answering the hotel phone?"

"I was passing the phone in the hallway when it started to ring and answered it. Reporter's instinct I guess."

"I tried your old cell phone number but the line went dead," Shanin said.

"That's not all that may be dead around here," said Vin.

"I figured you never sent me a new number. And of course there was nothing on you in 411."

"Yeah, my cell phone's been a bit of a problem lately," said Vin. His mood had changed 100 percent for the better upon hearing Shanin's familiar voice. "Listen, what are you doing now?"

"You mean right now?"

"Yeah. Can you come with me to the hospital?" asked Vin.

"Is everything okay? Is someone sick?"

"Maybe sick. Maybe dead. Either way I'd like to find out but I don't want to say very much over the phone."

"Vin, is everything okay? You're not in some sort of trouble are you?"

"No, it's not like that," said Vin, trying to allay her fears. "I'm not reporting crime anymore. I'm here on a travel assignment, a real soft feature. And there's an opportunity for you to work with me as photographer."

"What's this about Vin? Travel stories usually aren't set in hospitals," said Shanin, the tone in her voice shifting from concern to anger. "I haven't forgotten what it's like being involved with you."

"And I haven't forgotten what it's like being with you either. Why don't you come here? I'll fill you in."

"Look Vin, I'd love to but I just got in and . . ."

"And what?"

"I need a shower."

84

"Me too. I've been on the road all day. I've yet to see my hotel room, number 13. How unlucky is that?"

"Vin, you don't understand. I literally stink. I was on assignment for a commercial fishing magazine. I spent the whole night on a stinking fishing boat. I went down in the hole to photograph the catch and was up to my waist in fish. I've got to take a hot shower and then burn my clothes. I don't know how I get into these things."

"Shanin listen," said Vin, on the verge of pleading. "This can be a really big catch. It might be the job that gets you out of photographing fish. Or the whole thing might go down the hole. That's why I need you here."

"Vin, I appreciate the offer and ordinarily it would be great to see you but I can't go anywhere tonight. I'm exhausted and I smell."

"Look Shanin, you're not the only thing around here that stinks. There's another smell. One that's telling me that something's not what it seems. There's a winemaker who may have gone flat, a cop with mood swings who doesn't like reporters who show up where they don't belong and an editor who'd have better sent me a check or I'll be sleeping on the Long Island Railroad tomorrow night. That's all I can say right now. Please get here as soon as you can. You're the only person I know here and I need your help. You need my help. And I don't care what you smell like."

There was a pause before Vin continued.

"Shanin, one more thing.

"What is it?

"Don't forget your camera."

There were a few seconds of silence on the line followed by a click. Shanin had hung up. She did not say whether or not she would come to the hotel. He could not call her back because in the midst of the excitement he forgot to ask for her number and the old-style payphone did not display incoming numbers. Maybe he should heed St. Charles' warning and not further investigate things at the winery. Maybe he had been too pushy with Shanin. Maybe it was all too sudden. Perhaps he should not have insisted that she come right away to the hotel or that she work with him on the assignment. Would it make a difference if he waited a little longer to see her and gradually try to revive their relationship? Maybe like him, she was still hurting from their break-up and wasn't sure what to do. But it was too late to change things. He could not call Shanin back and tell her not to come. He'd have no choice but to wait. Vin decided to wait one hour. If Shanin did not appear during that time he'd try to get some sleep and then decide if he should pursue the winery story in a few hours as scheduled or call Pat Goode. Vin took one last look around the shabby lobby before heading to Room 13.

*   *   *

At the North Fork Harbor Police Station Sgt. Henry St. Charles had a bit more work to do before he could call it a night. The fact that Vin Gusto might be reporting on a possible murder in North Fork Harbor made him uneasy. Gusto, St. Charles remembered from his days with the NYPD was no ordinary reporter. Someone who preferred to go his own way rather than run with the pack chasing the "story of the day," Gusto was a bit of a throwback to old-time reporters who worked their subjects like police officers from a different generation worked their beats. They regularly observed their surroundings and took time to get to know those around them. They were alert and deliberate. They knew how to build trust and confidence with the public so when the time came they had reliable sources from which they could draw. Just like the dependable police officers who in unglamorous fashion almost always found the guilty parties, it was these reporters who usually got the stories the others didn't. They knew how to cultivate relationships and when the time came, just as importantly knew how to harvest the fruit.

Thorsen's parting remark about keeping things quiet had stayed with him and St. Charles then remembered a similar bit of advice an older officer had once given him during a public affairs course he'd taken in the New York City Police Academy. Don't let the press go hungry, said the older officer to the class. Feed them a story, otherwise they'll go looking for one and you probably won't like what they find.

St. Charles then ran an internet search on Vin Gusto. Vin had been actively reporting on city crime nearly until his last day at the Tattler but there were no serious clips for him from after the layoffs had been announced. His New York City reporting had suddenly stopped. The abrupt end to his reporting made St. Charles curious. What kind of effect would time like this have on such a prolific reporter? How would he react to the relatively slow pace of North Fork Harbor? Was he hunting for the story that might get him back into big-time reporting? And would he find it in North Fork Harbor?

Right now Gusto was only a minor annoyance but St. Charles wondered if he would stay that way. He was not the type of reporter who was easily scared or distracted. St. Charles was certain that despite his efforts to dissuade him, Gusto smelled a story and would be difficult to remove from the case. Gusto knew his way around a crime scene and so far hadn't broken any rules. As long as Gusto did not interfere with any forthcoming investigation and respected police procedure, St. Charles could do nothing to stop him from approaching the winery, asking questions or writing about Dr. Frank's case. If nothing else, Gusto would at the very least be a mental distraction to the officers working the case. They were not accustomed to reporters with connections to big-city dailies and national magazines asking questions about their work, especially one who was familiar with police procedures and knew his legal rights. His presence might make the officers anxious and this alone could disrupt any investigation. St. Charles always liked to hedge his bets and err on the side of caution when he planned strategy. That would not be decided until the circumstances surrounding Dr. Frank's death were made clear but so far St. Charles did not have a good feeling about how events were unfolding.

Gusto very likely knew that Dr. Frank was a significant personality in the international wine world. While the travel magazine might be paying Gusto a good fee for a charming feature on the village, St. Charles knew it was the rush of being on the edge of a potential blockbuster story that would get a reporter like him out of bed early in the morning and keep him out late into the evening on dark country roads. It would be hard to "feed" him another story that would excite him enough to pull him from this one—unless one of two things happened. If it was a simple open-and-shut case, Gusto would probably lose interest but as Thorsen said, the grapes threw off the equation. Plus Maria Lambrusco would soon be arriving. What impact would her presence have on any proceedings?

The other possibility would be to steer Gusto towards something else, so he could no longer pursue the Dr. Frank case. Gusto did not have a steady job. Maybe the local newspaper would like to add a former "big city" reporter to its staff. Could a regular paycheck, albeit a relatively small one be enough to take Gusto off the trail? At that point St. Charles made a mental note to phone Howard Gallant, publisher of The North Fork Harbor Reporter in the morning. He'd need to decide how much of his hand he'd be willing to reveal before talking to Gallant about Gusto. Even in sleepy North Fork Harbor the press and police department did not always see eye-to-eye.

As St. Charles prepared to call his wife Ellen to tell her that he'd soon be heading home for the evening he was fairly certain that he'd be seeing Gusto again, he just wasn't sure that when the time came if he'd be working with him or against him. St. Charles then called Officer Krupcheski to see if anyone else had come to the winery. Krupcheski had reported that no one else had been to the crime scene. St. Charles then again ordered the laid-back Krupcheski not to say anything about the case "no matter who asks," to make a note of anyone who inquires about Dr. Frank and to immediately contact him about those who did. It would most likely be some time before Dionasis would have any information. St. Charles was growing uneasy.

The all too familiar feeling of anxiety was starting to consume St. Charles. Despite what seemed like a lifetime as a police officer, unsettled business always disturbed him. Not one to take chances he was fairly certain the odds for a clean diagnosis on Dr. Frank were slight and in that case he'd need a plan. If foul play was involved and it almost certainly was, the police department would need an official statement, an investigation would be opened and a detective would be officially assigned to the case, probably the smart but ingratiating Thorsen. Plus there would almost certainly be an out-of-town reporter for St. Charles to control. This could become one of his biggest challenges. Keeping news of a violent crime from escalating out of the village would start with St. Charles and his ability to control Vin Gusto. This would require a different tactic then what was normally used by the North Fork Harbor police and local reporters.

As a precautionary measure, St. Charles thought further about approaching Howard Gallant regarding Vin Gusto. Could a place be made for a city reporter on his staff and get him off the trail of Dr. Frank? Gallant was a tricky person to read, even for St. Charles. While Gallant was born and raised in the area and had a vested interest in maintaining the towns' status as a quaint village, he also took his journalistic responsibilities very seriously. At times his staff vigorously reported on town scandals and controversies and other times did not pursue what St. Charles thought were stories worth reporting. As St. Charles did not like outsiders interfering with his men and their work he toyed with the possibility of Gusto becoming a local reporter. If it came to be, such a move would itself be considered news in North Fork Harbor as Gallant would be able to claim he'd gotten a reporter with big-city experience on his staff. Or would they each see through St. Charles' plan and call his bluff?

Since that time the two institutions had a less than cordial but sufficient working relationship. St. Charles made sure that reporters' press passes were issued and they gained access to most of the events they wanted to cover and for the most part, the reporters did not interfere in police business. If Gusto came on board all that could change. He'd have to be carefully managed—deliberately kept away from sensitive stories. Would Gallant want to deal with that?

What would be in it for Gusto besides a steady salary? Could he adapt to life at a slower pace? Would he meld into the country newspaper's culture? Would his relatively high-strung personality make him too disruptive a staff member? While St. Charles occasionally longed for the vibrant pace of a big city, he did find himself comfortably adjusting to a small-town lifestyle. He could not remember the last time he'd been stuck in traffic or had to wait on line more than a few minutes. St. Charles knew his neighbors and their families and they knew him. He enjoyed pulling his car into his driveway and seeing his children's toys on the front lawn and watching his wife Ellen tend to the sprawling flower garden that surrounded their mailbox at the side of the road. A person could fall asleep with their front door open in North Fork Harbor and wake up to find everything exactly as they left it. St. Charles took pride in this and often felt he and his fellow officers were partly responsible for the tranquility that enveloped the village and wanted to be sure his neighbors could continue feeling that way.

Who could tell what effect the news of a prominent, albeit reclusive winemaker's murder might have on the village's inhabitants? How would it impact the tourist trade—an important and growing source of local revenue? The local real estate industry? And what about the other winemakers? News of a murder in their backyard would almost certainly have negative repercussions for the local winemakers while crushing the weekend tourist trade, the wineries' main customers as well as that of the bed-and-breakfast inns, restaurants, gasoline stations and farm stands—virtually every North Fork Harbor business would be negatively affected. St. Charles, a former New York City police officer, did not like that a murder possibly took place on his watch in the sleepy village of North Fork Harbor. The idea of such a story hitting the media made him even angrier, yet each of these outcomes was a possibility.

Deciding it was worth the risk St. Charles left a message on Gallant's answering machine asking the publisher to call him at home. A newspaper publisher, even a country one, was accustomed to telephone calls at all hours. About 15 minutes later Gallant phoned back. While Gallant did not yet know about Dr. Frank or even why St. Charles was calling, he knew the sergeant well enough to expect that he was not one to engage in sensitive conversations over the telephone. Although telephone calls at police officers homes were generally not recorded, St. Charles would not say what the call was about nor did Gallant press the issue. By calling him at home at such an odd hour, Gallant knew it was a serious enough matter and the two made plans to meet early the next morning behind the abandoned white bait house at the docks.

St. Charles then ordered Officer Jeffrey Jonah who was now on the overnight patrol to stop at The Crashing Sea Gull. "Take a look-see," said St. Charles. "Take your time. Walk through the lobby. Let me know if you see anything suspicious. Ask the night clerk if he's noticed any unusual guest behavior."

It was his last order of business for the night and what St. Charles secretly hoped to gain was to subtlety pressure Gusto into thinking twice about pursuing the story. St. Charles liked giving these seemingly benign assignments to Officer Jonah. At six-feet, six-inches tall and about 250 pounds, Jonah's presence was hard to ignore.

CHAPTER 11

Through the Grapevine

At the Crashing Sea Gull Vin was putting the key in the lock and entering the small, dark hotel room while trying to make sense of the day's events. Upon entering the room he instantly turned on the light and put his bag in the doorway so the door would not fully close until he thoroughly examined his surroundings.

Vin's room contained a small bed in the center, a credenza, chair and closet. A television set was on a metal stand. The room actually smelled clean and looked as if it had been recently painted. A small bathroom was to the left of the door and there was a window that looked out to the docks and harbor. To the side of the window was a chair and small desk with a telephone and clock radio. After he checked the room he went and removed his bag from the doorway, made sure the door fully closed and locked it. He then took the chair and turning it around, shoved it under the door handle. Looking out the window Vin could see the green and red navigation lights of fishing boats on the bay. Vin decided to take a long overdue shower.

Vin then lied down on the bed and rolling over onto his stomach, set the alarm for 6 am. He ate the last of the brown bananas he'd brought while trying to scribble a few lines in his notebook but didn't get far. The long day which had started in the Bronx, winded through Manhattan and had ended near the eastern tip of Long Island's North Fork was finally catching up with Vin. He did not have the energy to write much but also strongly sensed that his assignment was about to drastically change and he would probably need his strength. Vin was thinking about what may have gone wrong at the winery when someone knocked three times at his door.

The staccato knocks came sharp and steady. Vin lay still, barely breathing, trying not to move a muscle. A few seconds later three more knocks followed in the same cadence. Again he did not respond but quietly and carefully reached for the telephone. There was then a voice.

"Vin, are you in there? I see a light on."

Vin thought he recognized the whispering, female voice but could not be sure.

"Who's there?" he asked.

"It's me."

Vin removed the chair and opened the door to see Shanin Blanc standing there. Vin instinctively opened his arms and moved to embrace her but she quickly stepped back.

"Not now Vin," she said. "Definitely not now."

"Funny, I don't smell fish," Vin countered, instantly reacting to her cool response. Standing about three feet apart they then stared at each other—each slightly stunned by the other's sudden appearance. A few seconds later the conversation abruptly resumed.

"Who's dead this time?" asked Shanin, still standing in the hallway.

"That's a helluva way to start a reunion, unplanned or not. Why don't you come in for a cup of what I'm sure will be very bad coffee?" he then asked Shanin. He did not feel comfortable discussing that evening's events in the hallway. And while Vin did not like how their encounter had started he was pretty sure she'd pass on the coffee, making it a no-risk gesture to improve relations.

"No thanks. I'm sure we can get equally bad coffee at the hospital. Let's get out of this dump," she said looking in at Vin's room. "It's not that it's not great to see you," she continued, "but we should get moving. I've got a busy day ahead of me. I'm taking you to the hospital and that's it."

"What do mean, 'that's it'?"

"I mean that's it until you tell me what's going on."

"Okay," said Vin, still uncomfortable with Shanin's demeanor. "I'll fill you in on the way. I don't want to talk around here. Just give me one second." Vin ducked back into the room to grab his gym bag which he already packed for the day ahead. It contained a note pad, pen, tape recorder and his old 35 mm camera which he had loaded with film.

"Let's go," said Vin. But before he locked the door he reached inside and slipped the Do Not Disturb sign over the knob—an old tactic for those wishing to be discreet about their movements. St. Charles had spooked Vin. Leaving the sign on the doorknob would discourage anyone from entering should he be out for a long time. He hoped Pat Goode's package with the advance would arrive but that was not a sure thing despite her promise. He'd been burned by editors before and learned that until the check was in his hands he could not count on getting paid. Until then, he felt the less management saw of him the easier it would be. He felt the same way about the North Fork Harbor police force. Once he had the door locked the two of them proceeded down the hallway.

"Why weren't you in the lobby?" asked Shanin.

"Why didn't you tell me you were coming?"

"Things don't always work out as planned. You should know that," she said.

"Let's not fight," said Vin. "With any luck they'll be plenty of time for that later. Right now I've got to get to the hospital."

They continued to the lobby with neither saying anything else. As they were approaching it Vin noticed a North Fork Harbor police car parking across from the hotel. He grabbed Shanin by her elbow and pulled her close to the wall.

"What the hell is it Vin?"

He pointed towards the window. Vin counted one police officer in the car.

"This is just like old times, isn't it?" said Shanin. "In town for one day and you already think the police are on your tail."

"News sure travels fast in North Fork Harbor."

"You really think he's here for you?

"I'm not sure but I don't like the odds. Where's your car?" asked Vin.

"Down the street. The red Camaro."

Looking in the opposite direction Vin could not miss Shanin's car.

"When did you become Mario Andretti?" Vin asked as he took in the sports car's form.

"This car and cable television are the two luxuries I've allowed myself as a reward for living out here."

"I thought you would've settled for hot water. Do you have to be so showy?"

"It's fast when I need it to be and in your case, you should be thankful for something that's got four wheels and can go uphill."

The red sports car was not the type of vehicle Vin liked traveling in for business. It was too ostentatious and easily recognizable, plus Shanin had parked diagonally across from where the police car was now stationed. Officer Jeffrey Jonah could clearly see it.

"There's an IGA not far from here?" Shanin said.

"A what?"

"An IGA, you know, a supermarket. It's on the next block. A two—to three-minute walk if you hurry."

"Is it still open?"

"Are you kidding? Around here they roll the sidewalks up at six pm. What do you want to do, buy groceries?"

"I want to get out of here without being seen. There's got to be a rear exit to this place."

"Go down the hallway and then through the door for the stairway," said Shanin. "You'll see a door that opens to the plaza overlooking the harbor."

At that moment they saw the police car door open and Jonah emerge. He was well over six-feet tall and walking towards the hotel's main entrance in broad, deliberate steps.

"How'd that guy fit in the police car? He's going to have trouble getting through the hotel doorway," said Shanin.

"That's his problem," said Vin. "I'll find the rear exit and you walk to your car like nothing's happening."

"What if he says something to me?"

"Try to avoid him. Check into the ladies' room for a few minutes."

"Okay but how will I meet you?"

"I'll find my way to the supermarket."

"Walk west along the waterfront. You'll see a sign for it on your right. There's an alleyway that leads to the street. Wait in the front of the alley for me."

"Okay," said Vin. "Just one question. Which way is west?"

Shanin sighed and pointed in the direction he needed to move. "Only you could turn a simple travel assignment into a clandestine operation."

"When you get to the car keep the passenger door unlocked and have your headlights off."

"One thing I forgot to tell you," said Shanin.

"What?"

"In case we taken captive I keep two cyanide pills in the glove box."

"Be careful what you wish for."

"Whatever you say Mr. Bond." The two of them then separated, Shanin to the ladies' room and Vin for the rear exit and pathway that ran along the waterfront. It was not the first time he had to quickly find his way in a strange place without much light.

While Vin was not sure if the officer was there to keep an eye on him, the idea made him uncomfortable. Vin wanted to avoid any unnecessary contact with authorities while on this assignment. If someone was looking for him and learned in which room Vin was staying he'd perhaps notice the Do Not Disturb sign and take it to mean that Vin decided to sleep in for the morning and would not be going to the winery as originally planned. It was a mild diversionary tactic intended to put some breathing room between Vin and the local police. He had no idea if it would work but he had nothing to lose by hanging a sign on the door.

The moon was full and bright that evening and Vin easily reached the waterfront. He briefly glanced at the stars that filled the harbor sky then took a deep breath and made his way as Shanin instructed. Walking briskly he regularly glanced upwards for the sign to the IGA's rear entrance. It was not long before he found it. The sign was large, perhaps so it could be visible from the harbor. Vin then carefully entered the dark alleyway. Having grown up in the Bronx dark alleys were not unfamiliar to him. He stealthily walked through the alleyway, winding his way past discarded crates, old newspapers, broken glass and other debris. Just before reaching the sidewalk he stopped and remained in the darkness. The surrounding buildings blocked out the moon's generous glow as he waited for Shanin.

Where could she be he wondered. He began carefully craning his neck outside the alley walls to look down the road for any sign. After a few moments Vin began worrying for her and hoped he did not cause her any trouble with the police officer. He was in strange territory and had no way of telling what could happen but besides Shanin there was no one else in the area he could trust. A few seconds later he thought he heard a motor in the distance but could see nothing down the road. He'd forgotten that he told Shanin to drive without the headlights. When she slowed to a stop Vin ran from the alley and into the passenger seat. She then continued west on the Main Rd. and when they got around the first bend put on the headlights.

"Anyone see you?" asked Vin.

"How do I know? How about you?"

"I think we're clear."

"It's been a while since I've driven in the dark without headlights," Shanin said.

"When you spend your time photographing kids in giant pumpkins there's no need to," said Vin. He almost instantly knew he again said something wrong. A few seconds later Shanin fired back.

"It pays the rent," she plainly said. "Besides, it's nice not living like a spy on the run. You should try it sometime."

"I'm sorry," said Vin. "I'm just a little creeped out by this whole thing."

"You're only here one day and already you suspect a conspiracy."

"I haven't even told you the story."

"You don't need to."

"What?!"

"I can summarize every Vin Gusto story ever written in about three sentences. Someone's gotten bumped off or hurt," she said. "And you suspect foul play. Then it's either conspiracy, robbery, jealousy or some other form of treachery but it's never an open-shut case with Vin Gusto."

"That's because it very often isn't," countered Vin. "In most crimes the victim knows the perpetrator. That's not me talking, those are FBI stats."

"Dog-bites-man is never enough for you. It's always why, why, why? Was the dog trained to attack? Did someone provoke it? Where was the owner? Did the man frighten the dog? When was the dog last fed? Was a controlled substance secretly added to the dog's food to make it more aggressive?"

"The last time I checked you were paid to shoot pictures and I'm paid to ask questions," snapped Vin. "I don't tell you how to work a camera, so don't tell me how to write stories. By the way, did you bring your camera?"

"Of course I did. I always bring it because you never know, I could be on my way to my big break," Shanin said, with an overdose of hostile sarcasm. "You never know which homicide victim, heart-attack sufferer, car wreck or crazed-psychopath photo is going to nail me a Pulitzer."

"It's better than shooting Little Miss Potato Festival," said Vin.

"Is it better than being called in the middle of the night by someone who's desperate about a travel-rag assignment and needs a ride to the hospital because he's just so successful and talented he doesn't even own a car?"

"I gave up my car and switched to mass transit. It's better for the environment," said Vin.

"You gave it up because you couldn't pay the tickets, insurance, inspection or anything. I'm surprised you had enough for train fare."

"You look like you're doing great too," said Vin. "Does taking a few pictures between baby-sitting jobs keep you going? The receptionist told me you're just a stringer, couldn't even make staff photographer. You must be so proud."

"And you're so unemployed."

"I was let go as part of a corporate restructuring. It's the way things go now. I'm an independent contractor," said Vin, trying to defend himself. "A professional freelancer."

"Me too," retorted Shanin.

"Then why don't you start acting like one?"

"Because I'm driving to the hospital in the middle of the night. You still haven't told me what we're to look for when we get there."

"That's a minor detail. In a small hospital it's easy to find out things. Let's stop this silly arguing. There's something I've been meaning to tell you."

"What's that?"

"It's great to see you. It really is, despite all the nasty things you just said about me," said Vin. "You look great and I haven't noticed any fish odor yet."

There was another pause in their conversation.

"Really?" she asked, ignoring the fish-odor comment. "It's nice to see you too. I'd forgotten how much you like to argue. It's been a while since I've been spoken to like that. Everyone here is so polite all the time."

"Not Sergeant St. Charles. He's tough to read. Have you had any experience with him?"

"Nothing unusual. He's issued me a press pass a couple of times. He's okay. I've never heard anyone complain about him."

"Do any of the reporters ever question him?"

"There's no need to. Nothing ever happens here."

"Maybe no one wants anything to happen here, anything unsavory," said Vin.

"There goes the conspiracy theory again," said Shanin. "This is a cute little town and people want it that way. What's wrong with that? Farming's down, fishing's down, real estate's down. If it wasn't for the tourists half the people here would be out of work."

"Something happened at a winery tonight and St. Charles wouldn't talk about it," said Vin. "That's why I'm hot on this story."

"But you said you're here for a travel assignment."

"I am. That's what brought me here," said Vin. "I'll get around to that. I don't want to invest too much time in it until the advance arrives. Pat Goode, remember her from the Tattler? I hadn't heard from her since the layoffs and all of a sudden she calls early this morning asking if I can take a rush assignment. She told me my subject, this winemaker would have a lot to talk about but now I'm not so sure. And then she wants pretty pictures of kids eating ice cream cones. My advance is supposed to come to the hotel. Until the advance arrives or I talk to Pat, I'd like to find out what I may have missed at the winery."

"I remember Pat," recalled Shanin. "Society girl. Never ate in the office cafeteria."

"Was she a vegan?"

"Maybe. Once in a meeting I offered her milk for her coffee and she shot me one of the dirtiest looks I've ever gotten. But other than that, she wasn't bad to work with."

"Remember anything else about her?"

"She spent most of her time in the office shopping online. I never saw Pat work very hard. She never worried about meeting a deadline. Came from a wealthy family. Pat went to one of those snooty all-girl colleges in Connecticut or New Hampshire or some place like that. My father knew a little about her family's operations from his business dealings."

"Your father did business with the Goode family?"

"Yeah. I remember him talking about them once or twice. Why?"

"What did he say?"

"Not too much. He didn't talk much about clients. I do remember him saying that they're an old industrial family with a pretty wide range of interests—publishing, manufacturing, some agriculture. Now I remember. My father sold them agricultural chemicals. WASPs I think."

"The chemicals were to kill wasps? Was there some sort of infestation?"

"Anyone ever tell you you're unbelievably dense? White-Anglo-Saxon-Protestants. Old New England money family. Charm schools. Summers at the Hamptons. New York City pied-a-terre. Like I used to be before I got in this business."

"You mean before you met me," said Vin. "Pat remembered you too. That's how I got you the photography assignment. We may get a possible cover out of this if we can get her 'happy photos.' Like the stuff you're shooting for the local paper."

"No problem," said Shanin. "Some of the people in this town are on perpetual happy mode. They act like they've found paradise on earth. The smile never leaves their face. I wonder what they're taking."

"I wish I could be like that," said Vin. "Be able to delude myself into thinking everything's wonderful all the time. What could be better? This job on the other hand, it brings out the worst in people. Just like Stine used to say."

"It's all a matter of perception," said Shanin. "Stine used to say that too."

"It's great being around optimists."

"They say the camera doesn't lie but the photographer might," Shanin said. "We can make the world look any way we like depending on how we hold the lens.

Out here, pretty pictures help sell papers. We'd rather put a pony on page one before we'd put a problem there."

"How'd a former city cop like St. Charles get here?" asked Vin.

"What I've heard is they needed to do some housecleaning in the PD. They wanted an outsider with big-city experience and no local ties."

"Who did?"

"The town I guess. Or whoever it is that the police report to."

"Was St. Charles getting the job more symbolic or does he really have power?"

"It's hard to say," said Shanin. "I've never gotten a clear idea on how this town's politics work. I'm too busy trying to pay my rent. By the way, you haven't told me what I'm getting paid on this job."

"Pat told me she'd pay the photographer separately. I didn't negotiate a rate for you."

"What are you getting?"

"That's confidential."

"People who are frequently broke usually don't make good deals," said Shanin. "You've never been able to hold onto money."

"That's because I never had enough."

"If you don't tell me what you're making I'll call St. Charles right now and tell him you're on your way to the hospital. I do that and you're definitely on the next train out of North Fork."

"And you'll lose your first cover assignment outside of the Crabapple Chronicle."

"I've made it this far. I can live without it."

"You wouldn't tell St. Charles what we're doing, would you?"

"If you piss me off enough I will."

"All right," Vin easily broke down. "I'm getting $5,000, including an advance and 'reasonable expenses' according to Pat."

"$5,000! That's more than I make in three months out here," exclaimed Shanin.

"But don't forget about the bonus you're getting," said Vin.

"Bonus?"

"You get to work with me again," he quipped. "You can't put a price on that."

"You're the one who tracked me down," countered Shanin. "I was doing fine on my own."

Shanin then slowed the car and pulled into a gasoline station stopping at one of the pumps.

"Why are you stopping here?" asked Vin.

"Why do you think I'm stopping my brilliant reporter? Since we're in this together and your 'reasonable expenses' are being covered you can give me $20 for fuel. This is the only station open around here at this time."

Vin looked across at the dashboard. "You've got a quarter-tank left," he said. "Let's get to the hospital."

"I want to fill up now. You never know, we may need it later and not have time to stop," answered Shanin. "Although your subjects usually aren't going anywhere."

"My advance hasn't come in yet."

"I've heard that before," said Shanin. "You couldn't have come out here flat broke."

"Take $15. It's all I have after my train fare. If the advance doesn't come I'll have to find an ATM. I still have to pay my hotel bill."

"I'm calling Pat tomorrow."

"You can't talk to Pat," said Vin.

"I have to."

"Why?"

"I've got to negotiate my deal."

"I'll negotiate for you."

"No thanks," said Shanin. "If you're getting $5,000 I'm worth at least double that. The photos tell the story. They're what build the fantasy. And fantasy sells magazines, especially travel magazines."

"You won't get $10,000 out of Pat Goode. The publishing business isn't what it used to be. She originally offered me $2,500. I argued that it's a rush job and worth more."

"And she gave it to you?"

"She said she would."

"Did you get a contract?"

"There wasn't any time. It's coming with the advance."

"Let's see what's inside when the envelope arrives."

There was a pause.

"The more things change, the more they remain the same," mumbled Shanin as she looked across at Vin.

"Don't look at me like that," said Vin.

"Like what?"

"Like you used to when we were working together. Like you did whenever something went wrong."

"And something always went wrong," said Shanin.

"I'm sorry. What were you doing yesterday? Photographing fish?" asked Vin. "That'll get you a Pulitzer."

"The last time I looked you had to be alive to get a Pulitzer."

"What's that supposed to mean?"

"I haven't been shot at or threatened, had to run from thugs or been turned away from an event since I've been here," answered Shanin. "And now I'm driving to a hospital in the middle of the night. Back where I started," said Shanin. "This will probably be the first travel story to take place in a waiting room. I can't wait to talk to Pat tomorrow."

"You've done nothing to move your career forward," said Vin.

"At least I sleep at night!"

"That's because that's all there is to do out here!"

"And why are you writing travel?" asked Shanin. "Because it's safe?"

"No, because it's lucrative!"

"You'd be the last reporter to thrive with a 'safe' assignment," she said. "And lucrative? You've never had a decent payday in your life. The Internal Revenue clerks must laugh when they see your tax return."

"I'm sorry. It must be tough to be a trust baby whose inheritance has run out. I wouldn't know. I just do what I have to do to survive."

"That money was from my father and for my education! That's how I used it."

"And my father died when I was 13!" said Vin. "He left me and mother with nothing. Not even insurance! She had to borrow money from neighbors to pay for his burial."

The former trust baby and hardscrabble writer then stared at each other for a moment. Without saying anything further, Vin got out of the car, paid the attendant and filled the tank.

"Let's get going," Vin said when he returned. "You should have a full tank."

"Thanks," said Shanin. She then turned the key forward without starting the motor, glancing appreciatively at the dashboard while watching the fuel-gauge needle rise. "A girl's got to do what a girl's got to do," she said before leaving the station.

"How far's the hospital?" asked Vin.

"We'll be there in about five minutes," said Shanin.

"Then let's get going please," said Vin.

"There's just one more thing before we go any further."

"What's that?" sighed Vin.

"You haven't told me who you think is dead."

CHAPTER 12

Peeling Back the Skins

Vin recounted what he knew about what took place at the winery earlier that evening as Shanin drove. Perhaps it was because she was focused on getting to the hospital or maybe things were happening too fast for her but surprisingly, Shanin did not appear shocked to learn of what may have happened to Dr. Frank. Vin told Shanin that while he was not exactly sure of Dr. Frank's fate he also mentioned the interest Pat Goode had expressed in him. Always a good listener, Shanin nodded as she drove.

When Shanin steered the car into the hospital parking lot Vin instinctively scanned the area for security personnel and other possible impediments to their entry. It was a big and modern-looking campus. Three separate brick buildings were joined through plexi-glass and steel skyway "bridges." They were surrounded by a sweeping parking lot which had a landing pad for helicopters and landscaped courtyards. It did not resemble the usually cramped big-city hospitals Vin was used to visiting. It appeared impressively modern and efficient and not what he expected so far in the country.

Driving through the parking lot they could see through the glass doors at the main entrance where a security guard was sitting behind a desk. A little further down was the "Emergency Personnel Only," entrance. An ambulance was parked a few yards away. It looked like the one that that Vin had seen at the hospital but he could not be sure. An attendant relaxed alongside the ambulance, leaning against the door as he talked into a cell phone, taking breaks to drag on a cigarette. Vin took note of the attendant and instructed Shanin to park in a dark area of the lot that was near the exit in case they had to leave quickly.

"It's my car. I'll park it where I want," she said.

Vin chose not to answer and instead gave Shanin a quick game plan.

"Let's act like we're Dr. Frank's relatives and see if he's here."

"Okay chief," said Shanin. "Who should we say we are, his long-lost son and daughter? Concerned niece and nephew? Housekeeper and aimless boyfriend?"

"Let's just say we're friends of the family."

"No can do," said Shanin.

"Why not?"

"Has one soft travel assignment blunted your memory? If the doc's in ICU or cardiac care the hospital won't give information to or let anyone but immediate family members see him. Besides family friends usually don't show up in the middle of the night, that's a time for immediate family."

"We'll worry about that later. Let's first get inside," said Vin. "He's probably still in the ER. Just keep the camera hidden."

"This isn't some big-city hospital," said Shanin. "It's a little different here. Everyone knows who's who. And if they don't know who you are they'll find out quickly."

"People are always visiting hospitals. Besides, Frank kept a low profile. No one would necessarily know if we're relatives or not. They may not even know he's some important wine guy," countered Vin. "An ER's an ER. Pat Goode told me to 'get inside his head.' Now I'm trying to find out if he's dead or alive. You get some shots no matter what."

"What if some real friends or family are already here?"

"It's doubtful. He's a recluse. Let's keep it simple. Get in. Nail this and get out. Let's go," said Vin reaching for the door.

"Just a minute," said Shanin. Vin looked across to see her slipping a tiny digital camera into her bra. This was in addition to the full-size camera, which she had covered in her shoulder bag.

"In case we get searched," said Shanin. "You've always got to have a Plan B."

An old photographer trick was to always have two cameras—one to hand to security and the other to take pictures. Once the first camera was handed over almost no one ever imagined there could be a second one hidden somewhere on the photographer's person.

Whether they knew it or not, Vin and Shanin instinctively made a good team—each always ready to cover for the other despite their bickering. There had been times when Vin was the one who actually got the photo and other times when Shanin overheard information that she relayed to Vin for his reporting. Shanin and Vin each knew it was doubtful that they'd be searched by any hospital staff at this hour so the chance of getting a camera inside was very good. Whether they could get close enough to Dr. Frank was still an unknown but things were usually a bit lax during the overnight shift.

Vin wanted to get into the hospital as quickly as possible. He had taken advantage of emergency room chaos numerous times during his career to get information on victims. His strategy was generally the same each time: get inside the ER or as close to the victim as possible and keep his eyes and ears open. He'd rarely disclose that he was a reporter and always kept a very low profile. Vin also found spending time in waiting rooms to be helpful when gathering information. Victims' friends and relatives could often be heard talking about what took place and sympathetic but irresponsible medical personnel frequently spoke with family members in such areas. Otherwise Vin would sit in the waiting room and pretend to be reading the newspaper. A person reading a newspaper in a hospital waiting room never aroused suspicion. Vin usually kept the paper open to the crossword puzzle page, filling in a few boxes as he waited. When he heard helpful information he would discreetly jot notes on the newspaper's margins, making a point not to look at those engaged in the conversations to which he was listening. If Vin had to phone something into his editor, he made sure he was well out of earshot when he did so. Other times he'd text bits of information into the office and an editor would use them to build a story. He was hoping he wouldn't have to employ any of those tricks tonight but get straight to his source.

Vin and Shanin went through the emergency room entrance, walking directly past the late-night waiting room visitors and then down a short corridor where a nurse and security guard were at a desk. The guard was seated behind the desk and the nurse was sitting on it holding a cup of coffee. A small area between one side of the desk and a wall that could serve as a passageway into the ER was blocked by a vacated folding chair.

"I'll see you Jimmy," Vin heard the nurse say as she rose. "My break's just about over."

"Goodnight Irene," Jimmy responded.

When the nurse noticed Vin and Shanin approaching she waited by the desk, watching the two of them come closer.

Vin briefly nodded at Shanin as they approached.

"Hi Jimmy," Vin said to the security guard.

"Hello," the guard said in response, looking Vin over.

"I'm here to see my uncle. He was brought in a little while ago."

"What's his name?" asked the guard, holding a thin stack of paper in this hand.

"Frank Lambrusco."

The guard looked down the top sheet of paper and then at the other sheets.

"No one here by that name."

"Are you sure?" asked Vin.

The guard looked again at the list. He then handed the papers to the nurse.

"I don't see anyone by that name either," said the nurse, returning the papers to the guard. The two couples then stared at each other until Vin broke the silence.

"Can I go in and have a look around? Maybe with the confusion your list wasn't updated."

"I'll call upstairs," said the guard. "If he's in the system, they'll have it. Wait here," he said, holding up his hand to indicate they go no further. Vin watched the guard punch a telephone extension into the keypad.

"Aren't you the newspaper girl?" the nurse then asked Shanin.

Shanin and Vin were each flustered—their cover possibly blown by a country nurse. The two of them looked at each other.

"Yes," said Shanin, smiling and extending her hand. "I'm Shanin. How do I know you?"

"I thought I recognized you. You took my daughter's picture, the one that was in the paper. You know, the kids at the Columbus Day Pageant. She was one of the Indians, I mean Native Americans."

"Of course," feigned Shanin. "What a nice day that was for the children. How's your daughter doing?"

"Oh you know, same old stuff except she hurt her ankle playing soccer. It's all swollen like a grapefruit," said the nurse, holding out her hands in an attempt to convey excessive swelling.

"That's too bad," said Shanin shaking her head up and down in her own attempt to appear sympathetic. "Fortunately at her age she'll probably be running across the soccer field in no time."

"There's no one answering upstairs," interrupted the security guard to the nurse, hanging up the phone.

"What did you say your cousin's name was?" the nurse then asked Vin.

"Lamburso, Frank Lambrusco, Uncle Frank."

"What happened to him, bad fall?"

"I'm not sure," said Vin. "He's an older man. English is not his first language so he may have trouble communicating. That's why my cousin called. She doesn't live in the area and asked me to come here to see if he needed help." Vin had a rudimentary knowledge of Italian and occasionally it had come in handy. This might be one of those times.

"I don't recall any older men coming in tonight. It was tonight right?"

"Yes," said Vin.

"You know Jimmy," said the nurse to the security guard. "They've had their hands full upstairs after that computer problem. I wouldn't be surprised if they don't have all the information yet."

"Could be," said the guard.

"I'll take him back with me," the nurse said, nodding at Vin. "That way if his uncle's here he can see if he needs anything."

"Okay" said the guard. Vin and Shanin then began to walk past the desk.

The phone on the desk then rang.

"Just a minute," said the guard, again holding out his hand. He then hung up the phone and rolling his eyes upward turned to the nurse and said. "That was Sgt. St. Charles from the police dept. He said there may be a reporter coming here and not to give out any information."

"Only one of you needs to go in. He's your uncle," he said nodding at Vin. "And you've got to sign-in," he added, sliding a clipboard with a pen attached by a length of string across the desk towards Vin.

"You'll have to go back to the waiting room," he said to Shanin.

"Shanin," said Vin."Can you sign-in for me? I'll probably just be a few minutes."

"Sure," she said.

The guard looked at Vin and then at the nurse who shrugged her shoulders. Without waiting for an answer Shanin took the pen and began writing onto the white boxes.

"Thanks," Vin said to the guard and he then turned to walk with the nurse. "See you in the waiting room," he said to Shanin.

"Does St. Charles like to give you a hard time?" Shanin asked the guard in an attempt to gain some insight into the local police-hospital security dynamics.

"Let's just say he likes to cover all the bases."

"You don't report to him, right? I mean you're not a police officer. You're a private security guard."

"True but we try to cooperate as best we can," answered the guard. "You don't want to be on the bad side of a man like St. Charles."

Shanin smiled before preparing to leave when the guard surprised her.

"If you don't mind, I've got a question for you."

Sensing their cover may be on the verge of being blown Shanin quickly felt anxious.

"Sure," she said, trying to appear regular.

"That your boyfriend?" the guard asked, pointing in the direction Vin had walked but was now too far down the hall to hear him.

"Sometimes," she sighed, a feeling of relief coming over her. She then handed the clipboard back to the guard and turned towards the waiting room.

"We all make mistakes," mumbled the guard as he watched Shanin walk down the hallway towards the waiting room.

*   *   *

Inside the ER Vin walked behind the nurse, glancing into the various patient areas separated only by thin curtains for a glimpse of Dr. Frank Lambrusco. As the nurses and technicians ran back and forth, often pushing trays containing equipment or medication, stopping to complete charts or speak with patients' family members, Vin tried to find his subject. In one of the patient areas he saw a doctor using a small light to look into the eyes of a handcuffed prisoner who was sitting on a chair. A police officer was sitting next to the prisoner, his hand on his baton. Vin kept walking, not wanting to be noticed although occasionally someone would look at him. But Vin, with St. Charles' latest warning to the security guard fresh in his mind, would stick to his business, working quietly and quickly, hoping to find what he needed and then leave just as quietly.

"We take in any old men tonight?" Vin heard Irene ask another nurse as they made their way through the ER. "This man's looking for his uncle," she continued gesturing towards Vin. "We got any older men who have trouble speaking English?" The other nurse just shook her head. Vin heard her ask similar questions to several other nurses and aides but each response was negative. When they reached the end of the small ER the nurse turned to Vin.

"I don't think we have whoever it is that you're looking for," said the nurse.

"Could he be in another area?"

"No. If he came in tonight he'd be here. And we've got no records of anyone by the name you gave being transferred to a room or to ICU."

"How about another hospital? Where's the next nearest hospital?"

"That would be Southampton. But it's not likely they'd bring him there when we've got beds here," she said, gesturing towards two empty beds. "It's nearly 40 miles away."

They both looked at each other.

"I've got to get to my station so I'm going to walk you back to the guard. He'll see you to the waiting room."

"You've been very nice but I can see myself out," Vin offered, now hoping to free himself from the nurse so he could further explore the hospital in search of Dr. Frank.

"No trouble. It's on the way," she said. "Why don't you give me a number where I can reach you? If your uncle comes in I'll give you a call."

Vin hesitated. He did not want to give the nurse his name and phone number should police come looking for him. Nor did he want to arouse any suspicion by declining her offer.

"I'm not sure if my cell phone's getting reliable service out here," said Vin showing her his ancient cell phone. "Why don't you call Shanin, you can reach her at the newspaper. She can always find me."

"I thought you said you didn't live too far away?"

"Well, I don't," Vin lied.

"Then if you get service at home you should get it here," said the nurse as they began leaving the ER.

Vin leaned close to the nurse. "I haven't been very good about paying my cell phone bill," he whispered. This time his excuse wasn't too far from the truth.

"I see," said the nurse, nodding her head. "If I hear of anything I'll get in touch with your lady friend."

"Thanks," said Vin. By this point they had returned to the security station. "You've been very helpful."

"You're welcome," she said as she turned to leave.

"Find who you're looking for," the security guard then asked Vin.

"Unfortunately no," he answered.

"The waiting room's right down the hall," the guard responded while gesturing in the direction he wished Vin would exit.

"Any other place they take old guys who might've gotten hurt around here?" Vin asked in a last, desperate attempt for an answer.

"If he ain't here he's either dead or still at home."

Vin paused for a second before asking, "You got a morgue here?"

"Yeah but it's only for patients who die in the hospital," said the guard. "It don't look like your guy was ever here."

"So when someone dies elsewhere," Vin said hoping the security guard would finish the sentence.

"Then he'd probably be in the county morgue in Patchogue. You know, next to police headquarters."

"Yeah," said Vin, trying to sound as if he was familiar with the area. "Thanks. Have a nice night."

The guard nodded while raising his eyebrows in Vin's direction.

Shanin rose as Vin entered the waiting room. He was walking at a brisk pace and did not stop. He gestured with his chin that they should head towards the exit. Shanin grabbed her bag and silently followed Vin out the door.

"What happened?" she asked once they were in the parking lot. She grabbed at his arm but Vin remained one step ahead of her.

"Not much," was all Vin said.

"What?" she asked, trying to get him to slow down long enough to hear what had happened inside.

Just then a police car entered the parking lot.

"Let's not say anything until we're in the car," said Vin, nodding towards the police car.

"Police are always around hospitals," Shanin said, grabbing Vin by the arm. "Calm down."

Vin continued to walk hurriedly until the two of them were safely inside Shanin's car.

"So, what happened?" she asked once inside the vehicle.

"The Doc's not here."

"Where is he?"

"How do I know? He's either at the county morgue or still at the winery."

"You're not sure?"

"I don't know."

"Damn. I hate when that happens."

"Me too," said Vin. "I never thought anyone would be able to hide so well in such a small town."

"You think he's under a different name?"

"No. Sick people usually don't think about changing their name," he said. "How far is it to this Patchogue?"

"Too far," answered Shanin. "Too far for me to drive now. Why do you want to know that?"

'That's where the county morgue is according to the hospital security guard and possibly where our subject is, if he's dead."

"We'll never get in there," said Shanin. "It's strictly employees, cops and next of kin. Besides, it's getting seriously late."

"Pat Goode said she wanted photos of the Doc. She didn't say whether dead or alive. This could be a deal breaker. What do we do now?" It was the first time Vin actually asked Shanin for direction since they had reunited.

"It's time to call it a night," said Shanin. "I've actually got an all-day assignment tomorrow."

"Photo job?"

"No, babysitting twins."

"Sounds like a headache waiting to happen."

"It can be but she's a single mom. I've been helping her for about a year now. She's become sort of a friend."

"What's she do?"

"She's a tech at a medical lab a few towns west of here. Lots of times they ask her to work overtime so she needs someone flexible to watch her boys. They fight a lot. She can't leave her job for something closer because she needs the benefits and the overtime. Her husband walked out before the kids were born. Doesn't know where he is."

"How's she treat you?"

"Good. Pays cash. Never haggles. Pays extra when I work overtime without me even asking," said Shanin as she drove from the parking lot and began heading back towards the village. "I feel sorry for her. She's always exhausted."

"She probably is and she's probably grateful she's got someone dependable like you."

"Yeah. Story of my life."

"What?"

"Always there when someone needs me but who's there when I need someone?"

"C'mon, you know I'm your friend."

"A friend who went missing for a long time."

Vin chose to turn from Shanin and stare straight out the window instead of responding and risking another argument.

"I'm taking you back to the harbor," Shanin continued. "Before you start giving me orders, I'm leaving you about a block from the hotel should you imagine anyone's watching and then I'm going home," she said. "I'll check with you some time tomorrow when I get a break."

"No problem," said Vin. "And thanks for putting up with me tonight."

"It was actually kind of fun," said Shanin. "It was the most excitement I've had since I've been out here. If you talk to Pat Goode let me know if we're still working together."

"Will do," said Vin. "I'll call you as soon as I know."

"Thanks," said Shanin. "It would be good if we can nail this assignment together."

"Sure would be," said Vin. "But right now we've got more questions than answers."

"That's usually how the good ones start," she said.

Neither of them said much more for the rest of the ride. When they got to about two blocks from The Crashing Sea Gull, Shanin as promised turned off the headlights, shut the motor and let the car roll to the side of the road without signaling. A few seconds later it was swallowed by the shadows cast from the slumping branches and broad leaves of the old oaks that lined the street, helping Vin to exit in nearly complete darkness. He slowly opened the car door with one hand while holding his other over the interior light.

"You really should remove this bulb," Vin said. "In the dark a small light like this can be seen from far away."

"See you tomorrow?" asked Shanin, ignoring his suggestion.

"I hope so," whispered Vin, gently closing the door and speaking through the open window. "One way or the other I'm sure I'm going to need someone."

Shanin looked away.

"Sorry, poor choice of words. Dinner tomorrow night?"

"As long as there are no dead guys or police involved, you're on."

"You pick the place," said Vin.

"I know a fish place that won't set us back too much," Shanin offered. "It's a little out of the way."

"That would probably be good."

"I gave the owner a deal on some family photos and he charges me the inside price whenever I go there, as long as I pay in cash."

"Sounds good," said Vin slowly walking round the car before talking to Shanin through the opened driver's window. "Let me know when you're free of the twins. And thanks again for coming out tonight."

"No problem."

Vin stood at the side of the car for a second, wondering if he should attempt to kiss Shanin goodnight. He then remembered what happened when he greeted her at the hotel. Instead Vin slowly turned and after waving once in her direction walked quickly towards the hotel. Shanin watched him disappear into the darkness before turning the car around to head home. At this point she wasn't at all concerned about how Vin was going to handle the assignment. Would he call Pat Goode and tell her their subject may be dead? Would Vin have to spend the rest of his time in North Fork Harbor avoiding the police? Would she get a good fee or would the assignment be cancelled? None of these things concerned Shanin because for the first time since she'd been living in North Fork Harbor her pulse had skipped a beat. She'd forgotten how that had felt.

CHAPTER 13

Pressing the Skins

Sgt. Henry St. Charles drove to the North Fork Harbor docks in his wife's car. He wanted to look as nondescript as possible. In worn jeans, boat shoes, a plain blue polo shirt, faded blue baseball cap and sunglasses St. Charles looked more like the tourist than veteran police officer. Before entering the harbor work area he double-checked his police gear which was locked in the trunk of the car. St. Charles then took a few seconds to survey the scene, making sure there was as little chance as possible that his identity would be discovered by any casual onlookers.

The North Fork Harbor docks were divided into two sections. The first and original section was for the commercial fisherman and their fleets. It was on the eastern side of the harbor. It was from here where crews sailed nearly year round, usually venturing into the eastern tip of Long Island Sound before heading into the Atlantic to fish the waters off Massachusetts. These docks were wide and made of thick, sturdy wood able to support the various machinery and equipment that was regularly transported in and out as part of the daily routines of bringing fresh fish to the trucks that would haul the loads to the market.

The second section was for the recreational fishing and tourist boats. These docks were narrower than their commercial counterparts. They were connected to a small parking lot that easily led into the village and tiny train station. They were lined with benches made from recycled plastic and carefully positioned so visitors could watch the harbor activity, take photographs or enjoy the water view. There was also a third dock at the western most point of the harbor. It was for the ferries that ran to nearby Shelter Island. It was a wide dock connected to a steel ramp that carried vehicles on and off the ferries. The new docks were an integral part of the plan intended to help the small town evolve from traditional fishing village to tourist destination. They were dotted with vendor booths selling items like postcards, sunscreen and t-shirts. There was also a tourist information section that handed out free maps of the village and coupons to local hotels and restaurants. Unlike previous generations of tradesmen skilled in once vital crafts, this generation of workers was trained in the art of providing friendly hospitality. They were there to cheerfully help tourists find everything from a dog kennel to a babysitter. The deliberate design helped the village's seaside tourist trade begin to flourish as its commercial fishing business steadily diminished due to a fateful combination of increased competition and regulation plus rising expenses.

The abandoned white bait house was between the commercial and recreational fishing sections. The small, one-level building had been vacant and for some unknown reason had so far been spared from the developers' plans. With its windows and doors covered in plywood, like the Crashing Sea Gull hotel, it was one of the last remnants of the village's past. Weeds had grown up around it and there was a tiny yard partially surrounded by a sagging stockade fence. Amid the debris that had been accumulating in the yard was an old wooden picnic table. Made generations ago, it was now faded, splintering and stained with paint but local harbor workers occasionally gathered around the ancient but still sturdy table. It was here in this fairly isolated spot that St. Charles would meet with North Fork Harbor Reporter publisher Howard Gallant to share with him some of his concerns and ideally agree on a plan to contain the news of Dr. Frank until they could be sure of what had happened and to try to devise a way to get Vin Gusto off the story.

St. Charles took a seat on the bench and poured some coffee from his thermos before unwrapping a corn muffin his wife Ellen had made the night before while he waited for Gallant. St. Charles had with him the major New York City dailies, including the Tattler. So far, none had reported on the Dr. Frank case, leading him to believe that Gusto had not yet filed anything—meaning so far chances were that no story had leaked. Having the newspapers and coffee also added to his cover. Should anyone see them in the yard, especially being out of uniform, it would look like nothing more than two men enjoying some breakfast together as he also had enough coffee and an extra muffin for Gallant.

"We've got to stop meeting like this," joked Gallant as he entered the yard.

"Nice to see you," said St. Charles as he rose to shake hands with Howard before gesturing for him to sit down and pouring him some coffee. "How's the news business?" asked St. Charles.

"Busy. How's crime in the country?"

"About the same," said St. Charles as he went to offer Gallant a muffin.

"No thanks," said Gallant, gesturing with his hand. "This is not my best time of day," he said, looking at the time on his cell phone as if for emphasis. Gallant had a natural apprehension towards authority figures and was uncomfortable around St. Charles. He just hoped it wasn't obvious.

"What's going on?" asked Gallant getting right to the point.

Ironically, it was reporters' questions that made St. Charles uneasy.

"Any openings at the paper?"

"You're looking for a new career?"

Now it was St. Charles' turn to fidget. He did not like asking for favors especially when the outcome was uncertain. "I know a reporter who might be looking for a new assignment," he said.

Gallant's sense of apprehension was growing. "When did you get in the business of helping reporters find jobs?" he asked.

"It's something that sort of fell into my lap."

"If you're serious you'll have to tell me more," said Gallant. "Business is down. There's no room in the budget for someone's niece or nephew looking to get into the business. The only exception would be a really extraordinary circumstance."

St. Charles saw his opening.

"This might fit the bill," said St. Charles who decided that he'd try to tell Gallant as little as possible about what had happened at the winery while still trying to win the publisher's cooperation. While neither man was entirely comfortable with the other, St. Charles was confident enough that Gallant would keep recent events a secret.

"We've got a situation," St. Charles continued. "And it's important we keep it under wraps until all of the evidence is in."

"Why's that?"

"Because we're not exactly sure what took place and if the wrong information were to leak out . . ." he stopped in mid-sentence.

"Yes."

"It would be very irresponsible," said St. Charles. "It could hurt a lot of people."

"Sounds serious."

"It is."

"It's not our job to keep things under wraps."

"No but it is your job to make sure you've got all the facts straight before you go forward with a story."

"Are you implying we've been less than accurate?"

"No, I'm just afraid we can't be accurate right now and I don't want anything inaccurate to leak. It would be a disaster."

"You don't want it to leak that the police aren't accurate?" said Gallant with a grin.

"Stop toying with me," said St. Charles, smiling briefly before returning to a grave tone. "We have a very serious situation and until we know more, need to keep it contained. There's a lot at stake."

Gallant nodded as neither spoke for a moment.

"So you want us to sit on a story?" asked Gallant.

"That's not all," said St. Charles. "There's a city reporter here. I suspect he's going to be a huge distraction for the investigation. I was hoping you could occupy him."

"How do you mean?"

"I was hoping you could give him a job at the paper. Keep him busy with other stuff. Send him on assignment on a fishing boat or something so he wouldn't have time to interfere with us."

"I wish I brought my tape recorder," said Gallant. "No one would believe this."

"This is an off-the-record conversation," said St. Charles. "Totally confidential."

"You're supposed to tell me that before we start talking."

"I guess I forgot. I'm a little stressed out by this whole thing."

"What's got you more stressed, the crime or the reporter?"

"No comment," said St. Charles who then tried managing a small smile.

"Henry," said Gallant, rising from his seat. "This is a very unusual request. I don't know if I can do it."

"The paper doesn't have the money?"

"No. The issue is I don't know if it's the right thing to do. Is it ethical? And even if I agreed, would the reporter come to work for us? By the way, who is it?"

"Vin Gusto," St. Charles plainly said. "Formerly of the New York Tattler."

"Gusto?" repeated Gallant. "Gusto's here? I know reporters in New York. They say he's crazy."

"He may be but he knows how to write crime."

"Forget it," said Gallant waving his hands. "Forget we had this entire conversation. Gusto's not our kind of reporter. Never could be. I can't even believe you'd dream up such a scheme. The guy's totally irresponsible."

"There wasn't a cop in the city who didn't read his page," countered St. Charles. "His name could help sell papers in a weak market."

"There probably wasn't a cop who didn't look at the Page Six girl either. Gusto's a loose cannon. He could totally torpedo the reputation of a small but well-respected paper. If he's so great why didn't any of the other New York papers grab him once the Tattler cut him loose?"

"I've no idea," said St. Charles. "All I know is he's here sniffing around where he doesn't belong. I'd like to quietly get him off the trail before things spiral out of control and people stop visiting North Fork Harbor. Like you said, he's a loose cannon and business is slow. Bad press would really hurt the village tourist trade."

Gallant just shook his head. He doubted whether St. Charles was sincere in his desire to help local business. He rightly sensed there was more to St. Charles' motives for stopping Gusto.

Realizing his gamble did not work, it was St. Charles who then rose from the table. "Thank you for your time Mr. Publisher," he said as he gathered his things from the table. "I thought you could help us but I was wrong. I understand. But I hope you understand that I can't afford to spend any more time on this with you. I've got an investigation to begin, one in which neither myself nor anyone else in the department will be saying anything further about."

For a moment the two men stood eye-to-eye, neither saying a word. St. Charles gathered his things before turning and quietly walking away. Gallant watched him for a few seconds before turning and walking in the opposite direction as he considered the impact of a new investigation, a tense police sergeant and rogue reporter each possibly about to collide with the other in the otherwise quiet village of North Fork Harbor.

/ / /

Near the far western tip of Long Island Maria Lambrusco had already landed. A limousine was waiting to take her nearly the entire length of the Long Island Expressway to North Fork Harbor. She had been filled with a whirlwind of emotions from the moment she received the telephone call from St. Charles. The shock was beginning to subside and was being replaced by a deep sadness. She knew it would return the instant she saw her father's body but for now, in addition to the sadness, she was emotionally and physically exhausted. She was afraid of what lie ahead as she wondered how her father died. Did he suffer? Did he go quickly? Could he have been saved?

If it was some sort of foul play, who she wondered, would be desperate enough to take the life of her father, a man who kept to himself and was widely respected. And if that were the case, how would she deal with the investigation? How would the perpetrators be brought to justice? And the question that hurt the most—would he still be alive if she had been there?

"Excuse me," she asked the driver as she opened the sliding door that separated the passenger from the front seat.

"Yes ma'am," he answered.

"How much longer 'til North Fork Harbor?"

"About 90 minutes."

"Thank you," she said as she closed the sliding door. She then slumped in the seat and with her face in her hands, allowed herself to cry until she fell asleep. The next thing she remembered was waking as the car abruptly stopped outside the gates of North Fork Harbor Vineyard and the door opening.

"Good morning Ms. Lambrusco," the driver said as he opened the door and leaned into the car to greet Maria. In the background she could hear police radio static. "This is as far as I can take you." The driver then stepped aside as the large hand of Officer Jeffrey Jonah was extended into the car, offering to help Maria.

Jonah's large frame nearly blocked out all of the sunlight that had entered the car a few seconds earlier. Taking his hand Maria stepped out of the car, her eyes taking a moment to adjust to the strong early morning sunlight. It was a warm, sunny morning, the kind of day her father would have appreciated.

"I'm Officer Jonah with the North Fork Harbor Police," he said, introducing himself. Maria nodded as she shook the officer's hand.

"I'm Maria Lambrusco, my father . . ." she suddenly stopped, not able to finish her sentence.

"I know," said Jonah. "We've been expecting you. I'm very sorry about your father."

"Thank you," she said.

"I'll need you to sign this," interrupted the driver, handing Maria a voucher. As Maria signed the receipt the driver unloaded her bags from the trunk of the car. Leaving them on the driveway he took the signed receipt. The driver then gave

Maria a copy and without saying anything further, got back into the limousine and drove away.

"What happened?" Maria asked Officer Jonah.

"Please wait here Ms. Lambrusco. Det. Thorsen will be right out." Maria began instinctively walking towards the winery but Officer Jonah quickly intervened.

"I'm sorry ma'am, no one's allowed in the winery. You can't go any further."

"It's my father's winery. I've got to go in."

"It's a crime scene. Please wait here," he said, extending his large palm in Maria's direction.

A second later the winery front door opened and Sgt. St. Charles emerged. He walked straight towards the head of the driveway where Maria and Jonah were standing. He was carrying the crime scene log book.

"Ms. Lambrusco," St. Charles called, extending his hand as he approached. "I'm Sgt. Henry St. Charles. We spoke on the phone."

Maria extended her hand and introduced herself to St. Charles.

"I'm very sorry about your father. He was a great man."

"Thank you Sergeant. I'd like to help in any way I can."

"There's a lot to do and I understand you're under a great deal of stress."

"I'd like to get into my father's winery. I might be able to help," she repeated.

"The best way you can help," said St. Charles, "is answer some basic questions. We're sill gathering evidence so we cannot let anyone into the winery."

Maria nodded.

"Detective Thorsen is handling the investigation. I'm sure he's going to want to speak with you. Right now he's preparing to interview persons of interest. You may be able to give him some insight. But I can help you with anything else. Do you have a place to stay?"

"I was planning on staying in my father's apartment. That's where I always stay when I'm here."

"I'm afraid that won't be available tonight," he said before pausing. "And I'm not sure if you'd be safe or if you'd want to stay there."

"What are you saying Sergeant?"

"Ms. Lambrusco," St. Charles said before pausing again. "We're not yet sure of what took place here. Det. Thorsen is the officer-in-charge. He'll explain everything to you. But if I can help you in any other way, like with a hotel room, a ride, someone to talk to, please let me know. We'd ask that you be careful who you speak with while you're here." He then handed her a contact card with his direct line at the police station. "I can be reached at any time through that number," he said. Without saying anything further Maria put the card in her shirt pocket.

At that moment the winery's main door flung open and Thorsen emerged, the tail of his brown suede overcoat swaying in the breeze behind him as he directly walked towards St. Charles and Maria. Thorsen was the officer-in-charge for the case and although he would collaborate with St. Charles's and the others, it was Thorsen who would have the final say on all investigation matters—including who was permitted on the premises and who could speak with persons of interest. So far he had only assigned such responsibilities to himself. St. Charles knew he had already overstepped his limits by giving Maria his contact information. He also sensed however, that Maria would probably not respond well to the brash Thorsen and wanted to give her an alternative contact. Not knowing how he'd react, St. Charles had not told the officer-in-charge that there was a big-city reporter trying to learn about the case or that earlier that morning he may have damaged relations with the local newspaper publisher.

"I'm Detective Conrad Thorsen, officer-in-charge of the investigation," said Thorsen with an unmistakable tone of authority in his voice. He extended his hand towards Maria.

Maria nodded while automatically accepting his hand. She did not notice the deliberately firm grip of his handshake as she stared out across the vineyard.

"Why don't we go into the patrol car," he said gesturing towards an empty police vehicle on the opposite end of the driveway. "I'd like to speak with you privately."

She nodded and he then put his hand against the lower part of her back, steering Maria towards the patrol car. He opened the passenger door for her and once she was seated, closed it. He then entered through the driver's side.

"Allow me to say I'm terribly sorry about all this," Thorsen said.

"Thank you," Maria said. "What exactly happened?" she asked.

Thorsen paused before taking a breath. He was accustomed to asking the questions and never liked answering questions from the victim's family until he was completely sure of what had happened, especially early in the investigation. He preferred letting family members and anyone else who could talk to do so, especially at the start of an investigation as they often indirectly provided bits of helpful information about the victim, sometimes intentionally, other times not. Background information, Thorsen learned was frequently very helpful when trying to determine motivations behind crimes. Although victims' families understandably craved information, one could never be sure how it might be received.

"Ms. Lambrusco," Thorsen said in the most considerate tone he could muster while trying to subtly take control of the conversation. "Things you may be able to tell us about your father might help us learn what happened. I'd like to start by asking you some simple questions."

"Of course, Detective."

CHAPTER 14

Preparing for the Harvest

As Thorsen prepared to speak, Maria turned from him and stared out across the vineyard. From where they sat she could see that the growing season would soon be coming to an end. The grapes were already hanging in heavy black clusters and the leaves were beginning to curl, a sure sign that a harvest was only a brief matter of time. Maria knew, somewhere among this field of ordinary-looking vines were the living proof of her father's pioneering work in agricultural cloning and perhaps the reason behind his death.

Sensing Maria's attention was shifting he called her by name.

"Ms. Lambrusco," Thorsen said. Maria slowly turned towards him.

"Yes Detective," she said. "I'll do everything I can to help."

While he knew he had a job to do, Thorsen himself was having difficulty concentrating. Maria's presence was hard to ignore. Tall and slim, Thorsen was captivated by her slightly curly black hair which framed a delicate face that was highlighted by deep brown eyes and full lips. She wore a tailored black blazer, white buttoned-down shirt, jeans and medium heels. Unlike most of the women in the North Fork Harbor community, Thorsen felt Maria would look more at home on a Mediterranean beach than at an eastern Long Island vineyard.

"I understand this is a terrible time for you," he began while mentally reminding himself to remain professional. "If you could answer a few questions we might get a better idea of what actually took place here."

"Yes, Detective," she replied. "I'll do whatever I can."

Thorsen liked to begin inquiries with simple questions, giving his subject a chance to build confidence and trust.

"Your father was very accomplished in his field."

"Yes Sir."

"No need to be so formal," Thorsen said, sensing a chance to build familiarity.

"You can call me Conrad," he said with a slight smile.

"Okay," answered Maria with a slight tone of hesitation. Like her father, she preferred to remain reserved until she had a better idea of what was happening.

"Whatever you're comfortable with," he said, sensing Maria's anxiety. "Getting back to Dr. Lambrusco, am I correct in saying he liked to keep to himself?"

"Yes," said Maria. "But not because he disliked people. He was very warm and generous once you got to know him but life had taught him to be cautious."

"Sounds a lot like my own parents," said Thorsen, again trying to win Maria's confidence. "Always looking over their shoulders."

"Yes, something like that."

"He kept his distance. He was 'old school'," said Thorsen.

"Very much so. It's how he was raised."

"How many languages did he speak?"

"Three I guess. Italian of course. Very good Spanish. He struggled with English but could manage."

"Do you think people may have mistaken his old-style manners, his being reserved as a sense of arrogance or rudeness, or maybe he felt uncomfortable with the language?" continued Thorsen.

"It's possible. What are you getting at?"

Thorsen was searching for motivation. He knew the officers would scour the winery buildings and grounds but it was his job to "get inside" of whoever was responsible for the crime and right now he had zero. The reclusive winemaker was a difficult starting point, nor was his daughter very forthcoming. The questions were about to get harder.

"Maria," he said, addressing her by her first name. "Do you know if your father had any arguments or disagreements with anyone in the area? An employee?"

"He never spoke of any."

"Did he owe anyone a large sum of money?"

"No, I always went over the books. All of his debts were current."

"Did he have a girlfriend? A love interest of any sort?"

"No. Not since my mother died."

"Were there any business rivals who might have liked him out of their way?"

"He was always guarded about his work," said Maria. "He felt people in the industry were watching him. Sometimes he thought they wanted access to his work which he would never give them."

Thorsen sensed a possible opening.

"How do you mean?"

"He was conducting a lot of research. Genetic research," she said, clarifying it for the detective.

"And . . ."

"He felt there were people who disagreed with his motives but wanted his research. He may have been a little paranoid," said Maria. "Growing up during the war made an impression on him. He was very secretive. But that's not a crime."

"No, it isn't," said Thorsen who then paused to consider what Maria had just said and to contemplate his next line of questions when she broke in.

"Did they find my father's computer?"

"What computer? The one in the office?"

"No, the handheld. My father always carried a handheld computer, usually in his coat pocket."

"According to the early evidence list," said Thorsen. "They found no handheld computer. Why?"

"That's where he kept a lot of his data. Each of the marked vines. The latest growing notes. It was all in there. He updated it almost daily. It's the key to the research."

"Whoever has this handheld can gain access to his research?" asked Thorsen

"Yes. It's password-protected but it wouldn't be impossible for a good hacker to decipher. He was a winemaker, not a software engineer."

"Let's double-check with the officers," said Thorsen sensing her urgency and possibly the first breakthrough of the case. Maria then exited the car with Thorsen following her. The first officer they saw was Krupcheski.

"Where's the evidence list?" asked Thorsen. The officer handed it to him. Slightly breaking with official procedure, he allowed Maria to look it over with him. There was no mention of a handheld computer.

"No one recovered a handheld computer?" Thorsen asked Krupcheski.

"Not that I know of Sir," said the flustered rookie.

"You finished searching the whole place?"

"Yes Sir. Did it myself," said Krupcheski, starting to feel uncomfortable from the pressure of Thorsen's aggressiveness.

Krupcheski did not give Thorsen confidence. "Did St. Charles sign-off on it?" the detective asked.

"He's in there right now, reviewing everything," said Krupcheski, gesturing towards the building.

Thorsen then took Maria by the arm and walking away with their backs towards Krupcheski asked her more questions.

"Maria, did your father perhaps have another hiding spot for his handheld?"

"Not that I know of," she said.

"What about at night?"

"When he went to sleep at night he'd put it beside his bed. It was always within his reach."

By questioning Maria, Thorsen had accelerated the investigation into the next stage. Thorsen was beginning to theorize that if the handheld had indeed been stolen, the information it contained and Dr. Frank's unwillingness to share it, may have been the reasons he had been murdered. Thorsen was starting to assemble a very preliminary "mental sketch" of his suspect but it was more than he had just a few moments ago.

"Maria," he said in his most understanding tone. "You've been very helpful. I'm very grateful for your time. I know you've been through a lot and had a long flight. I suggest you collect your things and get some rest. Sergeant St. Charles should be able to help you with a room."

Maria nodded.

"There's one more thing I should tell you," said Thorsen. "You need to know this."

Maria looked directly at him. Even for the calloused Thorsen the next bit of information was difficult for him to articulate.

"When we found your father . . ."

"Yes," said Maria, drawing closer as she anticipated new information.

"When we found your father, his mouth had been stuffed with grapes."

Maria just stared at the detective and then began to cry. After a few seconds Thorsen reached out to hold her but Maria pushed him away.

While Thorsen was pleased with what he'd discovered so rapidly he felt badly about what he just told Maria but saw no other alternative if he was to solve the case.

"I'm truly sorry," Thorsen said, extending his hand. "The Sergeant will be over in just a minute. I'll walk you to the front of the driveway and then St. Charles will take over. He can help you with a ride and anything else you may need. Once again, I'm very sorry about your father."

"Good day, Detective," Maria said. And then, squarely looking at Thorsen asked, "Do you think we'll find who did this?"

"Absolutely," said Thorsen without hesitation. He never worried about making promises he was not sure could be kept, especially around women, no matter how distraught they were. "St. Charles will be here in just a minute."

Maria then turned away from the winery and held Thorsen's arm as they walked towards the top of the driveway where St. Charles was now waiting inside a police car. Thorsen opened the passenger door and Maria sat in the front seat. Her bags were already in the back seat.

"We've arranged for you to stay at the Stilton," said Thorsen. The Stilton was a recently renovated hotel a few towns west of North Fork Harbor in the nearby town of Riverfront. More modern than anything else in the area, it had basic security although a police officer would be placed outside Maria's room and another would be stationed in a patrol car in the parking lot with a view to her room window. Until they had a better idea of what took place, Thorsen thought it was a wise precaution to take. St. Charles would be in charge of assigning the guards.

"Thank you for the ride Sergeant," said Maria. "You're very kind."

"Just doing my job," St. Charles answered. A few seconds had passed with silence between them when St. Charles interrupted.

"Do you know anyone out here Ms. Lambrusco?"

"How do you mean?"

"Any friends, relatives? It might not be the best idea to spend a lot of time alone."

"I really don't know anyone out here very well," said Maria. "But for now I do want to be alone."

"I understand," he said, nodding. "We'll be at the hotel in a few minutes."

Maria leaned back in her seat and resting her head closed her eyes for the rest of the ride. At the hotel, St. Charles checked Maria in while she waited in the patrol car, which he parked in the rear of the hotel. The police dept. had provided her with a false name and St. Charles checked her in using a department credit card. The hotel manager had been notified in advance and Maria was not asked to show identification. St. Charles and the manager then went around to where the car had been parked and escorted Maria in through the service entrance and directly to her room, with neither saying anything. As they approached the room a police officer was already standing outside her doorway.

"Good evening Sergeant," said the junior officer while saluting.

St. Charles returned the salute without saying anything.

The manager then opened the door. Maria and the manager, who with St. Charles had carried Maria's bags, then entered the room. Satisfied that everything was in order, the manager handed Maria his card, politely told her to directly call him if she needed anything and then exited.

Inside the room, a modernist print hung on the wall over the mini-refrigerator, on top of which there was a small electric coffee maker with gourmet selections in separate envelopes. There was a flat-screen TV on the wall directly opposite the bed plus a small desk complete with note paper, pen, desktop computer and a copy of the local tourist-guide magazine. Next to the television was a basket with some bottled water and fresh fruit.

St. Charles then shut the door and walked to the window. Slightly opening the curtain he gestured for Maria to join him. A patrol car had just entered the hotel parking lot, stopping to the side of the exit.

"In addition to the officer in the hallway," he said, gesturing towards the door, another officer will be on post, keeping an eye on your window." He then placed his business card next to the telephone by her bed. He quickly checked the closet, bathroom and under the bed.

"You think all this is necessary Sergeant?" she asked when he had finished his brief inspection.

"Until we have more information, this is a step we have to take," he said. "Are you sure you're going to be okay tonight?" St. Charles asked.

"All I want to do is sleep Sergeant," she said."

"Someone from the department will check on you in the morning," said St. Charles, firmly shaking her hand. "Call me if you need anything. I left another one of my cards by the phone for you. Goodnight Ms. Lambrusco."

After St. Charles exited Maria went to the door and closed the bolt lock. She then sat on the edge of the bed. Too tired to cry she got undressed and took a warm shower. Trying not to think about anything, she then put on the loose-fitting terry-cloth robe supplied by the hotel, pulled back the covers and fell into a deep sleep.

///

At about the same time that evening Dr. Damian Dionasis, the county medical examiner was finishing his preliminary study of the body of Dr. Lambrusco. Realizing the urgency of the case, he went immediately to work. While it would take some time before an analysis of the victim's blood and other bodily fluids would be completed the doctor was fairly sure he had made a discovery.

Trained in a time when physicians relied more on experience and skill rather than test results and computer analysis, as part of his standard procedure he meticulously examined every inch of the victim's lifeless body. Running his gloved finger tips over the body he noticed an unusual redness and slight spot of swelling almost squarely in the center of the victim's chest. While not certain of what he may have found he went to the phone and left messages for both St. Charles and Thorsen. Dr. Dionasis had discovered what he believed was a very small puncture wound, about the size of an insect bite, almost perfectly in the center of the victim's chest. He rubbed the tip of his gloved index finger over the wound and tried to think of what may have happened.

CHAPTER 15

The Crush Begins

"This is completely unofficial but it could barely have been placed more perfectly if it had been done by a physician in his office," said Dionasis on a conference call with Thorsen and St. Charles.

"What are you saying?" asked St. Charles.

"Lambrusco was injected. I'm ninety-nine percent sure this was done by someone who knew exactly what he was doing," said the ME. "Probably right around the time he died."

"How do you know that?" asked St. Charles.

"I think we agree Dr. Lambrusco was involved in a struggle with a physically superior opponent who probably surprised him," said the doctor. "In the course of the struggle the perpetrator, or perpetrators, managed to inject a needle into his chest before dumping him into the vat."

"And stuffing grapes in his mouth. We're going to need more than that," said Thorsen, prodding the doctor. "Anything else?"

"Normally I probably wouldn't be able to detect a mark from an injection but there was either a reaction to it or the heat from the fermenting wine or the alcohol content irritated the wound, which is how I found it."

None of the men said anything as Dionasis continued speaking.

"We won't have chemical-test results on the body fluids and organs until the end of the week," he said. "The full autopsy will take at least another day but this is my early prognosis. I wanted to let you know before you start interviews."

"We'll have to chase that down," said Thorsen who was intentionally downplaying the significance of Dionasis's alleged discovery. "Let's fast-forward this discussion. The winemaker's daughter said a very important handheld computer may be missing. Whoever has the handheld will probably be able to fill in the blanks."

"You're sure it's missing, not just lost or misplaced?" asked St. Charles.

"It hasn't turned up anywhere and she says he always had it at his side."

"What else?" asked St. Charles.

"It holds some special grape data," said Thorsen. "The daughter thinks that's what whoever did this may be after."

"I guess that destroys the crazed-loner theory," said St. Charles.

"Even crazy loners believe their actions have purpose," Thorsen quite seriously said. Then, to Dr. Dionasis he said, "Excuse me Doc. But a needle to the chest? That's not a normal procedure. It's not something someone would ordinarily get while on a regular check-up, is it?"

"Not normally, no."

"And I'm guessing it's not an easy shot to make in a struggle either. The dead Doc probably put up some fight."

"He could've been injected after he was subdued," answered Dionasis. "He did suffer a head wound."

"Going back to the injection, could it be an insect bite or some other skin irritation?" asked Thorsen.

"Remote," said Dionasis. "It's almost a perfect bull's eye over the heart."

There was a pause as Thorsen contemplated his next move.

"Doc, you can hang up now," said Thorsen. "Call us when you have anything else."

"Yes Sir," said the doctor. "Good night gentlemen."

The detective and sergeant waited for the click.

"What do you think of the Doc's discovery?" asked St. Charles.

"Not sure yet," answered Thorsen, not wanting to reveal his early thoughts to St. Charles. "I'm still putting this together."

"So what's our game plan?" asked St. Charles.

"Crime scene's been covered right?"

"Yes Sir. Photographed, videotaped, dusted for fingerprints, footprints, tire tracks, evidence gathered."

"Anything from the security cameras?"

"Nothing anywhere. We have nothing solid to go on at this point," said St. Charles. "It's too early to say without a trace but I feel similar to Dr. D. Someone knew exactly what they were doing, planned it well in advance but at some point their emotions got hold of them, that's how the grapes wound up in the winemaker's mouth."

"Precisely," said Thorsen. "You may have a future in criminal psychology."

"Just been doing this for too long," St. Charles sighed.

"But you forgot one thing," said Thorsen.

"What's that?"

"If the perpetrator really wanted to cover his tracks he would not have iced the winemaker when he did."

"Why not?"

"Because he was leaving for a conference," said Thorsen. "That's why the limo driver was there, to take him to the airport for some conference. I checked it online. He was a featured speaker. When he doesn't show up, people are going to start asking questions. The first place they'll probably call is the winery."

"Maybe he didn't know about that or didn't care."

"No. He probably knew the Doc's schedule," said Thorsen. "That's why he was there when he was. Thought it was worth it or maybe there was some time pressure to do the deed. We need to speak with anyone who had access to his schedule."

"What about the daughter?" asked Thorsen.

"She's staying in a hotel. Two officers are standing guard."

"Think she's ready for an in-depth interview? She's pretty hot-looking."

"You talked with her earlier," said St. Charles.

"Yes but I should talk to her again ASAP just to be sure. I'm not sure how long she'll be staying here."

"Yes Sir," said St. Charles, shaking his head.

"Let's set a follow-up interview right away with Maria Lambrusco and line up any other persons of interest, workers, suppliers and business associates," ordered Thorsen. "I'd be surprised if there's a witness considering how careful the perpetrator was but you never know. Have the office call for a Spanish interpreter for the migrants. We'll speak with them at the winery. But put Maria first, there's a good chance she can give us more information after she's rested and becomes more comfortable with me."

"Anything else?" asked St. Charles.

"Dismiss the officers at the winery before the workers show up. Remove the tape. Let's see who fills the winemaker's vacuum."

"I'm sure the daughter will run the winery."

"I doubt it," said Thorsen.

"What do you mean?"

"Where's your psychological acumen now?"

"Please stop toying with me Detective. It's been a long day."

"Toughen up Sergeant and think for a minute," said Thorsen. "If someone was aggressive enough to kill the father why would they let the daughter stand in their way? She may take over temporarily but I bet that will change."

"It depends on what they're after," said St. Charles. "If the perpetrator was an outsider, a pro, not from the area, and only wanted the handheld he can be 1,000 miles from here by now. If he got what he wanted, he couldn't care less about who runs the winery. Considering Dr. D's comment that it was a nearly perfect puncture wound to the center of the chest and so far we have no leads, I'm thinking he's an outside contractor. The perpetrator may even have a little medical experience if he can operate a hypodermic so accurately. But if he's local, he may try to continue with business as usual, not arouse any suspicion or suddenly vanish without explanation. Those types are usually discovered. Anyone moving to run the winery would be too obvious."

"Correction Sergeant, he did not only want the handheld."

"How do you mean Sir?"

"The mouthful of grapes throws off the equation. That's where this gets personal. Whoever did this is not a pro but very smart and slightly psycho, bent on some sort of revenge. He knew the layout, the alarms and Dr. Vino's habits. He's settling a score. What we don't know is why. Who might be driven to do something like this? In any case we need to check the winemaker's medical records," said Thorsen.

"Yes Sir," said St. Charles.

"I'll find who his physician is when I speak with the daughter. Then we'll see if he recently took a hypodermic to the chest. Doesn't sound likely but we've got to check. Put that near the top of your to-do list. We've got to talk to his doctor. People often confide in their physicians. You never know what he may say."

"Dr. Lambrusco was not the confiding type," said St. Charles.

"Someone's going to have some ideas. That's why we interview."

"One more thing," said St. Charles.

"What?"

"A reporter was around the scene," said St. Charles.

"A local guy, already?"

"No. A city reporter," said St. Charles. "Said he was on assignment. Supposed to interview the winemaker this morning for some big-time magazine."

"He just showed up in the middle of the night after a probable murder?" asked Thorsen.

"When I spoke with him he didn't know there was a possible murder. I got him out of there ASAP and warned him about hanging around."

"Be careful how you handle that. We don't want to make enemies with the press. The perpetrator may want others to know what he did. Let's not help him."

"Yes Sir."

"Otherwise, remind your officers and all PD personnel that no one's to have any comment regarding this investigation. That's standard procedure but make sure they tighten up. No talking about this to friends, relatives, wives, girlfriends, bartenders, shrinks, pastors, rabbis, waitresses whoever. No exceptions. After we nail this there will be plenty of time for talking."

"Yes Sir."

"On second thought, maybe we should bring in the reporter for questioning."

The suggestion did not sit well with St. Charles.

"Detective, I suggest we let sleeping dogs lie as far as the reporter goes," said St. Charles. "The news business moves fast. His assignment may get cancelled and he can be on his way back to the city in no time. Plus we have nothing on him."

"I don't know how important this winemaker really is," said Thorsen. "But if some reporter with big-time connections is looking around and Dr. Magic Grapes is missing at the conference I want this wrapped up ASAP. Otherwise I'm going to look bad."

"Yes Sir."

"If the reporter becomes a distraction or tries to make me look bad we're going to have to do something," said Thorsen.

"Yes Sir," repeated St. Charles.

"I'm starting to think this case may make us look like champs or chumps. Which do you want to be?"

"Champs."

There was a pause as St. Charles was getting another glimpse into the unpleasant side of Thorsen.

"Anything else Sergeant?"

"No."

"Very good. Then let's plan on meeting near the end of the day."

"Yes. Good . . ."

Thorsen had hung up the phone before St. Charles could finish his sentence.

St. Charles's theories regarding the perpetrator were similar to those of Thorsen's but he did not want to share them this early in the investigation with the detective. He'd worked with Thorsen on enough cases to know he was only too eager to take information but very slow to share credit. The North Fork was St. Charles's territory. He did not like the vain detective's flamboyant mannerisms and cavalier attitude towards other professionals like Dr. Dionasis and despised his shallow compassion for victims and their families. St. Charles also felt it was too early to speculate. Things were changing however as Thorsen was sensing that this could very quickly become a high-profile case and wanted to be sure he was on the right end of it. Mentioning the reporter had put Thorsen in a foul mood. The detective was suddenly more concerned about his reputation than solving a crime and wanted the sergeant to help protect it. Unlike most of his co-workers, Thorsen included, St. Charles understood the pressure the media could create from his days in New York City but he also knew that this type of attitude often led to a sloppy investigation. He would not compromise his work to rush an arrest, whether it made Det. Thorsen look bad or not.

/ / /

Vin rose about six that morning thanks partly to a bright ray of sunlight that relentlessly peered through a seam in the thin curtain and partly due to his nervous nature. While Vin had gotten a few hours of sleep quite often it was his nearly endless supply of nervous energy that got him through the day. After washing his face he made himself a cup of coffee in his room and then sat on the edge of the bed to once again review his plan for the day.

Although Vin did get a few hours of sleep, the fact that he presently had more questions than answers combined with his rough encounter with St. Charles and not knowing whether the magazine would continue with the assignment if he could not interview the winemaker made relaxing difficult. While Vin was typically tense, he was even more so than usual. The unknown was making Vin anxious. He needed a strategy, a concrete plan covering the alternative outcomes to put his mind at ease. To better organize his thoughts Vin began entering a few lines into his notebook.

He was fairly certain something bad had happened to Dr. Lambrusco. Vin knew St. Charles did not want him looking into the story and would probably like to see Vin leave town. He did not know if he was going to have enough money to pay his hotel bill. On the plus side, it was nice to be out of the city and it was great to see Shanin.

Sitting up in bed and tapping his pen onto the paper Vin knew his first order of business was to find out what had happened to Dr. Lambrusco. In a small town like North Fork Harbor, Vin did not think it would be too difficult to learn what had actually taken place. He might be able to overhear some gossip in the hotel lobby or while waiting in line at a deli. Shanin knew people at the local newspaper. They would probably know in a reasonable amount of time. Vin estimated by about noon the next day he'd have a reliable idea of what had happened. By then his advance would arrive and he'd hopefully be able to continue the assignment, spend more time with Shanin and collect a nice fee when he returned to New York.

Vin needed to get to the winery. Learn what, if anything had happened to Dr. Lambrusco, avoid the police and with any luck, have dinner with Shanin that evening. With the exception of dinner with Shanin, he did not have a good feeling about the forthcoming day. Vin also had to decide what and when he would tell his editor Patricia Goode while still managing to get the advance. Vin then quickly dressed and trying to be as discreet as possible, planned to leave through the rear exit leading to the docks. If no one saw him leave the hotel he'd consider that a good start to the day. Vin hoped that when he'd return to the hotel his advance would have arrived as it would only be a matter of time before the hotel clerk discovered Vin had given him a bad credit card.

Vin managed to exit the hotel unseen. He then quickly made his way along the waterfront to the IGA only stopping briefly to look at the boats dotting the sparkling bay. He wondered what it would be like to enjoy a relaxing day on the water but as Vin approached the grocery store his thoughts returned to business. As Vin anticipated, there was a good amount of local people going in and out of the store. He lingered around the self-serve coffee station and near the store's deli counter hoping to pick up bits of gossip that might provide a clue to what may have happened at the winery. Vin fixed himself a cup of coffee. The young woman behind the counter smiled at him when he paid for it. Vin thanked her and then asked her for a receipt which he slipped into his shirt pocket. He slowly finished the coffee in the store, all the while watching, waiting and listening as various pick-up trucks and work vans pulled in and out of the neat parking lot when he noticed a pay telephone. Vin went to the telephone and dialed Shanin's number. Leaving a message, he asked her to scan the internet that day for any news on Dr. Lambrusco. He didn't think it would be likely that she'd find anything but knew there was a chance that something may have leaked.

While Vin had overheard lots of conversation bits in the store, he heard nothing about a winery mishap. So far, thought Vin, St. Charles had been doing a good job of keeping things quiet. And while he realized that Shanin may have been right, that he may be overreacting, his reporter instincts told him otherwise. Not willing to suppress his instincts, Vin decided to wait and listen a little while longer at the coffee counter before trying to find a ride to the winery. He actually had little choice. If Dr. Lambrusco was hurt or dead, he may no longer have an assignment. If he was alive and well, then he'd have to shortly be at the winery for the interview—a perfect cover. Vin liked his odds.

He looked at his watch. It was 7 a.m. Vin needed to be at the winery in 30 minutes. He could return to the phone booth and call Lefty's taxi or better yet, maybe save some money by getting a ride from someone heading in the same direction. Vin remembered the counter girl who smiled at him. Maybe she'd help. Vin approached the side of the counter and when she was between customers spoke to her.

"Excuse me," said Vin to the young woman.

"Everything okay with the coffee?" she asked.

"Coffee's great," Vin said. "Best I've had since I've been out here. I'm trying to get to North Fork Harbor Vineyards."

"Just take the Main Road west," she said pointing in what Vin trusted was an westerly direction. "You should be there in no more than 15 minutes."

"I'm not driving. I don't have a car," said Vin. "Any other way I can get there? Maybe a bus?"

"You could get to China faster than you can get anywhere around here by bus," she said while serving the next customer. "Hold on a minute. Tugboat!" she yelled in the direction of the front door. A man about to get into a delivery truck turned. She waved for him to come into the store.

"Watch ya want?" the driver said as he entered the store. He was a husky man in high boots. He wore a worn blue denim jacket with the logos of different bakery products sewn into the fabric. He had a burly beard and wore big, rounded glasses.

"You headin' west?" the counter girl asked.

"Why? You gettin' off early?" he said with a wry smile revealing a row of chipped and brown-stained teeth.

"Can you take this gentleman with you?" she asked glancing in Vin's direction. "Where you goin' again?" she asked, turning towards him.

"North Fork Harbor Vineyards," answered Vin in the direction of the driver. "Got room for me?"

"I like coffee too," the driver responded while tilting his head in the direction of the coffee station. "Black, no sugar."

"How about a large?" asked Vin taking the hint.

"See you out front," said the driver.

"Thanks," said Vin to the counter girl while leaving the money for the driver's coffee on the counter.

"You bet," she quickly said without looking up from the register while serving the next customer.

The driver waved to Vin from the van, his husky arm hanging out the opened window. Vin climbed into the passenger seat and handed the driver his cup of coffee.

"Thanks for the coffee," said the driver. "You from the city?"

"Yeah," answered Vin. "How can you tell?"

"Just by how you walk, how you carry yourself. By the fact that you don't know your way around here and you ain't got a car," said the driver.

As was usual with Vin, he was not comfortable when the other person was asking most of the questions. Vin made note of his surroundings. The van was full of paper scraps, old newspapers, empty coffee cups and cigarette packs. It had the mixed odor of perspiration, tobacco smoke, exhaust and fresh bread. Vin kept his window opened half-way during the entire ride.

"Why do they call you Tugboat?" asked Vin, in an attempt to change the subject.

"When I was a kid I used to pull all the other kids on my bicycle," said the driver. "I was always kinda husky, you know? They started calling me the tugboat and it stuck," he said with a big grin. "My real name's Vincent. I'm Vincent Tucker."

"Me too," said Vin extending his hand. "It's always nice to meet another Vincent."

"The funny thing is," continued Vincent the driver. "I never been on a tugboat in my life." Each man smiled a bit in response to the observation.

"Which do you prefer to be called?" asked Vin "Or does it matter?"

"I'd like to be called Vincent or Vince, even Vinnie. I'm getting' tired of Tugboat. I know nobody don't mean nuthin' by it but I'm just getting' a little tired of the nickname. It's been a long time since the fourth grade."

There was a slight pause as neither man said anything.

"You got friends or family out here?" asked Vincent the driver.

"Sort of a girlfriend," said Vin. "It's kind of on-again-off-again."

"I know what you mean. It's tough to hold onto a woman," said Vincent. "What kind of work do you do?"

"Writer," said Vin.

"You mean like books and stuff?"

"No, more like newspaper articles."

"Ever meet anyone famous? Anyone I might've heard of? Race car driver? A president?"

"Not really," said Vin. "I mostly do local stuff but I would like to write a book one day."

The driver nodded as he took another sip of his coffee.

"The vineyard where you're goin' is right around this bend," said the driver gesturing with his chin. "I'll pull over in a minute."

"Great," said Vin. "I really appreciate the ride."

"No problem," said Vincent the driver. "I don't get to talk to writers much. Maybe you'll write about me in your book one day. It don't gotta be much. I'd be happy with a small thing."

"You never know," said Vin. "I'll keep it in mind."

The driver signaled as he steered the van to the side of the road. Vin exited and while standing on the roadside but still holding the door he spoke through the opened window.

"Where's a good place to hang out around here at night?" asked Vin. "Maybe have a burger and a beer. Watch some NASCAR."

"The best place is the Apple Tree," said Vincent the driver. "It's about a mile back east of here, opposite side of the road," he said, nodding his head back to clarify the direction. "On the south side of the Main Road. Things don't get busy there 'til about 8. It's kind of a late crowd."

"You gonna be there?" asked Vin.

"You might catch me there."

"If I do, you and your buddies got a beer on me," said Vin, closing the door. "Thanks again for the ride Vince."

"You bet," he said, giving Vin a thumbs-up gesture as he steered the van back towards the road to resume his route. Nothing would make him more insane than a night watching NASCAR but Vin was always thinking of places in which he might find information. He learned nothing in the deli that morning. The bar might be more useful and if the advance came he'd happily buy a few beers in exchange for information.

Vin methodically walked towards the top of the winery driveway, the sound of gravel crunching beneath his rubber soles. Vin decided he was going to directly walk into the winery office, state that he has an appointment to interview Dr. Frank Lambrusco for Travel & Pleasure magazine and act as if he fully expected to complete his assignment. He decided his best strategy was to behave as if he had no knowledge of the previous night's events and see what he could learn.

As Vin approached the winery all appeared to be operating normally. In the distance he could see workers tending to vines in the field. Other workers were cleaning equipment outside the barn. A few cars, Vin assumed they belong to the workers, were parked at the side of the building. The entranceway was relatively empty. Unlike other wineries there were no framed press clippings on the walls of reviews, no free tourist magazines and no t-shirts or cookbooks for sale. No information about tours, tastings, winery events or marketing material of any kind. This was strictly a place for those in the business of wine. He opened the door and stood in the building's dark entranceway. In front of him was a wooden stairway. The only light came from old windows high on the wall or through the small window in the door. Underneath the stairway were stacked a few cartons of empty bottles and some agricultural-chemical containers. Vin could hear a woman's voice coming from the upstairs. She was ending a telephone conversation. "I'll give him the message," Vin heard the woman say before hanging up the phone.

"Hello," came the female voice from upstairs.

"Hello," responded Vin.

He heard steps and then saw a pair of female legs walking down the stairway.

"Are you from the magazine?" she asked.

"Yes, I'm Vin Gusto. Travel & Pleasure. I'm here to interview Dr. Frank Lambrusco," said Vin, smiling while he extended his hand.

"I'm Cindy, Dr. Frank's assistant," she said, shaking Vin's hand.

"I was just on the phone with the magazine people. They want you to call the office right away. Here's the number," she said, handing Vin a slip of paper. "There's an extra phone in my office you can use. Sometimes cell phone service is not too reliable here."

"Sure," said Vin before following Cindy up the stairs to her office.

Vin called the magazine's office from a phone on a separate desk across from Cindy's. A young man identifying himself as Giorgio answered.

"Hi, this is Vin Gusto. I'm a writer on assignment. I just got a message from Pat Goode."

"No you didn't," said the voice on the other end.

"Yes I did," countered Vin. "I was just handed this message with this number."

"I'm sure you did," Giorgio said. "Pat didn't call. I did. I'm her executive assistant. I tried calling your cell phone but it didn't go through. Service must be weak where you are."

"Yeah. I guess. Can I talk to Pat?"

"She's not in today," said Giorgio. "She's at home with a migraine, lying on the couch with a cold compress over her forehead I hope. I think it's from the new cappuccino machine they installed this week. The poor thing's been drinking the stuff like it's going out of style. I kept telling her to slow down but . . ."

"Giorgio," Vin interrupted. "Can you please give me the message?"

"Your assignment's cancelled," he flatly said.

"Cancelled? Why?"

"Your advance was sent yesterday to the hotel, the Crashing whatever. I brought the package to the mailroom myself. You're to keep the advance as your kill fee. The assignment letter in your package has some clause about that."

"The assignment's cancelled?"

"We just went over that, didn't we? Pat said to tell you and I quote, to 'drop it immediately and enjoy the rest of your time out there.' I've said all I can. Any more questions you can e-mail me and I'll forward them to Patty and she'll respond when she's feeling up to it. Have a nice day."

Giorgio then hung up the phone and Vin did the same. Cindy had been watching him through the entire conversation and spoke first.

"It seems like there's been some sort of mix-up," she said. "Dr. Lambrusco left last night for his flight. There was no way he could have been here for the interview. Sorry."

"He left last night?" repeated Vin.

"Yes. I was just filing the order from the car service," she said quickly flashing a copy of the receipt. Vin noticed it was issued by Country-City Limousine but she did not hold it out long enough for him to read any of the other information on it.

"So no Dr. Frank," Vin said to Cindy, still a bit shocked. "Don't you handle his schedule? Couldn't someone have noticed this before?"

"I do handle his schedule but sometimes he does things without telling me. I'm sorry for the inconvenience. And I'm sorry about your assignment," said Cindy. "Maybe you can reschedule something once Dr. Frank returns. Are you staying on North Fork Harbor or did you drive out for the day?"

Vin did not answer. He had difficulty believing that Dr. Frank's secretary would not know his schedule before leaving on an important trip.

"If you need a ride I can call you a cab," she offered, putting her hand on the phone.

"No thanks," said Vin thinking quickly. "I was really looking forward to this assignment. Would it be okay if I had a look around the premises? I'm from the city. I've never seen a real winery before."

Vin noticed a slight change of expression when he asked Cindy if he could tour the winery.

"We don't permit that sort of thing," she said shaking her head. "I cannot allow you to do that."

"Even if someone escorted me?"

"We're not what you would call a 'tourist winery.' This is a working winery, a business operation. Workers handling equipment. Trucks coming in and out. Vines being sprayed. We don't give tours. We have no tasting room and we're not covered for non-authorized persons on the property. Those are Dr. Frank's standing orders."

"I am authorized," countered Vin. "I had an assignment. I'm here on business."

"But your assignment's been cancelled," she said with a slight tone of condescension in her voice. "I can't spare anyone to show you around. We're really shorthanded and approaching our busiest time of year, not to mention all of the other stress and confusion around here."

"What do you mean?"

Cindy hesitated before speaking. "It's our busy time of year," she blurted. "I'm sorry but you'll have to leave."

Vin sighed loudly as he thought about what to do next.

"The other wineries offer tours and tastings," Cindy offered, turning cheerful again. "Some are free and others charge. I don't know which ones do which. You can grab one of the tourist guides at a supermarket or hotel lobby and you'll see information on each of them. Or you can go online."

Vin was not comfortable with how Cindy's mood and tone shifted. Since it was clear she would not meet his request for a tour and wanted him off the property he decided to retreat. Vin didn't actually care to see the winery. He was hoping he'd be able to get information by touring the premises. The fact that Dr. Lambrusco was not available combined with the sudden cancellation of his assignment did not sit well with him. At the same time he noticed through the window behind Cindy a car sporting the Lefty's Taxi Service logo had entered the driveway.

"I understand," he said to Cindy who nodded with a fake smile. Just then her telephone rang. "I'll see myself out," said Vin. "Thank you anyway. Maybe we can reconnect in the future, after Dr. Frank returns."

They shook hands and he left her office but it was apparent that Cindy's attention had fully shifted to the incoming phone call. Vin slowly walked down the stairway and stood alone by the landing. This time he could hear Cindy on the phone.

"What? Maria Lambrusco's here."

Vin sensed an opening.

CHAPTER 16

Sowing Seeds of Discontent

Vin stood on the winery's front porch and watched as the driver opened the rear door of the car, allowing Maria Lambrusco to exit. The sunlight was now shining through the treetop canopy that lined the driveway and glistening off the bright green vines that surrounded the property. Vin watched Maria, tall and slim, she was wearing sunglasses, a rose-colored, silk scoop-neck t-shirt, white form-fitting dress pants, white sandals and black blazer. Her hair was pulled back from her slightly tanned face. As Maria exited the car she briefly thanked the driver before precisely heading towards the front entrance where Vin was standing. With her head down she walked purposely along the driveway. Vin noticed she was carrying a designer handbag but did not recognize the logo. He sensed he should initiate contact with her but also knew he had to be careful. But it was Maria who spoke first.

"Can I help you?" she asked as she approached the doorway.

"I'm Vin Gusto," he said. Breaking from his usual procedure he thought it would be best to tell Maria why he was there. "I'm a writer."

"A writer?" repeated Maria. "We're not giving any statements."

"I'm not seeking a statement," said Vin. "I was supposed to interview Dr. Lambrusco." He then removed his New York City press badge from his pocket and showed it to her.

Maria stopped and while looking in Vin's direction, sensed she was actually looking past him. She had the glazed look of someone not fully aware of their surroundings. Maria then briefly looked at Vin's badge. While she may have had her father's sense of apprehension before she could say anything further the door opened and Cindy appeared.

"Maria, I'm so sorry," Cindy said as she put her arms around her in a gigantic show of affection.

Vin thought he heard Maria mumble a "thank you." He watched as Cindy then quickly ushered her inside the winery, the door closing behind them and wondered about what he had just heard—the idea of "giving a statement" from Maria followed by condolences from Cindy. As Cindy would be occupied with

Maria, Vin thought it would be a good time to try to take a self-guided tour of the winery.

Noting on which side of the main building was Cindy's office, Vin began his tour walking around the opposite end. As Cindy had said, it was very much a working winery and apparently they were not accustomed to visitors. Vin found it hard to be inconspicuous as he had no idea to where he was walking or no real purpose for his presence there. Some of the workers briefly looked up from what they were doing as Vin passed, quietly acknowledging a stranger in their midst while others appeared not to have noticed. None of them said anything to him as they tended to vines or equipment. With his reporter's gear still in his duffle bag, Vin wondered if anyone was truly paying attention to him and how long it would be before Cindy learned he was on the premises and would send someone to escort him off the property. In any event, it would give him something to do while he thought about how he'd get back to the hotel, get his kill fee and then figure how he was going to spend the rest of his time in North Fork Harbor when another car entered the winery grounds.

Vin stepped back into the shadow cast by a shed and watched as a black, four-door Ford Crown Victoria swung across the top of the driveway and made its way down, abruptly stopping just outside the winery office entrance. From the driver's side emerged a tall man in a fairly bad suit. Recognizing the vehicle as something used by police crews and noting his attire, Vin correctly identified the man as a detective. From the passenger side emerged Sgt. St. Charles in uniform. The two men walked quickly into the building.

Vin did not like the idea of another encounter with St. Charles. While St. Charles could not prevent him from doing his job, Vin would rather avoid the sergeant and thought about making an inconspicuous exit. Behind the shed was a dirt trail that led down a small hillside and into the vineyard. Vin wondered if it might offer a safe way off the premises or at least a temporary hiding spot. While Vin liked keeping a low profile, as it generally helped him get the story he was after, he wasn't the type who liked to hide. While avoiding a possible encounter with a police officer was not his way he thought at this time it might be the wiser thing to do. Vin then walked quickly from behind the shed and down the dirt road. He soon found himself between seemingly endless rows of grape vines and a cloudless blue sky. It was a good day to be out of the city.

While the sun's rays felt hot on his back, the brown earth was soft and cool beneath the soles of his sneakers. After he'd walked for a few minutes Vin stopped to look where he was. Around him was nothing but bright green grape leaves and twisting brown and gray vines strung along tight wires. Thick clusters of plump grapes hung down all around him while near the base of the canes he could see the tiny spouts from the underground drip-irrigation system, giving the vines the right amount of water when Mother Nature was unreliable. This was an extraordinary environment for a boy from the asphalt playgrounds of the Bronx.

Vin picked a few grapes. The actual berries were much smaller than the table grapes he was accustomed to seeing on city fruit stands and were full of seeds. But the fruit itself was very sweet and full of juice. He spit the seeds and wiped the thick juice that had mixed with perspiration on his chin with the back of his hand. Vin then thought about the subject of his interview. Where was Dr. Lambrusco? From what Vin knew, the man had given a good part of his life to the field where he was now standing. And what did Maria Lambrusco know? What might she tell St. Charles and the detective? How would he make contact with her?

Vin then heard voices in the distance. While he could not understand what they were saying, as they drew closer Vin made out the sounds of men speaking in Spanish. He had a slight knowledge of Spanish and combined with his rudimentary Italian was sometimes able to make himself understood by Spanish-speakers, depending on the subject matter. He waited for the men to get close before approaching them. Vin knew foreign workers, illegally in this country or not, were often reluctant to speak with outsiders but it would be to his advantage to be friendly towards them, otherwise they might report him to someone in the winery office and Vin would be escorted from the premises.

Vin waved at the men. Some were shirtless and others were wearing just thin t-shirts in an attempt to beat the heat. Some were fanning themselves with wide-brimmed hats. They looked at him but offered no response. They were carrying farm tools and seemed determined to go about their duty while paying little notice to Vin. He approached them and again holding up his hand asked for Dr. Lambrusco.

"*Signor Lambrusco,*" Vin said. "*Donde esta hoy?*"

The men looked at Vin and then at each other. None of them said anything. Vin repeated the question, being sure to keep his tone friendly in an attempt to earn their cooperation.

"*No hoy,*" one of the workers answered, shaking his head and staring at the ground.

"*No hoy?*" Vin repeated.

The workers gave no further response. Some of them stared at Vin, who detected a feeling of apathy. Vin then heard the hum of a motorized vehicle heading in their direction.

"*La polizia aqui?*" asked Vin in an attempt to learn if St. Charles or any his force remained at the winery.

"*Si,*" the same worker answered.

"*Estoy aqui?*" Vin asked gesturing at the ground.

The workers shrugged their shoulders and remained where they were standing.

"*Gracias,*" said Vin as the noise from the approaching vehicle grew louder. Vin's presence did not seem to affect the workers and he sensed that they would not report him being in the field. Migrant workers understood what it was like to be an outsider and Vin was counting on their sympathy. To play it safe, he stepped back a few rows and crouched down behind a leafy cluster of grapes and vines, trying not to move.

A small, all-terrain, off-road vehicle soon appeared on the same dirt road Vin had taken. It was pulling an empty cart and had a plow blade attached to its front. It was being driven by one of the American workers. The driver, who was wearing short pants, a wide-brimmed hat and a long-sleeved, white shirt stopped and gestured to the migrant workers each of whom then automatically entered the cart. Vin watched the driver from behind his spot among the vines. He appeared to say nothing to the workers as they continued down the dirt trail.

Vin remained where he was behind the vines and thought about what he had seen that warm morning at the vineyard while contemplating his next move. Convinced he would not learn anything further at the winery that day, he decided he needed to get back to his hotel, cash his advance, settle his bill and get in touch with Shanin. The more immediate concern was how to leave the winery unseen. From the position of the sun Vin could tell that the dirt road the vehicle driver had taken veered west. Recalling St. Charles' remarks on the local geography, Vin theorized that the winery buildings and main entrance were nearly directly south from where he now stood. If he walked north he guessed he'd eventually reach the end of the vineyard and hopefully find a road and from there make his way to the hotel.

/ / /

In the winery office Det. Thorsen had begun speaking with workers with very little success. Each provided the same basic responses. They expressed shock over Dr. Lambrusco's sudden death. None knew of any altercations in which he may have been involved. Each said he was generally a pleasant albeit quiet employer. Other words used to describe him were smart, considerate and secretive. It was the last adjective that got Thorsen's attention and it had come from Larson, the boisterous mechanic.

"There was nuthin' wrong with the Doc," said Larson to Thorsen. "But you never knew what he was thinkin'. Kept to himself a lot."

"Professionally," asked Thorsen. "How did he treat you?"

"Okay," said Larson. "Always paid on time."

"Did he have any business enemies?"

"None that I know of."

"Did he have any friends?"

"Not around here," said Larson.

"All of the employees spoke highly of him," said Thorsen.

"Sure if you ask them Mexicans. What do you think they're gonna say? They're praying they ain't gonna be deported."

"You're saying one of the migrant workers may have been involved?"

"No, it's just that they gotta watch their step. Any little thing and they can be headin' south of the border if you know what I'm sayin'. I wouldn't be surprised if they start takin' off on account of this."

"But he treated the workers well according to what I've heard today."

"Look Detective," said Larson, stretching his large, grease-stained palms across the desk that was between him and Thorsen. "I'd like to help you."

"So what's holding you back?" pressed Thorsen, sensing a psychological opening. "If you and the Doc never had any disagreements and you said he was a good customer, why wouldn't you want to help us?"

"It's true me and the Doc had some arguments," he stopped in mid-sentence.

"That's not a crime," said Thorsen. "People argue every day, ask any husband and wife," he said with a smile in an attempt to cut the tension. "And you said he was a good customer."

"It was never anything personal," said Larson. "It was just normal stuff."

"Are you a good mechanic?" asked Thorsen, changing the subject.

"I keep busy."

"How's business?"

"I pay my bills."

"How'd you learn how to repair vineyard equipment? It's pretty complicated stuff."

"Self-taught. Trial and error. Ain't no magic to hard work."

"Someone with good technical skills like yourself could work in a lot of industries. Ever work in any other field? Say medical, pharmaceutical?"

"No. Been around tractors my whole life."

"A lot of this equipment's very sophisticated. A lot's computer-controlled. What does a mechanic like you do when the computer breaks down?"

"I usually don't mess around with that end of it."

"How do you mean?"

"When the computer breaks down, I just pull it out and it gets sent back. I'm strictly a nuts-and-bolts guy. I don't mess around with none of that software. That's a different trade. When the new one arrives, I plug it in."

"Who handles the computers around the winery?"

"Cindy I guess."

"When you say 'send it back,' you mean to the manufacturer, correct?"

"I guess."

"Who sends it back?"

"I don't really know Detective. Maybe the Doc. Maybe Cindy. Can I go now?"

"Do you work for any other winemakers in the area?" asked Thorsen, ignoring his request to leave.

"A little," said Larson.

"Any of them ever mention Dr. Lambrusco?"

"Sometimes," said Larson, who did not like authority figures and was growing uncomfortable with the detective and his line of questioning.

"Are they angry when they discuss him? Envious? Curious? He apparently had great knowledge about growing grapes but you said he was 'secretive'. Maybe he didn't share information with them."

"Look around. No one needs help growing grapes around here. These guys are grape-growin' experts. I guess with you not being from around here you might not have noticed that," said Larson, rising to leave the room.

"I wouldn't be so fast to leave," said Thorsen who quickly grew agitated by the mechanic's arrogance and moved to even the score. "Right now you're not a suspect," he lied. "But if you walk out of this room before I'm through there's a good chance you'll be receiving a subpoena in the near future."

Thorsen understood that most people did not know much about how the legal system worked and the subtle threat of receiving a subpoena was often enough to get a sensible person to cooperate, especially if he was innocent. And so far, Larson had given Thorsen more information than anyone else he interviewed that day. He wanted to keep the stream of information flowing, despite his arrogance and was not beneath using an empty threat to do so.

Larson stood with his hands on the back of the chair exposing husky biceps beneath short sleeves. He was squarely facing Thorsen who took a good look at the mechanic. Judging Larson by his size, it was likely that he would have had a relatively easy time physically overpowering the much older and smaller Dr. Frank, especially if he had done so by surprise, which was almost surely the case. He was boisterous, opinionated and confrontational but he was an intelligent mechanic and businessman. Thorsen did not think Larson was guilty. Nor did he think any of the migrant workers were responsible. Each had too much to lose.

"So how much do you know about computers?" Thorsen asked.

"I already told you, not much," he said.

"One's missing," continued Thorsen. "A handheld that belonged to the Doc."

Larson shook his head and stared down at the desk. Thorsen took a risk letting Larson know about the missing computer but felt it was one worth taking.

"You see someone using a handheld who you never seen using one before or you see someone offering one for sale, maybe to a competing winemaker, you let me know right away. Understand?"

"Yes Sir."

"People like secrets but they don't like not knowing them," said Thorsen. "Especially if they can be making money from them. Do you think that may have been the case with Dr. Frank?"

"I don't know," said Larson.

"I think you may know a little bit more," said Thorsen who for the first time in his conversations of the day used a slight but unmistakable tone of anger. "If you've got nothing else to say you're free to go Mr. Larson. But if you know something I expect you to submit it. Doing anything less is a crime. And you can share that bit of information with your friends around the winery as well."

"I ain't got no friends around here."

"I know what you mean."

The two men stared at each other for a moment.

"Thank you," said the tall Larson, rising from his seat.

"No, thank you," said Thorsen quickly changing his tone to a more positive one as he rose and opened the door. "You've been so helpful we may find it necessary to contact you again. Have a good day," he said smiling as he held the door for him. Thorsen made sure he thanked Larson loudly enough so that Cindy, who'd been working in the reception area would be able to hear him. Larson walked quickly from the office, forgetting to acknowledge Cindy. Thorsen was using slight psychological intimidation on what was so far, his best source. He hoped that in a short time, Larson would reconsider and come forth with more information.

While Larson acknowledged that Dr. Frank was a good client, indicating that he would have little motivation to harm him, he also added that he worked with a lot of his competitors. Although not very personable, Larson ran a good business and was a respected mechanic. Even if he felt no remorse for Dr. Lambrusco he was too smart to get in the way of an investigation. It was doubtful that Larson would have been able to give competitors the information they wanted but as someone who regularly was in contact with many of the local vineyard managers, he could be a valuable source.

Thorsen was also beginning to feel the pressure mounting despite the fact that they were very early in the investigation. He wanted a quick resolution. Thorsen despised the fact that he was given an assignment in the backward East End—wine country or not. While his colleagues were either unraveling the crimes of the rich-and-famous in some of Long Island's more prosperous areas or getting high-profile cases in the glamorous Hamptons he was interviewing truck mechanics and office workers. The fact that a reporter was interested in the case only made him more anxious to quickly find the culprit and bask in any publicity it might generate if the public was actually even interested in this case. But if that's what was needed to get elevated to solving the more high-profile crimes, then that's what he'd do.

As Thorsen stood in the doorway watching Larson leave, Cindy looked up at the Detective.

"Tough customer," she said to him.

"A pussycat," answered the detective, allowing his gaze to rest on her for a few seconds. He liked making people uncomfortable, including police officers and fellow detectives, but during investigations he particularly liked to do so. He felt the subtle pressure helped bring people forward. People preferred taking the road of least resistance he believed. Disagreeing with Cindy on the perception of

Larson would surely make an impression on her. It would also let her know he was not intimidated by the loud and large mechanic as he kept him in the office for a relatively long amount of time.

"Was Maria Lambrusco here earlier?" Thorsen asked Cindy.

"Yes, but she left," the receptionist answered.

"Where'd she go?"

"I don't know," Cindy said. "She understandably was pretty upset, the poor thing. She left without saying anything."

"Any word on that handheld?" asked Thorsen.

"None that I know of," she said.

"Who's running the winery now?" he asked.

"I don't know," said Cindy, somewhat flustered by the question. "I can handle the day-to-day office business and Andy can manage the vineyard. That's how it works whenever Dr. Lambrusco's away."

"Who's Andy?"

"Andy LaBroom. He's the vineyard manager," said Cindy. "He knows every inch of this farm."

"Farm?" repeated Thorsen. "I thought this was a vineyard."

"It used to be a potato farm," said Cindy. "In fact it belonged to Andy's family. Sometimes we still call it that. Sentimental I guess. I haven't seen Andy today but his truck is here."

"Why is it that he's not on my list?" asked Thorsen.

"He's probably in the fields," said Cindy. "They don't get cell phone service out there."

"Please get word to him that I want to meet with him ASAP," said Thorsen. "And you and I need to set some time to talk as well."

CHAPTER 17

Surveying the Harvest

After about 30 minutes Vin reached a paved road. Like most of the major roads in the area it ran east-and-west. With his head down and tired from the heat, he began walking in an easterly direction, betting eventually it would take him towards his hotel. When he heard a vehicle approaching he'd turn to face it, extend his thumb and gesture for a ride. He was nearly astonished when a pick-up truck pulled over. The driver extended his arm from the window, gesturing for Vin to approach the truck.

"Can you give me a lift?" asked Vin.

"Can you pay your bill?" the driver responded. It was the hotel clerk. "You got a 'Do Not Disturb' sign on your door and here I find you walkin' on the side of the road."

"Sorry about that," said Vin. "Did a package come for me?"

"What do I look like, the postman?"

Without waiting for an answer Vin walked around the truck and entered through the passenger door. "I appreciate the ride," he said.

"You ain't even asked where I'm goin'?"

"I like my chances," said Vin.

"And I got a vested interest in you."

Vin was too exhausted to worry. "Listen," continued Vin. "I know I owe you for last night. When I get to the hotel there should be a check for me in an overnight package from the magazine. They told me they sent it. If you could cash it for me I'll pay you on the spot."

"Sounds like a deal," said the clerk.

"So how was the fishing last night?" asked Vin.

"Pretty good. We got our limit of bass and lobster."

The mention of fish reminded Vin about his date later than night with Shanin. In addition to being low on funds, he was in desperate need of a shower and some rest. He was quietly thankful that the advance would cover a few nights in the hotel and his dinner bill with Shanin, relieving him of at least some financial worries.

"Where you comin' from?" the clerk suddenly asked Vin.

Not wanting to reveal where he'd been Vin waited a second before answering. "Just out gathering information for my assignment. Getting the lay of the land, that sort of thing."

"You hear what happened at the winery you asked me about last night?"

"No, what?" asked Vin.

"It's kinda preliminary but they're sayin' the winemaker was murdered."

Vin just stared out the window for a few seconds, tying not to look like the news he'd just heard was too important to him.

"What?"

"That's what they were sayin' down at the docks. Don't know if it's true."

"They know who did it?" asked Vin. "Any suspects?"

"None that I know of," said the clerk. "That's the police's job."

Not one to tip his hand Vin tried to remain relatively emotionless and continued staring out the window. "When do you think we'll be at the hotel?" he asked.

"Not long," said the clerk. "If we get there in time you might be able to get your room cleaned today. The maid might still be around."

Vin said little else as he thought about the alleged murder. While there had been no official word, the news had confirmed what Vin had suspected. When he arrived at the hotel he saw an overnight package protruding from the mail/shoebox near the front desk. He stood by the desk and opened it. It contained the contract which had been signed by Patricia Goode. The "kill-fee clause" mentioned by her assistant had been highlighted in yellow. Inside was a business-sized envelope. Vin opened it and found a check made out to him in the amount of $350 with the words "kill fee—North Fork article," handwritten on the memo section. There was nothing else in the envelope. Holding the check in his hand Vin sat on a chair in the lobby to plan his next move.

"You get that check?" called the clerk who was now standing behind the desk.

"Yeah," said Vin. "It's right here."

"You want me to cash it? Save you a trip to the bank and we can settle up like you said."

"Sure," said Vin, rising from the chair to hand the check to the clerk.

"Sign it while I go in the back room to get the cash from the safe," said the clerk who left the check on the counter for Vin to sign.

"It's for $350," said Vin.

When Vin went to take the pen from his shirt pocket something had gotten attached to its clip. It was the business card of Nadia Rivera, editor of Travel & Pleasure's competitor Travelzonia that he slipped into his shirt pocket during their Penn Station encounter. Vin looked at the card. Did he now have a reason to call Nadia? She promised her readers a radical view into the world of travel and asked Vin to call her if "anything happened" during his trip. But did she mean it or was she merely being polite? His original assignment had been cancelled. His main subject was probably murdered. Would Nadia be intrigued by a story of an up-and-coming wine region nestled in a quaint seaside village just east of New York City with the possible murder of a renown winemaker as its backdrop?

Just then the clerk returned from the back room. In his hand he had a small white envelope containing Vin's cash. He handed it to Vin who immediately opened it.

"There's $150 in here," said Vin flipping through the bills. "The check was for $350."

"That's right," said the clerk.

"Two-hundred's missing," said Vin.

"How long you plannin' on stayin' here?" asked the clerk.

"I'm not sure," said Vin.

"The original reservation was for three nights," said the clerk. "You already stayed one which you ain't yet paid for plus two more makes three. I'm cuttin' you a deal. Three nights for $200. But it's gotta be cash only."

"What if I check-out now?" asked Vin.

"Then I'm chargin' you the full rate for the night you already stayed . . . $150. That's got to be cash too 'cause your credit card didn't go through and I ain't tryin' it no more. Or I can call the police and tell them I got a guest here passin' around a bad credit card."

Vin considered the offer. The clerk had the cash and was going to keep nearly half of his kill fee whether he remained at the Crashing Sea Gull or not. He wasn't sure if the clerk would actually call the police but getting them further involved would obviously be a bad idea. While Vin's assignment had been cancelled, two more days out of the city was still an appealing proposition. Plus, if he stayed there was the chance to rekindle things with Shanin. It was worth the extra $50 but he did not want to give in so quickly to the clerk.

"I see you got some troubles so I'm offerin' you a special rate," continued the clerk.

"Before I answer I'd like to ask you a question?"

"Shoot," said the clerk.

"Why'd you pick me up today?" asked Vin.

"Because you looked terrible walkin' under that hot sun and you owed me money," said the clerk. "I did a good deed but was protectin' my own interests."

"I'll stay the two more days under one condition," said Vin.

"What's that?"

"I'm sorry about the credit card I guess it was just a mix-up." said Vin. "Since we're even, if you promise not to call the police I'll be sure to write something nice about this hotel in my article. Maybe even include a photo if you're lucky. Look at it as free advertising."

"You got a deal," said the clerk who extended his hand across the counter.

"Okay," said Vin. The two men shook on their new agreement and Vin then put the remaining $150 in his pocket and headed to his room but not before stopping at the lobby payphone to leave a message for Shanin. Using the phone card he asked her to meet him that evening outside the IGA at 8 pm for a late dinner. It would be dark by then, giving them less chance of being seen as well as ample time to rest. He also called his mother. The answering machine came on after the third ring. Vin said in his message that he was on Eastern Long Island in the beautiful Crashing Sea Gull Inn on special assignment and that he hoped to be done by the end of the week. Vin left her the hotel telephone number and then hung up the phone.

When he got to his room, the "Do Not Disturb" sign was still hanging from the door knob. His room had not been cleaned. Vin didn't care. He wanted to rest, fill Shanin in on that day's events and plan his next move.

///

On his drive home from North Fork Harbor Det. Thorsen made an unannounced visit to Maria Lambrusco. Without stopping at the front desk he went straight to the hotel manager's office, showed his badge and asked in which room he would find Maria Lambrusco.

He then went alone to the elevator and directly to her room. Outside her door he spoke briefly with the officer on duty.

"Is she inside?" was all Thorsen asked the officer while nodding his head in the direction of the door. He did not bother showing his badge to the officer.

"Yes, Sir," said the officer.

"Has she had any visitors?" Thorsen asked.

"No Sir," said the officer.

"Sent out for a meal?"

"No Sir."

"Open the door."

The officer knocked on the door.

"Who is it?" came the voice from inside the room.

"Detective Thorsen is here," said the officer.

The door slowly opened.

"Hello Detective," said Maria. "I wasn't expecting anyone."

"I'm sorry I didn't call first Ms. Lambrusco," said the detective, the tone of his voice becoming much more pleasant when speaking to Maria. "There are some follow-up questions I'd like to ask. I hope it's all right if I come in to talk with you alone for a few moments."

Maria's dark eyes opened wide. Her black hair was loose and undone. She was wearing a white button-down silk blouse open at the neck, a pair of creased jeans and was barefoot. Thorsen would have a difficult time keeping his eyes from her. She was tall, slim and walked with a definite purpose, even during this trying time.

"You can come in," said Maria, opening the door and nodding at the officer. Once Thorsen entered Maria closed the door behind him and went to turn off the television she had been watching.

"I was just watching a little television," she said. "Trying to relax."

"You can keep it on while we talk," said Thorsen. The detective actually preferred to have the television on while he was in the room. It would help prevent the officer outside from hearing any of their conversation. He reached over and turned it back on, keeping the volume on a medium-low setting.

"Why don't we sit at the table," Maria offered as she gestured to the small wooden table and two chairs that were at the other end of the room. The basket of fruit from when Maria arrived was still on the table. It was largely untouched.

Without removing his coat, Thorsen sat on the chair closest to the window. Maria took the opposite seat.

"I'm sorry if the room's a little messy," said Maria, still a bit flustered by the detective's sudden appearance. "I wasn't expecting anyone."

"That's quite all right Maria," said Thorsen. "I wanted to come by and see how you were doing."

"That's very nice of you," she said.

"This is a nice hotel for out here," Thorsen said. "This it's the first time I've been in any of the rooms," he lied. "I've always passed it from the road and knew it had to be better than that other place out in the Harbor, the Seagull's Nest or something. That place looks like it hasn't been renovated since the Second World War."

"I'm okay I guess, you know, for under the circumstances."

"It looks to me like you're doing quite well, for as you say, 'under the circumstances'," said Thorsen "I also wanted to bring you up to date with where we are in the investigation and see if perhaps you can help us fill in a few blanks. I want you to know we're working very hard on this."

"I'll do everything I can," she said.

"I spoke with some of the winery workers today," said Thorsen. "They each said basically the same things. They were shocked to learn of your father's death. They liked and respected him and no one could offer a clue regarding suspects or persons of interest."

"Has my father's handheld been located?"

"Not yet," said Thorsen. "Did you know your father was to attend an agricultural conference?"

"Yes, he was to be a speaker there."

"Has anyone called to ask why he was not there?"

"Not that I know of Detective. But they'd call the office, not me."

"I suppose so," said Thorsen who then rose to walk around the room as he continued talking. Maria chose not to watch him but instead looked out the window.

"So you're convinced whoever did this was after the data in that handheld?" asked Thorsen.

"I'm not completely sure but I'd say it's a strong possibility," said Maria. "Why take the handheld and nothing else?"

"So far it has not turned up on the evidence list. The men are keeping an eye out for it." Thorsen paused.

"Detective," said Maria.

"Yes?"

Maria paused while tapping the tip of her index finger on the desk.

"What is it?" pressed Thorsen.

Maria, with eyes opened wide then with voice cracking asked, "What about the grapes?"

Thorsen looked down at the desk. It was one of the rare times when he was not ready and chose not to answer her.

"I spoke with most of the workers," he said, avoiding the issue. "Except for Cindy the secretary and a LaBroom."

"They're longtime employees. My father never had any complaints about them," said Maria. "I'm not sure what they'd be able to tell you that you haven't already learned."

"They're on my list for tomorrow," he said. "Now that you say that I wish I had gotten to them today. This is a long drive for me."

Maria nodded as Thorsen rose from his seat to pace across the room.

"You said you wanted help filling in some blanks. Can I help you with anything else?"

Thorsen came up behind Maria and placed one hand over each of her shoulders and began rubbing them.

"What are you doing Detective?" asked Maria, brushing his hands away and turning to look at him.

"No need to be alarmed," said Thorsen, stepping back. "I know you're tense. I just want you to know you have a friend in me."

Maria continued to look at him. "There's a police officer just outside the room," she said.

"They work for me," Thorsen lied again. The officers reported to St. Charles who was in charge of the investigation's personnel. "I'm running the investigation and suggest you cooperate."

"You said you have a long drive. I suggest you get started," said Maria, who rose and began walking towards the door.

Thorsen grabbed his coat, "Thank you for your time. I'll see myself out," he said, extending his arm to prevent her from reaching for the door. "Goodnight Ms. Lambrusco. I'll let you know as soon as we recover that handheld."

Thorsen opened the door himself, went through the doorway and quickly shut it. Ignoring the officer on duty he went straight to the elevator. Inside the room Maria reached for the business card of Sergeant St. Charles.

CHAPTER 18

Barreling through Obstacles

At exactly 8 pm Vin saw Shanin's car emerge from the shadows of the Main Rd., headlights off. He stepped from the alleyway and entered through the passenger door. To keep noise to a minimum Vin held the door close rather than slamming it shut which might call attention on the otherwise still North Fork Harbor night.

"Is it always this quiet around here?" Vin asked.

"What happened to: 'Hi, nice to see you. How was your day? Thanks for coming'?"

"Sorry," sighed Vin. "Just a little wound up. A lot happened today. How was your day? It is nice to see you, as always."

"I'm okay, just teasing you," said Shanin.

"Let's talk strategy in the car," said Vin fast-forwarding the conversation. "You never know who may overhear us later. Let's hold the small talk for when we're at the restaurant, okay?"

"Sure boss. You really know how to get a girl in the mood for a wonderful evening."

"Sorry, again. I'm in the car for less than a minute and I've apologized twice. That may be a new record."

"Before we go any further there's something else you should know," said Shanin.

"What's that?"

"In ten seconds this car will self-destruct."

"Joke if you want but I've got serious news."

"And I've got a serious question," interrupted Shanin.

"Ladies first," said Vin.

"Did the advance come?"

"Yes. Dinner's on me tonight, as long as it's reasonable."

"It's cash-only at the restaurant if we want the insider price."

"Got it," said Vin. "The advance wasn't everything Pat Goode promised but the good news is that my hotel bill's been paid for the next two nights. The clerk made sure of that. Now for the other news." Vin then told Shanin about the strong suspicion of Dr. Lambrusco being murdered, Maria Lambrusco's arrival and the cancellation of his assignment. He also informed Shanin of his encounter with Nadia Rivera and her offer to contact her in the event of a breaking story.

"That is a lot for one day," said Shanin. "No wonder you're tense."

Without being asked to do so, Shanin parked her car behind the restaurant in the area reserved for employees' vehicles. Once inside she spoke with the owner who directed them to a semi-private table near the back of the dining area that was less dimly lit than those in the other parts of the restaurant.

"If business comes up we should be able to talk pretty safely here," said Shanin. Vin instinctively took a chair from which he could see the restaurant entranceway before opening the menu. "I already ordered the seafood platter for us when I talked with the owner," Shanin continued. "Whenever I do that he usually sends a pretty big variety of things. It's definitely enough for two. I didn't think you'd mind."

"That sounds great," said Vin. "I've barely eaten since I've been out here."

"I also ordered some wine for us," said Shanin. "You look like you could use a drink."

"That's great too. It's not white zin is it?" asked Vin.

"Certainly not," said Shanin. "But it is Long Island local. That's all they serve here. When did you start drinking white zin?"

"Never," said Vin. "It's Pat Goode's favorite. I was supposed to bring her a few bottles and meet her for lunch when I finished this assignment."

"That would be a pretty picture," Shanin joked. "You sipping white zinfandel with Pat Goode."

"It would be pretty," repeated Vin. "Pretty weird."

"Any encounters with the police today?"

"Not yet," said Vin. "They were at the winery when I was there but I managed to stay out of sight. I hitchhiked back to the hotel."

"Anyone else there?"

"Not that I know of."

"Without an assignment how are you going to interview people."

"Travelzonia may be interested. I'll call the editor tomorrow," said Vin.

"You're still on shaky ground," said Shanin. "We don't know for sure if the Doc was murdered or how it happened or if Travelzonia will buy the story."

"We said we wouldn't discuss this in the restaurant," said Vin changing the subject and fidgeting in his seat. "Tell me about your day. How was watching the twins?" Vin reached for the menu and as Shanin talked he opened it, looked downward and pretended to be reading it when he thought he recognized someone entering the restaurant.

/ / /

St. Charles was having dinner with his family at home when his cell phone rang. He answered on the first ring. He regularly kept his cell phone close by for just such occasions. The ID on the screen indicated: "Private Number."

"Sergeant, I hope I'm not disturbing you."

He immediately recognized the voice of Maria Lambrusco.

"That's all right," he said as he rose to leave the table and take the call in his backyard. Key figures in investigations often chose unusual times to talk and he was as always, ready to listen.

"What's going on?" continued St. Charles. Just then one of his daughters entered yard. "Daddy," she said. But before she could say anything further he put his index finger over his lips, indicating he could not be disturbed. His young daughter, already accustomed to such behavior, immediately returned to the dinner table.

"I need to talk to you," said Maria.

"Go ahead," said St. Charles.

"I can no longer work with Detective Thorsen," said Maria.

"What's wrong?" he asked.

"This afternoon he stopped at my hotel room, unannounced."

"Yes," said St. Charles.

Maria stopped speaking.

"Please go on and I'll do my best to help you," said St. Charles, trying to coax her to continue. "I didn't know he was planning on visiting you. What did he want?" asked St. Charles."

"I'm very uncomfortable with him."

"I'm sorry to hear you feel this way Ms. Lambrusco," said St. Charles. "May I ask why or what specifically happened?"

"It's a personal matter," she said. Maria had originally planned on telling St. Charles the entire story but suddenly found herself unable to do so.

St. Charles sensed what Maria was trying to say. She would not have been the first woman to lodge a complaint about the detective's behavior but she would be the most prominent. The fact that her complaint came in the middle of a very important investigation in which they so far had made no substantial headway only made Maria's cooperation more vital. St. Charles could not afford to lose the cooperation of the person who was closest to the victim.

"I'll talk with him tomorrow Ms. Lambrusco and see what I can do."

"No Sergeant, I want him off the case," said Maria, her voice becoming firm for the first time during their conversation. "I insist. His intentions are in the wrong place. If you want my help this is not negotiable."

"That's quite a request. I'm not sure if I can do that," said St. Charles. "I need to have a valid reason and then I need to make the request to the Detective

Sergeant. I'm not sure if he'll cooperate." While St. Charles wanted Maria's cooperation he did not want to take orders from her. Nor did he want to deal with Thorsen any more than was necessary. Maria's request, if it were to be carried out, would certainly make an already difficult investigation more troublesome.

"If I have to make a formal complaint I will," said Maria.

"I see," said St. Charles.

"There's something else," she said.

"Yes."

"I'm hiring private security for myself. I'll have a bodyguard and professional driver for the rest of the time I'm here," said Maria. "They'll be licensed to carry firearms and will only be responsible to me. Starting tomorrow you can remove your officers from the hotel. I appreciate your efforts and sorry to have troubled you but this is the best course for my own protection."

It was clear to St. Charles that whatever Thorsen had done that afternoon had a severe impact on Maria. While Thorsen was running the investigation, it was actually St. Charles who was in charge of all personnel. He had the authority to call headquarters and request a new detective in light of Maria's demands. If Maria meant what she said, and he was certain she did, he'd have to seriously consider this but he was reluctant to do so.

"Ms. Lambrusco," said St. Charles. "While I have you on the phone, I was hoping you could give me some information about your father's handheld computer."

"I'll try."

"Do you have the serial number? Make? Model? Most of us don't register these things but if we could see a photo of it, maybe from a brochure he may have kept, it may help us identify it."

"I bought it for him as a gift a few years ago," she said. "I'll see what I can find."

"Ms. Lambrusco," continued St. Charles in as understanding a tone he could muster. "Perhaps we should talk tomorrow. I understand Thorsen can be irritating but he's a very good investigator. Removing a detective in the middle of an investigation may cause more harm than good and I can't guarantee that headquarters will support such a move."

It didn't matter. Maria had hung up the phone.

/ / /

"Big cop just walked in," Vin said to Shanin from his seat in the restaurant. "Don't turn around. It's the one who was at the hotel the other night."

"Jonah the Giant?" asked Shanin. "Are you sure?"

"That guy's hard to miss," said Vin. "He's alone at a table and has a good view of us. I don't like the odds."

"Maybe he's just here for dinner. Stop being so paranoid."

"Young guy having dinner alone, not likely. Guys usually get takeout, it's cheaper, no tipping. Then they go home, watch whatever sports are on TV and eat over the sink."

"Not everyone's like you," said Shanin.

"Let's make our order 'to go'," said Vin, unconvinced. He quickly rose and after dropping his napkin on the table put some bills next to his plate. "This ought to cover it," he said. "I'll meet you in the car."

Shanin watched Vin leave through the rear exit. She then looked at the money and food on the table before taking a drink of wine. There was a time in her life when she was not unlike Pat Goode. She had been a rising society girl who could've had it all and never would've had to work too hard but due to events beyond her control was now barely earning a living in a small town. She hated being alone about as much as she hated struggling to pay her rent and other expenses each month. But nor was she sure if staying with Vin would be a wise decision. While Vin was a great reporter he was as poor as she was plus had a hyper-personality with traits of paranoia. What type of future would the two of them have? She hadn't had thoughts like these since when she first broke off with Vin but she hadn't had much luck either since then. Shanin recalled the week when after much deliberation, she left her job and boyfriend to pursue a new life in the country as a professional photographer. At the time, a change of scenery seemed like exactly what she needed. The deadline pressure of working for a daily newspaper plus the tension that naturally accompanied time spent with Vin made the move look like a sensible choice. At first, assignments were plentiful but as the economy slowed, the freelance photography market declined as well. Looking back, except for the scenery, things hadn't changed that much for Shanin. A place that had brought her great joy and serenity as a child could not sustain her adult ambitions. Shanin's job prospects, finances and personal life were each about as poor as they were when she chose to leave the things that seemingly rooted her to New York City and move alone to North Fork Harbor. Now she wondered was Vin's sudden appearance a sign that things were to improve or was it a momentary interruption, a meaningless detour or a reminder of her former life? Shanin took a deep breath and rose to pay the bill. When she turned to head towards the register she noticed that Officer Jonah was no longer at his table.

"Wasn't there someone at that table a minute ago?" Shanin asked the young woman behind the counter while pointing to the now-vacant seat.

"I honestly don't recall," she responded. "We've been so busy tonight I can barely remember my own name."

Shanin nodded, took her package and went to meet Vin who was waiting beside her car.

"Sorry you had to stand here but I guess I instinctively locked the doors when we went into the restaurant," said Shanin who handed Vin the shopping bag full of take-out cartons while she sifted through her own bag for the car keys.

"No. I locked them," said Vin. "You never know, someone could've bugged the car while we were inside having dinner."

"A few minutes ago I would've said you were totally paranoid to say something like that but considering how that police officer suddenly disappeared, now I'm not so sure. How does a giant vanish so quickly?"

"This package looks heavy," was all Vin said. "Your friend gave us a lot of food."

Shanin said nothing as she opened the doors and started the car.

"I feel really bad I made us leave so suddenly," continued Vin as they sat in the car. "I knew something was not right."

"I was mad at first but you may have been on to something," said Shanin. "That guy was probably following us but I don't see anyone in the mirror."

"Let's finish this meal someplace where we won't be watched and then maybe we can go get a drink when the coast is clear," offered Vin.

"Sounds good," said Shanin.

"But if they followed us here I'm sure they'll be someone at the hotel or outside your place," said Vin.

"There's a lot of food here," said Shanin. "Why don't we visit my baby-sitting client? I'm sure she'd appreciate some grown-up company and no one would think of looking for us there. Later we can go for that drink."

"It's okay if we just drop in on her?"

"As long as she's not too exhausted," said Shanin. "With all this food she won't have to cook. And I'm sure her boys, if they're still awake, will probably enjoy seeing an adult male at the house."

"You make me sound so important," said Vin.

"You can play video games with them."

"Whatever you say."

As Shanin steered the car from the parking lot, she suddenly accelerated and then just as quickly stopped over a deep puddle, remaining there for a moment.

"What's going on?" asked Vin.

"If someone stuck a bug underneath the car, this water might knock it out."

"Do you seriously think the police would do something like that?"

"Who said it had to be the police?"

"Now that sounds like my old partner," said Vin. "But let's get going. The smell of this food's making me hungry."

CHAPTER 19

Pressing Out the Truth

Sensing the seriousness of Maria's tone and her importance to the case, St. Charles immediately put a call into the Chief of Detectives, Louis Stimmel, informing the night-duty clerk that he had an urgent matter to discuss with him. St. Charles never liked working with the ingratiating Thorsen but respected his ability. However, the idea of losing the cooperation of a key person could severely impede the investigation. The idea that Maria Lambrusco was hiring private security guards did not sit well with him either, while he'd still have access to her for police business it indicated that she did not trust the local officers to protect her and he was therefore concerned over how forthcoming she'd be. And he was sure this decision by Maria was the result of Thorsen's surprise visit to her hotel room. If he'd stuck to business he'd be a great detective thought St. Charles about Thorsen. But St. Charles, the experienced veteran, knew no investigations run without incident and deciding what to do with Thorsen was just another decision that would need to be made in the course of duty. He'd make his case to Stimmel and then see if the department would cooperate by providing another detective.

Stimmel called St. Charles back within half an hour. St. Charles pled his case but Stimmel was barely moved.

"Thorsen's been on the force a long time," said Stimmel. "He's solved a lot of big cases. A victim's family member doesn't decide who's working the case. I don't care how good-looking or rich she is."

"I'm afraid if we keep him on we'll lose the cooperation of a key person in the investigation," argued St. Charles. "She's the only person with in-depth knowledge of the victim. Prior to Thorsen's surprise visit to her hotel room she was very cooperative. Now she wants to hire private security. She doesn't want to talk."

There was a pause.

"Here's what we'll do," said Stimmel with an unmistakable tone of anger. He knew no one liked Thorsen but couldn't tolerate interference in an investigation and came up with a temporary compromise. "I'm keeping Thorsen on the case technically but I'll keep him busy in headquarters or assign him to help on another case but only temporarily. I've reviewed the files on the Lambrusco case," continued Stimmel. "You're off to a good start and some of this has to be attributed to Thorsen. If that California girl wants to go back home and drink wine she can get on her surf board and leave tonight. We'll solve the damn case without her. It wouldn't be the first time a victim's family member refused to cooperate but it would be a damn stupid thing to do."

"Yes Sir," said St. Charles.

"You know police work ain't a popularity contest."

"Yes Sir," repeated St. Charles.

"I'll give you a few days because I respect your judgment and you've only got a few years left," said Stimmel. "But if you don't make any real progress Thorsen will be back out there. I don't give a rat's tail if some California broad doesn't like him. We're trying to find who killed her father. She at least could appreciate that."

"Thank you Chief," said St. Charles.

"You're welcome," he gruffly said in return. "And one more thing," he added. "This is between you and me. You breathe a word of this to anyone and you'll be back patrolling the cotton candy stand at Coney Island before you can turn in your badge."

St. Charles knew he did not have an ideal relationship with the police headquarters staff but felt it was worth taking the risk. St. Charles could never prove it but often thought it was because he was an outsider. Unlike the gigantic New York City Police Dept., which had a certain amount of anonymity within its vast ranks, most of the headquarters staff personally knew each of the Suffolk County police officers, even those in remote North Fork Harbor, especially since many were children of former officers and relatives of other police department employees. The relationships tended to span generations. St. Charles was one of the striking exceptions and it was a line he could never fully cross. Being brought into sleepy North Fork Harbor on the heels of a local scandal that would have barely raised an eyebrow in New York City had never endeared St. Charles in the hearts of his fellow Eastern Long Island officers. Stimmel was at the head of that group. Blown out of proportion by the press and subsequently chastised by the public, St. Charles always felt that in the chief's eyes he was a reminder of what had gone wrong in an area to which he should have been paying greater attention, the sting of the embarrassment never having fully disappeared while bringing any form of career advancement to a halt for the Chief. Stimmel's mention of St. Charles only having "a few years left," was an indirect threat to his retirement from the force. It was a warning that was sporadically used against older officers. While it was doubtful that Stimmel could return St. Charles to "Coney Island," a reference to his New York City days, he could make his remaining years on the local force uncomfortable for him. And why mention that Maria Lambrusco was "good-looking" and "rich"? A statement like that could only have come from one source thought St. Charles. But at least for the foreseeable future and for better or worse, St. Charles was going to be running the investigation free of Thorsen.

He actually had mixed feelings about this decision. While he would not miss his sarcasm and condescending attitude, St. Charles did appreciate Thorsen's acumen, especially his seemingly always high energy level and ability to build a reasonably accurate psychological profile of a suspect with minimal information. He was sure the case would move forward, he just wasn't sure how they'd get Maria Lambrusco's full cooperation. If they did not make any meaningful progress, as Chief Stimmel warned, Det. Conrad Thorsen would surely make a return appearance to North Fork Harbor.

/ / /

Shanin took Vin down some dark roads. The humidity from being so close to the bay was rising and the smell of the fish dinner was beginning to grow thick within the car's small interior.

"How much longer 'til we get there?" asked Vin. "Or are you secretly kidnapping me?"

"You got me," joked Shanin "I'm actually a double-agent. I'm taking you to a secret hideout."

"I haven't been in places this dark and isolated since I was covering the Purple Gang."

"Whatever happened to them?"

"The same thing that happens to nearly every gang," said Vin. "Most of the members are either sent to jail, killed or become so injured that they're useless and the gang falls apart. It's not easy to regularly be fighting or chased by police," added Vin before pausing. "Why does your client live in such an isolated area?"

"She and her former husband bought this as a vacation home," said Shanin. "When he left her she thought her boys would be happier here."

"Kind of like you," he said.

Shanin paused. "Yeah, maybe," she said.

Shanin then turned the car down a dirt road. The entire area was unlit except for porch lights from a few homes nestled alongside the dirt-and-gravel road and bright moon. Shanin steered the car onto a dirt driveway and shut the motor. A few lights were on inside the house.

"This is it," she said. "I'll knock on the door to make sure it's okay."

A moment later Vin watched as the screen door opened and saw Shanin speaking with her client/friend. After another moment Shanin turned and waved for Vin to join them. Not before instinctively locking the car doors and carrying the heavy take-out bag, Vin walked across the dark, narrow driveway. He noticed the door on the mailbox was dangling by one screw. Then walking across the spotty lawn Vin sidestepped a beach ball, a small bicycle, various toys and some scraggily bushes in the semi-darkness. He then ascended the cement steps as Shanin held the screen door open for him.

"I'm Barbara Brandywine," a tall, blondish and barefoot woman wearing what appeared to be hospital scrubs said as Vin entered the small house. She and Vin shook hands. Like the front yard, the entranceway of the house was littered with signs of children. Articles of children's clothing and toys were seemingly everywhere. "Shanin's told me a little about you," said Barbara. "I'm always happy to have a few grown-ups around. But we've got to keep it a little quiet, I got the boys to sleep early and don't want to wake them."

"I'm surprised Shanin considers me a grown-up," said Vin. "I hope it's no trouble having us."

"No trouble at all," said Barbara. "Just the other day I was fantasizing about a real fish dinner. The closest I get to it with two little kids is fish sticks." Barbara took the bag from Vin and began setting the cartons on the small wooden kitchen table as Shanin removed plates and glasses from the cabinet. "Maybe you can open the wine," said Barbara, handing Vin a bottle of locally made pinot grigio and corkscrew.

Vin looked at the quirky label as he held the bottle with his left hand and drove the cork screw in with his right. The main image on the label was an illustration of a woman's face but her hair became roots that led to what appeared to be a vine full of grapes. Her face displayed an expression of a tortured or stressed individual. Not the most appealing of images, perhaps the wine would be more pleasant he thought. Vin then pulled down on the lever and when the cork emerged with a slight pop the women came forth with a small applause. Vin then proceeded to pour the wine into plastic wine glasses as Barbara and Shanin put the food onto brightly colored dishes decorated with illustrations of various super heroes.

"I'll bet it's been a while since you ate off a Spiderman plate," Barbara said to Vin.

"It's a nice change of pace," he said. "It brings back memories. Peter Parker and Clark Kent were heroes of mine. They worked for newspapers too."

"Too bad the boys are sleeping," said Shanin to Vin. "They'd love talking about the Super Hero Universe with you."

"Maybe it's not too bad they're sleeping," said Barbara. "We'd never get to eat a whole meal sitting down. It was such a crazy week at the lab."

"It was a crazy week all over North Fork Harbor," said Shanin.

"We actually helped the police lab with some analysis work," said Barbara. "Talk about pressure."

Vin and Shanin looked at each other. "What happened?" Shanin asked Barbara.

"They needed verification for a toxicology report on an agricultural chemical," said Barbara. "Something about a poisoning case."

"Any idea about the poisoning?" asked Vin. "Was it some sort of accident?"

"They don't tell us that sort of thing," said Barbara. "It's just some scuttlebutt I overheard."

"Did you do the actual analysis?" asked Shanin.

"I assisted on some of the lab work. Everything had to be triple-checked." Then, turning to Shanin she said: "You might appreciate the work, being a former chemistry major."

"What was it?"

"I'm not supposed to say this," said Barbara. "It was a very obscure agricultural chemical, tetrachlorodyne. It's a synthetic insecticide. Highly lethal. Supposedly tough to come by."

"Was it a fatal dose?" asked Vin.

"Apparently it was a pretty rough dosage," said Barbara.

"Any antidote?" asked Shanin.

"None known but it would've barely mattered."

"Why not?" asked Vin.

"With the dosage we're talking about, it was probably a five-minute kill time. Ten the max."

"Deadly stuff?" asked Vin.

"Absolutely," said Barbara.

"So the victim barely had a chance," said Shanin after a pause.

"Victim?" repeated Barbara. "What do you mean by victim? The police are calling it an accident."

"If it was an accident," interrupted Vin. "How did it get into the person's body? I thought you said it was a 'poisoning case'."

The conversation stopped as the three of them looked at each other.

"I don't know," said Barbara, realizing the misstep. "That wasn't made available to us. The police don't give us any information. We're to verify the results of their analysis. Whatever else I hear is like I said, speculation."

"Do they want a second opinion a lot?" asked Vin.

Barbara reached for her glass before answering. "Hardly ever," she said.

"Do you think they'd go through this trouble for just an 'accident'?" probed Vin.

"I can't say," answered Barbara. "Why are you so curious?"

"He's always asking questions," interrupted Shanin. "I can never get used to it either but it's his reporter's nature." Then changing the subject she said. "We're just about finished. Why don't I help you clean up? I'm sure you're tired."

"Good idea. You're always the thoughtful one. It is getting late," said Vin to Shanin backing his chair and rising from the table. Then turning to Barbara he asked, "Do you have a computer I can use for a moment? I'd like to check the Long Island Rail Road schedule. My hotel doesn't have a good internet connection and my cell phone service is not great out here."

"Sure," said Barbara rising from the table as she began collecting the now empty take-out cartons. "It's in the playroom down the hall. Just try not to get distracted by the kids' computer games."

Alone in the playroom Vin immediately began scouring the internet for information on tetrachlorodyne. He quickly located some information but found little more than Barbara had told him. It was a very powerful synthetic insecticide, fatal to nearly any living organism but had been outlawed years ago. Shanin then appeared in the playroom doorway.

"I think we should get going," she said with a nod.

"Sure thing," said Vin, understanding her subtle signal. But before shutting down the computer Vin was sure to erase his search history.

Vin and Shanin then returned to the kitchen, quickly thanked Barbara for her hospitality and headed to the car, each remaining uncharacteristically silent as Shanin drove down the dark dirt road. It was Shanin who broke the silence.

"I know you think it was the Doc who got poisoned?"

"I'm not totally certain but in my toy room internet search I discovered that farmers used to buy that stuff. It's possible they had it at the vineyard and someone there knows how deadly it is."

"I understand you want to solve this and restore your career," said Shanin. "But you can't jump to conclusions. That's gotten you into trouble before. A vineyard's a farm. It wouldn't be unusual to have chemicals on the premises and for people there to know how to use them. Do you think the Doc just stood there and let himself be injected?"

"No one's poisoned accidentally," countered Vin. "The Doc's dead. The police are calling it an accident as a cover-up."

"You have no idea if this is connected to the Doc," argued Shanin.

"And you have no idea if it isn't."

"You need proof Vin. Now's no time for speculation."

"He wasn't at the hospital right?"

"Yeah. So what?"

"They took him straight to the morgue. There are too many coincidences," he said.

"You can't base a story, especially a possible murder, on coincidences," argued Shanin. "The Doc was a well-known guy who suddenly died. It makes perfect sense that they'd have an autopsy to be safe."

"Here's how I see it," said Vin. "I've got two nights left at the hotel and nothing else going on. I can go home early and sweat in my tiny apartment banging out nonsense assignments or stay here, try to learn what actually happened, write about it and possibly get my career back on track."

"Even if you did find out what actually happened," said Shanin. "You've got no assignment. Pat Goode killed it."

"That's not necessarily true," said Vin reaching into his shirt pocket to show Shanin the business card of Travelzonia editor Nadia Rivera. "Nadia said, 'if anything happens,' on this trip to call her. A possible murder of a famous winemaker with some knockout bug juice in a vacation town may qualify as news to a competing editor."

"People generally don't vacation in areas where there's been a murder," said Shanin. "If there even was one. And if this other editor doesn't want the story, then what? You can't peddle a murder story that's based on speculation."

"What do you mean?"

"How long are you planning on chasing stories Vin? Maybe this is a sign that it's time to move on with your career, leave journalism. Do something else. When I'm with you I feel like a lab rat in a giant maze who can't find his way to the cheese."

"My career's fine," said Vin. "Things are just a little stagnant right now."

"Stagnant? Your career's not stagnant. It's going backwards."

"What do you want Shanin? Journalism's all I know. It's all I ever wanted to do, from when I was a little kid delivering papers."

"It's the middle of the night and we're chasing a story that no one wants. We're still not sure what happened. Neither of us has a real job."

"Look," said Vin, taking a breath. "I know where you're going with this. Right now there are more questions than answers and I'm not just talking about this story. But if this story turns out to be true, I can be back in the game. So can you."

"It's not a game Vin. It's your life. It's my life."

"I never told you to move here," said Vin. "That was all your idea. It's not my fault your life is nowhere."

"And you came looking for me."

"An opportunity brought me here. You're a bonus."

"A bonus you'll never receive."

"I'm taking a shot on this story. If you can hang in there you can share in the glory. If not, then I wish you the best but I don't feel good about a woman like you settling in a place like this."

"Vin, you're still making my head spin," said Shanin. "I'm too tired for this. I'm taking you back to your hotel and heading home to sleep. Maybe things will be clearer in the morning."

Vin did not say anything further but as they drove along the Main Rd. in the direction of the hotel, he spotted The Apple Tree. "Slow down," he said to Shanin.

Vin scanned the parking lot and surveyed the scene. "What about that drink we mentioned earlier?" asked Vin. "Let's check out the Apple Tree. Looks like a big crowd. C'mon, you need a break. We each need a break."

"Since when did you like hanging out in a crowded bar?" asked Shanin.

"When I'm hunting for information," he said. "Pull in, please. I'll buy you a beer or a white zinfandel."

Shanin cooperated, the look of exasperation on her face. "I hate white zin," was all she could say as she steered the car into the crowded lot.

There were two windows in the front of the bar with flashing red neon signs. The front door was between the two windows. The sign in the left window read:

World's Best Chili. The other noted: NASCAR Tonight. Vin entered the bar first, with Shanin closely following. The entranceway walls were paneled in driftwood with fish nets hanging from them. Inside, race car memorabilia including ancient black-and-white plus color photos of racers from previous generations donned the walls. Shelves held copies of famous racing trophies and autographed helmets. A few big-screen TVs kept the patrons updated with race news. The crowd around the bar was deep and each of the tables was occupied.

"I don't think I've ever been in here," said Shanin, looking around the wide room and at its patrons, most of whom were wearing shirts or jackets adorned with racing logos. "Now I know why."

"It doesn't look like a white zin kind of place," said Vin. "I'll get a couple of beers. Wait here." The seafood dinner had made them thirsty and the idea of a beer was a welcome one.

Vin snaked his way to the bar and after a few minutes was able to place the order. By the time he returned Shanin had found some standing space on the side of an empty fireplace. He joined her there and began recounting his meeting that morning with Tugboat.

"This is the kind of place where we might find out something," said Vin to Shanin who rolled her eyes. At about that time a burly young man holding an opened bottle of beer approached them. "A friend of yours?" asked Shanin nodding in his direction before he got too close.

"Tugboat, I mean Vincent," said Vin extending his hand. "I was hoping I'd bump into you."

"Hey man!" said the jovial Tugboat. "I didn't think a big-city writer would drink in a place like this."

"This is Shanin," said Vin gesturing towards his partner.

"Good to meet you," said Tugboat to Shanin, extending his heavy hand while introducing himself. "My name's Vincent too." Vincent then proceeded to wipe his mouth with his sleeve as Shanin pulled back.

"You from the city too?" Vincent asked Shanin.

"Used to be," said Shanin. "I've been out here for a few years. I shoot for the paper."

"So that's why you two are together," said Vincent before turning to Vin. "I thought maybe she was the one you told me about in the truck."

Shanin looked at Vin. Picking up her signal he turned to Vincent and rolled his eyes. Vincent winked back in return.

"Pretty good crowd tonight," Vin said to Vincent.

"Yeah, it's a big race. That brings everyone out," he said. "If you were to live out here this is where you'd probably be hangin' out."

"It's not so bad," said Vin, turning to Shanin who pretended to be interested in her beer. "Vin," said Shanin. "I'm really tired. I'd like to head home soon."

Vincent looked at Vin. "Hey man," he said. "I can drive you back to your hotel. Why don't you hang out? Let your lady friend retire for the night. This party will break-up pretty soon after the race ends."

"You'll take me back in your van?" asked Vin.

"I got my bike out back. It's the 883 Harley Sportster," said Vincent. "A guy my size needs a monster of a bike. It's got enough muscle to take the two of us. I got an extra helmet. I'll have you back in a flash."

"You drive a motorcycle too?"

"Sure do. Used to fix 'em too but I got out of that business. Customers never satisfied. Too many headaches. Bikes ain't never hurt no one, it's the drivers who are crazy. Doin' stunts, takin' curves too fast. They wind up in the hospital or worse and everyone blames the bike . . . or the mechanic. Driving a truck's a lot easier."

Vin and Shanin looked at each other. Vin wanted to stay at the bar. He sensed he'd have a better chance of making progress on his story in the bar than alone in his hotel room. Shanin sincerely wanted to get going.

"Do you mind?" Vin asked Shanin.

"You don't need my permission," she said, shrugging her shoulders. She then put her half-finished beer on the fireplace mantle, said a quick goodnight to Vincent and turned. Vin followed her, neither saying a word until they got to Shanin's car.

"I'm going to hang around here. I might find out something," said Vin as he opened the car door for Shanin.

"Sure, I'm beginning to think we can do better separately." said Shanin getting into the driver's seat. "Enjoy your motorcycle ride." Shanin then closed the door, attached her seatbelt and started the car. Vin watched her drive out of the gravel parking lot and thought he noticed a slight burning odor before returning to the bar.

/ / /

Henry St. Charles had just gotten into bed, next to his wife Ellen who was already sleeping, when he heard the ring from the fax machine in their small home office. St. Charles immediately sprang from the bed. The cover sheet indicated it was from the office of the County Medical Examiner, Dr. Damian Dionasis. Besides the confidentiality and legal notices, the only mark on the sheet was a large, handwritten capital "D." St. Charles stood before the small desk to read the autopsy and toxicology report for Dr. Frank Lambrusco.

CHAPTER 20

Spilling the Juice

St. Charles immediately went to the summary section of the report which would include the cause of death and any other pertinent information. The cause of death was determined to be sudden cardiac arrest brought on by a hypodermic injection of tetrachlorodyne near the center of the chest. The cause was determined by an autopsy and an outside laboratory had confirmed the diagnosis.

Small abrasions were found on the victim's fingertips and there were signs of slight asphyxiation, probably administered by hand as there were no friction marks on the victim's neck that would have been left had the perpetrator used a rope, belt or other such object. The report also noted that a white thread, nearly one-half an inch in length, probably from clothing as it was determined to be cotton, was found between the victim's two front teeth. The total period between struggle and time of death was estimated to be 7-15 minutes.

St. Charles immediately phoned Dr. Dionasis. Relationships between medical examiners and police officers varied from county to county. But St. Charles and Dr. Dionasis shared a healthy, professional rapport that allowed them to collaborate at a fairly deep level.

"Thanks for sending this Doc," said St. Charles. "What do you think?"

"I had the toxicology results confirmed by an outside lab because it was such an unusual poisoning," said the doctor. "I checked everywhere and could not find any records of death by tetrachlorodyne injection. It basically paralyzes the heart in about five minutes, possibly a bit more. I've never seen a heart destroyed like this one."

St. Charles took a breath as he considered what Dr. Dionasis had just told him. "What about this thread between the teeth?"

"I'd surmise that further indicates signs of a struggle," said Dr. Dionasis. "Lambrusco was probably grabbed from behind, maybe in a headlock-type position and the perpetrator's sleeve was over the victim's mouth at one point. The victim may have inadvertently bitten off a thread of the perpetrator's clothing during the struggle. Between that and the slight asphyxiation I'd say the victim was held by the perpetrator until it was clear that the poison was going to have the desired effect. Then he was probably thrown into the vat, which is likely when he hit his head. Unfortunately because the body was moved when pulled from the vat, this is very hard to definitively determine. There may have been some fragments or other material beneath the victim's fingernails but the wine washed anything like that away. The thread, the full report and everything else will be in your office tomorrow."

"Do you think this was a one-person job or a team?"

"It could be either," said Dionasis.

"Based on the evidence you've uncovered, do you think the perpetrator was significantly stronger than the victim?"

"Yes, to a degree," said Dionasis. "But don't forget Lambrusco was an older man. He may not have had any glaring health problems but a younger and determined adversary, acting with the element of surprise would have a significant advantage."

"But to aim that needle into the center of Lambrusco's chest would have required the perpetrator to have great physical control over the victim."

"That's true, but the asphyxiation weakened him and then there was the bump on the head. We don't know if that came before or after the needle was administered. Each of these took a toll, quickly weakening an older, surprised victim. Like the poison he used, the perpetrator worked very fast."

"Do you think the perpetrator may have had some medical training or experience? Maybe in the military?" asked St. Charles, trying to build a suspect profile.

"It's possible," said Dionasis. "Or he could have learned on his own. If he was capable of engineering this crime, he could have easily learned to administer a hypodermic."

"But then how did he get the needle? And how did he learn to fill it with the insecticide?"

"He may have tapped into some medical waste and found a hypodermic in good condition," said Dionasis. "That sort of thing isn't monitored as well as it should be. He could've easily learned online how to fill and use needles or could have found it in a medical book or video in the library. If he had outside help, someone could've gotten it for him and shown him how to use it. In any event, we don't have the needle."

"It's probably been destroyed by this point," acknowledged St. Charles who then paused to think about the contributions Dionasis's work had made towards moving the investigation forward and where they would go from here.

"How's it going on your end?" Dionasis then asked, breaking the brief period of silence.

This last question was an unusual one for a medical examiner to ask but considering the relationship the two men as well as Dr. Dionasis's respect for the victim, St. Charles did not mind answering it.

"Unfortunately we've got very little to go on," said St. Charles. "Nothing unusual was found with the fingerprints or tire impressions and shoeprints don't show up well on a concrete floor. The employee interviews did not turn up much."

"Were the Spanish-speaking workers interviewed?"

"Yeah. The Department sent an interpreter but they basically said the same things the other workers did."

"How about the guest log?"

"No visitors that day," said St. Charles. "And Thorsen blew up the relationship we were cultivating with the victim's daughter. Technically she's still cooperating but realistically I'm not too hopeful about her participation."

"Any blood on the victim?" asked St. Charles.

"Impossible," said Dionasis. "The wine took care of that. What about when you drained the vat?"

"Nothing.

"This is beginning to look like a very well planned operation," said Dionasis.

"Apparently," said St. Charles. "Plus the victim's handheld computer remains missing. Still more questions than answers."

"Get the medical records?" asked Dionasis.

"Yes. The Doc had had some minor heart trouble a few years back but recovered nicely. He was on a mild blood thinner but his pressure, weight and other vitals were under control. This could have possibly passed for a heart attack if it wasn't for the grapes in his mouth."

"Anything else missing?"

"Yeah," said St. Charles. "A motive. The data in the handheld may be valuable to someone but this is more than a murder. Why would anyone stuff grapes into a dead man's mouth?"

"It had to be done before the body was thrown into the vat."

"The killer waited to be sure he was dead," added St. Charles. "He's not the type to take chances. That's clear from how this entire crime unfolded. Usually some sign of force is left behind after most break-ins. There was no forced entry. Nothing else was stolen or damaged."

"And there are almost no clues," said Dionasis.

"But he wanted to communicate something," said St. Charles. "That's our biggest clue."

"You believe there's a meaning behind placing the grapes in the victim's mouth?" asked Dionasis. "That he's not deranged. That the perpetrator's making some sort of statement?"

"Maybe slightly deranged, temporarily insane. Maybe a sociopath who was seeking some sort of revenge by way of the killing," said St. Charles. "Murdering Lambrusco wasn't enough. He felt the need to say something more."

"Lambrusco led an interesting life. Who knows what type of characters he may have come across," said Dionasis. "Revenge killings, feuds, vendettas, they still happen in certain parts of Europe. But then why take the handheld? Why now?"

"If the perpetrator's working for someone else, they wanted the data. Perhaps that was the perpetrator's initial motivation," said St. Charles. "There may have been others but he also left the grapes in the victim's coat pocket, probably because he had no need to take grapes or anything else. But if the perpetrator wanted something more, that's where placing the grapes in the mouth fills some sort of psychological void. Otherwise there's a good chance he could've succeeded in making it look like Dr. Frank suffered a heart attack and fell in the vat. But he wasn't satisfied with that."

"We could use Thorsen's psychological profiling right now," sighed the doctor.

"The piece of thread you recovered," said St. Charles. "Get it to a lab for a DNA analysis."

"Will do," said Dionasis.

Whether it was someone working alone or as part of a larger group, St. Charles was not yet certain. Whoever it was however either had inside information about the security workings of the winery as well as Dr. Lambrusco's habits, was familiar with the system used to guard the premises or had enough electronics knowledge to bypass the code. The idea that the perpetrator was an electronics whiz as well as killer was very unlikely thought St. Charles. Nevertheless he made a note to order Krupcheski to check for all break-ins during the past 24 months where the same security system was in use, to check for all known criminals in the area with an electronics and/or medical background and to get a complete inventory of each insecticide and herbicide stored at the vineyard. He also had him visit the nearby landfills and check for any handheld computers that may have been deposited at the e-waste sites.

While Thorsen's acumen may have been useful, with him temporarily out of the way, St. Charles was able to focus on the investigation rather than on managing individuals. Until he had to take back Thorsen, he was going to put himself into the mind of the perpetrator. The two certainties surrounding the case were that it was a poisoning and that there was a handheld-computer still missing. While the murder may have been the work of one individual, St. Charles believed others were involved in some supporting role. An employee may have passed on information about the security system or of Dr. Lambrusco's schedule. He also thought it was very likely that someone may have offered a large sum of money for the data in the handheld. He felt this was probably what he would describe as the "initial motivation" which served to inspire the perpetrator to commit the crime. St. Charles was beginning to theorize that whatever was contained in the handheld computer was what the perpetrator was technically after and nothing was going to stop him from getting it but he also felt it was important to leave behind a signal, a sign that this was about more than money or information. He was convinced he was dealing with a smart and very strong-minded adversary, possibly determined to the point of temporary insanity. Not necessarily an adversary with a criminal past but certainly an intelligent and highly motivated one, probably seeking revenge. If a third-party put the perpetrator up to this, he may have realized he had a very determined accomplice at his disposal. Any money obtained from selling the handheld, he theorized may have been what originally inspired the perpetrator to plan such a crime but St. Charles was certain this was about more than money. He also knew that intelligent, determined perpetrators frequently were the trickiest to catch.

/ / /

Vin returned inside the Apple Tree to look for Vincent. He had a seat at the bar with a good view of one of the television sets broadcasting the race.

"Hey Vincent," said Vin, pulling up next to him at the bar. It was a big crowd and space around the bar was at a premium. While Vincent had come alone to the bar that night, he was friendly with many of the patrons.

"That's your girlfriend, right?" asked Vincent when Vin returned.

"Like I said in the truck, right now I'm not so sure," said Vin to a smiling Vincent.

"That's all right," he said. "I've been on-again, off-again with my old lady for about eight years now. I still can't figure her out," said Vincent. "Country livin' ain't so bad, right?" Vincent continued. "On Saturday nights they got line dancin' here. You should check that out too. That would be good to write an article about. Ain't too many places left with line dancin'," said Vincent slapping Vin across the shoulder with his heavy hand. "Let me get you another beer." Vincent was drinking the locally made brew, Capt. Kidd Lager, a tribute to the region's pre-Revolutionary heritage when pirates and shady merchants plied Long Island's waters.

"It's nice," said Vin. "Looks like a friendly crowd. Everyone seems to be having a good time."

"You should try the chili," advised Vincent. "It's the best around."

"Maybe next time," said Vin. "I just finished a fish dinner."

When the bartender served them, Vin immediately paid the tab to Vincent's surprise and left ample cash on the bar for more.

"You didn't have to do nuthin' like that," said Vincent. "I invited you here."

"No problem," said Vin. "You helped me and I'd like to repay you."

"Are you rich or something?" asked Vincent.

"Hardly," said Vin. "I've been pretty poor my whole life but I got an advance and I'm a little flush so I'd like to repay you."

"What are you writin' about anyway?"

"Just a travel piece about how nice this place is," said Vin. "By the way, have you heard anything about an accident at one of the wineries?"

"No but I'll tell you who might," said Vincent, nodding towards two men standing together at the end of the bar. "The tall one's Larson. He's a mechanic. Can be kinda ornery. The short one's Andy. Used to be a potato farmer. They work for that secret winery. The one that don't want no visitors. Where you was goin' the other mornin'. They tend to keep to themselves but if you want I can introduce you."

"Sure," said Vin.

"Let me hit the men's room first," said Vincent rising from his seat and yanking his jeans up by the waist. "And then I'll get the three of you together."

Vin waited at the bar as Tugboat stopped to say a few words to the men. In the meantime Vin tried to get interested in the race on one of the television sets above the bar.

"They stop by?" asked Vincent returning to the bar a few moments later.

"No," said Vin as he looked in the direction where he saw the men standing a few minutes before.

"He said he was going to come by," said Vincent. "I even said you'd buy them a beer," he added half-kiddingly. "Maybe they're on their way."

"Probably," lied Vin. A seasoned reporter, Vin theorized that if the men were no longer in sight, they probably were not interested in speaking with him.

"Did you tell them I'm writing a story about North Fork Harbor?" asked Vin.

"Yeah, I did," said Vincent. "I thought they'd be a good source for you. Andy's family's farmed out here forever."

"Sometimes when people hear I'm a writer, they get uncomfortable," said Vin. "Let's wait a few minutes. Finish our beers. Enjoy the race. Maybe they went outside to check cell phone messages or have a cigarette."

"Good idea. Race is almost over." said the affable Vincent. "They're kind of an odd couple anyway. Andy probably wouldn't have said much and Larson would've gotten into an argument over some dumb politics. He can't take no one who disagrees with him."

"I know someone like that too," smiled Vin.

As Vincent watched the closing minutes of the race with intensity, Vin pretended to be interested in it. He would have liked to talk with the men as they worked at the winery. It would have been Vin's first chance to speak to someone with firsthand knowledge of Dr. Lambrusco but he did not want Vincent to sense his disappointment, hence he chose not to pursue the issue. As Vin stood there he began thinking of how he left Shanin earlier that night. Excusing himself, he went to the pay phone. He did not want to call her in case she was sleeping. Instead he dialed his hotel room to see if she had perhaps called him. He had a new message. Maria Lambrusco wanted to talk to him.

///

Vin returned to the bar just as the race was ending. He found it hard to concentrate knowing Maria Lambrusco had called. Vin was not sure why she called but he could only believe Maria would be able to fill in some of the blanks for him. His mind was racing but he needed to get back to his hotel, call Maria and figure what his next steps would be. At the bar Vincent was closely watching the race replays, including several crash highlights played from multiple angles, plus the finish, which apparently had been very close.

"Vincent, would you mind if we headed back to the hotel?" asked Vin. "I am supposed to be working while I'm here."

"Sure thing," said Vincent as he swallowed the last bit of beer from the bottle. Wiping his mouth with his sleeve he turned and said, "Let's go. Thanks for picking up the tab."

In the parking lot Vincent handed Vin his spare helmet. "Without this we're almost sure to get stopped by the cops," he said. "That's the only reason you got to wear it. I'm a very safe driver. Twenty years, no accidents, although I have gotten a few speeding tickets."

"No problem," said Vin, strapping on the helmet. It was a little large for him and his head felt loose in it but it was better than not wearing one he thought. As they each mounted the bike it occurred to Vin he'd never before been on a motorcycle.

"I've been riding motor bikes since I was this high," Vincent said, placing the palm of his hand at about the height of the bike's rear tire. "Just hold onto my waist. If you hold onto the seat or anything else you'll throw off the balancing."

Not knowing otherwise Vin put his arms around Vincent's large waist. Vincent then started the bike. Sitting on the rear of the seat, the roar from the motor was louder than Vin ever imagined and he quickly began to feel the heat rising against his legs. He pulled the helmet's visor over his face as they left the parking lot and headed east on the Main Rd. towards the hotel. As Vincent had promised, they arrived very quickly. Between the darkness that enveloped the winding roads and the speed at which Vincent drove, Vin could barely remember anything about the ride except that it was loud and fast.

"Good hanging with you," said Vincent, extending his hand as Vin gingerly stepped off the motorcycle, still not comfortable with it. "Hope things work out with your girlfriend. I don't know how much longer you'll be out here but if you see me again be sure to say 'hello'."

"Thanks," said Vin returning the spare helmet. "I'm not sure how much longer I'll be here either, depends how the assignment goes. It was great hanging out with you too and thanks for the rides."

"Hey," said Vincent. "When you write that book, don't forget to say a few nice words about me."

"Will do," said Vin. "Thanks again."

Vincent then turned and drove into the darkness. Vin took a deep breath and surveyed the scene. He could hear the motorcycle's roar gradually diminish as Vincent seemingly vanished into the overwhelming darkness. As there were no police cars that he could see parked outside the hotel or signs of anyone else who might be watching his movements, Vin went straight to the lobby, which was as empty and silent as the town outside it and called Maria Lambrusco from the pay phone. When the recording came on he began to leave a message.

"Hello Ms. Lambrusco, this is Vin Gusto, returning your call. Hope I'm not calling too late . . .

Maria then came to the phone, interrupting Vin before he could finish his message.

"Hi Mr. Gusto," she said. "Thank you for returning my call. I hope I'm not bothering you."

"No trouble at all," said Vin. "But I have to tell you I haven't been getting good cell phone service here so I'm calling from a pay phone. We have to talk quickly, before I run out of nickels."

"That's fine," said Maria. "Are you busy right now?"

"Not really," he said. Vin was never too busy to speak with a promising source, no matter what the time.

"Why don't I send a car for you?" suggested Maria. "I know you came by the winery. I'm not sure how much longer I'm going to be here. We can talk in the lounge. It's fairly private. That is if I'm not putting you out too much."

"That would be great," said the slightly shocked Vin.

"I can have my driver there in about 30 minutes. Will that work?"

"Sure," said Vin. "I'll be waiting by the hotel lobby front door. Tell your driver to wait in the car and I'll come out as soon as I see him." Vin wanted to be as discreet as possible and thought it would be best if Maria's driver did not enter the lobby, enabling him to make as fast an exit as possible.

"I'm at the Crashing Sea Gull," said Vin.

"Yes," said Maria. "See you soon Mr. Gusto."

Vin could hardly believe what had happened. In a short while he was going to have a private meeting with Maria Lambrusco. He tried to organize his thoughts as he quickly walked to his room. Once inside Vin scribbled a few random notes on a scrap of paper. This practice had the effect of calming his nerves. He then took a fast shower before stuffing his camera, tape recorder and notebook into his bag. Vin wrote down a few more notes and then hurriedly returned to the lobby where he waited for the arrival of Maria Lambrusco's driver.

In the lobby Vin had difficulty keeping still and constantly paced across the small space, occasionally stopping to jot down a note on the slip of paper which he'd then fold and put into his shirt pocket. What would he ask Maria? Where would they begin? How was her emotional state? What did she know about what happened to her father? How was the investigation progressing? Who's going to run the winery? Should he tell her that his assignment's been cancelled and that he's sometimes been followed by the North Fork Harbor police? And most importantly: why did she want to see him now?

CHAPTER 21

Tracing the Roots

Vin immediately left the lobby when he saw a black limousine arrive. As he approached the driver's window opened.

"From Maria?" was all Vin asked.

"Mr. Gusto?" the driver responded.

"Yes," said Vin.

The driver nodded as he stepped from the limousine. He was a tall, husky man with short, dark hair and heavy hands.

"May I see some identification?" requested the driver.

Vin reached into his jacket and removed his wallet, producing his driver's license.

The driver looked it over for a moment and then wrote down the license number before handing it back to Vin. "Please sign this," he said, handing Vin the same clipboard and pen he'd used to note his license number. Vin signed his name beneath a paragraph that basically noted that he was who he claimed to be.

"May I examine the contents of your bag sir?"

Vin handed the driver his bag. While he didn't like the idea he knew that if he did not cooperate, there'd be a good chance his meeting would not take place. After examining it and handing it back to him the driver noted its contents.

"Please spread your legs shoulder-width apart sir," said the driver. "And place your hands behind your back." Vin again cooperated as the driver patted him down.

"Is this how Maria Lambrusco usually welcomes her guests or this special treatment is just for me?"

"This is standard procedure sir," said the driver. "If you refuse to cooperate I'll have no choice but to return without you." The driver then stared blankly at Vin before opening the passenger door and gesturing for him to take a seat in the rear of the limo.

Once inside Vin asked the driver where they were going through the grating in the heavy glass partition that now separated the two men.

"I'm sorry sir, as a security service we're not allowed to disclose client information. Your host will be able to answer your questions once we arrive at the destination."

Vin saw no point in continuing the conversation as he peered into the rearview mirror, trying to study the driver. Although it was late at night, the driver was wearing an unusual style of dark glasses and a dark suit. There was a gray wire running from a plug in his right ear into his vest pocket where Vin noticed a significant bulge. Inside, there was no two-way radio that was typically used in such vehicles. Vin's compartment was complete with dark curtains, a sound system, television and lots of leg room. Feeling safe in his surroundings, an unusual feeling for Vin, he leaned back in his seat and closed his eyes, hoping to get a bit of rest before his meeting with Maria Lambrusco.

/ / /

After speaking with Dr. Dionasis, St. Charles decided to go to the police station and review the entire Lambrusco case file from beginning to end. He wanted to check for irregularities, missing information, incomplete statements and any flaw in the process that may bring him closer to finding the perpetrator. St. Charles parked his car behind the station house and took the rear entrance before walking directly into his office. At that time of night the dispatcher and desk sergeant were the only other police personnel present in the station house along with a few assorted individuals confined to the holding cells for various minor offenses.

St. Charles was pleasantly surprised to see that Krupcheski had left on his desk the list of known area criminals with medical, electronic and military backgrounds. He was not pleased, however to see that the lists were each very short, just a few names in total. While petty criminals generally were not a well-educated group these were small lists even by relatively low standards. Out of the three with some electronics knowledge, one was presently incarcerated and the other two had left the area. The medical background list contained only two names each with "whereabouts unknown." The military lists contained names of three men, each of whom was gainfully employed with no subsequent criminal activity—one as a truck driver, another on a fishing boat and a third in a local vegetable-processing facility.

Putting that information aside, St. Charles went to work on the case file, poring over each line of data, reviewing interview notes and re-examining medical and personnel records. Lambrusco had what police would call a "clean file." No history of threats or disturbances. No arrest record. No suits of any kind against him or his company. From a superficial standpoint, it was hard to imagine anyone would be sufficiently motivated to commit such a crime. St. Charles however, knew about Lambrusco's genetic research and his so-called "super vines." He understood that there could be others who would be desperate for the genetic code. But he needed to know more. He needed to know who and he needed to know how. But most important, he needed to know why. Dionasis's comment about settling old scores also weighed on his mind. St. Charles knew people were capable of holding vengeful motives for years, sometimes across generations waiting for a chance to act. At this point, anything was possible. Just then there was a sharp knock on his office door. As he rose it opened about halfway.

"I saw the light on so I thought I'd drop in," said Thorsen.

"Detective, what are you doing out here so late at night?"

"I couldn't sleep. Want to get a cup of coffee?"

"Sure," said St. Charles. The two men walked down the short hallway and into the tiny kitchen where St. Charles boiled water for instant coffee. They then returned to St. Charles office. After they both entered, the detective closed the door.

"I can't believe you drink this," said Thorsen after tasting a sip. He then put the cup down on St. Charles desk.

"Only when I have company," said St. Charles. "It must be some case of insomnia to bring you to this neck of the woods in the middle of the night."

"I've been thinking about the case," said Thorsen. "How can you let that broad tell you how to run the investigation?"

"Why are you visiting her hotel room unannounced and alone?" St. Charles responded. "I couldn't afford to lose the cooperation of a key person. She's the only one with intimate knowledge of the Doc and you scared her off."

"And has she shared any further knowledge with you?"

"You know I don't have to answer that," said St. Charles. "You're virtually suspended from the case but I'll break from protocol for your sake. The answer is no. Maria Lambrusco hasn't helped much since your private visit to her hotel room. In fact, she's hired her own security. She won't trust our men with her safety."

"Considering what happened to her father, I don't blame her," said Thorsen.

St. Charles wasn't sure if Thorsen's last remark was a serious or sarcastic one.

"Look," said St. Charles. "I've got work to do. If you've got something to offer regarding this case I'd appreciate hearing what it is. If it's helpful, I'll call Stimmel and ask to have you back on this case, if that's what you want."

St. Charles was lying in order to see what Thorsen had to offer but it was difficult to trick the cagey detective. He'd prefer not to have Thorsen back on the case but his desperate thirst for any information that may help him overpowered his pride. He wasn't sure if Thorsen was holding back something or it was St. Charles's own ego that was getting the best of him.

"I'm not here for a favor," said Thorsen. "Headquarters is keeping me very busy."

"Then what have you got?" pressed St. Charles. "What's your theory? What's the motive? Why show up at our humble country police station in the middle of the night?"

"The motive is revenge," said Thorsen.

"We know," said St. Charles. "Revenge for what?"

"For growing too many grapes," said Thorsen.

"Then where's the Doc's handheld computer?"

"By now it's either in the hands of whoever bankrolled this thing or on the bottom of Long Island Sound."

"Not in a landfill?"

"Doubtful, this guy's too smart. Wouldn't take that kind of chance. Leaving something where it might be scavenged. Where someone might recognize him or steal the data. Or where police sometimes check for evidence. No reason for that."

"So you think someone else is behind this?"

"Absolutely"

"Any proof?"

"None whatsoever."

"Then why are you here?"

"To see how far I can push the envelope."

"Detective," said St. Charles, it was now his turn to provide the irritating comments. "I was under the impression your visit here was a meaningful one, that you'd have something useful for us to move this investigation forward. If you haven't noticed, I'm still waiting."

"And if you haven't noticed, while others have, you haven't moved forward since I was removed from this case," countered Thorsen. "You're staring into a pile of papers in the middle of the night. You're not going to find your suspect in some file," said the detective.

The grizzled, former New York City cop and the street-smart detective who's convinced himself that he's too good for the assignments he's given momentarily stared at each other.

"How do you expect to find a suspect who hasn't left a fingerprint or footprint? There's no video image, witness or tire track," said Thorsen. "Not even a piece of hair or broken fingernail. You don't have a shred of evidence," he said, reaching over the desk and slamming the file shut before shoving it towards St. Charles. "Is this how you famously found punks in New York City, sifting through files in the middle of the night."

"And where do you suggest we look for him?" asked St. Charles.

"Up here," said Thorsen, tapping his middle finger on his temple. "You're dealing with a very determined mental case. A closet sociopath."

"You don't know that," countered St. Charles. "No one does."

"None of us will ever know until he's apprehended but I'll tell you this. Either that sucker's left the country by now or he's right under your nose. I'll bet it's the latter because ninety-nine percent of psychos want to get caught. That's my personal theory I developed after years of chasing all sorts of criminals. But you never know, you may be chasing the one percent that throws off my curve, the one who gets away. But what do I know? I'm just an old detective who makes people angry. But even I have to believe in something. If I didn't, my life would be too bland, like this warm brown water that passes for coffee."

Then St. Charles spoke.

"You guys blow into here in your fancy suits and cars at all hours of the day and night and expect to find an audience that just hands you everything," said St. Charles who was on the verge of boiling over in the face of the condescending detective but was also sensing a bluff in his subtle threats. "You have no idea where we are in this investigation. Neither does headquarters. It's lucky you're good with dead people, because you're pretty bad at handling live ones."

Thorsen leaned back and took a breath, whether what St. Charles said was true or not, he was unaccustomed to being spoken to in that manner, especially from a man in a police uniform.

"Anything else Sergeant?"

"Yes sir. If you'd ever spent any time walking a beat, talking with people, instead of looking down your nose at them, you might've learned that you can get more bees with honey than with vinegar."

Thorsen sat back and took a deep breath. He was not interested in St. Charles's opinion or analogy.

"The simplest definition of insanity is when someone is incapable of distinguishing the basic difference between right and wrong. The one thing you've got to hand over is a suspect," said Thorsen. "Your suspect believes what he did is right. Therefore, in his mind, he does not believe he committed a crime or that what he did, criminal or not, was justified in his own warped morality."

"That's why we found a mouthful of grapes," agreed St. Charles.

The detective nodded, indicating a modicum of common ground between the two professionals. "Something really motivated this guy. That's your key. Find the motivation. Find the suspect. It's called need-driven behavior. That's today's Psychology 101 lesson. Class dismissed."

"Ego-driven?" asked St. Charles.

"Possibly," said the detective. "I'm convinced he wanted to accomplish some sort of outrageous goal. The grapes in the mouth were the signal that he achieved what he set out to do. Why did some ancient tribesmen scalp their victims? They were already dead. For that brief moment passion overpowered logic. The perpetrator went for the trophy. He wanted the scalp."

"Do you think he's a serial killer?"

"No evidence points to that. No pattern," said Thorsen. "No records of crimes with this sort of injection."

"What else do you think?" asked St. Charles.

"Whoever it is has executed a nearly perfect crime. No real clues yet. He spent a lot of time planning this. Judging from the care that went into this he's probably some kind of control freak, watching from a distance. Right now he's still delighting in the fact that no one's got any idea who he is. I'm willing to bet after he was done he secretly did a little victory dance, treated himself to a little vacation, bought himself a gift of some sort. But I'll bet that's what will do him in."

"Exactly what do you think will do him in?"

"His fatal flaw," said Thorsen.

"His what?"

"His fatal flaw," Thorsen repeated. "We've all got one. Some of us have multiple ones. Like a bad habit or character trait, very often this is what leads to our demise."

"So you think he won't be able to keep it a secret? He'll want credit for his actions."

"Eventually he's going to want some attention, some recognition or reward. Ego gratification," said Thorsen. "Doesn't look like he trusts many people, so he's probably going to need to be prodded in some fashion, drawn into the open by an event beyond his control. Nothing makes a control freak crazier than something he can't control. And if he feels he's losing credit, being forgotten or passed over, in some perverted way he'll do something to get that recognition. The ancients did a victory dance when they returned home with their scalps. What good's a trophy if no one sees it?"

"And the criminal always returns to the scene of the crime." Now it was St. Charles's turn to be sarcastic.

"Not the good ones. Only the amateurs," responded Thorsen in complete seriousness.

"Anything else?" St. Charles then asked.

"Considering the way you just spoke to me, I've given you more than you deserve but there is one more thing you should know."

"Go ahead," said the Sergeant.

"This ain't the New York City PD where they've got thousands of cases to process on any given day. I'm here to tell you that the whisperings in the hallway are that Stimmel isn't happy. He has no love for this town and is going to want some real answers soon. Remember what I told you," he said, again tapping his temple with the tip of his middle finger. "Motivation," he repeated. "Any more questions?"

"Just one," said St. Charles. "What's your fatal flaw or don't you have one?"

"Mine?" asked Thorsen. "I've actually got several flaws. I know this because I regularly engage in deep introspection."

"I'm listening," said St. Charles, not sure if Thorsen was toying with him or not.

"It's probably never occurred to you but the thing that will do me in is not the typical stuff, not what you might think. Not women or booze or money. What'll do me in is well for one . . . I'm too generous. Always helping others at the expense of myself. Like I did for you just now. I've actually helped others at my own expense. It's definitely hurt my career. Who does that nowadays?"

"I do. Anything else?" asked St. Charles.

"You really want to know which flaw will do me in? The truly fatal one?"

"Sure, since we're on the subject."

"Isn't it obvious?"

"Isn't what obvious?"

Thorsen held back for a moment, exhaling a deep breath.

"I'm just too smart," he said in complete seriousness.

Not sure if Thorsen was being sincere St. Charles stared at him for a moment before saying anything. "I'll keep that in mind. Thanks for stopping by."

"There's one more thing you should know about me," he added.

"You're giving me a lot more than I bargained for."

"I forgive but I don't forget. You wanted me off the case, you got it," said Thorsen. "Have a good night Sergeant."

Thorsen then turned and left the office as St. Charles rose to close the door behind him. He then returned to his desk and slammed his fist on the file. Even when he tried to be helpful and was somewhat pleasant Thorsen had a way of ingratiating everyone, including the otherwise nearly unflappable St. Charles. But what truly irritated St. Charles was the fact that despite his difficult personality Thorsen was a good detective. He had an insight into people's minds that was highly refined from years of investigating all sorts of suspects. What did he mean by the one percent that gets away? Did the detective know something that St. Charles didn't? Was he baiting him to get St. Charles to request to have him returned to the case? At times St. Charles had to consider his own ego. Could Thorsen return and help solve the case or was he trying to indirectly help him with his mention of motivation and his psychological profiling? Was he withholding information or would he truly like to see St. Charles fail? Thorsen had given his card to those he interviewed. It's possible one may have called him to offer some information. By withholding any such information he himself would be guilty of committing a crime. Thorsen surely knew that as well but might be enjoying the feeling of power and control having such information could provide. Or was he bluffing? St. Charles had no background in psychology but understood ego was a sensitive thing. He was also well aware that the case hadn't progressed much and perhaps Thorsen was toying with St. Charles's frayed nerves to fortify his own ego which had been damaged after having been removed from the case. In any event, St. Charles knew he had to produce some answers soon or he'd again be working with Thorsen who'd quickly take credit for any progress made with the investigation whether he was responsible for it or not. St. Charles also knew there was two winery staff members who Thorsen neglected to interview. He clenched his teeth. It was a thin thread of hope but he was not going to let it slip through his fingers. St. Charles reached for his telephone. It was time for him to consider new tactics as he thought about ways to draw out the killer.

/ / /

The black limousine quietly pulled in front of the rear entrance to the hotel. Vin's door was opened by another man dressed very similarly to the driver.

"Right this way, Mr. Gusto," said the guard, extending his hand to Vin. "I hope you don't mind but we're taking you in through the service entrance." Vin nodded and followed with the driver walking behind him in single file. Vin followed the first man through a brightly lit, cinderblock lined hallway. The brightness in the hallway made him squint as his eyes adjusted. Along the way he got a quick glimpse into the hotel kitchen where a few workers were beginning preparations for that morning's breakfast. Through another door they emerged into a much darker lounge area. A long, oval-shaped bar padded in black leather was in the center of a dimly lit room. The bar was surrounded by several booths of various sizes where patrons could sit in relative privacy. A piano-jazz medley was being piped in through the sound system. Leading him to the booth that was farthest from the bar Vin could make out a partial silhouette of the back of a woman's head. She had black hair with a slight curl that fell slightly above the collar of a black shirt. As he got closer he could see she was wearing a small black hat as well. Just then the first man gently took Vin's elbow.

"Ms. Lambrusco," he said. "Mr. Gusto is here."

Maria rose from her seat and extended her hand. A glass of red wine was on the table.

"Very good to see you again," Maria said. "Thank you for coming on such short notice."

"That's quite all right," said Vin taking her hand. "It's a great pleasure to truly meet you and allow me to say I was very sorry to hear about your father. I had been looking forward to meeting him."

"Thank you," said Maria. "Please sit down."

The two of them took seats facing each other and Maria dismissed the guards who then occupied a nearby booth, one positioned to watch the lounge entrance and the other fixed on the table at which Maria and Vin were sitting.

"That's quite a team, you've got," said Vin, nodding towards the guards.

"They're very professional," said Maria. "I use the same firm in California. I sleep well when I know they're nearby. I'd be pleased to refer them to you."

"Thank you but that won't be necessary," said Vin.

"You never know," said Maria. "Things can change very quickly. Would you like a drink?"

"Sure," said Vin. "I'm sure you know your wine. I'll have a glass of whatever you're drinking."

Maria gestured towards the guard who'd been watching the table. Holding up her glass and pointing towards Vin, she subtly gave the order for more wine. Maria then turned back to face Vin and spoke directly to him.

"I saw from my father's appointment book you were scheduled to meet with him. You don't have to answer any of my questions if you don't want to but considering what happened to my father, I'm trying to get some answers," she said.

"Sure," said Vin. "I'd be happy to help you."

"One more thing. We're speaking off-the-record tonight. Nothing we say goes into print anywhere, unless I give my permission, agreed?"

"Agreed," he said.

Vin had had off-the-record conversations with subjects before and was not surprised by Maria's demand plus he did want to help her. She then extended her hand and Vin shook it. He would keep his word with Maria.

"Can you tell me how your visit to my father's winery came about?" she asked as the guard placed a glass of wine for Vin on the table.

"I received a sudden assignment from Travel & Pleasure magazine to interview your father as part of a longer North Fork Harbor piece. Soon after I got here it was canceled."

"Did they give you a reason why?"

"No. I got a very brief message from the editor's assistant and a minuscule kill fee," said Vin. "But it was enough to allow me to hang around here for a few more days."

"Who was your editor?"

"Patricia Goode," said Vin.

Maria nodded as if making a mental note.

"Why stay after your story's been canceled?" she asked.

"I've got a friend here. We've been spending some time together, catching up" said Vin. "Plus I was curious. I'd like to know what actually happened to your father. It's unfinished business for me. I was sent here with an assignment and have nothing to show. I did get a kill fee but I didn't come here for a kill fee. I came for a story. But unless something breaks soon I should be heading back to New York in about two more days. That's all the kill fee will allow and I've got other assignments waiting for me."

"I understand but what could 'break,' as you say?" asked Maria.

Vin hesitated to continue. He did not want to make idle talk with Maria or give her false hopes but he did not know what to say. To buy himself time he picked up the glass by the stem and held it under his nose. Swirling the liquid within the bowl of the glass Vin could smell the deep, rich bouquet. He knew very little about wine but could tell this was a strong one. Vin took a sip, then a second and returned the glass to the table. He thought that maybe he should not have intimated that there might still be the possibility of a story. "I'm not sure," Vin then said, hoping to cover his tracks. "But if there's something I could help you with let me know."

Maria held her glass by its stem and stared into it before speaking. "You said a moment ago you came here for a story. Is that why you came in the middle of the night to see me, someone you don't know because of the chance of getting a story?"

"Possibly," said Vin. "I didn't know what I'd find when I got here but I also thought you might need some help."

"There may actually be something," she said looking up at him.

CHAPTER 22

Untangling the Vines

"Mr. Gusto," continued Maria. "I was all my father had and he was all I had."

"I understand," said Vin. "I lost my father when I was young. My mother and I struggled ever since."

"I'm sorry," said Maria. "But your parents must've done something right. You're an esteemed journalist who came out in the middle of the night to help a stranger. I can see you're a good person. You can take some consolation in that."

"Journalist, yes," said Vin. "Esteemed, I'm not so sure. But thank you just the same." He chose not to respond to the "good person" portion of Maria's comment. There was then a pause in the conversation. "You haven't told me how I can help you," he said.

This time Maria turned to look at her body guards before turning back to face Vin. She then leaned across the table to get as close as possible to him.

"Mr. Gusto," she said. "My father was murdered."

Vin blankly stared at her.

"Are you sure?" he asked.

"Yes. He was attacked in his fermentation room and injected with a poison. There was an autopsy."

"This must be terrible for you," said Vin.

"It's a horrible nightmare," she said. "My father was a good man. He believed science should help others. Someone wanted him dead. I'm here talking to you but I'm still in a state of shock. This whole affair has been somewhat surreal."

During his career Vin had heard many people describe recently deceased family members in lofty terms but from what he knew about Dr. Lambrusco he believed what Maria was telling him. Plus her announcement had confirmed what he had heard elsewhere.

"Why do you think someone wanted your father dead?"

"Because of his experimental work," Maria said. "He was a pioneer in agricultural genetics, especially grapes and was on the verge of a big announcement."

184

"That's why he was going to the conference?"

"Yes. He was going to make his announcement there."

"What was the announcement? Can you tell me?"

"My father had created SG-10. It's a scientific abbreviation but we called it the Super Grape. The name sounds silly but it was a very serious project. Imagine a fruit that could grow almost anywhere. Survive nearly any conditions, insects, drought, freezing cold, intense heat, pollution, floods. He was very possibly on the verge of a true breakthrough. This experimental strain is full of vitamins and the vines grew quickly. They'd reach full production in two years versus five. And there's barely a spot on earth where they will not grow. As my father used to put it, if an area can sustain people, SG-10 will thrive there. My father remembered what it was like to be hungry. He never wanted anyone else to be hungry. That was his motivation."

"Why grapes?" asked Vin who also knew what it was like to be hungry. "Why not a more staple crop like corn or wheat?"

"My father grew up around grapes," said Maria. "Some of his earliest memories were picking grapes with his family. In agriculture school he specialized in grape propagation. He traveled the world studying grapes. It was only natural that that's where he would focus his work."

"Was he going to make an announcement about this at the conference? My editor vaguely mentioned something about that," pressed Vin. "So that's why someone wanted him dead?"

"Word had gotten out about his work. Some people did not like the idea of a super strain. The worldwide grape crop is worth billions of dollars each year. If his research could be transferred to other crops, if it made growing crops too easy, which very possibly would have been a side effect of his work, it could crush the world commodity markets. Others may have wanted the formula for their own personal gain. My father wasn't interested in getting rich. He only wanted enough so that he could live comfortably while he continued his work. He wanted to help people."

"Are you sure?" asked Vin. "You've been under a great deal of stress Maria. Maybe you need time to come to terms with this."

"About my father, I'm absolutely sure. At his age, with his accomplishments he was no longer interested in money. The idea of helping others is what got him out of bed each morning," she said. "But there's something else."

"What's that?"

"His handheld computer, which contained the genetic code, the locations of the vines he planted around the world, all of the harvest and propagation data is missing. I think whoever killed him was really after what was in his computer. At North Fork Harbor he kept only a few experimental vines."

Vin shook his head and looked down at his hands which were spread out as he tapped his fingers over the table. Whenever he spoke with people without holding a pen and notebook he quickly became restless and fidgety.

"What I need is help. I need justice," Maria continued. "I need to push this investigation forward and catch whoever it is who did this."

"Why me? I'm just a reporter."

"I'm not satisfied with the pace of the investigation. I don't think the police fully realize what's taken place here. They send an obnoxious detective to see me. My father wouldn't have shared a glass of wine with that type of man," said Maria. "The big picture, bigger than my father's murder are the ramifications. In that handheld are that results of years of work, a potentially groundbreaking experiment may be in the wrong hands. Someone wanted the data and murdered a scientist to get it."

"I still don't understand what you want from me."

Maria looked down at the table while pushing a napkin back and forth with her index finger. "I'm thinking that if the world knew about this story justice could be done. Whether the police solve the case or not, I cannot go quietly with this."

"So you think someone wanted the data," said Vin. "Wouldn't your father have given it to whoever it was? Save his own life?"

"Yes, of course he would have," said Maria.

"So you think even after the perpetrator got the handheld he still wanted your father dead?" asked Vin.

"Yes," said Maria staring back into her wine.

"Why don't you go to the newspapers yourself?"

"I'm not a writer," she said. "They'd see me as a hurt, angry daughter with very little evidence. You're an established reporter."

"I'm a reporter without a paper," said Vin. "And I don't have any more evidence than you do. I'm a former reporter for The New York Tattler, not exactly a bastion of journalistic integrity. And what about the autopsy?"

"Despite my complaints about them, I still need the police," said Maria. "I've embarrassed them enough by hiring my own security and cutting off communication with them. Besides, coming from a reporter the news would be more objective. It would have greater impact."

"What else?" asked Vin.

"My father had a very elaborate security system in the winery," she said. "Someone figured a way to bypass it. Someone had inside knowledge."

"You're sure about that?"

"Yes."

"You don't trust the people who worked for your father."

"Not now I don't. How could I? But my father did."

"How are you handling that?"

"I'm still the grieving daughter," said Maria. "But my eyes are open. I'll be stopping unexpectedly at the winery, staying for different amounts of time. Someone's got to run the harvest and the crush. The grapes are very good this year. It would be a shame to let the crop go to waste."

"What about after the crush? Don't you have business in California?"

"Mr. Gusto, I'm staying for as long as I can stand it. Until this case is closed," she said holding back tears.

Vin kept his gaze on Maria as she started to cry. Not sure what to do Vin reached across the table and placed his hand over Maria's. "I'm really sorry about your Dad," Vin said. "I'll do whatever I can to help you. Maybe you need to take a little time." He removed his hand as Maria looked up at him.

With her watery eyes opened wide she nodded and tried to smile. "There is no time. A harvest does not wait. But thank you for coming. My driver will take you back to your hotel now," she said. "Would it be all right if I call you tomorrow, around noon? We can compare notes."

"Sure," said Vin but remembering his cell phone status added: "It might be better if I call you."

"Okay, but one more thing," said Maria. "I realize you're a working person. Consider this when you return to your room tonight. If you think we truly can do something and you need help with expenses, if you have to put other things aside, I'll have my office send you a check."

"Thanks but I could never consider that. I may not have known your father but I admired him," said Vin rising from his seat. "Let's see how things unfold. You never know, something may happen."

Maria nodded and rising as well, shook hands with Vin before signaling for the driver. "Please take Mr. Gusto back to his hotel," she said. "He's a good man." Maria then turned and left the lounge.

As Vin was leaving the hotel lobby with Maria's driver and security guard he noticed a man delivering a bundle of newspapers to the hotel. Parked nearby was a white van with The North Fork Harbor Reporter logo on its side.

"I'd like to get a newspaper," Vin said to the driver. "Just wait here a minute." Before the driver could answer Vin sprinted in the direction of the delivery van. A young boy was seated on the passenger seat. Vin was anxious to see if there was any news of Dr. Lambrusco.

"How about a paper?" asked Vin, handing the boy a dollar bill. Without saying anything the boy took the bill and gave Vin a newspaper. Vin began walking back towards the driver when the page one headline made him suddenly stop.

VINCENT 'TUGBOAT' TUCKER KILLED IN MOTORCYCLE CRASH

Vin could hardly believe what he was reading. Above the small article was a photo of police officers examining the accident scene. Noting the late time of the accident and the newspaper's press time, the article was very brief but it offered a theory for the crash. Tucker it reported, was heading west on the Main Rd. when he lost control of his motorcycle. While police were not sure at press time of the exact cause of the accident they did report the discovery of a sizeable pool of motor oil on the road which may have caused the driver to lose control. The report did not mention his blood-alcohol level. Tucker, the report's authors theorized was traveling at about 60 miles per hour when he was thrown about twenty feet from the motorcycle and broke his neck upon crashing into the pavement. Paramedics pronounced him dead at the scene. The police were asking for anyone with information about Vincent Tucker's activities or whereabouts that evening to contact them.

Vin could hardly believe what he was reading and was unable to move when the driver approached him.

"Everything okay Mr. Gusto?" he asked.

Vin handed him the newspaper. The driver quickly glanced at the front page before folding the paper and tucking it under his arm. "Come along Mr. Gusto," he said, taking Vin by the elbow. "We've got to get you to your hotel."

/ / /

The sudden news about Vincent was too much for Vin to take. Maria's driver took the same road to the hotel that Vincent and Vin had taken earlier that evening. Vin had to interrupt the driver, asking him to stop the car so he could exit and vomit on the side of the road. By the time they passed the scene it had been cleared by the police. There were no signs that an accident had taken place. But the image of the happy and well-meaning Vincent remained fresh in Vin's mind and he became overwhelmed with guilt over his sudden death. Perhaps his accident could have been avoided if he had not given Vin a ride to the hotel.

Vin barely remembered reentering the car or returning to the hotel that night but when he got back into his room he immediately went to the bathroom and vomited again. He sat for some time on the bathroom floor, eventually grabbing onto the sink to pull himself up. He then looked at himself in the mirror wondering what happened to Vincent. He tried reconstructing the events as best he could, grasping for some logic in an otherwise hopeless situation. Vincent was an experienced driver who knew the road. Vin wasn't sure how much he had been drinking but felt secure during the motorcycle ride to the hotel. Why didn't they hit the oil patch on their way to the hotel? As he stared at himself in the mirror the telephone in his room rang.

"Hello," said Vin into the receiver.

"Vin, it's me," said the female voice. Vin did not respond. "Shanin."

"Hey," was all Vin could say in response.

"You okay?"

"Yeah," said Vin. "What's up?"

"Did you hear the news about Tugboat?"

"Yeah," repeated Vin. "How'd you find out?"

"I couldn't sleep," said Shanin. "I wanted something to read and got up in the middle of the night to check the paper's website. I'm really sorry Vin. I know you two sort of became friends."

"He was a nice guy. He was a stranger who helped me. I feel like I just said goodbye to him and now he's dead. The whole thing makes me sick," said Vin.

"It said in the paper that the police are seeking information. Are you going to go to them?"

"I probably will. It'll help relieve some of the guilt. And I owe it to Vincent. Maybe you can drive me to the police station tomorrow," he said.

"Yeah, except my car gave off an awful stink on the way home."

"What do you mean?"

"I was barely halfway home from the Apple Tree when smoke started coming from under the hood and there was a tapping noise I never heard before. It felt like the engine was dying," said Shanin. "I got home o.k. I'll bring it to my mechanic in the morning."

"I'll go with you," volunteered Vin. "Mechanics have a way of swindling women."

"He's a friend of Barbara's," said Shanin. "He's fair but I've got to get there early."

"No problem. I'll still go with you," said Vin. "It's been a crazy night. We'll catch up but don't call me. Come to the hotel on you're way to the mechanic and ask someone at the front desk to call me. I'll come right down no matter what time it is."

Shanin sighed before they each said goodnight and hung up the phone as Vin collapsed onto the bed.

CHAPTER 23

Preparing for the Harvest

Sgt. Henry St. Charles telephoned the North Fork Harbor Vineyards office and left a message on its answering machine requesting separate interviews that morning with Cindy Murphy and Andy LaBroom. He deliberately did not make his request with a sense of urgency but instead politely explained that they were the last remaining staff members to be interviewed as a matter of procedure and he was going to have to speak with them as Det. Thorsen was temporarily unavailable. Nor did he state a time beyond the next morning. St. Charles wanted to be somewhat vague, almost casual in his request as he thought he might be able to get more information by psychologically disarming his remaining subjects rather than by taking a more hardnosed approach. The fact that some time had passed before Cindy and Andy were interviewed could be an obstacle to the investigation. It was considered most effective to speak with anyone of interest as soon as possible, within 24 hours of the crime. St. Charles then spent the rest of the night in his police station office, reviewing the case, thinking about the crime scene, considering Thorsen's observations and the autopsy results while scouring the files for anything that might help him make even a small amount of progress.

The next morning was uncharacteristically warm with the temperature approaching 100 degrees on Long Island's North Fork before noon. Even the otherwise reliably cool breezes from Peconic Bay and Long Island Sound were not enough to take the edge off the day's heat. When St. Charles arrived at the winery the first thing he requested was a drink of ice water from Cindy Murphy, who cheerfully greeted him when he entered the winery's air-conditioned office carrying a brown leather briefcase. The two of them then sat down for a closed-door meeting. St. Charles quietly put the briefcase on the floor and removed a small notebook and pen from his jacket pocket. After exchanging pleasantries it was actually Cindy who first spoke.

"Can you tell me even a tiny bit of what's going on?" she asked.

"You mean in terms of the investigation?" St. Charles asked.

"Yes," Cindy said, again with a smile.

"I'm afraid I can't tell you anything besides the obvious," said St. Charles. "The investigation is still open but I expect it to end soon," he lied.

"How do you mean?" she asked.

"If no progress is made the case will remain open but inactive, which basically means it's dead and business-as-usual will resume," he said. "I'm sure you've noticed the detective's already off the case. That's usually a sign from headquarters that they've got more important things to do. They generally don't like spending much of their resources out here with us East Enders." St. Charles was sticking with his game plan to lull her into a false sense of security.

"How then can I help you?" asked Cindy.

"Just a few formalities," started St. Charles. "I'm going to take a few notes as we talk. How well did you know Dr. Lambrusco? I understand those closest to him called him Dr. Frank. By which name did you call him? How long have you worked here?" St. Charles deliberately dropped three seemingly insignificant questions on the outwardly unsuspecting Cindy in his attempt to disarm her.

"I've worked here for a couple of years," she said, taking the last question first. "I called him Dr. Frank. He asked me to call him that," she lied.

"Then this must be very difficult if you two were somewhat close," he said, trying to initiate feelings of empathy with Cindy while seeking inconsistencies in her statements.

"It has not been easy," she sighed. "He was a nice man."

"Any quirks? I've heard he kept to himself," said St. Charles. "I've tried to get some of his wine over the years. This is the closest I've come."

"At times he could be a little hard to communicate with," she said.

"What's been the most difficult?"

"Just getting on with things, trying to manage the winery in Dr. Frank's absence. Not knowing what's going to happen next."

"Why were you out sick on the day in question?"

"Backache," she said. "I occasionally suffer from sciatica."

"Seeing a chiropractor for it? I know good one right here in town."

"No," she sighed. "It seems to pass after I put heat on it and lie down for a while."

"Hasn't Dr. Frank's daughter been around?" asked St. Charles. "From what I understand she knows something about the wine business."

"She's been here but I don't think we can expect Maria to take over," said Cindy. "She's been through a lot."

"Have you had much conversation with Maria? Do you think she might know anything about her father's private dealings?" asked St. Charles. "An unhappy business associate is always a possibility."

"Not that I know of," said Cindy shaking her head.

"Not that you know of what?" repeated St. Charles suddenly leaning forward in his chair and adding a tone of seriousness to his voice. "What Maria Lambrusco may know about any unhappy business associates?"

Cindy pulled back, alarmed by St. Charles's sudden change in tone.

"Sorry Cindy," he said, returning to his sympathetic tone. "I must've gotten caught up in the conversation. I thought we might've been onto something. I've been working too hard. You were saying . . ."

"I'm not sure about what Maria knows," said Cindy, regaining composure. "I've only seen her a few times around here. I don't know of any angry business associates."

"How about Larson, the mechanic He works here doesn't he?"

"He's here a lot but he's not a winery employee," she said. "He repairs the equipment."

"He's got a temper right? I know that for a fact."

"I guess," said Cindy. "He's always been nice to me."

"Why wouldn't he be?" asked St. Charles. "I can see you're a nice person. You'd never be mixed up in anything unseemly like what we have here. But your boyfriend Andy, he and Larson are friends right?"

"They're friends yes but Andy's not really my boyfriend," she said. "We dated a few times but nothing came of it."

"I had a few relationships like that in my day," St. Charles said with a smile. "So you wouldn't have any real insight into him?"

"I guess not. Nothing besides the normal stuff," she said. "He's a nice guy. Kind of quiet. Dr. Frank trusted him with a lot of things."

"Like what?"

"He's the vineyard manager," Cindy said. "He's pretty knowledgeable about growing grapes. Knows irrigation, how to test for sugar in the lab, maintain the equipment, stuff like that. This used to be his family's farm."

"So he 'knows the land,' as the farmers like to say."

"Every inch. Dr. Frank bought it and he hired Andy. We sometimes used to joke Dr. Frank got the farm and Andy."

"Andy would have had access to agricultural chemicals?"

"Yes," said Cindy. "But why are you asking me about Andy? He didn't do anything."

"Sorry Cindy, there's no telling how a conversation will turn," said St. Charles. "You can relax. I'm just about through. Just one more minute. I have a statement for you to sign. It's standard stuff. It just says that you and I spoke at this time and place. It could be helpful to you later. It shows you cooperated." St. Charles reached into his briefcase, removed a folder and began writing on a sheet of paper.

"Did anyone have to sign a statement with the detective?"

"I don't think so."

"Guess that's the price I pay for being last," she sighed.

"Andy's last," said St. Charles, looking up from the desk. "Let me just add a few notes and you'll be free to go."

"I might be able to help you try some of that wine," said Cindy.

"Really," said St. Charles without looking up. "I'll keep that in mind. Now if you'll just sign here," he said sliding the paper across the table. "This is a sworn statement noting that we met today."

Cindy leaned over the table to read the statement.

"Is that all?" she asked.

"Yes but I left out your offer for the wine. That wouldn't look good," he joked.

"Okay," Cindy said as she signed her name to the statement.

"Thanks," St. Charles said. "Thank you for your help."

Cindy left the room without saying anything further.

"Ms. Murphy," St. Charles called in a friendly manner. "Please let Mr. LaBroom know I'm ready."

As St. Charles remained in the room waiting to hear when he might meet Andy LaBroom he received a call from Officer Krupcheski who had a telephone message for him. Police Chief Louis Stimmel wanted St. Charles to call him right away. Thorsen wasn't kidding thought St. Charles who instructed Krupcheski to call the Chief's office and tell him he was interviewing persons of interest and he'd phone him as soon as he was through. A few minutes later Cindy reappeared.

"Andy's asked if he could meet you later or tomorrow," she said. "He's with some equipment that's broken down on the far end of the vineyard and he's waiting for Larson, you know, our mechanic, to get here. He said he can't leave the equipment because it's sinking in some mud. He and some of the workers are trying to keep it from sinking further until Larson can haul it out with his truck."

"I see," said St. Charles remembering his plan to psychologically disarm the remaining persons of interest. "It must be a very valuable piece of machinery."

"It is," said Cindy. "It's a special grape harvester from Germany. It cost a few hundred-thousand dollars when Dr. Frank bought it new. Andy can't just walk away from it."

"If the harvester's sinking how are they going to get a truck out there?" asked St. Charles.

"Balloon tires," Cindy quickly answered.

"How would you know a thing like that?" pressed St. Charles while maintaining his friendly tone.

"Happens all the time around here" she shrugged.

"Where'd all the mud come from? Hasn't rained in a few days?"

"Broken irrigation head that ran all night," she said. "It flooded the field."

St. Charles nodded while pretending to write a brief note.

"Tell Andy if he wants to see me later to stop by the police station," said St. Charles in as unthreatening tone he could manage under the circumstances. He did not like the fact that Andy would not meet with him that day but refused to show it. St. Charles needed the investigation to move forward as quickly as possible. "I'll be there until three. I'm sure our talk will only take a few minutes. Otherwise I'll be here the same time tomorrow morning. If I don't see him today I'll have to talk with him tomorrow without fail. Be sure he understands that."

"Will do," said Cindy, leaving the room in a hurry.

/ / /

Vin was already outside when Shanin pulled up in her car which was nearly engulfed in a cloud of blue smoke.

Vin walked to her side of the car. "Shut the motor," he instructed as soon as she rolled down the window.

"I don't know what's going on," she said getting out of the car. "It was running fine all day yesterday then last night it started erupting."

Vin opened the hood, tried to wave away some of the smoke and pulled out the dipstick. A pungent, burning odor permeated the air. "You don't have a drop of oil in here," he said stepping back from the fumes and showing Shanin the bare dipstick. Shanin shrugged. "Maybe we can get some oil at the IGA," said Vin. "You can't drive it like this. You'll be lucky if you haven't cooked the engine."

As they walked to the IGA Vin mostly lectured Shanin on the importance of motor oil. When they returned to the car Vin showed Shanin how to add the oil to the engine and then check the level by using the dipstick. But when he pulled the dipstick from the engine to show Shanin how to measure it, the stick remained clean. No new oil appeared on the stick which was still at the empty level after adding three quarts.

"That's strange," said Vin. "After three quarts of oil the level should have started showing up on the stick."

"I'm calling my mechanic," said Shanin. "Sometimes he'll make a roadside call."

As Shanin stepped away Vin noticed a pool of oil seeping towards where he was standing. He bent down and touched it with his fingertip.

"This oil's cold," he said to Shanin who had just returned from calling her mechanic. "And it's fresh," he said rubbing the slippery film between his thumb and index finger. Vin then knelt down and looked under the car.

"Your oil plug is missing," said Vin. "I've never seen that happen before."

"What do you mean?" asked Shanin.

"This brown liquid on the ground is the oil we just added. The oil plug is like a big screw," said Vin pointing to a small brown puddle on the road where they stood. "You remove it only when you're changing the oil. After the old oil drains you replace the plug and add the fresh oil. You've got no plug so the car can't hold any oil. Keep running this motor and it'll overheat in a hurry."

"That's what's making the smoke and the smell?" asked Shanin.

"Yes," said Vin who then knelt down again and this time ran his finger around the slippery perimeter of the hole where the oil plug should have been.

"When was the last time you had your car's oil changed?" he asked, wiping his finger on a napkin Shanin had taken from the self-serve coffee stand at the IGA while Vin bought the motor oil.

"I don't know," said Shanin. "A long time ago I guess."

"That's very odd," said Vin.

"Could it ever just fall out?" asked Shanin. "Like from vibrations or something."

"No," said Vin. "Unless it's been tampered with."

"You mean vandalized?"

"Possibly," said Vin.

"Allen, my mechanic, is on his way," she said. "He'll help us."

"He serviced the car last?"

"He's the only one who's ever serviced it. But like I said, I haven't been to see him for some time."

"Call your mechanic back," said Vin. "Tell him you need an oil plug and five quarts of oil. The car's not holding any oil. If you drive it anymore you'll risk blowing the engine if you haven't already done so."

"Right," said Shanin reaching for her phone. "By the way, how'd you learn so much about cars?"

"When you're poor, like we were, you learn how to fix things in order to survive," said Vin. "We repaired everything we could ourselves. By the time I was 14 I was on a first-name basis with the guys in the auto parts store."

Growing up Shanin had never as much as looked under the hood of a car.

After about a half-hour wait, Allen arrived in his Ford F-150 pick-up truck.

"I could smell that thing from down the road," he said. Allen was tall and slim with a scraggily brown and gray beard and deep-set eyes. His fingertips were stained black from grease.

"You say you ain't got an oil plug?" asked Allen. Like Vin, he knelt down to look under the car and ran his finger over the hole where the oil plug should have been. "I've never seen a car with no plug," he said standing up. "I got a universal plug in the truck. I'll screw that in and then we'll see if she holds oil."

"They make a universal oil plug?" asked Shanin.

"Yeah," said Allen. "The size is pretty standard. Lucky for you I got one in the truck. Once it's in we'll add the oil and test the motor."

Allen inserted a replacement plug made from heavy, black rubber. He then took a jug of motor oil from his truck and began filling the car's reservoir.

"Think I damaged my motor?" asked Shanin.

"Only one way to find out," he said. "Sometimes these big motors can go a little longer on low oil 'cause they run cool." Allen looked again under the car and ran his finger over the newly inserted plug. "Start the engine," he said without removing his gaze from under the car.

Shanin turned the key and the motor started. After a few seconds the tapping noise stopped, as did the blue smoke and foul odor. Vin bent down to look under the car as well.

"She ain't leaking a drop now but you're going to have to watch it over the next few days. This is very preliminary. See how she does under pressure," said Allen. "You know how to check the dipstick?" he asked Shanin.

"I do now," she said.

"She sounds all right. You might've gotten lucky. Maybe caught it just in time," he said. "Be alert as you drive for the next few days and don't run no air conditionin'," Allen continued. "If you get that smell or hear that tapping noise again pull right over and shut the motor. If you don't get nuthin' like that come by next week when you get a few minutes and me or Sparky will give it a good look-see, make sure you're gettin' the right compression. No charge for today," he then said climbing back into his truck. "I got to hurry and get me some parts and get back to the shop before the customers start askin' where I disappeared to and why their car ain't ready."

"Thanks," Shanin said as Allen headed off in his truck. "See," said Shanin turning to Vin. "He didn't even charge me."

"Nice guy," agreed Vin. "Since you're taking a test drive can you get me to the police station? I want to tell them what I can since I was probably one of the last people to see Tugboat. We can listen to the motor as you drive."

"How can I turn down an offer like that?" asked Shanin. "I hope you don't mind if I don't stay," she continued. "I've got a job taking a family portrait tonight and have to prepare. I'll drop you at the police station and come back in about an hour."

"That should work," said Vin.

The drive to the police station was a short one and Vin did not have time to fill Shanin in on his meeting with Maria Lambrusco.

"Have time for lunch today?" Vin asked as Shanin stopped on the side of the road across from the police station. "It shouldn't take too long here and I've got to finish telling you about last night."

"Sure, as long as my car holds up and you've got some cash. I may need to save some funds if I need a car repair."

"No problem," said Vin. "It will be my pleasure. I'll probably need some lunch after this. You pick the place."

Vin then said good-bye to Shanin and entered the North Fork Harbor Police Station.

Chapter 24

Seeking Clarity

Upon entering the police station Vin went directly to the desk officer on duty and said he had information regarding Vincent Tucker. After taking Vin's name and contact information the desk officer asked him to take a seat as he made a telephone call to one of the officers working on the case. A few seconds later Vin heard his name called. He looked up to see the towering figure of Officer Jeffrey Jonah.

"Follow me," said the very tall Jonah. Vin rose from his seat and followed Officer Jonah to a small meeting room. They each took a seat facing the other around a small wooden table. The room was completely bare except for the two chairs, table, a telephone and an overhead light.

As Jonah opened a notebook he began the conversation by asking Vin basic personal information such as permanent address and telephone numbers. Almost the same information he'd given the desk officer.

"Why are you here in North Fork Harbor?" was the first question.

"I'm here on business," Vin flatly said.

"What do you have for us regarding Tucker," Jonah then said.

"I was talking with him in the Apple Tree when he offered me a ride back to my hotel. It was about 11 pm," said Vin.

"Which hotel?"

"You've got to be kidding," said Vin. "The same one at which you were watching me a few nights ago."

Jonah just looked at Vin quizzically.

"The Crashing Sea Gull," Vin said.

"I know the place," said Jonah.

"I thought so," said Vin.

"Used to summer there with my family."

"So Tucker offered me a ride back to my hotel," Vin continued, ignoring Jonah's personal reference.

"The entire ride probably took no more than 20 minutes, maybe less," said Vin.

"Had he been drinking?"

"I saw him have two beers," said Vin.

"Anything else? Drugs of any sort, prescription or street drugs? Cold medication? Anything that might make him drowsy or might not mix well with alcohol?"

"Nothing I know of."

"Did he mention anything like maybe he was tired or in a hurry?"

"No," was all Vin said.

"When he took you back to your hotel, how would you rate his driving?"

"I didn't notice anything out of the ordinary," said Vin. "He wore his helmet. He made sure I wore one too. I thought he drove fine, very well in fact."

"No tricks? No showing off on the bike?"

"No, nothing like that."

"You probably know from the newspaper article that we think he skidded on some oil on the road," said Jonah. "Did you experience any problems with him driving over that same area?"

"No," said Vin. "I didn't notice any problem. But we were on the opposite side of the road. When I was on the motorcycle we were heading east."

"The slick covered each side of the road," said Jonah.

"I didn't notice," said Vin.

"Did he mention he may have some enemies? Anyone who might want to harm him in some fashion?"

This was the first question that did not directly point to Tucker's actions on the motorcycle that evening. Vin waited a few seconds before answering.

"No," he said shaking his head. "He was a very pleasant, easy-going type."

"Anything else we haven't covered that you think may be helpful?" asked Jonah.

"No Sir," said Vin.

"Is there anyone else who might have information for us who was with Tucker that night?"

"None that I know. I saw him briefly talking to a couple of guys at the bar but it looked like friendly conversation."

"Just friendly banter?"

"I would think so."

"Then thank you for your time Mr. Gusto," said Jonah rising from his seat. "If you should think of anything further please give me a call. We're investigating this very vigorously," he said handing Vin his card.

"I understand," said Vin. "I'll do whatever I can but I have a question."

"Sure."

"Can you tell me about how much oil was found on the road where Tugboat skidded?"

Jonah looked through the file. "It's estimated to have been a little better than a gallon. About five quarts according to this," he said.

"I see," said Vin.

"Thank you for your time Mr. Gusto. If you'll excuse me I've got to complete this report. You're free to go," said Jonah, gesturing Vin towards the meeting room door which he then opened for him.

"Thanks," said Vin as he exited the room.

Jonah closed the door behind him, remaining in the small meeting room to complete his report on his meeting with Vincent Gusto.

///

While driving into the police station parking lot Sgt. Henry St. Charles was mentally preparing for his call with Chief Stimmel when he thought he saw a familiar figure leaving the front exit. He stopped the car, rolled down the window and called out to Vin Gusto.

"Hey writer," he called. Vin turned around to see who was calling him.

"Oh no," Vin muttered when he saw Sgt. St. Charles.

"I want to talk to you. Stay right there," said St. Charles, his hand extended from the opened window and moving in an up-and-down motion as he spoke in a most emphatic tone. Vin nodded at St. Charles before looking down the long, narrow road as he went to park the patrol car. Vin was hoping Shanin would suddenly appear and he'd be able to get in her car and leave. He was not required to stay and speak with St. Charles at this time, despite the Sergeant's sudden command but leaving might be seen as refusing to cooperate and that would not be good in a town as small as North Fork Harbor. So Vin reluctantly waited for St. Charles who as promised, reappeared after a few minutes. Walking briskly he did not stop as he approached the station entrance.

"Come with me," was all St. Charles said to Vin as he entered the building, not waiting to see if Vin was following him. Vin took one more look down the road. There was no sign of Shanin. Vin could either continue standing outside or follow St. Charles. He chose the latter.

Once inside the police station there was no sign of St. Charles. Vin never felt comfortable inside a police station and to be at the same one twice in the same day did not sit well with him. He approached the desk officer with whom he earlier spoke. Without looking up from his paperwork the desk officer simply gestured by extending his thumb and thrusting his hand in a backward motion, implying a general direction in which he might find St. Charles. Without saying anything further Vin walked alone down the hallway thinking either he'd see St. Charles or the Sergeant would see him. If neither occurred, Vin would find the nearest exit and leave the building, hopefully for good.

"Hey writer," someone called. Vin turned and saw St. Charles in his office. "Come in here." Vin entered the small, cluttered office. "Close the door," said St. Charles. "Take a seat."

Vin sat on a hard wooden chair and looked directly at St. Charles. Growing up in the Bronx Vin was never comfortable around police officers. He'd already told Officer Jonah what he knew about Vincent Tucker but did so more to relieve his guilt than to help the police. His tolerance for police was waning and he had little desire to help St. Charles with the Lambrusco case. Vin was sure that was the reason St. Charles called him into his office.

"I'd thought you would have gone back to the big city by now," said St. Charles.

"I've been spending some time with a friend," said Vin, trying to give St. Charles as little information as possible.

"How's Maria Lambrusco?" asked St. Charles.

"No comment," said Vin. "How can I help you Sergeant? I've got someone coming to pick me up in a little while. I just came over to provide what I could for the Vincent Tucker accident."

"Did you know Tugboat?"

"Slightly," said Vin. "He gave me a couple of rides."

"So you thought you might have some information for us?"

"I was probably one of the last to see him alive. I had just come from speaking with Officer Jonah when you saw me outside."

"That's very nice of you," said St. Charles. "We appreciate the help."

"So what do you want to talk about?" pressed Vin who sensed the Sergeant was wasting time rather than getting to the point.

"How's your article coming? The one about North Fork Harbor."

"Sergeant I don't think you called me in here to talk about my assignment. What is it that I can do for you? I have someone coming for me shortly."

"Don't worry," said St. Charles. "We can always get you to your appointment. You city people are always in such a hurry."

"You remember how it is," said Vin.

St. Charles had no reason to hold Vin. He was in his office strictly as a courtesy but what insight could Vin have that might help him find the murderer? As Thorsen said, a control freak can't handle something he cannot control. Was Vin Gusto possibly something they could not control yet be useful in helping to find the murderer?

"Seriously," resumed St. Charles. "How's the North Fork Harbor article coming?"

"Seriously?" repeated Vin. "You really want to know?"

"Yes," said St. Charles.

"It was canceled," said Vin, still not sure why he was having this conversation with St. Charles.

"So then you've been out here just passing the time all this while?"

"Yes," said Vin. "In fact the friend with whom I've been passing time should be coming by shortly. So if you don't mind, I may have to end this meeting soon."

"I thought reporters like you didn't have friends," said St. Charles. "Aren't people uncomfortable around someone who might be writing down whatever they say?"

"Not everyone's like you," Vin shot back. Vin clearly didn't like St. Charles's tone. He strongly sensed St. Charles was trying to provoke or trick him into inadvertently disclosing information and rose to leave the room. Not wanting to let St. Charles think he could be intimidated with one foot crossing the office threshold he suddenly stopped and turned to face St. Charles.

"I've got more on this case than you do," said Vin, whose patience was wearing thin.

"What?" asked St. Charles, who was caught off-guard by Vin's comeback.

"I've got a story," said Vin. "You don't even have a serious suspect."

"You don't know that," said St. Charles, rising from his seat.

"I'll tell you something else. I don't think Tugboat's death was an accident," said Vin.

"Why not?" asked St. Charles, somewhat amused by this new turn in the conversation.

"He was an experienced driver, knew the roads."

"He'd been drinking."

"Barely enough to affect a man of his size."

"That cannot yet be confirmed until the blood work's back, besides, no such thing as a minor motorcycle accident," countered St. Charles.

"In The Apple Tree he'd been talking with two guys who worked at Lambrusco's winery, the mechanic and a friend of his, a short guy," said Vin before pausing. "That same night, probably just before Tugboat left the Apple Tree, a woman's car that had been in the same parking lot suddenly lost all of its oil, just vanished from the motor, about five quarts."

St. Charles sat back down considering the information.

"Did she report it?"

"No."

"Why not?"

"I don't know," said Vin. "But that doesn't mean the two events aren't connected."

"Doesn't mean they are. She probably just burned out her oil," said St. Charles. "Women have a tendency not to maintain their cars."

"The plug was missing and the car was serviced not very long ago," said Vin.

"You two have a lot in common. She doesn't have any oil and you don't have a story," said St. Charles who let out a deep breath followed by a grin. Local reporters didn't talk to St. Charles the way Gusto had. He then leaned back in his

chair and glanced out his office window which overlooked the station parking
lot as he quietly considered what Vin had just told him. Vin however, was not a
local reporter. He had too much experience reporting on criminal activity for St.
Charles to casually dismiss his observations, despite the seemingly relaxed manner
in which he was outwardly treating this recent news.

"How do you know I don't have a story? Is that what your spies at the hotel and
the restaurant said?" asked Vin.

St. Charles continued gazing out the window, not wanting Gusto to think that
his last remarks were important. "I think your ride is here," St. Charles calmly said
after a beat without turning to look at Vin. "I'll be seeing you Mr. Gusto."

This time Vin left without saying anything further. As St. Charles tried to
focus his attention on the papers on his desk Officer Krupcheski entered his
office. Closing the door behind him he handed St. Charles a sealed envelope
containing the DNA testing results. Before he opened the envelope St. Charles
ordered Krupchski to immediately seal off the parking lot to the Apple Tree, scour
the grounds and send another team to the Tucker accident scene to do the same
thing. The item they'd be searching for—an oil plug.

As Krupcheski exited St. Charles opened the envelope. In it was the small
white thread in a sealed plastic bag plus a brief written report. The thread had
been sent to the New York State DNA Databank at the Suffolk County Crime
Laboratory in Hauppauge, part of the New York State Police Forensic Investigation
Center (FIC) but no match was found. Intermingled trace amounts of saliva and
blood were found on the thread. After matching them against blood samples taken
at the morgue, they were each determined to be from the victim.

But St. Charles had little time to further consider the evidence. Chief Stimmel
was on the other line.

/ / /

"Great news," Shanin said as Vin entered her car.

"What's that?"

"The car's running fine, no smoke, no noise and my photo shoot for tonight's
been rescheduled. One of the kids is sick. So I was thinking we can go to this great
place for lunch I've been meaning to try. It's in Westhampton Beach. It's about an
hour's drive from here. We can take our time."

"That sounds great," said Vin. "Westhampton Beach? I may know someone
there."

"Somehow I'm not surprised," said Shanin as she drove out of the police
station parking lot and headed west on the Main Rd. For the first few minutes Vin
listened to the engine for any unusual noises. "When we get to Westhampton we
can check the oil," he said.

"You sure know how to have a good time," said Shanin.

"Just looking out for you," said Vin.

"Who do you know there?" asked Shanin.

"A magazine editor," said Vin. "Maybe she'll want to come by and meet us for a coffee. As a freelancer I've got to keep up with my connections."

"Use my cell phone," said Shanin.

"Where are you taking me?" asked Vin.

"The West Bakery and Café. I've heard they make a great seafood salad. I'm going to top it off with a chai latte. It's right in the village and we won't have to worry about anyone watching us have lunch. We'll be way out of their area."

"This may be the first time I can actually relax since I've been out here."

Vin removed Nadia Rivera's card from his shirt pocket and dialed her cell phone number. To his surprise she answered on the first ring.

"Nadia," said Vin. "This is Vin Gusto, the writer you met at Penn Station. I'm staying over in North Fork Harbor."

"Yes, hi Vin, of course I remember you," said Nadia. "But listen I can't stay on long. I just finished an emergency conference call with the office and I've got some work to do if I don't want to be on the next train back to New York."

"Sounds big," said Vin. "But if you get a minute swing by the West Bakery & Café in Westhampton."

"Only if you've got a story for me, otherwise I'm going to be pounding the phone, trying to avoid cutting my vacation short," said Nadia with an unmistakable tone of anxiety in her voice.

"I may have something for you," said Vin sensing an opening. "How about a possible double-murder at a winery on the outskirts of an otherwise quaint seaside village?"

"Sounds like you're selling a murder-mystery screenplay rather than a travel article."

"There's a lot more to the story. You want the exclusive come by the café in about an hour," said Vin. "I've got a photographer on it too."

"You're kidding me right?" asked Nadia. "Are you writing for Travel & Pleasure or some new reality TV show?"

"A stodgy magazine like that can't handle something this hot," said Vin trying to sell Nadia on the story. "This is cutting-edge travel but I've got to tell you Nadia, you're not the first editor I've talked to about this."

"Don't tease me Vin. It's been a rough day."

"I never tease when it comes to a story, you know that. What happened in the office?" Vin wanted to pull information from Nadia while waiting for the right moment to make the case for his story.

"Something went wrong with a new section they're launching," she said. "At the last minute before press time the publisher started complaining that the editorial's not exciting enough. Wants to change things. Typical self-inflicted, ego-driven, last-second publishing emergency that's got to happen while I'm vacationing."

"I know what you mean," said Vin trying to empathize and win her support for his story idea. "Since you're on a working vacation text your assistant that you're meeting with a writer and photographer who've got a useable story that might get you out of this jam. Besides, you sound like you could use a chai latte."

"That does sound good," said Nadia. "I'd love to see you and meet your photographer. If things work out, I'll see you there in about an hour. If not, I'll probably be on the next train to Penn."

"Great," said Vin. "Hope to see you later. We'll save you a seat."

Vin handed the phone back to Shanin.

"Are you crazy?" asked Shanin. "You're trying to sell a story to a national magazine about a murder that may not have taken place."

"Two murders," said Vin.

"It's all speculation," argued Shanin.

"People only care if it's a good story," countered Vin.

"Let's not let details like facts get in the way," she said. 'You're not writing for The Tattler anymore. Stine's not here to bail you out."

"I intend to be completely honest with Nadia, if she shows up," said Vin. "Besides, there was a murder, possibly two. I've got to fill you in on my latest conversations."

"I'm really going to need that latte," sighed Shanin, rolling her eyes as Vin used the remainder of their time in the car to tell her about his meetings with Maria Lambrusco and Sgt. Henry St. Charles. They reached Westhampton Village just as Vin finished informing Shanin of the most recent developments but before they could leave the car he left her with a warning.

"Shanin, if these events are connected, I'm concerned about your safety."

"Stop Vin. They're not related."

"Oil plugs just don't fall out of cars. Experienced drivers don't run off roads they've taken thousands of times," said Vin. "If they struck your car they probably know where you live. Whoever's behind this is smart and sneaky. That can be a dangerous combination."

"I don't want to talk about this anymore for the rest of the day," said Shanin. "I want to enjoy my lunch. You're creeping me out."

"Two innocent men have gotten killed," said Vin. "Maybe you can stay somewhere else for a while, like with your friend Barbara. But if the police can't catch him then I've got to break the story somewhere. Draw some attention that people can't ignore."

"Maybe you can just quietly leave, go home and try to live a calm, normal non-dangerous life. Like I had before you showed up."

"Don't try denying it. You're in this with me Shanin, almost as deeply as I am. I'm worried about your safety and I'd like to see whoever's responsible for this sent to jail. So would Maria Lambrusco. So should you."

"Maria Lambrusco's wealthy enough to hire her own private investigators," said Shanin. "Why don't you leave police work to the police?"

"If Nadia Rivera joins us maybe you should wait in the car."

CHAPTER 25

Planting Seeds of Change

Sgt. St. Charles exhaled before grimacing as he took the call from Chief Stimmel.

"I was about to hang up," said the sarcastic and seemingly perpetually annoyed Stimmel. "I know how busy it can be out there in Blue Crab Cove. I thought maybe you forgot about me, overwhelmed planning security for the next potato festival."

"Impossible to forget you," said St. Charles. "I was actually finishing up with someone regarding the winery case."

"I don't give a rat's ass," said Stimmel, his tone growing more hostile. "I'm calling to tell you that you'd better make progress on this case. I can't spare Thorsen. Some Southampton society broad was killed. The maid found her face down in the swimming pool this morning which is behind the tennis courts but before the horse stables. Now we got two murders. What a way to kick off the summer in Vacation Land USA. You makin' any progress on the dead winemaker? I don't need any more unsolved murders showing up on the evening news."

"Yes Chief," said St. Charles in as confident tone as possible. "I'm preparing my report for you this afternoon. You should have it in the morning." He chose not to mention the death of Vincent Tucker as it was still considered to be a traffic fatality.

"Everyone been interviewed?"

"Yes sir," lied St. Charles.

"Any serious suspects?"

"I think so," he lied again.

"Any new evidence?"

"It'll be in the report sir."

"I'll call you after I've reviewed the report," said Stimmel.

"Very good sir," said St. Charles. "One more thing."

"Go ahead."

"So far we've managed to keep this out of the papers but I don't know how much longer I can manage that."

"That's your problem," said Stimmel. "You know how I feel about your town. Make this thing go away." There was then a click as Stimmel abruptly ended the call.

There were four lies in one conversation thought St. Charles, a result of the mounting pressure. If there was any good news it was that it didn't look like Thorsen would be returning to North Fork Harbor any time soon. Since he promised Stimmel a report for the morning he was immediately going to have to meet with Andy LaBroom to complete the initial interview process. Just then his desk phone rang again. It was Krupcheski.

"Sarge, guess what," said the junior officer.

"I've got no time for guessing. What is it?"

"We may have found something."

"Stimmel just hung up on me. I'm in no mood for small talk. Are you going to tell me what it is or do you still think I'm going to guess?"

"We got an oil plug."

"You do. Where?"

"Right here, in my hand."

"I mean where did you find it?"

"I didn't find it. One of the other guys did."

"Are you trying to give me a heart attack? Where the hell was the plug found and you'd better have put it in an evidence bag. We can't afford sloppy prints."

"It was in some tall grass on the side of the parking lot," Krupcheski said. "We picked it up with the tongs and put it right in the bag."

"Good," said St. Charles. "Bring it in here and have it checked for fingerprints. Then call the officers at the other site to let them know they can stop looking."

"Yes sir."

A recovered oil plug could be the first concrete step towards proving Gusto's theory but it was far from conclusive. But as of now, it was the only potential piece of hard evidence they'd acquired since the discovery of the thread in Dr. Lambrusco's mouth and it was yet to be proven if the two instances were connected or if the oil plug was indeed involved in the spill that resulted in the death of Vincent Tucker. But if the events were connected, this could be the first mistake made by the perpetrator to be discovered by the police. St. Charles then reached for his phone. He telephoned the winery and told Cindy he needed to meet with Andy LaBroom that afternoon.

"I'm not sure if I'll be able to see him before the end of the day," she said.

"Make sure you tell him if he doesn't come to the police station by 5 pm this afternoon I'll send a car to pick him up, wherever he is."

"He's still out in the north end of the field."

"I don't care if he's in Siberia," St. Charles firmly countered, growing inpatient and now sensing that Cindy might be helping LaBroom avoid meeting with him. "Look Cindy, you didn't strike me as the type who wouldn't want to cooperate with the police but like I said, if he's not here by 5 we're coming to get him and we may bring you in as well for good measure." These were empty threats made by St. Charles but he used them to convey a sense of urgency and responsibility. Cindy had admitted dating Andy LaBroom and he felt there was a possibility she'd try to help him.

"I'll do what I can," she said.

"Thank you," said St. Charles who then hung up the telephone. He then looked at his watch. It would most likely be a few hours before he met with LaBroom. He then left a message for Krupcheski to send the oil plug for fingerprint testing and to see which model cars it fit. St. Charles then decided to head home to check-in with his wife Ellen and enjoy a quick dinner before returning to the police station for what he hoped would be the concluding interview of the Lambrusco case. He left word with the desk officer to call him immediately should Andy LaBroom arrive at the station before 5 pm.

"Sergeant," called the desk officer as St. Charles was preparing to leave.

"Yes."

"There's a package at the desk for you. Must've come in today's mail."

When St. Charles went to the desk the clerk handed him a large, brown envelope. The return address contained only the initials M.L. It was from a California-based post office box.

St. Charles returned to his office to examine the package. Carefully opening it, inside he found a brochure and other literature regarding the handheld computer that Maria Lambrusco had bought for her father. From the brochure cover photo he could see the model, although only about four years old, it had probably become obsolete by current standards. It was gray in color with a small screen and large buttons, better suited for a person with heavy hands and who was probably not comfortable with technology than someone who'd grown up around these sorts of things. The sales literature described it as a "rugged" model suitable for those working outdoors in such areas as construction, landscaping and agriculture. He continued to sift through the literature and soon found what he was after. On the cover of the instruction manual was the serial number for Dr. Lambrusco's handheld computer.

Turning to his desktop computer, St. Charles went to the Stolen Computer Registry site. He entered the serial number and other information only to find as he suspected that it was not registered with the national agency which tracks stolen computers. He then registered the computer, noting it was stolen. He entered the case number and contact information, listing Maria Lambrusco as owner and himself as the law-enforcement contact. Should someone obtain the computer and try to sell it there was a chance it would surface on the registry. The merchant would then be obligated to confiscate the computer and he would be notified.

On his drive home St. Charles realized he would pass Allen's garage. The only auto mechanic in North Fork Harbor, Allen ran a one-man operation and serviced

St. Charles's personal car as well as police department vehicles. St. Charles drove his car onto the lot and entered the garage. A hood on a car was opened and Allen was working on the motor. He did not hear St. Charles approach.

"Hey Allen," said St. Charles.

"Who's there?" asked the mechanic, not looking up from his work.

"It's Henry St. Charles. You got a minute?"

"Sure," said Allen turning around and wiping his hands on an already dirty, gray cloth that was on the car's left fender. "Don't tell me your car ain't runnin' again."

"I'm afraid I'm here on police business."

"What's up?"

"I've got a mechanical question. I got word that about five quarts of oil came out of a woman's car the other night. Is that likely?"

"I think I know who you're talking about," he said. "I got a call someone needed an oil plug. Luckily I had a universal in the truck. I was able to patch it up."

"Is that sort of thing likely? Say on an older car perhaps?"

"No. It ain't likely at all, old car or not" said Allen. "It's the first time I ever seen it and you know me, I've been fixing cars since I was 14. In fact, I changed the oil last on the car if we're talking about the same one."

"We probably are. Whose car did it happen to?"

"That photographer girl from the newspaper, Shanin," he said."Nice kid. Comes in here from time to time. Don't got much money so I try to patch up her old tank as best I can."

"Would that plug fit other cars?"

"Sure," he said. "It would fit a lot of GM cars. Pontiacs. Oldsmobiles, stuff like that."

"A Camaro?"

"Sure."

"So they don't fall out easily?"

"Only two ways they come out. Someone screws 'em out or they ain't put in right when the oil got changed. And like I said, as far as I know yours truly changed the oil last on that car so it went in right. I checked my records 'cause it was so unusual. I changed that oil about three months ago. She wouldn't have been able to drive for so long if I hadn't put the plug in right. And I don't think that young lady got down under the car and started messin' with it."

"So you think someone may have fooled with it?"

"I don't know. Who's gonna go under a car and screw around with an oil plug except a mechanic or someone who wants to be one. It's a messy job. She had a guy with her when I met her on the road. He seemed to know a little about cars. Maybe he botched the job and was too embarrassed to say so."

"Could she maybe have hit something on the road?"

"Not really. That thing's protected pretty good from stuff like that the way it's positioned."

"Would you happen to have a spare one around that I can borrow?"

"Sure," said Allen. He then walked to a shelf where he had a wooden box containing miscellaneous parts. He rummaged through what looked like thousands of random screws, bolts, nuts, washers and assorted metal pieces. "Here you go," he then said, handing St. Charles what appeared to be a thick, heavy screw with a washer that had a slit in it under the head of the screw.

"You see here," said Allen, pointing a grease-stained finger at the washer. "This here's what they call a lock-washer. It stays with the plug 'cause it don't come off unless you screw it off on account of this washer. You get what I'm sayin'?"

"You're saying once this goes in it's going to stay in 90 percent of the time."

"Ninety-nine-point-ninety-nine percent of the time," he emphatically said. "The engineers who design these things know what they're doin'."

"Will this fit that girl's car that lost the oil?"

"Yeah. It'll fit."

"Can I hold onto this for a few days?"

"Yeah, keep it for as long as you want. I got a few around," said Allen. "Bring it back when you're done. It ain't likely I'm gonna use 'em but you never know."

"Okay," said St. Charles. "I'll let you get back to your work. Thanks for the information and the sample."

"You bet," said Allen returning to his previous position under the opened hood. "I got to get this baby hummin' before the customer shows up."

When St. Charles got back into his car he studied the oil plug. Holding it between his thumb and index finger he could see it was dirty and scratched but still contained a faint odor of motor oil. He tore a sheet of paper from his notebook and wrapped the plug in it. He then wiped his fingers on the same sheet of paper, started the car and resumed his drive home all the while thinking about showing the plug to Andy LaBroom in a few hours and asking questions about his friend, Scott Larson, the mechanic.

/ / /

Vin and Shanin were completing their lunch and discussing what to have for dessert when Vin noticed a vaguely familiar figure coming through the café doorway. Recognizing the oversized straw sunhat from their chance encounter in Penn Station, Vin rose from the table to greet Nadia Rivera. Bringing her to the table he quickly introduced her to Shanin. Without asking, Vin then ordered chai lattes for the women and a plain espresso for himself. After finishing their coffees and making some small talk, Shanin announced she was going to do some window shopping in the village and would rejoin Vin in about one-half hour. Vin took it as a sign that he should move the conversation with Nadia to business.

"So are you going to have to cut your vacation short?" asked Vin.

"Listen Vin," said Nadia leaning forward with her hands folded across the table. "Don't repeat this to anyone in the business. My publisher is driving me crazy. I don't know what he wants for this new section. I haven't had a real vacation in two years, since we started this magazine. The first time I'm away the office is calling me. The way I feel right now I may never go back."

Nadia had provided Vin with the ideal opening but he did not want to look too anxious in his dealings with her.

"Be careful what you wish for," warned Vin. "I sometimes used to feel the same way about the Tattler but working on your own is tough. Assignments can be hard to come by. Pay is usually slow."

"But you've got your freedom," countered Nadia. "I envy that."

"Everything's got its price," said Vin. "You've probably got health insurance."

"A minimal plan," she said. "Everyone's cutting back wherever they can."

"That's where I may be able to help you," said Vin. "Has the publisher given you any guidelines?" Some sort of direction or vision for this new section?"

"Not really," she sighed. "He almost seems like he's running this project on emotion and adrenalin. I think he has a lot riding on it too. Upper-management's watching very closely from what I hear and although we're doing well for a new magazine he can't afford to make a mistake. There's a lot of money at stake. And as you well know, Travel & Pleasure's the monster that's got this space smothered."

"I know what you mean," said Vin. "But even T&P will stumble from time to time."

"How do you mean? The magazine's beautiful."

"It is," said Vin. "If you're reading it in the nursing home, which is where most of its readers will be in a few years. You can't publish a winning magazine with a backward-looking editorial."

"That's how we feel too," agreed Nadia. "But we haven't hit that home run yet. We need that story that will really set us apart to start gaining circulation. But I thought you were writing for Pat Goode."

"It didn't work out," said Vin. "I didn't get a reason, just a call from Pat's assistant and a small kill fee. No sooner did I get out here than the story was canceled. I hadn't written a word. Barely taken a note but I did uncover a lot of stuff for what might be a very unusual travel article."

"What do you mean Vin?"

"Pat wanted a 'happy story'," said Vin. "Kids on ponies, sailboats, girls on the beach and an interview with a winemaker," he said. "Instead I think I've got a murdered winemaker and possibly a second murder in this otherwise cute seaside village. If your publisher's looking to rock the travel world I think I can help you," said Vin.

Nadia admitted she was intrigued and asked Vin to tell her everything he knew about the possible murders. She produced a pen and small pad from her bag and took notes as Vin recounted nearly everything that had happened to him since his arrival in North Fork Harbor.

"That's a pretty amazing story," Nadia said when Vin finished. "You're sure it's all true."

"Absolutely," said Vin. "Do we have a deal?"

"Not yet," she said. "I've got to 'sell' it to my publisher if he hasn't yet had a nervous breakdown or found something he likes better."

"Okay," said Vin. "What else?"

"I'm going to want to talk to Maria Lambrusco," she said. "Plus the story's got to be exclusive to us and I want exclusive photos and statements from Maria. In fact, I'm going to want to meet with her and I want you to talk to one of the police officers involved in the investigation. We need their perspective."

"That's a tall order," said Vin, leaning back in his chair.

"Look Vin," said Nadia, rising from her seat. "I'm reaching the point where I don't care. I've got to get going. I am still on vacation."

"Wait a minute," said Vin. He wasn't sure if Nadia was bluffing but he was absolutely sure that he could not afford to lose another assignment. "I didn't want to spoil your vacation. I just thought I could help."

"Go ahead then," she said.

"Before I set up a meeting between you and Maria I've got to be guaranteed you're taking the story. I'm not sure I can get the cooperation of the police department," countered Vin. "Plus you haven't said what you'd pay me and the photographer."

"The highest I can go is $6,000," said Nadia, returning to her seat.

The conversation then came to a sudden stop. Vin looked down at the table. Shanin would be back soon he thought. It would be helpful if he'd made a deal with Nadia by the time she returned. This was $1,000 more than what Pat Goode offered. He wasn't sure if he could get Maria to cooperate but didn't want to tell that to Nadia.

"What about 'selling' it to your publisher?

"I'll handle my job, you handle yours," she said. "If he doesn't like it, I don't care. I'm about this close to quitting," she said, holding her thumb and index finger close together for emphasis. "I'll shove the story down his throat if I have to."

"I'll need a 25 percent advance within 48 hours," pressed Vin. "That's fair under the circumstances."

"We can do that," said Nadia. "I'll need the story and photos in about a week. I'll be back in New York by then and won't be able to go much further out on the schedule."

Vin wasn't sure if he'd have all the information necessary to meet her deadline but couldn't take a chance on losing the assignment.

"No problem," he said.

"When do you think you'll start writing?"

"As soon as I get the advance," he said. "Then it's a deal, right?"

"Absolutely," said Nadia with a smile.

The two then shook hands across the small café table.

"The payment includes the photographer's fee. I don't care how the two of you divide it."

In his excitement to close the deal Vin had forgotten about Shanin's share but time was running out. He wouldn't be able to afford to stay much longer in North Fork Harbor without a fresh cash infusion and was sure Shanin would agree to a fifty-fifty split on a previously canceled assignment.

"When will you be certain about the advance?" Vin asked.

"Within 24 hours," she said. "Probably sooner. I can call you on your cell phone or leave a message at your hotel. I'll give you the exact due date then as well. And don't be late or I'm cutting 25% from your fee. I'll need the money for a good sedative."

"Why don't you leave a message with Shanin?" said Vin. "I'll give you her cell number. Mine's been a little shaky out here and the hotel hasn't been too reliable. Have the office overnight me a check to the hotel. Once I get it I'll start writing." Vin wrote down the hotel's address on a slip of paper, copying it from his receipt.

"When do I get to meet Maria?" she then asked.

"After I get my advance," said Vin, using the lure of the meeting as leverage to ensure prompt payment.

"Fine," agreed Nadia who then began to again rise from her seat. "I'm going to go back to my room, sort this out and tell the publisher he can breathe easy. I know I've got the story he's after," she said. "I don't really have any other choice. I can return to the office and be just as frustrated as I am here. And it's much more pleasant to be frustrated in Westhampton with an ocean breeze blowing through my window than in the office with a crazed publisher breathing down my neck. Wouldn't you agree?"

"Absolutely," said Vin. "If I were in your designer flip-flops I'd make the exact same decision. But I do have one more question."

"What's that?" asked Nadia.

"How can you be so sure your publisher will agree?"

"Because I'm going to personally guarantee that Vin Gusto's going to deliver a killer story that's going to make Travelzonia copies fly off the stands and at least for one month crush T&P. It's called 'editor's prerogative'," she said. "And there's one more thing."

"What's that?"

Nadia looked directly at Vin, briefly hesitating before speaking.

"I refuse to cut my vacation short," she said. "Don't you think it's a little silly that the editor of a travel magazine can't get away for a few days?"

"I completely agree," said Vin. "Thanks for coming by. I'm really looking forward to working with you."

"Same here. Thanks for thinking of me," she said before turning to exit.

Vin couldn't wait to share the news with Shanin.

CHAPTER 26

Assessing the Harvest

Vin waited until they were in her car and heading back to North Fork Harbor before giving her the news.

"You're going too far with this," said Shanin when Vin told her about his agreement with Nadia.

"And you're not going far enough," he replied. "Shanin, we have an opportunity to revive our careers. I'm going ahead with the story."

"Nothing's proven Vin," she pleaded.

"It's still an interesting story," he said.

"You can destroy what little integrity you have left."

"I've had enough for one day," said Vin. "Please take me back to my hotel. I need to arrange a meeting between Maria Lambrusco and Nadia Rivera. If I can make that happen I may then get the police to provide a statement or two. And with any luck when I get to the hotel I won't find my bags out on the street."

Shanin had no response and kept driving.

"I don't want you staying at your place tonight," continued Vin. "Did you call Barbara or is there another place you can stay?"

"If I had a decent boyfriend, one with a paying job, maybe I could stay at his place," she said.

"I don't even feel safe at the Crashing Sea Gull," said Vin. "I'm certainly not going to have you there. It's not my fault there's no good hotel here."

"Maybe we can sleep in the car," she said. "I know a parking lot with a 24-hour security guard. How's that for accommodations?"

"Give me Barbara's number," said Vin. "I'm calling her right now to see if you can stay there."

"I'll take care of myself," she said.

"And maybe tomorrow I'll have to find a new photographer too."

"Yeah," she said. "Maybe I'll quit. Unlike you I find it easy to leave a job that hasn't paid me."

"Nadia's having a check sent in 48 hours."

"If her publisher agrees."

"She said it was practically a done deal. We shook on it."

"You know what you're trouble is?"

"I have a feeling I'm about to find out," answered Vin.

"You're too trusting. A handshake doesn't mean anything. Wait until you get the check before arranging meetings. You should never have trusted Pat Goode. Look where that's gotten you."

"I never trusted Pat but there was no reason not to trust her," countered Vin. "I took the assignment because that's what writers do. I don't think Pat knew what was going to happen. Besides, this hasn't been so bad. We got to spend time together and now I'm writing for a new magazine."

"And two people are dead."

The two of them then said nothing for a while until Vin spoke.

"You've never gotten over it, have you?" he asked her without warning.

"Gotten over what?"

"The death of your father," said Vin. "And how your life changed because of it. He was your security blanket, wasn't he? And you've never been able to replace him."

"I'm sorry Dr. Freud, therapy's not in session right now. Can you come back at a different time?"

"I can sense it," said Vin. "Maria losing her father. Me showing up without warning. All of these unconnected, sordid events. This whole affair's got you confused over things which you thought were settled or which you chose not to confront."

"I'm so glad you majored in journalism," she said. "You would've made a terrible psychologist."

"I'm not sure about that. There's no one left who knows you like I do."

Silence then returned and neither of them said anything further until they reached the hotel. Shanin stopped the car under a streetlight near the main entrance. There were no police cars in sight.

"Listen," said Vin, with his hand on the door and staring straight ahead, not looking at Shanin. "I'm sorry if I went too far. I guess I'm a little stressed myself. I want you to finish this assignment with me. Collect a good fee. But I can't do it if you're not going to be safe."

Vin turned to look at Shanin. He was struck by the tears that were running down her face. She lifted her hand to wipe them with her sleeve.

"I don't know what to say Vin. It was bad enough losing my father but then my mother, in a way, left me too. I never hear from her unless I call first. Not even during the holidays. I barely know her husband. I occasionally talk to my brother but he's busy with his own family. At least you and your mom stuck together."

Vin reached over and put his arm around her. "It's not easy," was the only thing he could think to say.

"How'd you do it?" she asked. "You and your mom, with no money, no real help."

"We struggled," he said. "I grew up fast. I learned pretty quickly that my mom and I needed each other. Somehow we made it work."

"Once my father died my family practically disappeared," she said. "There was enough money but our family ended."

"I don't know which is worse," he said.

"Being alone is definitely worse," said Shanin. "A person can find a way to make money but it takes more than one person to make a family."

"I'm really sorry," said Vin. "I had no idea you felt this way." He leaned over further and kissed her on the lips before pulling himself away. "This probably isn't the right time," he said. "But I'm serious about you not being alone tonight. Did you call Barbara?"

"No but it worked out," said Shanin. "Barbara called when I was walking around Westhampton. She has to work late tonight and asked me to watch her boys. I'm going there now. She said I could stay overnight. Didn't ask why. I'll be fine but I'm worried about you. She said you could stay over too, in the basement."

"It's better if we separate for tonight. I'll be fine in the hotel," he said. "I'm going to be up late writing, organizing my notes. No one will surprise me. I've got an assignment. I'm going to call Maria Lambrusco in the morning and see if I can arrange for her to meet with Nadia even though you think I should wait. If anything happens call me right away."

"All right," she said. Vin then exited the car and Shanin watched him enter the hotel lobby before driving away.

Vin came through the unlocked front door and stood alone in the lobby. There was no one behind the front desk but on the counter he spotted a small envelope with his name scrawled across the front of it. He reached for the envelope and opened it. Inside was a small slip of paper with two words written on it: "Call Gloria."

///

As Sgt. St. Charles left Allen's garage he decided to make one more stop before heading home. Andy LaBroom was apparently reluctant to meet with St. Charles, nor was he required to do so, but there was nothing stopping St. Charles from visiting him. Instead of going through the main entrance St. Charles drove along the road that paralleled the north side of North Fork Harbor Vineyards. Cindy had earlier told him that LaBroom was with some equipment that had broken down on the north side of the vineyard. If the breakdown was as serious as Cindy had described and with his understanding of the local terrain, St. Charles didn't think it would be too hard to find where LaBroom might be. He drove for a while, scanning the neat, well-manicured rows of vines until he saw what he was looking for. St. Charles then drove the police car onto the side of the road, discreetly parking it behind a cluster of wild maple trees. Before exiting the vehicle he took the oil plug Allen had given him, putting it in his pocket before quietly closing the car door. He quickly walked through the rows towards the disabled equipment he had earlier spotted. St. Charles expected to find at least a small group of men clustered around the equipment but instead could see only one man.

"Hey there," St. Charles said, emerging from one of the vineyard rows.

The man who looked up was not Andy LaBroom.

"Hey Sergeant," said Scott Larson, remaining by the equipment but watching St. Charles. "What do you think I did now?"

"Nothing," said St. Charles. "How are you managing in this heat?"

"Not bad. I try not to think about it."

"You working solo today?"

"Yeah," he said, turning his back to St. Charles to continue with his work. "I can't get no helpers who want to help."

"Andy LaBroom around?"

"Not no more," said Larson. "He was here a while ago but he took off."

"Know where he went?"

"No. If you really got to find him ask Cindy the secretary. She usually knows where everyone is."

"I did. She told me I'd find him out here."

"Like I said Sergeant, he ain't been around for a while. Soon after I showed up he took off."

"Any idea where he was off to?"

"Andy don't say much. He don't have to."

"Maybe I'll give Cindy a call. There could have been a change of plans," said St. Charles. "Listen," he continued, reaching his hand into his pocket and removing the small wad of paper. "You know what this is?" he asked Larson, revealing the oil plug Allen had given him.

"Sure," said Larson. "It's an oil plug."

"You know from what kind of car?"

"Could be anything from General Motors. They got plugs that fit a lot of models."

"You want to look more closely at it?" asked St. Charles, holding the plug in the paper on the palm of his hand towards Larson, hoping he would take hold of it and leave a fingerprint. "Maybe you can tell me specifically what type of car it's from."

"No. I don't need to see it no more," he said. "I know what the hell it is."

"Let me ask you another question. These things fall out of cars very easily."

"Never."

"One just like this was found outside the Apple Tree," said St. Charles. "It may be a part of the Tucker accident."

"I already told you," said Larson. "I didn't do nuthin'."

"You might not have done anything but you may know something."

The two men then stared at each other, neither saying anything.

"Withholding information is obstruction of justice," continued St. Charles. "By impeding a police investigation you can be charged as an accessory. You're a smart man. You're a respected mechanic and businessperson. There's already an out-of-town reporter snooping around. This isn't going to go away until it's solved."

"I got work to do Sergeant," said Larson, turning his back. St. Charles, reacting to Larson's insulting behavior stepped forward and grabbed the larger man by the back of his shoulder and spun him around. "I got work to do too. Tell Andy I came by to see him," he said. The two men stood alone in the vineyard facing each other. The larger Larson, a heavy wrench in his hand, could easily have brushed St. Charles back in the isolated vineyard but he remained still. Realizing Larson would talk no further St. Charles removed his hand, turned and left the vineyard.

Back in the patrol car St. Charles telephoned the station to see if Andy LaBroom had arrived.

"Negative," said the desk officer who added that there was a message from Officer Krupcheski. "A partial fingerprint had been found on the oil plug the police officers recovered. It was run through the data base but no match was found."

St. Charles thanked him and hung up the phone. He had a partial fingerprint with no match and no LaBroom. He then called the winery office but got no answer. Next he called LaBroom's personal telephone number and again there was no answer. He chose not to leave a message each time. LaBroom was not required to meet with St. Charles. Perhaps his fake threat that afternoon with Cindy backfired. He would have to submit his report to Chief Stimmel without comments from LaBroom. While it didn't prove anything and certainly was not a crime, it was nevertheless odd for an innocent person who was close to the victim to refuse to cooperate with investigators.

Why did Larson refuse to touch the oil plug and what did he mean when he said he didn't do anything? Was he referring to the Lambrusco murder, the sabotaging of the car which may have led to the death of Vincent Tucker, or was it simply a thoughtless comment made by a gruff mechanic who did not appreciate an unannounced visit by an interrogating police officer on a sweltering afternoon? He had gambled in his exchange with Larson, disclosing information in an attempt to increase the pressure. St. Charles knew Larson and LaBroom were together the night Vincent Tucker died after talking with Vin Gusto. While too experienced to expect Larson to reveal anything in the vineyard he also knew when people with knowledge of crimes had time to think things over they often cooperated, especially if they were innocent and had something to lose, like a reputation or their freedom.

///

Vin immediately went to the payphone and dialed his mother's home number. She answered on the first ring.

"Hi Mom, it's me Vin."

"Are you still on Long Island? I got your letter."

"I'm in North Fork Harbor, eastern Long Island, on assignment. How are you doing?"

"I'm fine. I went by your apartment late this morning to drop off your mail."

"How was inside the apartment?"

"The inside was the usual mess. When are you coming home?"

"I'm not sure, in a few days. Anything else?"

"The hallway was kind of dirty. There were actually a few grapes on the floor by your door. I guess they fell out of someone's grocery bag."

"Grapes?" Vin repeated.

"Yeah. Not big grapes like you get in the supermarket. These were small, really dark, almost black grapes. There was just a few."

"Did you save them? What happened to them?"

"The super got rid of them. They could attract rodents."

Vin stopped talking for a moment, allowing the news to settle.

"Try to go back and get one or two of those grapes. Save them for me. Don't eat any. I'll call you when I have a better idea of when I'm coming back but if anything else happens to my apartment or you find any more grapes call me right away."

"It would be a lot easier if your cell phone worked."

"Service isn't good out here."

"It's not good anywhere if you don't pay the bill."

"This assignment could be a sign of bigger and better things to come for me."

"I hope so, you deserve it."

"As soon as I get back we'll go to dinner and I'll tell you everything that's happened. Is everything good with you?"

"Sure. I'm fine," she said. "I'm just worried for you."

"There's nothing to worry about Mom. Thanks for getting my mail. And Mom, one more thing."

"What's that?"

"Any checks come?"

"None that I can see."

"Okay. Thanks again. I'll see you soon."

Vin hung up the phone and quickly walked to his hotel room.

/ / /

Before entering his hotel room Vin quickly surveyed the perimeter around the door. Not noticing anything unusual he quickly inserted the key into the lock and opened the door. He then grabbed the waste basket in the room and slipped it over the threshold, preventing the door from closing behind him as he examined the room's interior. He checked under the bed, inside the closet and in the bathtub but found no signs of anything out of the ordinary. He then quickly removed the waste basket from the threshold and locked the door. Vin then took the chair in his room and turning it backwards, lodged it under the doorknob. He then took a fast shower and while disturbed by the news his mother had given him, tried to put it out of his mind as he began preparing to write his first article for Travelzonia. He felt confident Nadia would get the assignment approved and would need to be ready to begin as soon as he received the final word as the deadline would be very close. It would be his first assignment in a mainstream publication since leaving the Tattler and he could not let this chance slip away—no matter what distractions, threats or obstacles that may lie before him. Vin instinctively knew that this could be a major career opportunity and had every intention of making the most of it.

Since the room's only chair was being used to block the door Vin knelt down on the floor next to the bed and taking out a pad and pen, began reconstructing the events of the past few days as best he could, making notes in the margins to describe local scenes such as vineyards, ferries, fishermen and children playing on the beach. He made a note to write something favorable about The Crashing Sea Gull as well as to mention the supportive nurse at the hospital, the friendly woman behind the counter at the IGA and the helpful mechanic. There was a jovial man named Vincent Tucker who met a sudden and tragic end to include and of course the death of Dr. Lambrusco, the grapes found in his mouth, the despair expressed by his daughter Maria and the little progress made in solving either case. In his mind Vin tried to connect the two deaths but could find nothing substantial. He thought about the tone he would take in his article, which he realized would be quite an unusual tack for a travel magazine. And then, as he so frequently had in the past, Vin thought about Shanin and what she revealed to him in the car earlier that evening. There was a hole in her life. He had not been aware of the pain it had caused her. What made Shanin suddenly break down and tell him how disappointed she was with what took place in her family after the death of her father? Could he somehow fill that void?

CHAPTER 27

Growing Heavy for the Vintage

Now fairly certain that Andy LaBroom was not going to come to the police station to be interviewed, St. Charles nevertheless had to prepare the report for Chief Stimmel. He checked-in with the desk clerk, poured himself a cup of black coffee and went to his office to complete the report. On his desk was an envelope from the crime lab. He opened it. Inside was the blood alcohol content (BAC) report for Vincent Tucker. It was 0.07%, a fraction below the New York State legal maximum of 0.08%. While important, it did not make for a compelling case of driving-under-the-influence, especially for an experienced driver on a familiar road. More importantly, it underscored what Vin Gusto had told him about Tucker's driving ability the evening he crashed. Tucker and Gusto had driven the same route a few minutes earlier in the opposite direction without incident. Sometime between leaving Gusto at his hotel and Tucker making his return, an oil slick appeared. Coincidentally earlier that same night, about five quarts of oil suddenly disappeared from the car belonging to Gusto's companion. Did the oil come from her car? It was impossible to tell at this point as the road crew had cleaned it from the area. It was similarly impossible to know if the oil plug that Krupcheski and his team recovered was the one from her car.

Was the death of Vincent Tucker an accident or was it deliberate? St. Charles's logical side still did not think it was likely that the deaths of Tucker and Lambrusco were connected. But experience also taught St. Charles that people aren't always logical, especially when murder is involved. They're often motivated by abstract factors like passion, greed or revenge he believed. As the men earlier theorized, it may have been the work of someone settling an old score. Lambrusco had lived in many parts of the world and possibly was engaged in a controversial experiment. That theory, if true, would seemingly have no connection to the death of Tucker but might have made the reclusive Lambrusco vulnerable.

St. Charles removed a pencil from the glass jar he kept on the far corner of his desk. A multi-colored crayon drawing one of his daughters made in art class was taped to the outside of it. He couldn't remember which of his daughters made the drawing or for how long he'd had it. The drawing consisted of two stick figures, a small and large one. The larger stick figure was mostly colored in blue. He wore a holster and gun on his waist and a flat, triangular blue hat. The smaller one appeared to be wearing a yellow dress and black curly hair. The rest of the drawing consisted of a blue sky, a yellow kite and a large orange sun. On the bottom of the drawing was a note written in dark blue letters. It read: World's Best Daddy.

Removing his gaze from the drawing and holding the pencil upside-down, St. Charles tapped the end on the report he was about to prepare for Stimmel. He'd soon have to file a similar report for Vincent Tucker. There were no substantial clues or motivations in either case, simply a few coincidences. In fact, one of the few things the two cases had in common was that there were very scant clues for each. Was Tucker's death simply an accident? Was he an innocent victim of a fatal twist of fate or was St. Charles's own paranoia asserting itself? While St. Charles didn't think Stimmel would care, he did not want to submit an incomplete report on the Lambrusco case but the fact was he did not have the cooperation of LaBroom, a key person of interest, nor did he have any concrete reason to suspect him.

Had someone come to North Fork Harbor and committed the perfect crime? St. Charles did not believe it was possible to commit a perfect crime. Crimes are committed by human beings, each of whom, as Thorsen noted, is flawed. St. Charles also believed that there was a solution to each crime and it often was the discovery of this flaw that lead to a resolution. Many cases were left unsolved and perpetrators never caught not because their acts were perfectly committed but because law-enforcement organizations often did not have the resources to commit to solving the number of crimes which regularly take place. Individuals such as he often had to decide whether to continue pursuing a case or declare it "inactive," a police classification indicating that the case was unresolved but no longer being actively investigated. Maybe his unwillingness to give up, to refuse to recommend that the Tucker case be classified an accident and the Lambrusco murder be moved to the "inactive" file was his fatal flaw? St. Charles did not like unsolved cases or unanswered questions. In this respect he was a lot like Vin Gusto.

///

Vin had written by hand nearly everything he could think of for his story. Once he received his advance he'd need a computer. He'd wanted to check-out of the Crashing Sea Gull and do the majority of his writing in a more secure location but still needed to stay in or near North Fork Harbor. Perhaps Shanin's friend Barbara would let him use the computer in her home. He estimated it would take him about two full days to complete the story. While he had not yet made the call, he was certain Maria Lambrusco would agree to meet Nadia Rivera as it was Maria who asked that Vin try to get a respected publication interested in the story. He was not so sure about getting anything more than an official statement from the local police department. But after he'd submit his story to Nadia, his schedule would be fairly open. Vin could then return to his Bronx apartment and resume his prior life as a freelance reporter or maybe new opportunities would present themselves.

Vin then took a long shower but still had trouble sleeping. The time on the clock radio was 12:15 am. He didn't want to leave his room. There was however, one person he could call and leave a message for at that time. Someone would answer the telephone at the police station where he could leave a message for Sergeant St. Charles seeking a statement. St. Charles would definitely want to know for which publication Vin was writing. How would St. Charles react when he heard a national publication was taking his story? Vin found the telephone number for the North Fork Harbor Police Station in the telephone directory in his room.

"North Fork Harbor Police Headquarters," the voice on the other end answered.

"I'd like to leave a message for Sergeant St. Charles," said Vin.

"One moment please."

Vin stayed on hold for less than a minute when a new voice came on the line.

"Sergeant St. Charles speaking."

Vin was surprised to hear St. Charles's voice. "This is Vin Gusto," he said. "I'm sorry to bother you at this late hour but I was actually planning to leave a message."

"Gusto, the writer," said St. Charles. "Can't you sleep? Maybe it's writer's block."

"I've never had writer's block. In fact, I'm actually writing about the Lambrusco case," said Vin. "I was wondering if I could ask you a question?"

"Will this be on-the-record or off? asked St. Charles.

"I'd prefer it to be on," said Vin.

"I'd prefer if you spoke to the headquarters media person," said St. Charles. "He can give you the official statement."

"I'd prefer a statement from you. A comment from the local police officer running the investigation is worth far more than a bland statement from some guy in the community-relations office," said Vin.

"Who are you writing for?" asked St. Charles. "Did you get that job with the local paper?"

"I'm writing for Travelzonia," said Vin. "I don't know anything about a local job."

"Travel what?" St. Charles repeated. "For a minute I thought you were serious."

"It's a relatively new publication," said Vin. "But it's nationally circulated."

"Can't anyone mind their business? You know no one in any police department's going to talk about an open investigation."

"That's too bad. Maybe someone should," said Vin. "Everyone else is. I think they'd want their viewpoint included. Otherwise it's going to be pretty one-sided."

"I see," said St. Charles. "I'm actually finishing a report. Can I get back to you tomorrow?"

"Yes, of course," said Vin. "That's what I meant when I said I was planning on leaving a message."

"Fine," said St. Charles. "I'll call you at this number tomorrow. Sometime late morning. I don't know if I'll be able to give you a statement but I'll call either way. How's that?"

"That would be fine," said Vin. "Thank you."

"Anything else new?" St. Charles asked.

"Yeah," said Vin. "You might be interested to know my mom found grapes outside my apartment door in the Bronx yesterday."

"What?" was all St. Charles could say in response.

"She said there were a few small, dark grapes outside my apartment door."

"You're kidding me, right?"

"No," said Vin.

"How far's your apartment from mid-Manhattan?"

"About 30 minutes by subway."

There was a pause then until Vin resumed speaking.

"I told my mother to report it to the police but I'm not sure if she did. You remember how it is in the city. People there aren't too keen on going to the police. They prefer to solve their problems themselves."

"Is there a security camera in the building?"

"No," answered Vin. "We're lucky we've got working locks. And I doubt if there's a witness. Before you ask, my mom did not save any of the grapes. She figured they were trash, which I think is what most people, except maybe you and me, might think."

"Fair enough," said St. Charles. "I'll speak with you tomorrow."

Pleasantly surprised by St. Charles's relative cooperation Vin actually breathed a small sigh of relief. At the most, he expected a very brief exchange with St. Charles. He then lied back on the bed, closed his eyes and fell asleep. By now, even Vin was too tired to worry about what St. Charles might be thinking.

While Vin may have now felt relieved St. Charles did not. He was frustrated enough by his inability to make progress with the case and did not want to be known beyond the North Fork Harbor boundaries as the lead investigating officer of what would surely be portrayed as an inept and outwitted small town police force in a national magazine. St. Charles also knew headquarters would not cooperate with a journalist on an open investigation and at the same time knew he would be blamed if the department was not positively portrayed in the article. Nor was he sure if Gusto was telling the truth about the grapes outside his apartment door. Maybe he was trying to needle him in response to the way St. Charles treated him earlier in the week. Aggravated by Gusto's call and LaBroom's failure to cooperate, St. Charles decided not to submit his report to Stimmel and instead prepared to leave the station. On his way out he curtly told the desk clerk he was going home for the evening but not before putting a blank report form and new pen in his briefcase. While LaBroom may have chosen not to see St. Charles, there was nothing stopping the sergeant from visiting him.

/ / /

St. Charles slowed the police car as he approached the North Fork Harbor Winery entranceway. Stopping at the head of the driveway he shut the headlights. He could see a light on in the winery office. Still with his headlights out he parked the car on the side of the driveway and walked to the office. Even during the short walk down the driveway the nighttime heat and humidity was making St. Charles uncomfortable. His clothes began to stick to his skin as his body responded with perspiration in the steamy night air. When he reached the door he soundly knocked on it with his night stick.

"Anybody home?" St. Charles loudly asked when no one came to the door. "Police," he then announced. St. Charles could hear footsteps inside approaching the door.

"Coming." It was a man's voice. "Sergeant," said a seemingly surprised Andy LaBroom opening the door.

"How you doing Andy?"

"Not bad," he said. "A little tired you know, my head's still spinnin' after all that's happened around here. Cindy gave me your message. I was in the city the other day and just haven't been able to find the time to call you."

"No problem," said St. Charles, surprised by the sudden rambling from the normally taciturn LaBroom. "I'm glad I found you. Maybe you can help me. Can I come in?"

"Sure. We can sit in the reception area," Andy said, gesturing towards two available chairs in front of the receptionist's desk.

Andy was wearing a white shirt that was a bit large for his frame. The sleeves were rolled but St. Charles noticed a tear on the left one.

"Why are you wearing long sleeves on a night like tonight?" asked St. Charles who also noticed two small abrasions on the same wrist. "And what happened to you? Your sleeve is torn. Your wrist is scratched. You got a frisky cat at home?"

St. Charles sensed a nervousness which he was going to try to exploit.

"I don't know," said Andy. "Guess I just ain't gotten around to changin', been so busy and all with the harvest creepin' up. Guess the shirt got caught on a vine or fence post. I been so busy I didn't even notice."

"What about those red marks?"

"Probably just bug bites," said LaBroom, looking down at his wrist.

"In a line like that? Must be pretty smart bugs."

"Whatever," LaBroom shrugged.

"I didn't know running a vineyard was such hazardous job," St. Charles tried to joke.

"Look what happened to the Doc," he said leaning forward. LaBroom then reached for a scissor on Cindy's desk and trimmed off the loose threads. He then turned to deposit the threads in a waste basket and return the scissor to the desk. LaBroom did not notice when a small piece of thread from his sleeve slipped onto the table. While he had his back to him St. Charles quickly grabbed the loose thread and slipped it into his shirt pocket.

"How can I help you Sergeant?" asked LaBroom returning to his chair across the table from St. Charles. His torn left sleeve was now fully unrolled, covering his wrist.

"You're not a suspect. You can relax," St. Charles lied. "But I would like to talk to you. If you've got a few minutes you'd help me complete my report. They're screaming for it over at headquarters. You know, procedural stuff. They don't care if the case is solved. They just want to see some paperwork filed."

"What about my rights?"

"You've got the same rights as anyone else. You're entitled to a lawyer if you like but right now you're just helping your local police officer."

"In that case I'll do what I can."

"You must've had big business in the city to leave during such a busy time," said St. Charles.

"Yeah, not bad I guess."

"So what's going to happen here without Dr. Lambrusco?"

"I don't know," said LaBroom. "Guess the staff will pitch in as best it can. The Doc never did much of the actual work. He supervised. Anyone can do that."

"I know what you mean," said St. Charles, trying to build a false sense of empathy with him. "We have the same problem in the police department. I understand you handle the farm chemicals. Know anything about tetrachloradyne?"

"It's a synthetic."

"What do you mean?"

"It's a synthetic insecticide," explained LaBroom. "Was outlawed years ago. Very powerful. We might've had some in the shed."

"You keep an inventory of your chemicals don't you?"

"Yeah but that stuff's so old it grandfathered into inventory. Could've evaporated by now. We don't use it no more. It's too harsh. A lot of environmental restrictions these days."

"Can anyone get into the shed or is it limited access?"

"Workers go in and out of the shed every day. That don't mean they're touching the chemicals. We got tools, equipment in there too."

"Ever use it yourself, even years ago?"

"No, not really."

St. Charles paused to consider his next line of questioning.

"The Doc took a lot of notes in his handheld computer didn't he?"

"Yeah," said LaBroom. "He was one of those specific types. Everything always had to be just right."

"Any idea where that handheld may be?"

"No. I didn't even know it was missing. Did you check with the daughter?"

"She doesn't know either. Any idea who might want something like that?"

"No. I think he wrote in Italian, you know, native language. Whoever tries to read it will need to deal with that."

"That's not surprising," said St. Charles "Besides, a translation program's pretty easy to come by."

The two of them sat still before St. Charles continued the conversation. He remembered the earlier discussion about disrupting the control freak.

"You've got nothing to hide," he said, leaning across the desk. "What do you think happened to the Doc?" asked St. Charles.

There was another pause. LaBroom looked down at his hands.

"The Doc was a suspicious type," said LaBroom. "No matter how good a job you did he never trusted anyone, except his daughter. There must've been a reason."

"A reason for what?" asked St. Charles, sensing an opening.

LaBroom paused. "For whatever it was that happened to him."

"Yeah, maybe," said St. Charles. "How about Tucker? You heard about him right?"

"I saw him drinkin' in the bar that night," said LaBroom. "Must've had a few too many."

"Not according to the blood work. He was under the limit."

"Bad luck then I guess."

"I'll say," agreed St. Charles. "So where were you when the Doc died?"

"Home."

"Any idea if someone had an ax to grind with him? Angry business associates? Unhappy former employee? Anyone he owed big money?"

"I'm not involved in any of that stuff Sergeant. I just grow the grapes."

"But you hear things."

"Not out in the field."

"You talk with Cindy. You dated her. You must've talked. And Larson, the mechanic, he's your friend. You must've talked about Dr. Lambrusco now and again."

"Nuthin' like what you're sayin'."

"Didn't your family once own his land?"

"Yeah," said LaBroom. "Land don't kill no one."

"It must be nice to be on the land your ancestors farmed."

"Land's land. It don't matter who's farmin' it. I got plans Sergeant. One of these days after I make my score I'm going down to Latin America, Chile or Argentina. Buy a spread and raise potatoes or cattle. I got experience doin' both. You can get a thousand acres down there for the price of a hundred here. At least that's what I hear."

"I wouldn't know," St. Charles casually said. "I know everyone dreams but that's a big move. If you're really serious about that how are you going to make your big score?"

"I don't know," LaBroom said, looking down at his feet as he shuffled them.

"You speak Spanish?"

"Not really. Just a few words and phrases for what we need around the vineyard."

"Then how are you going to make it in Latin America?"

"We got a whole barn full of Spanish-speakers here," said LaBroom with a slight laugh. "If they can make it here I can do it there I guess."

"Have you ever been to Latin America?"

"No but I been hearin' a lot about it. I'm gonna check it out."

"Is Larson going with you?"

"No way. That guy don't like anything that ain't American."

"Is that why you went to New York the other day?"

"C'mon Sergeant. I'm just a farm kid but I can dream too, can't I?"

St. Charles took a breath. He didn't like LaBroom's evasive answers but was trying not to show it.

"You ever work anyplace else Andy? Any other area besides farming, medical maybe? Spend any time in the military?"

"I'm strictly a local farm kid," said LaBroom. "I wanted to enlist in the army when I finished high school but my parents wouldn't let me. Being the only son left they needed me around here."

"They needed the money? They needed you to work?"

"Yeah, it was tough in the years before they sold the farm. The bank was pressurin' them and potatoes weren't making the profit they used to make. Somethin' had to give."

"You ever wish your family still owned it?"

"Yes and no. It bothered me at first, you know when I was younger. I got ancestors buried in that land. My older brother Anthony is buried out there. But it's okay now. I got other opportunities."

St. Charles knew it wasn't unusual for some of the oldest families in the area to bury their dead in the far reaches of their property. The tradition quietly continued among some of the families, apparently including LaBroom's.

"How did your brother die?"

"Motorcycle crash. Was a crazy kid drivin' too fast and lost control. Ain't no such thing as a small motorcycle accident. Kinda like Tugboat."

St. Charles stared at LaBroom for a moment.

"Are you frustrated about spending your whole life in the same town?" he then asked.

"Not no more. I been around a little. This ain't a bad place but like I said, I'm going to be movin' on one day. Nuthin' holdin' me here but this job and who knows how long that's going to last with the Doc gone. My parents are fixed okay now. Everyone does what they have to at the time."

"How's it going with Cindy?"

"Not much is going on. She's a nice girl but we'll have to wait and see. She don't know what's going to happen with her job either."

St. Charles jotted a few notes before speaking again.

"We're almost done," said St. Charles, taking a breath. "I just need you to sign this form. It says that I was here and we spoke. It could make things better for you. It shows that you cooperated. You never know how this may turn out. I heard the winemaker's daughter's considering hiring private investigators and there's some magazine writer snooping around."

LaBroom looked up after St. Charles's last remark which was intended to make him uncomfortable. St. Charles looked at him curiously before removing something from his briefcase. "I've even got a new pen for you," he said with a slight smile. He gestured for LaBroom to take the pen which was still in its plastic wrapper.

LaBroom looked at the pen still in St. Charles's hand—a cheap ballpoint model in a silver-colored metal casing. He took the pen as St. Charles placed the form on the table.

"Just sign at the bottom," instructed St. Charles. "By the way, since you mentioned it earlier, there's an Advice of Rights paragraph at the bottom."

"In the fine print," LaBroom said with a slight grin.

"Actually it's the same size print as the rest of the form," said St. Charles. "I'll fill in everything else back at the station tomorrow. It's late and I want to get going. I'm sure you do too."

Instead of removing the pen from its wrapper, LaBroom pushed the top button, forcing the tip through the bottom of the plastic wrapper.

"I've never seen anyone use a pen like that before," said St. Charles.

"I don't want to dirty your new pen. I been in the field all day."

LaBroom signed his name where St. Charles instructed. He then returned the pen still in its wrapper to St. Charles who discreetly tried to hold it by the tip as he quickly deposited it into his shirt pocket. St. Charles then took the form and slipping it into his briefcase, rose to shake hands with LaBroom.

St. Charles deliberately provided a firm handshake and LaBroom responded in kind.

"Thanks again for your time," said St. Charles.

"You bet," said LaBroom, making direct eye contact with St. Charles as he did so.

"One more thing," said St. Charles. "I almost forgot. Maybe you can help me with this." St. Charles returned his briefcase to the floor and reaching into his shirt pocket removed a small wad of grease-stained paper. He unfolded it and held it in the palm of his hand for LaBroom to see. "Know anything about this?" asked St. Charles moving his hand that was holding the plug directly towards LaBroom as he spoke.

"No," said LaBroom, leaning slightly back.

"You know what it is, right?"

"Yeah. It's an oil plug."

"It's the same type of plug that was found after Vincent Tucker died. One of our officers found it outside the Apple Tree. Traces of motor oil were found on the motorcycle tires. We think Tucker skidded on oil and lost control of the bike."

"A freak accident I guess," said LaBroom.

"Either that or a homicide."

LaBroom shook his head and looked down at the floor.

"I've got to get going," said St. Charles. "Thanks again. If you hear of anything be sure to call me. And if you take any trips out of the area try to let me know ahead of time. You're the guy who knows all the comings and goings around here. We're going to be closing in on this soon and I may need your help, you never know. You could wind up being a hero."

"You bet," said LaBroom.

St. Charles then left the office and as he walked to his car heard the sound of a door slamming behind him. But he did not have time to look back. He wanted to pressure LaBroom, confuse him a bit in an attempt to disrupt the control freak, if indeed he was one as Thorsen theorized. But he also wanted to get to the police station and have the shirt thread sent to the lab for a match against the piece recovered from the victim and compare the fingerprint he hoped would be on the pen wrapper with the partial print taken from the oil plug. Like Larson, LaBroom refused to touch the oil plug. And what about the marks on his wrist? Would they match against Lambrusco's dental records?

CHAPTER 28

Navigating the Wine-Dark Sea

As soon as he returned to the police station St. Charles called Dr. Dionasis.

"I had a meeting with Andy LaBroom, Lambrusco's field manager," said St. Charles. "He was the last one outstanding on the persons-of-interest list. His shirt sleeve was torn. I managed to get a piece of white thread from the shirt. I'm sending it to the lab to see if it matches the thread you found during the autopsy. Maybe they'll be some DNA on it."

"Unless they find some blood or saliva on it, which would be difficult at this point, you know that would just be circumstantial evidence," said Dionasis. "Thousands of shirts are made with the same type of cotton."

"I may have gotten a fingerprint sample and noticed two reddish marks almost in a straight line, about one to two inches from each other on the underside of the same wrist."

"Possible bite marks? I've got Lambrusco's dental measurements on file. I can check them against that. Anything else?"

"I've heard he doesn't say much but he was pretty chatty with me."

"Could be nerves. Anything else unusual about him?"

"He said he had business in New York City the other day. That was one of the reasons he gave for not being able to talk to me."

"Must've been big business?"

"He intimated that it was big for him. Then he backpedaled, saying it wasn't," added St. Charles. "I'm going to get in touch with the financial crimes unit tomorrow and see if he's had any unusual account activity."

"You think this might be the guy?"

"A lot of coincidences," said St. Charles. "But nothing solid. I'm going to call the District Attorney's office tomorrow and see what my odds are for getting a Motion to Compel. I don't think I've got enough for a subpoena."

"Probably not."

"He evaded me. I got very few solid answers. The most consistent thing I have is inconsistency. I don't like the odds."

"Everything's circumstantial right now, except the bite marks, if that's what they are," cautioned Dionasis. "The only DNA on the thread in the victim's mouth was his own. I'll send you the dental measurements first thing tomorrow. You'll have to get him back somehow to see if the marks match and you won't have a lot of time. They'll heal soon. They've probably started healing already. You don't think there's a chance he'll leave the country do you?"

"Maybe. He mentioned buying land in Latin America. Could've seen a lawyer for that when he went to New York."

"If he went to New York. My grandfather always said he was going to move the family back to Europe. It never happened."

"I'll bet he was never a suspect in a murder case. That can be quite motivating. If he's got a wad of cash in a foreign bank he may be able to persuade an immigration agent to let him stay, avoid extradition. It's happened before. "

"Stand by. I'll get the dental records to you right away but bite-mark analysis has never been viewed as reliable evidence in court. It can have a very high error rate. I've seen statistics claiming error rates as high as 60 percent."

"That means 40 percent are correct. I'll take my chances," said St. Charles.

"You can't take chances on a possible murder accusation. We don't even know if it's a human bite mark. What you need is DNA. That's nearly irrefutable."

"What are you saying Doc?"

"You can't do the bite test without his cooperation. It's an elaborate test. First the bite-mark area is wiped with sterile swabs moistened in distilled water. We used to use cotton swabs but there's a new technique using swabs made from yarn. They could be more effective in getting any saliva that was left behind. The swab is then air-dried and placed in a sterile tube. After that, a control sample is taken from another place on the victim's skin. Then a dental impression or mold is made of the upper and lower set of teeth and a computer image formed. You'll need a forensic dentist to corroborate everything and it's still not irrefutable. Any good lawyer will point to dozens of cases where bite-mark convictions were overturned."

"I thought you were on my side."

"I'm trying to help you build a strong case."

"You've got a funny way of doing it. We won't know what we may find until we take a look. Today it's the teeth, maybe tomorrow it'll be DNA."

"Okay. I'm standing by if you need help with the bite test or anything else. We'll catch whoever did this."

"Absolutely we will," he said hanging up the phone.

As St. Charles began processing the latest paperwork his logical side emerged to remind him that Dionasis merely pointed out what he actually knew but had lost sight of in his excitement to move forward. Everything he'd collected so far was nothing more than circumstantial, not nearly enough for a subpoena. The possible bite marks might be enough to justify a Motion to Compel, but he could not be sure of even this. He thought again about his conversation with LaBroom, repeatedly running the nuances and nearly endless possibilities through his mind. LaBroom was a type who largely kept to himself. How did he know Dr. Lambrusco wrote his notes in Italian? Why disclose his plan about going to Latin America? Was it just a smokescreen meant to throw St. Charles off his trail? Was he indulging in a fantasy or did he actually have concrete plans to do so? Similarly, did LaBroom truly have business in New York City or was he simply hiding someplace, hoping to avoid being interviewed? But if he had nothing to hide, why not be promptly interviewed?

Although unruly as a teenager, LaBroom had no police record, a steady work history and came from a stable family with deep roots in the community—not the stuff of which criminals are typically made. While there was no solid reason to hold LaBroom, St. Charles also personally knew of many people guilty of committing crimes who bypassed the justice system due to insufficient evidence. The Lambrusco murder was not a typical crime. There were no records of murder by tetrachloradyne. And while they had seemingly covered a lot of ground in their interviews with the winery workers they came away with neither a motive nor any substantial clues. Was Dr. Lambrusco's murder a crime of passion committed by an otherwise seemingly stable individual or was it actually the work of a skilled professional who left the scene with barely a trace? If it was the latter then Vincent Tucker's death would almost certainly have been a freak accident. In any event, St. Charles would quickly need to clarify these points. If not, he'd have to temper his own personality.

Whether deliberate or not, St. Charles was frustrated by LaBroom's evasive answers. Had this been a careful strategy designed to thwart the investigation or were St. Charles's own insecurities coming to the surface? Was he becoming willing to accept insubstantial clues and circumstantial evidence in an increasingly desperate attempt to solve the case? At that moment St. Charles had become aware of his own racing pulse. He then stepped back from his desk and taking a deep breath, realized that his inability to collect sufficient facts was what was frustrating him. He then decided that his next steps would be to administer the bite test to LaBroom and contact the Financial Crimes Unit. He knew these steps had flaws as well but also knew they might reveal something worthwhile. Acknowledging that the evidence he currently had was inconclusive, whatever results the bite test and financial investigation might reveal would help him decide whether or not to continue pursuing LaBroom.

///

Vin woke early that morning, partly from the sun streaming through his window and partly due to his nearly steady supply of nervous energy. He dressed quickly and went to the lobby to call Maria Lambrusco from the payphone. Surprisingly she answered on the first ring.

"I knew you would get back to me," Maria said answering the phone.

"How'd you know it was me?" asked Vin.

"The name of the hotel was on the caller ID. You're the only one I know staying at that wretched place."

"I guess that makes me special. It looks like I've got a magazine interested in your story," said Vin. "But the editor wants to meet with you today."

"Are you writing the story?"

"Yes," said Vin.

"Then why does she want to meet with me?" continued Maria. "I only want to deal with you Vin. This is very personal. I thought you understood that."

"I do but the editor doesn't," said Vin, suddenly afraid that the meeting and assignment might unravel. "Maria, I understand you're going through a terrible ordeal but this is a small request. I've never worked with this editor before. She's under a bit of pressure herself and wants to be sure everything's accurate. And as someone who lost his own father, I urge you to do this. We can have a brief meeting this morning someplace discreet. She's in Westhampton and she's very nice, very professional."

"I'm not sure Vin if this is the right thing to do."

"Maria," said Vin. He wasn't sure if Maria meant the story or the meeting when she mentioned the "right thing" and couldn't take a chance. Trying not to sound desperate but feeling the tension rise he pushed harder. "I went through a lot of trouble to make this happen. You've got to do this or there won't be a story. I can guarantee it."

"Okay," relented Maria. "I trust your judgment. It's got to be someplace discreet. When I see you later I'll tell you why. I'll pick you up in one hour outside your hotel and you can tell us the location then. We won't be in the limo. Watch for a blue Pontiac sedan. I need to be back in North Fork Harbor by noon."

"Fine," said Vin. "That'll work. See you in an hour."

Vin then hung up the phone. He had no idea if he could make the meeting happen. He needed to get in touch with Nadia and find a discreet place for the three of them to meet. Perhaps Shanin could recommend a place. He dialed her cell phone number but got neither an answer nor an outgoing message. After a few rings the line went dead. He tried again and got the same result. Not having much time he then called Nadia. Thankfully she was able to meet that morning and suggested a small café on Shelter Island—about a 15 minute ferry ride from North Fork Harbor. Vin found the café's number and called to get directions from the ferry terminal. He then ran back to his room, got his journalist's gear in order and prepared for the meeting. He'd reconnect with Shanin later that day.

Maria's car arrived outside the hotel exactly when she said it would. Vin, who'd been waiting in the lobby walked quickly outside. He sat in the rear alongside Maria. She was wearing plain, slightly worn, straight-leg blue jeans, shiny black high heels and a white silk blouse opened at the neck where Vin saw what appeared to be a very heavy silver necklace holding a pendant in the shape of a bunch of grapes. Vin didn't know but figured Maria was dressed in designer clothing. She had a large, brown leather bag that was placed between where they each sat. On the brief ride to the North Fork Harbor Ferry terminal Vin handed the address to the driver before giving Maria details about their upcoming meeting.

"Nice to see you again," said Maria as Vin settled into the black leather backseat. "I changed cars not to attract attention and I'm down to one body guard-driver. The security service thinks the threat level is not as high as it was before."

"How do they figure something like that?"

"They think whoever it was got what they were after."

"What do you think?"

"I'm not sure. I still don't know why anyone would want to kill my father. Listen," Maria continued. "I'm not convinced doing this interview is the right step to take. I don't want my father's death to be exploited just so someone can sell some extra magazines but I do want to turn up the heat on the police. I can't allow this to be buried in some file and forgotten about."

"It won't be like that," said Vin. "I'm writing the story."

"What about controlling the message? You'll submit it to an editor. How will they handle it after you're finished and paid?"

"For one thing, I'm in your corner. I respected your father's intentions. Not meeting him is one of the biggest disappointments of my career but if it's any consolation, I'm glad I've had the opportunity to help you. The second thing is, according to Nadia, there's not a lot of time. The magazine's got a tight deadline and Nadia's not the type of editor to sensationalize things. I doubt if they'll have the time to change the story in any substantial way. There's not a lot of available information about your father's case. As far as sources there's you and you're not talking, there's the police and they're definitely not talking and there's me. Besides, why would a magazine pay me only to change it?"

They were then silent as each thought about what the other had said. By this time the car had boarded the small ferry and begun its journey to Shelter Island. The ferry ride would take only about 15 minutes to get across the channel. Vin looked out the car window and watched a flock of sea gulls dive into the bay in pursuit of a school of fish. In the distance were impressive looking houses nestled in the hills and between the lush, green trees that rimmed most of the island. Vin then briefly remembered losing his own father and how the suspect was never charged. Vin then thought about Shanin and how the sudden loss of her father impacted her and changed her family. The thought reminded him that he had been unable to reach her earlier that day.

"Can I borrow your phone Maria?"

She fished the phone from her bag and handed it to him. Vin called Shanin's number and again the line went dead. But by this time the ferry had reached

Shelter Island and it would not be long before they'd meet Nadia at the café. Vin handed the phone back to Maria.

"She's not there?" asked Maria.

"How'd you know I was calling a woman?"

"From your facial expression. You look anxious. Or maybe you're just concerned about this meeting and your assignment. Don't worry Vin. You're going to be fine."

"I've always been a bit of a nervous type," said Vin. "I guess it's from my upbringing."

"Vin," said Maria. "I know I gave you a bit of a hard time but I want you to know I appreciate your efforts. Maybe one day you can do some communications work for the winery. I'm going to be personally taking it over, at least through this upcoming harvest. And I'm going to be doing things a little differently from my father, raise the profile of the operation a bit. We may be able to use a man who's good with words and has some media connections."

"You're going to run the winery?" repeated Vin.

"I owe it to my father's legacy," Maria said. "We made a succession plan some time ago. Now it's time to put it into action."

"Sounds like a lot of advanced planning."

"I cannot let my father's work whither on the vine. I mean that in every way imaginable. I've got the data for this year's crop. It has the potential to be a very good wine, perhaps a vintage. Tomorrow night I'm leaving for California. After taking care of some business there I'll return in time for the harvest and crush. Perhaps you and your girlfriend can join us for the crush? It's pretty exciting. Tons of grapes going in the top. Next year's wine coming out the bottom."

"Thanks. If she's still my friend then maybe we will," said Vin.

"I thought she was a little more than your friend."

"Sometimes I'm not so sure."

"If you think she's somebody special Vin don't let her slip through your fingers or you may wind up like me. Like my dad, your mom won't be around forever and being alone is terrible, especially in a time like this."

Vin politely nodded. It was the second time a woman had mentioned being alone to him in just a few days. He wasn't expecting the sudden advice and until then had not seen the parallel between himself and Maria. The car then slowed as the driver pulled to the side of the road. They'd reached the café. The ride after departing the ferry was much shorter than Vin had expected. The aroma of freshly roasted coffee was in the air and for some unknown reason it made Vin feel optimistic. It was the first time he'd felt that way in several days.

"Maria," said Vin. "You haven't told me why you need to be back by noon."

"That's right," she said. Maria then advised the driver to wait in the car outside the cafe. "I don't plan on this being a long meeting," Maria said to the driver but loud enough for Vin to hear. "I'll meet this editor. Have a quick coffee and then head back to the winery office." Then turning back to Vin she said, "Let's go inside."

Nadia Rivera was already seated in the small café when Maria and Vin entered. She rose from her seat at a small table and gestured for them to join her. The two women shook hands and after Vin made the formal introductions, took over the conversation. From what Vin could gather, it seemed that each woman wanted to make sure the other was genuine. Maria wanted to be sure she was dealing with a sincere editor who wouldn't take advantage of her father's death while Nadia needed to be reassured that Vin had Maria's cooperation. The meeting went well and was surprisingly brief.

"We each have a lot riding on this story," Nadia later said at the table.

"That's okay," said Maria. "I have to be clear. I don't want my father's death to be exploited. You can't use our images for any commercial purposes."

"I understand," said Nadia. "I won't let that happen and Vin will give us a quality piece that will help both of us, nothing sensational. In fact, I was going to ask you Maria, if you could loan us a photo of your father, or several if you wish. That's an important part of the story. What you select will make an impression. I'll give you full control over them provided the photos and story, including what you disclose to Vin, are exclusive to Travelzonia for use with this article. I'm afraid I can't go forward if you tell your story to other news organizations."

"Okay," said Maria as she nodded. "I'll send some to Vin and he can submit them with his story. But you get one-time use only."

"We're each gambling a bit and at the same time relying on each other," said Nadia.

"That can create the best partnerships," said Maria. "I expect this story to make quite an impact, in your world as well as mine."

"I hope you're right," said Nadia. "I'll have a usage agreement sent to your office spelling out the terms. Providing you're okay with it, sign it and send a copy to me."

Nadia and Vin then reviewed what she expected in the story. When it came to photos they each stopped and looked at Maria. "You should take photos tomorrow," she said. "I'll be there then. That way you can be sure you'll have full access to the winery and vineyards."

"You haven't told me who the photog is" said Nadia.

"Shanin Blanc," said Vin.

"Of course, we met in Westhampton," said Nadia. "Lovely person. You mentioned her the other day. I wanted to confirm that you two will be working together on this."

"We used to work together in the city but she lives here now. She's got a sharp lens. Stine knows her too."

"I also think she's Vin's girlfriend," said Maria grinning. It was the first time Vin had seen Maria smile since he'd met her.

"That's fine," said Nadia. "As long as you each meet the deadline with quality work."

"It'll be awesome. I mean we'll each be awesome," said Vin, fumbling a bit with his words as he got over the embarrassment caused by Maria. "The story and photos will be awesome. Don't worry about a thing."

"I'm not," said Nadia. "Speaking of Mr. Stine, it turns out your old editor and I have a mutual friend. I checked you out after we met in Westhampton. Stine said I wouldn't be able to find anyone better for this story, especially if it's on a tight deadline."

"I'll be sure to thank Charlie when I get back," said Vin. The waitress then came with the check and Nadia reached for it before anyone else could take it.

"Did he say anything about Shanin?"

"Nothing I can repeat here," Nadia said with a smile. "I've got this," she then said.

"Are you sure?" asked Maria.

"Absolutely," said Nadia. "I'm expensing it back to the office. It's the least they can do after making me work on my vacation."

The three then rose and shook hands one more time and the women exchanged business cards. On their way out Nadia quietly slid a plain white envelope into Vin's hand. He stopped to briefly peer inside. It was the check she had promised, in the full amount.

"Why do you look so shocked?" she asked. "Haven't you ever gotten paid before?"

"I thought it was going to be fifty-percent."

"It's one-hundred percent. Don't tell me you have a problem with that."

"Not a bit. Just a little surprised, that's all."

"I trust you'll split it with Shanin."

"Absolutely," he said slipping the envelope into his notebook. Vin had every intention of doing so. "Thanks. We'll do a good job."

"I know you will. That's why I'm not worried about the money."

Vin shook his head. He could barely remember a day when he did not worry about money.

CHAPTER 29

Getting to the Roots

When the ferry returned to its dock at North Fork Harbor Vin was relieved to see Shanin waiting there. He exited the car and walked directly to meet her.

"I tried calling you twice and each time your line went dead," Vin said as he approached her.

"Is that how you greet me?" she responded. Shanin was well dressed, making a better appearance than during any other time Vin had been with her on this assignment. Her hair was brushed away from her forehead, held back with a black band. She was wearing black shoes with a slight heel, a black suede skirt that extended past her knees, a white cotton shirt and a string of pearls.

"You look really nice," remarked Vin. "Anything special on your schedule today?"

"Thanks and no, nothing special. Since I'm not working today I thought I'd upgrade my image a bit. Thanks for noticing."

"Something's special on my schedule," said Vin.

"What's that?"

Vin reached into his notebook and handed Shanin the envelope with the check.

"Nice but where's mine?"

"This is yours," said Vin.

"It's made to you."

"We're supposed to split it but I'm giving my share to you. It's for putting up with me these past few days. Just give me enough to cover what's left of my hotel bill and a few dollars to hold me over until I get back to my apartment. There should be a few checks for me there."

"No Vin. Absolutely not," said Shanin. "It's your money too. I'll take my share but no more. You do the same. I wouldn't have gotten this job if it wasn't for you."

"And I wouldn't have come here if it wasn't for you."

Just then Maria's car stopped by them. They suddenly ended their conversation as they were transfixed by the descending car window. "Is this that special someone?" Maria asked Vin with only the slightest hint of condescension.

240

"Yes," said Vin. "The woman with the dead phone."

"And I'm with the man with no phone," said Shanin.

"He was worried for you," said Maria. After a second they each laughed and Vin then introduced Shanin to Maria.

"You two have work to do. I'm sure Vin will explain. Good meeting you," she said. "Let me know when you want to come by the vineyard." As Maria left Vin and Shanin slowly walked towards her car which was on the opposite end of the parking lot the ferry terminal shared with the last Long Island Railroad station, the same one Vin arrived at a few days before.

"You were worried about me?" asked Shanin.

"Yeah," said Vin. "A little. With so much happening lately can you blame me?"

"Now you know how I feel when I can't get in touch with you," she said. Vin then took Shanin's hand as they continued their walk towards the car. "Maria's going to give us full access to the vineyard and winery so you can shoot exclusive pictures. I thought we could go together. I'd feel better that way. But we've got to work fast. Maria may change her mind. Anything can happen. Can you do it tomorrow?"

"Sure."

"Great. You can pick me up in the morning."

They each then stood still, looking only at each other.

"I really should start writing," said Vin after a brief pause. "But I'd like to take care of this check. If I sign it can you cash it at your bank?"

"Probably," said Shanin. "That's one of the nice things about small-town living. Everyone knows each other, even the people in the bank. They trust each other. Let's go to the bank and after that get some lunch. Then I'll take you back to the hotel so you can start writing."

"What are you going to do?"

"The first thing I'm going to do is pay your cell phone bill and get your service restored."

"And after that?"

"Isn't it obvious? I'm going shopping. I'm overdue."

"I should've known," he said. They then got into Shanin's car and headed to the bank.

/ / /

St. Charles began planning his next steps that evening. He wondered if LaBroom was bluffing about business in New York. Did he really have so much sudden money to deposit that he couldn't use a local bank? Was he truly hiding something? The County Financial Crimes Unit was located in the same office as Police Chief Stimmel and while it would be the place to open this end of the investigation a call to them would have to come from the detective assigned to the case, which meant getting Thorsen back involved. If that's what it would take to move the case along then St. Charles would make the call to the flamboyant and irascible detective. It was his responsibility to move the case forward. It would only be a matter of time before headquarters would demand that he make progress or move the investigation into the inactive file as resources were not unlimited. Further, he knew Vin's article would be forthcoming and did not want to think about how people at headquarters, namely Stimmel would react. His goal of retiring with a virtually spotless career history was only a matter of time. He did not want to be remembered as the head of an investigation that had no real answers in what would certainly be portrayed as a very high-profile case, perhaps the most spectacular case in the otherwise relatively quiet history of rustic North Fork Harbor. St. Charles then looked at LaBroom's Social Security number on the statement form he completed. This would be the key piece of information to initiate any financial investigation. St. Charles then wondered if it would be enough as he determinedly dialed Thorsen's telephone number.

/ / /

"I'd been wondering what happened with the chicken-coop murders," said Det. Thorsen to Sgt. St. Charles's. "I've been so busy tracking down the killers of Long Island's rich and famous that I haven't had much time to devote to solving Dr. Vino's untimely death."

"Your dedication is only matched by your professionalism," said St. Charles in as sarcastic a tone as he could muster.

"Seriously," said the detective. "I've been thinking about the case each morning as I traverse the Long Island Expressway. What I think you've got is some sort of mythic-creature, maybe a grape-like Lochness Monster or Big Foot lurking about. Some half-human, half-beast creature. Whatever it is hides in some remote part of the vineyard and the Doc probably saw it one night eating grapes so the monster had to kill him to maintain its secrecy."

"I'll be sure to put that in my report," said St. Charles. "But before I recommend sending you for a psychological evaluation I need you to put a call into the Financial Crimes Unit. I'm trying to verify whether a large amount of money was deposited by one of the persons of interest, possibly into a foreign bank with a New York City office."

"I didn't know anyone had that kind of money out there."

"Normally they don't, not farm workers. Not if he's telling the truth. That's what I need you to find out."

"Well," said Thorsen taking a breath. "Considering that there are probably only about a thousand foreign banks with offices in New York City and how you didn't want me on the case and how HQ has got me hop-scotching across Long

Island, this should be no problem. I'll make it my top priority. You'll have the information in about thirty to forty-five days. How's that?"

"Stop screwing around," said St. Charles. "This is my investigation. I decide how it runs. You've got to respect that. I need this information in 48 hours. I'm going to fax you the suspect's Social Security number in a few minutes."

"Take it easy Sergeant. I didn't say I'd do it."

"No you didn't," said St. Charles. "I did."

"Are you telling a detective what to do?"

"Yes," said St. Charles. "And here's something else. Be sure to provide your full cooperation. Anything less will be seen as an attempt to impede an investigation. Like I said, I'm faxing you some info momentarily and need responses in 48 hours. It'll be in my report to Stimmel which he's been hollering for. I can't hold him off indefinitely."

"Anything else I should know?"

"I got the serial number to the Doc's handheld and filed it with the Stolen Computer Registry. If it should surface I'll be notified."

"Good idea. How's it going with the suspects?"

"No real suspects yet, just a lot of circumstantial evidence. Dr. D's going to do some DNA work for me on a thread I recovered and a bite mark test with this same worker who may have deposited a large sum of cash somewhere. Whoever did this is either a million miles from here by now or right under our nose."

"Could be a combination," suggested Thorsen.

"What do you mean?"

"An outsider with an interest in the Doc's work hired a local guy to do the job."

"Anything's possible."

"Okay. Send me what you've got," said Thorsen. "I'll get in touch with the financial-crimes people. As you might guess, I'm on good terms with one of the young ladies there. I'll try to get her to move this to the top of her to-do list."

"Thanks Detective."

With that he hung up the telephone and punched the fax number to Thorsen's office into the machine. As he watched the sheet of paper containing Andy LaBroom's information slide through the feeder slot he thought about what his next move might be. The reference to Chief Stimmel was intended to ensure Thorsen's cooperation and St. Charles was fairly certain he'd get it as he had something at stake in this investigation as well. His statement about Stimmel demanding the report was an exaggeration designed to convey a sense of urgency to the unflappable detective. It wasn't always easy to motivate people, thought St. Charles even among professionals who were supposed to be cooperating with each other. Therefore, it sometimes had to be done by unusual means, especially in Thorsen's case.

/ / /

Vin and Shanin arrived early the following day at the winery. They checked-in at the office. Maria was not yet there but she had sent word to Cindy that a writer and photographer would be coming and that they were to have access to the vineyard for photo-taking purposes. Maria, without letting anyone at the winery know, was on her way back to California. As she had disclosed to Vin, she had some business to attend to there and would then return to North Fork Harbor in time to supervise the harvest and crush. Disappointed in the search for answers to her father's death but not willing to give up, she was secretly hoping that the forthcoming magazine article would pressure the local police to find the killer.

"I'll have to talk with Maria before I let you two go anywhere on the property," said Cindy Murphy when Vin and Shanin arrived at the winery office. Cindy dialed Maria's cell phone number. "Nothing's going through," she said, hanging up the office telephone. "Maybe you can come back later?"

"We're on a deadline," said Shanin.

Cindy simply shrugged while continuing to stare at them. "Her father never liked outsiders walking unescorted around the property."

Realizing that Cindy was trying to keep them from accessing the property Vin reluctantly made a suggestion with the intention of calling what he sensed was a bluff.

"Then why don't you get us an escort?" he suggested.

"I suppose I can do that," said Cindy. "How much time do you think you'll need?"

"Not sure," said Vin. "At least half a day."

"I can't spare anyone for that amount of time," she said. "I'll call you once I hear back from Maria?"

Sensing the stonewalling Vin made another move. "I have a few calls to make," said Vin. "We're going to go to the car. We'll check back with you in a little bit."

Cindy nodded as she held the office door open.

"This is a big stall tactic," said Shanin once they were back in the car.

"It could just be a miscommunication," said Vin who for once was not being the suspicious one.

Just then Vin's cell phone beeped. It was a text from Maria: "Not coming to office. Cindy's expecting you and Shanin at winery."

"It was a good thing I got your cell phone service restored," said Shanin. "Let's get back inside, take our pictures and get out of here. I don't like hanging around a place where I'm not wanted."

"I've got a better idea," said Vin. "We're on a deadline. Let's skip checking-in with Cindy. She doesn't want us around whether she knew we were coming or not. I'll forward this text to Cindy. Let's take our own tour of the facility and if anyone stops us we'll show them Maria's text."

"Okay," said Shanin as she removed her photography gear from the car. "It's not the first time we're working in a place where we're not wanted."

"I may take a few notes along the way," said Vin. "I've got a few holes to fill."

"I've never photographed a winery before," said Shanin. "Do you have any idea what Nadia wants in terms of photos?"

"No. We made the deal so fast that photo details were never discussed. Try to shoot a variety. Grapes, workers, sunsets."

The two of them then began walking down the dirt road that led deep into the vineyard. The road was rutted on each side from the equipment that went over it nearly each day. Shanin walked on one side and Vin on the other. Shanin carried the camera in its protective bag while Vin took the tripod. Small clouds of dust rose from beneath their heels as they walked.

Shanin soon began taking pictures from every conceivable angle—long, scenic vistas, close-ups of dew glistening on grape clusters, vines reaching towards the sky, she even got a photo of a small, red fox scurrying through a vineyard row. When they thought they had enough photos they spotted a group of workers in the distance.

"We don't have many people shots. Let's see what they're up to," said Shanin.

She and Vin began walking in the direction of the workers when Vin noticed a familiar figure. "Hold it," Vin suddenly said to Shanin, extending his arm to stop her from walking further.

"What's wrong?" asked Shanin.

"I think I recognize one of those guys," said Vin gesturing towards the group of about six workers. "Take a couple of quick shots before they know we're here," he said. "Then put your gear in the bag."

About one hundred yards from where they stood a group of farm laborers were tending to a row of vines. Vin thought he recognized Andy LaBroom from the Apple Tree the night Vincent Tucker died. He was the tallest and only non-Hispanic in the group. "Make sure you get the tall guy," he said. Shanin worked fast, taking about six varied shots in less than a minute. They then quickly packed her gear before approaching the group.

"Who is he?" Shanin quietly asked Vin as they walked forward.

"I'm not sure," said Vin. "But Tugboat knew him. He was in the bar the night of the crash. He wasn't too friendly."

"That seems to be the order of the day around here," said Shanin.

Most of the workers turned and looked at Vin and Shanin as they approached, including Andy LaBroom.

"Hi there," said Vin. The workers and LaBroom continued to stare at them.

"Hi," Vin repeated.

"This ain't a tourist farm," said LaBroom, approaching the pair. "This area's closed to the public. Sorry."

"We're not tourists," said Vin. "We're journalists. Maria Lambrusco said we could walk around." Vin then showed LaBroom his press pass.

LaBroom briefly studied the pass and then looked back at Vin and Shanin. Some of the workers continued to watch the encounter and others returned to their jobs. LaBroom then remembered that St. Charles had mentioned that a journalist was in the area.

"I think I remember you," Vin then said. LaBroom looked at him "You were in the Apple Tree, talking to Vincent Tucker a few nights ago."

LaBroom looked at Vin. "You were there?" he asked. "You knew Tugboat?"

"I didn't know him well," said Vin. "But I had a beer with him."

"It's too bad about him," LaBroom said, looking at the ground. "I knew him practically my whole life. I can't believe he's gone."

"I liked him too," said Vin. "Poor guy didn't have a chance."

"It's true," said LaBroom. "You were on the bike that night?"

Vin nodded.

"You're lucky you're here. Listen," continued LaBroom. "I've got to finish with this crew but feel free to walk around. Any questions you got about this place let me know. I know every inch of this land. What's your name?"

"I'm Vin and this is Shanin. She's a photographer."

"You even got the same name as Tugboat. I'm Andy." The three of them then shook hands. "Do what you gotta do," said Andy, gesturing towards the land behind him. "If you want a ride back to the office be here in about an hour. We should be breaking for lunch about then. We can give you a lift back in the truck."

"Thanks," said Vin. "We'll keep that in mind."

"How about a shot of you and the crew?" interjected Shanin.

LaBroom hesitated but then after a few seconds relented.

"Okay," he said. Andy then organized the workers in front of the truck. He stood at the side of the group with his hands folded across his belt. Andy then instructed the workers to smile for Shanin who took several shots of the group from different angles. When she finished Vin again thanked Andy and with Shanin, walked further into the vineyard.

"For a guy who's not supposed to be friendly he turned out to be pretty nice," Shanin said to Vin as soon as they were beyond listening distance.

"It didn't start that way. That kind of sudden change in behavior always makes me uneasy," said Vin. "We have enough photos. I say we get off this property before anyone changes their mind."

"I didn't want to ride in their truck," said Shanin. "You, me and all those guys in the middle of nowhere. I don't like the odds. I'll bet that LaBroom can turn nasty just as easily as he got nice. Let's take the long way back by foot. Besides, you never know what we'll see."

"And how could he assume I was on Tugboat's motorcycle the night he died?"

"Are you going to tell that to St. Charles?"

"Maybe," said Vin.

Vin and Shanin then looked at each other as they considered this last exchange with neither saying anything. The pair then quietly continued its walk away from the work crew towards the parking area outside the winery office. They would each breathe a sigh of relief once they drove off the vineyard property. From inside the office Cindy watched Vin and Shanin enter the car and leave the premises.

CHAPTER 30

The Wrath of Grapes

Even Sgt. Henry St. Charles was slightly startled the following morning when he received an e-mail notification from the Stolen Computer Registry. St. Charles dialed the telephone number listed on the e-mail and after supplying his identification information, spoke with a representative who told him that Dr. Lambrusco's handheld computer had been recovered and was being held at a retail shop in New York City that buys, refurbishes and sells used computers and related equipment. The representative then gave him the telephone number of the shop plus the other information he would need to take possession of it. As it was identified as stolen merchandise it would be held at the store until it was turned over to a law-enforcement agent and was not available for sale. St. Charles, after getting the store's location, called Det. Thorsen. He was a lot closer to New York City than anyone on St. Charles's force and since he might be going there to see about LaBroom's banking activity he'd also be able to obtain the handheld, ideally getting additional information from the representative who acquired it at the same time.

"They found the Doc's handheld," St. Charles said as soon as Thorsen answered his phone.

"What?"

"That registry found the handheld computer that belonged to the dead winemaker. It's being held in a store in New York City."

"I've got some information for you too."

"You're not retiring are you?"

"No such luck. I won't retire until they show some appreciation for me around here, now you'll see why. I called the girl in financial crimes. She referred me to FinCEN, the Treasury Department's financial clearing house. The federal, state and local levels are connected for money crimes. You should know that. After going through about a million passwords and inputting all sorts of data I was finally able to enter the Social Security number you gave me. It belongs to an Anthony LaBroom, North Fork Harbor, NY."

"Are you sure?

"Of course I'm sure. I've got the information right here."

"Anything else on it?"

"No financial activity if that's what you mean. No account connected to it. But it's still early. That's only preliminary. I've got an alert on it so if there's any activity associated with it I'll be contacted."

"I wouldn't wait by the phone for that."

"What do you mean?" asked Thorsen.

"Anthony LaBroom died years ago in a motorcycle crash. There's got to be a mistake somewhere."

"Read me the Social Security number again," requested Thorsen. St. Charles complied. "That's what I've got," he confirmed.

"Nothing else?" asked St. Charles.

"That's all for now."

Each man then paused until St. Charles resumed the conversation.

"I'm going to send you the information about the handheld. Try to get hold of it within the next 24 hours. I was hoping you could go because I wanted a trained investigator, someone who knows how to talk to New York City people. See what we can learn about how they came to get it. The first thing is to see if they've got information on who brought it to the store. The registry only notes where it is."

"You're a former city boy. I thought you'd want to do make that trip. Maybe visit your favorite café on the way home."

"Ordinarily I'd love to but I've got too many murders to solve."

"If only I had a nickel for each time I heard that line," sighed Thorsen.

"I knew you'd understand. Whatever happened with the Southampton woman-murder case?"

"We solved it in about five days. The husband thought she was getting together with an old boyfriend. He had just gotten off the phone with the life insurance company when we showed up to cuff him. Said it was a heart attack but we found signs of a struggle. He confessed before crying like a baby to keep it off the evening news."

"Was the husband right?"

"Yes and no. She was having an affair but not with an old boyfriend. She found a new boyfriend, her personal trainer. The trainer thought she'd divorce the husband, run away with him and they'd get the house and some money. Confessions usually come easily in these love triangles. Listen," continued Thorsen. "About that Social Security number. The guy may be dead but the number may still be alive."

"What?"

"The names of dead people have been used in crimes before," said Thorsen. "It's not unreasonable that someone would use a dead guy's Social Security number if they're trying to hide something. It's pretty obvious as to who would use this particular guy's number at this particular time."

"I'm going to request a Motion to Compel for Andrew LaBroom as soon as we end this call," said St. Charles.

"One more thing before you go," requested Thorsen.

"What's that?"

"Did you send your report to Stimmel?"

"Not yet," said St. Charles. "I've somehow managed to keep it from him. Don't worry. When we solve this case we'll share top billing. It may get you enough recognition to think about retiring. Maybe go on the talk-show circuit."

"Now you're talking. Thanks Boss."

"You'll get there by tomorrow?"

"You bet."

St. Charles had given Thorsen all the motivation he needed.

///

Early the next morning, at about the same time when St. Charles was preparing to have Officer Krupcheski deliver a Motion to Compel to Andy LaBroom, Det. Thorsen, already on his way to New York City, received a notification from FinCEN. Banc di Basil, a Switzerland-based bank with a New York City office had opened a new account with the Social Security number of Anthony LaBroom.

For a moment Thorsen was uncharacteristically unsure of what to do next. Should he continue to the computer retailer or visit the bank? Should he make a surprise visit to the bank or should he call ahead? Had there been any activity in the account? What about the handheld? Would the clerk be able to help him locate the person who brought it to the retailer? Thinking that there was probably some time to spare at the bank since the account had been opened within the last 24 hours, Thorsen decided to proceed to the computer retailer as planned. It was located on West 27th St., in the heart of New York City's wholesale and import district. The neighborhood largely consists of narrow streets lined with old grey-brick buildings and is nearly choked during business hours with delivery trucks, workers carrying large boxes and various merchants looking to buy and sell everything from electronics to blue jeans to jewelry. Thorsen parked his unmarked car on an angle between two delivery trucks and then tossed his detective plate on the dashboard, indicating he was there on official police business and preventing his car from being towed by the virtually insatiable New York City parking patrol. He quickly found the store. It was located on the basement level of an old building. The outdoor stairway was made of cement and had a wrought iron guard rail and banister that led below the sidewalk. Thorsen quickly walked down the stairs, entered the store and went directly to the counter. A dark skinned man with horn rimmed glasses was barking orders into a telephone in a language Thorsen did not recognize. He paid little attention to the detective, barely acknowledging his presence. After about 30 seconds of waiting, Thorsen flashed his detective's badge. The man then hung up the phone and approached the detective.

"Sorry to keep you waiting Sir. I was on an overseas call. How can I help you?"

Thorsen showed the man his identification before speaking. "You're holding a handheld computer for us. I'm here to take possession of it."

"Yes. I have it right here. One moment." The man then walked into a back room and a few seconds later emerged carrying a small cardboard box which he placed on the glass counter in front of Thorsen. There were two pieces in the box—the computer and the hard drive.

"Why was the hard drive removed?" asked Thorsen.

"That is how we received it," answered the clerk. "I'm not even sure if that's the hard drive for that computer but they must have come in together, otherwise they would not be like that."

"Did you destroy the data on the hard drive?"

"No. That is not our job. But if we had sent it out it would have been destroyed. You are lucky."

"This will go a lot easier if you just answer the questions and keep the commentary to yourself."

Thorsen then checked the serial number on the hand held case. It matched the one in the report. The hard drive had a serial number on it but there was no mention of one in the report.

"The manufacturer may be able to tell you if that is the hard drive that went into that computer. They will have that information. Or you can reconnect it yourself and try to retrieve any data."

"How'd you get this?" asked Thorsen.

"I have done nothing wrong," said the man. "I run a legitimate business."

"That remains to be seen," said Thorsen. "For now, as long as you cooperate you probably won't be in any trouble. Where'd you get this?"

"A woman came in looking to sell it. That's our business. We buy and sell used computers. Sometimes we buy and sell them here. Other times we send them out to be refurbished. Sometimes we sell them for scrap. But we run everything through the data base. I'm guessing that's what brought you here."

"That's correct. I'm sorry if you paid money for this but that's your loss. This is stolen property. It's also evidence. Therefore it has to be confiscated. I'll also need the information of the person you got it from."

"That's confidential. I don't have that information."

"Which is it?" asked Thorsen leaning closer. "Confidential or you don't have it?"

"I pay cash and the people, they leave. Many come here each day to sell electronics. They need cash. I don't have to ask where the merchandise comes from."

"I already told you this is stolen property and evidence. If you don't cooperate, produce some records, I'll get a subpoena for your arrest. We'll haul your ass out of here and padlock your store until we release you."

"I'll get a lawyer, my nephew," said the man reaching for his telephone which was lying on the same counter. Thorsen placed his right hand over the man's which was already on the telephone. With his other hand he then pulled back his coat, revealing his badge and pistol.

At that moment a customer entered the store. Upon seeing what was taking place, he immediately turned and exited.

"I'll arrest you right now for impeding an investigation. Take you out to Hauppauge, Long Island for booking. Send you back on Long Island Rail Road late tonight if you're lucky. That ought to keep your store closed for at least a day." said Thorsen. "Unless you show me who bought this, unless you want to personally visit your friend from that overseas call . . ."

"Yes Sir," the clerk then said. He then withdrew his hand from beneath Thorsen's and reaching below the counter produced a thick vinyl binder full of small, yellow slips of paper. He spilled them out on the counter and began sorting through them. Another customer entered the store with an armload of electronics.

"Store's closed," said Thorsen, flipping his badge in the direction of the customer. "Come back later." The man immediately turned and left, taking the electronics with him.

After several minutes of sifting through miscellaneous receipts the clerk produced the correct one.

"This is it," he said, handing it to Thorsen.

There was a name, address and a barely legible signature on it: Carlita Melendez. The address was for a building a few blocks away.

"That's all I have," said the man to Thorsen.

"Do you know what she looks like? Does she come here frequently?"

"I don't know Sir. So many people. I'm very honest."

"For an honest guy you have a funny way of showing it."

"I can do nothing more for you."

This time the detective was satisfied. He took the receipt and the hardware in the cardboard box. "Thanks for your cooperation," he sarcastically said as he turned to leave the store but not before dropping his card on the counter. "If this Carlita Melendez comes back or if anyone comes looking for a handheld computer like this one be sure to call me." The clerk did not answer but simply stared at the card as Thorsen left the store. He then picked it up and placed it in the vinyl binder with the receipts. Thorsen, returning to his car, locked the box in the trunk and then double-checked the address on the receipt as he went to look for Carlita Melendez. He decided he could visit the Swiss bank's office after at least trying to locate Carlita Melendez and learn how she came in possession of a handheld computer that belonged to a murdered winemaker.

A few minutes later Thorsen was parked outside the building matching the address on the receipt. Not bad for New York City traffic he thought. The address led to an office building on Park Avenue South, a thriving business district of law firms, advertising agencies and hi-tech start-ups, as well as some avant-garde restaurants. Thorsen exited his car and entered the building. A husky guard with a crew cut wearing a dark blue blazer sporting the seal of a security firm was sitting behind the security desk at the end of the hallway in front of the elevator bank. As Thorsen approached the desk he flashed his badge, making sure the guard could see it before saying anything to him.

"Good morning. I'm looking for a Carlita Melendez," Thorsen told the guard.

"Good morning Detective," the guard replied, removing his gaze from the badge. "It doesn't sound familiar. I'll check the building directory." The guard then punched characters into a key pad and watched names scroll across a computer screen. "Nobody here with that name," he said.

"Are you sure?" asked Thorsen.

The guard again stared at the screen. "No Sir. You're sure this is the building?"

Thorsen showed the guard the receipt. The name of the computer reseller ran across the top of the receipt. "Are you looking for a computer place?"

"No," said Thorsen. "Someone brought a stolen computer to this place," he said, pointing to the store's name on the receipt. "They gave this address. I need to find who that is."

"That's one of those places that buys and sells used electronics right? I pass it on my way home."

"Yeah," said Thorsen.

"It's probably one of the cleaning people. We get reports on stuff missing from people's offices all the time," he said. "You can get anything cheap in that neighborhood, especially electronics. You have a photo of her? Maybe I'll recognize her."

"Negative," answered Thorsen.

"Your best bet then would be to talk to the cleaning-service people. Let me get you their number."

After sifting through a sheaf of papers the guard then wrote a Brooklyn-based number on a slip of paper. "You can call this number. They manage the cleaning people. I don't know any of them by name but they start showing up here around four o'clock. They have a room in the basement with their supplies. They usually hang out there before their shifts start."

"How will I know who she is?"

"They've got to sign-in and most of them speak a little English, even if they act like they don't."

"Thanks for the info. You've been very helpful," said Thorsen. "Maybe I'll be back around four."

"Yes Sir."

"You're a good son," said Thorsen. "Do me a favor. I'm not sure if I'll be able to be back here later so I'd appreciate if you didn't tell anyone I was here. This is an open investigation."

"Yes Sir," the guard repeated.

Thorsen, not sure if he could trust the security guard, then exited the building, went to his car and opened the trunk. He stared at the handheld and hard drive still in the cardboard box. He put on one of the rubber gloves he kept in his investigation-equipment bag and picked up the handheld, hoping he might learn something by examining it. What did it contain he wondered that would make someone commit murder? He then thought about whose fingerprints might be on it, what they were after and how it came to be found in a used-electronics store in New York City.

///

At about the same time Thorsen was traversing New York City, Officer Nicholas Krupcheski was preparing to personally deliver a Motion to Compel to Andrew LaBroom. St. Charles liked having Krupcheski deliver such items. An affable young man from a locally well-known family, Krupcheski was often welcomed by the townspeople as he had been his entire life. Upon seeing him they would unknowingly drop their guard, enabling him to deliver bad news to them. Conversely, local people were often apprehensive when St. Charles approached any of them. At times they'd pretend not to be home. He often noticed house lights turn off and hear locks turn in doors as he walked up driveways. Krupcheski rarely faced such obstacles, making him the ideal courier. It was early in the morning and Krupcheski hoped he'd find LaBroom still at home. Typically, it was less embarrassing, as well as less stressful, to serve someone in the privacy of their home rather than in a public place or at their job. Less embarrassment generally meant less hostility towards the police and the overall justice process. This often translated into greater cooperation and more efficient procedural work. When done in this manner recipients would often eventually come to realize that the police officers were only interested in doing their jobs, not in embarrassing or making examples of them. While dressed in uniform, to minimize attention he drove his pick-up truck to LaBroom's home that morning rather than park a patrol car in the driveway. Before knocking on the front door to the home of his former high school classmate, he noticed Andy's truck was not in the driveway.

"Nicholas," said Mrs. LaBroom as she opened the front door. "What brings you here so early?"

"Good morning Mrs. LaBroom. Nice to see you. Is Andy home?"

"No. I'm afraid we're both looking for him. He didn't come home last night. He's not in some sort of trouble is he?"

"Do you have any idea where he is?" Krupcheski asked, deliberately evading Mrs. LaBroom's question and natural concern for her son.

"I left a message on his portable phone about two hours ago but haven't heard back," she said before leaning forward as if to confide in Krupcheski. "He runs around with that Cindy Murphy. Sometimes they're on, sometimes they're off. She's no girl for a boy like Andy, don't you think?"

"Do you think he's at the vineyard?" asked Krupcheski, trying to keep control of the conversation.

"I hope so. He has done that."

"Done what?"

"Caroused all night and gone straight to work," she said. "Sometimes he'd tell me he worked all night but I think he was running around with that Cindy. I wasn't born yesterday. She's got a place of her own in town, above the hardware store. He thinks I don't know. A mother knows," she said, tapping her index finger to her forehead. "I don't like a girl with a place of her own. No good can come from that."

"I'm going to try the vineyard," said Krupcheski. "If you talk to him ask him to give me a call Mrs. LaBroom. Sorry to bother you."

"Come here Nicholas," Mrs. LaBroom said. Krupcheski drew closer to the woman he'd known since childhood. "Andy's in trouble isn't he? I can see by the look on your face."

"I didn't say that Mrs. LaBroom."

"You didn't have to."

"Has he been acting strange lately?"

"No, not really. I haven't seen much of him."

"Then why are you concerned?"

"Have you forgotten I'm his mom? Whatever it is I'm sure that Cindy's got her hand in it. Andy's bright but he can be manipulated by girls."

"Andy's not so bad," Krupcheski said, not wanting to leave Mrs. LaBroom on a bad note. "When I see him I'm sure we'll get everything straightened out. And I'll tell him to call you."

"Thank you Nicholas," she said. "You're a good boy."

Krupcheski returned to his car. He noted the time and place of his meeting with Mrs. LaBroom and that she did not know her son's whereabouts. He also noted that Andy's truck was not in the driveway, lending credence to what Mrs. LaBroom had said. Krupcheski then made his way to the vineyard.

///

The overnight flight carrying Maria Lambrusco from California touched down at LaGuardia Airport early the same morning Officer Krupcheski was looking for Andy LaBroom and Det. Thorsen was pursuing leads in New York City. She had received a report from Cindy Murphy on the condition of the grapes. According to the numbers supplied by Cindy, the Brix, or average sugar-level measurement of the red grapes was 24. The average pH level was nearly 4. Each number represented nearly optimum harvest conditions and according to the calendar, had reached these points ahead of schedule. As a result, the crush date would need to be moved up as well. By reviewing the report Maria was also able to see from which vines the sample fruit had been taken. Some of the vines were the experimental ones cultivated by her father. They registered higher levels of sugar than the others, indicating that they had matured faster, as her father had designed. It was impossible for anyone without the proper data to tell which vines represented the experimental varieties. Until now that data had existed only in Dr. Lambrusco's handheld and in Maria's computer in California. As she stared at the data supplied by Cindy she wondered who else would now be able to decipher the codes.

When the passengers had disembarked, Maria went to the rental car area. She had decided to forego her private driver and security personnel for this trip. She would drive herself to the vineyard and stay in her father's apartment. She'd also call Vin Gusto to see if he was still in North Fork Harbor and if he'd like to take part in the crush.

CHAPTER 31

The Fruit of the Vine

Unfazed by the "full" sign, Det. Thorsen drove his car into the parking lot beneath the office building that housed the Banc di Basil, directly steering the vehicle in a vacant space next to the small and unmanned attendant's booth.

"Yo! You can't park there," the attendant yelled while emerging from the other end of the driveway. "We're full. Get that car out of here."

Thorsen waited until he was nearly face-to-face with the animated attendant.

"I told you man, move that car!"

"Do you talk to everyone like that?" Thorsen quietly asked.

"Hell yeah, 'specially those who don't listen. Now get that car out of here or I'll put it out on the street for you."

"You touch that car I'll shut this place down," Thorsen said, flashing his badge for the third time that morning. "I'll be upstairs doing some banking. I'll be about an hour. Don't expect a tip. Do we understand each other?"

"Yes Sir."

"I thought so. Where are the stairs to the lobby? And by the way, I'll be holding onto the keys, that's an official vehicle."

Without saying anything further the now-deflated guard pointed in the direction of the stairs. A few minutes later Thorsen was inside the building lobby. Once he located the floor upon which the bank was located from the wall-mounted directory he immediately proceeded to the turnstiles.

"You can't go through there without ID man," a security guard from behind a counter said in his direction without looking.

Again the detective flashed his badge. "I'm going to the second floor. Beam me up Scottie." The guard complied, quietly releasing the turnstile arms as Thorsen made his way to the elevator.

The second floor was a maze of corridors and closed doors with the names of various companies printed on them. Thorsen followed the numbers on the doors until he came upon the bank. He pressed his ear against the door and heard no noise coming from the other side. He attempted to turn the door knob but it was locked. He then pressed the buzzer switch and was given entry without anyone checking who was at the door.

Inside he walked down a short hallway and stopped at an unmanned reception desk. He stood there expecting someone to greet him. The air was full with the strong smell of coffee. A moment later a tall young man appeared at the end of another hallway and walked briskly towards Thorsen. The young man had thick black hair, was clean shaven and was wearing what Thorsen thought, had to be a custom-tailored suit. The Europeans sure know how to dress he thought.

"*Bonjour*, may I help you sir?" the young man asked in a heavy German accent.

"I hope so," said Thorsen extending his hand. "I'm a detective. I'm here on official business. I'd like to see your branch manager."

"Yes. Your name please?"

"I'm Detective Conrad Thorsen, Suffolk County Police."

"Do you have an appointment?"

"No. I don't need one. I have this," he said, again revealing his badge.

"Yes *Signor* Thorsen. Please have a seat," the young man said gesturing towards some plain, straight-backed chairs lined against the wall. "May I take your coat?" Thorsen removed and then handed him his trench coat. "I am Max. Can I get you something?" he offered.

"That coffee smells good," Thorsen said.

"Right away sir and I'll see about Mr. Rinaldi for you. He's our manager but I must warn you, his English is not as good as mine."

"Thank you," said Thorsen as he took a seat.

A few moments later Max appeared with a small cup of hot espresso. "I hope you like your coffee black," he said. "It is the only way we serve it here."

"Perfect," said Thorsen, taking the small cup and saucer. The surroundings weren't great thought Thorsen but the service was so far excellent.

"*Signor* Rinaldi will be with you in a few moments. He is on the line with the home office."

As promised, a few moments later Thorsen watched Max walk down the hallway with a smaller and older man behind him. As they drew closer Max stepped to the side and the older man then walked directly towards Thorsen. It was clear they had exercised this protocol before. As he extended his hand Thorsen put the cup and saucer on the seat next to him and stood in response.

"Good morning Detective. I am Christian Rinaldi. How may I help you?"

"I have some questions. I'm here on official business. Is there some place we can speak privately?"

"Yes. We can adjourn to my office. Please follow me. Max," he then said turning to his aide. "You will wait outside the door if I have trouble with English. Okay Detective?"

"Okay," answered Thorsen.

Rinaldi's office was the polar opposite of the waiting area. It was a large, lavishly decorated room complete with a big-screen television, Oriental rugs, a mahogany desk, artifacts from seemingly around the world and a great view of Park Ave.

"Please have a seat," Rinaldi said as he closed the door. "How may I help you?"

"We have a little problem," began Thorsen but before he could continue Rinaldi interrupted him.

"You are not with FinCEN? Rinaldi asked. "Nor the FBI, correct?"

"That's right," said Thorsen. "I'm with the Suffolk County PD. Long Island." He handed him his business card.

"That is not affiliated with the New York City Police Department, no?" he said, staring down at the card.

"No," Thorsen repeated. "But I'd like to talk with you about an account opened here."

"I do not have to talk with you."

"You don't," said Thorsen, his tone turning serious. "But I would recommend that you do."

Rinaldi then sat back in his chair and looked up at the ceiling. He put his hand into the vest pocket of his blazer and withdrew a silver cigarette case. "Do you smoke Detective?"

"When I'm under stress, yes," he said.

Rinaldi smiled and extended the now opened case towards him. "Would you like one? They are from Geneva. It's okay to smoke in the office here, we are exempted as an international company from the smoking laws," he lied.

Thorsen took a cigarette, smelled it and then put it to his lips. Rinaldi leaned forward and lit it with a gold-plated lighter that sported the Swiss flag on its side. "Very good," the detective said as he puffed, leaning back and blowing smoke towards the ceiling.

"You cannot get these in your country. My mother sends them to me. I can always get you a carton. So you say I should talk with you about a private client. That is against our laws. I'm sure you know that."

"What does your law say about opening an account using the identification of a dead man?"

"I do not understand," said Rinaldi, leaning closer.

"We have very good information that a man came in here last week and opened an account under the name of Anthony LaBroom."

"Maybe. We have many accounts. I cannot personally know each one."

"Anthony LaBroom died years ago."

"That means nothing to me."

Thorsen turned and admired the view down Park Avenue.

"How does a bank like this usually get its customers?" he then asked. "You don't advertise on the subway."

Rinaldi smiled. "You are very charming Detective. Most of our new clients come by referrals from existing clients. That is how private banks typically operate."

"So if I found a wad of cash and didn't want anyone to know, I could just walk in here with a couple of shopping bags full of money."

"No, no, no," said Rinaldi, crushing his cigarette in an onyx ashtray. "It is not like that. We have compliance procedures. We need to know where the money comes from. We do not accept money involved in criminal enterprise." Thorsen did not believe what he had just been told but gave no indication of his apprehensions.

"But banks like these have a reputation for helping their clients, and their clients' friends."

"Remember what your American writer Mark Twain said about friends."

"What's that?" asked Thorsen.

"*When we think about friends we call their faces out from the shadows.*"

"So you come out from the shadows to help your clients?"

"If we need to."

"Why are you in the shadows in the first place?"

"I do not understand."

"Remember what the French writer Balzac said about money?"

"No, I do not."

"*Behind every fortune there's a crime.*"

"Maybe in your business but not in mine."

The two men then stared at each other for a moment. Thorsen then extinguished his cigarette next to Rinaldi's.

"So I do not have to talk to you," said Rinaldi. "But you recommend that I do."

"*Oui, oui,*" said Thorsen, offering a fake grin.

"And why would I do that?"

"Because if you don't it will only be a matter of time before I do get FinCEN or the FBI in here. They like coffee and fancy cigarettes too. And they like to know where sudden deposits into banks like yours come from."

"We've committed no crime. I assure you. This is a small but proud bank with a great tradition in Europe. We have customers whose families go back to before the French Revolution."

"Not cooperating with an investigation is a crime here, whether one's a citizen or not. We have a law here called the Patriot Act. Among other things it's to prevent international money laundering. So tell me how your office opened an account for a dead man."

"I do not know what you are talking about. Do you have an account number for this person? Each of our clients has a numbered account and it is highly confidential. We work with discretion. We are on the honor system."

"Maybe your honor system is not as honorable as you say it is. I have a Social Security number. That should be enough to begin the search. Apparently you have the same number somewhere in your files. What we want to know is how it got there."

"Your hypothesis is highly doubtful Detective."

"Since we're seemingly at an impasse I'm going to give you some time to think things over. I've got an appointment on the other side of town at 4 today. I'm going to get there a little early. I'll need to find parking of course. I've also been up since early this morning. I'm about due for lunch. Maybe while I'm out you can look into that name I gave you. Call your home office if you like. I'll return here in about two hours. I work with discretion too but only for a limited time. If you don't have anything helpful for me when I return, I'll be back tomorrow with a warrant and maybe a subpoena to seize your records. Perhaps we'll hold you in a cell for a while. And at the same time I'll make sure to call FinCEN, the FBI, the NYPD Financial Crimes Unit and the newspapers too. That'll impress your home office and your upstanding clients, your name in the paper for withholding information, not cooperating with an investigation. I'm investigating a murder *Signor* Rinaldi. How's that for discretion?"

"I see," said Rinaldi, staring down at his desk. "Anything else Detective?"

"Yes actually. I'd like you to recommend a good French place nearby for lunch and have fashion-boy Max fetch me my coat, *pronto, s'il vous plait.*"

Rinaldi then rose and silently left the room, walking directly past Thorsen who was now standing by the window. He left the office door open and Thorsen heard him talking rapidly with Max. While Thorsen did not understand what the two men were saying there was no mistaking the tone of urgency in Rinaldi's voice. A few moments later Max appeared with his coat.

"*Merci,*" said the detective.

"Good day Detective," said Max. "And this is for you."

He handed Thorsen a slip of paper. It contained a few words written in French.

"What's this?" asked the detective.

"It is *Signor* Rinaldi's regular French restaurant. It is only a few blocks from here," he said pointing to the address. "You can walk there. Hand this to the *maitre'd* and everything will be taken care of."

"I'll take it under consideration," said Thorsen. "Please thank *Signor* Rinaldi for the recommendation."

Max then accompanied Thorsen to the elevator and neither said anything further.

/ / /

When Officer Krupcheski reached the head of the North Fork Harbor Vineyards driveway he shut off the truck's engine and let the vehicle quietly roll into the parking area, choosing a spot alongside two other small, unoccupied trucks, one of which he recognized to be LaBroom's. Experienced at delivering bad news, Krupcheski learned it's best to be discreet whenever possible.

He exited the truck and after quietly closing the door, walked behind the winery office building to look over the vineyard. Perhaps he thought, he'd see a work crew and be able to directly find LaBroom, call him aside and quietly hand him the Motion to Compel while privately explaining to him the seriousness of it. He had after all, grown up with LaBroom in the small town of North Fork Harbor, warranting he felt, some discretion in their dealings. But Krupcheski could see no work crews amid the long rows of vines, giving him no choice but to knock on the office door.

Andy LaBroom himself answered the door. "Hi Nick," was all he said.

"Hi Andy, I've come to deliver something to you."

"What's that?"

Krupcheski looked past LaBroom. He could see Cindy the secretary and his sometimes-girlfriend watching the scene from behind her desk.

"Is there a place we can talk?" asked Krupcheski.

"Sure," he said shrugging his shoulders. "We can go in my truck."

"Okay," said Krupcheski.

Without saying anything to Cindy, LaBroom walked with Krupcheski to his truck. Each man separately opened their respective door and entered.

"Andy, you and I have been friends for a long time but as a police officer of this town it's my duty to hand this to you in person," said Krupcheski as he slid an envelope into LaBroom's waiting hand. LaBroom took it and somberly placed it on the sun visor of the truck without opening it.

"I know what it is Nick. They want to talk to me at the police station, don't they?"

"Yes. St. Charles wants you to come in for a talk."

Neither man spoke for a few seconds until Krupcheski broke the silence. "You can save everyone, including yourself, a lot of time and trouble if you tell me what you know, right here, right now," offered the young officer, trying to coax a confession.

"I already told your boss, that St. Charles, the great cop from the big city, everything I know."

"St. Charles ain't so bad," said the junior officer. "He gets wrapped a little too tightly sometimes, that's his personality I guess from all those years of lookin' over his shoulder."

Again there was a pause broken by Krupcheski.

"They found the Doc's handheld the other day Andy," said Krupcheski. "They got some pretty smart guys workin' on this case. They'll put the puzzle together one day. I just come from your Mom's place. She's worried for you."

LaBroom remained silent, rubbing a small stain on the truck's dashboard with the tip of his thumb. "How long before I got to show up at court?" he asked.

"It's not court. That's a subpoena. You generally have 24 hours to report from when it's handed it to you," said Krupcheski, looking at his watch. "I don't give legal advice. I just do what they tell me. Which reminds me, I've got to get to work myself. Think things over carefully and give me a call if you think of anything you want to tell me," he said to his friend while exiting the truck. "And don't leave town."

While Krupcheski tried to get a confession from LaBroom he was not completely forthcoming with his troubled friend. Krupcheski neglected to tell LaBroom that he was not legally required to comply with the Motion to Compel. Unlike a subpoena, it's voluntary. But sensing LaBroom's ignorance, Krupcheski mentioned a 24-hour response time, which is generally used for subpoenas, in an attempt to prod LaBroom into going to the police station. LaBroom however, remained in the truck, hands now at his side while staring directly ahead. He did not watch Krupcheski get into his own truck and leave the property. He chose to instead listen to the sound of Krupcheski's truck starting, followed by the cracking of the tires over the gravel. Not until he could no longer hear Krupcheski's truck did he exit and walk directly out to the vineyard, over the very same land his ancestors farmed and to the spot where his brother Anthony was buried.

/ / /

When Det. Thorsen returned to the offices of Banc di Basil after lunch he was personally greeted this time as he stepped from the elevator by Rinaldi. Not wanting to look like he was seeking favorable treatment or risk being watched, Thorsen avoided the restaurant recommended by Rinaldi and instead ate at a small Chinese place he had passed earlier that day.

"Did you have a pleasant lunch detective?" Rinaldi asked when he saw Thorsen.

"Yes, very nice."

"You did not visit the bistro I recommended?"

"No. Sorry I changed my mind at the last minute. But I did get a fortune cookie."

"And what did it advise?"

"It said: *The rabbit keeps many holes.*"

"Maybe that's very good advice. Please follow me."

Thorsen accompanied Rinaldi to his office. The manager waited for the detective to enter before firmly closing the door behind him.

"I trust this is the information for which you have come Detective," said Rinaldi, pointing to a thin file on his desk. "The reason I did not have the information previously is that the account is so new it is not yet in the bank's computer system."

Thorsen wasn't sure if he should believe Rinaldi's explanation but decided to withhold offering any opinion until he saw what the file contained.

"We have a new account featuring the Social Security number you provided," Rinaldi continued.

"How did you get this account?" Thorsen asked.

"From a referral, I'm sure. If you'll just wait a moment . . . yes, here it is. It came from a Mr. Paxton Goode."

"An existing client?"

"Yes, a very respected businessman and a longtime client. There is no reason to doubt his integrity."

"A US citizen?"

"A dual-citizen. Switzerland and the USA. Your country and ours. So he is afforded certain protections."

"That depends on which passport he uses."

Rinaldi nodded.

Although Thorsen felt the banker was trying to quietly intimidate him he chose to ignore his erroneous statement about certain protections afforded to someone he was beginning to increasingly believe was a key suspect. Internally his patience was wearing thin. "Can you guide me through this file please?" he asked.

"Certainly," said Rinaldi. "It will only take a moment once you understand the codes."

"Here is the date it was opened," said Rinaldi politely referring to one group of numbers on the account form. "And here is the type of account," he said, pointing to another. "It is a general account right now, meaning nothing has been established as to its purpose, such as retirement, investment, discretionary etc. This is very typical new-client behavior."

"And where's the money?" asked Thorsen.

"Very good question," said Rinaldi, breaking into a grin. "It is a shell account. It's been created, it has an account number but it has not been funded until this morning. The account had been empty."

"What about this Paxton client?"

"I'm sorry I cannot disclose information about any other bank clients. Everything I can tell you is in this file," Rinaldi said.

"Was the account opened in New York?"

"Yes," answered Rinaldi, who pointed with his index finger to a signature at the bottom of the account-opening form. "Anything else detective?"

"What did you mean when you said the account 'had been empty'?"

"Coincidentally, while you were having lunch I discovered there was some activity in this account this morning. An inter-bank deposit had been made into this account from our Buenos Aires office."

Thorsen studied the account form. It had been opened only a week ago by: Mrs. Cynthia LaBroom, with a Buenos Aires, Argentina postal box as an address and Anthony LaBroom's Social Security number.

"I'm new to international banking. Help me with this."

"Certainly."

"Here's how I see it. A mystery woman in New York uses a dead man's Social Security number with an Argentine address to open a numbered account but does not deposit any funds into it. Then a deposit suddenly is made from one of your bank's other offices. Was anyone in your bank planning on filing a Suspicious Activity Report?"

"That is what I meant when I told you the account was not yet in our computer system. Once that would have occurred an alert would have been issued and a report would have been filed with FinCEN."

"Why so long?" asked Thorsen. "Seems like your record keeping's a little weak. Any info on the wife? Social Security number? Photograph? US address? Driver's license? Passport number? Fingerprints? Let me see her signature."

Rinaldi hesitated before showing Thorsen the woman's signature. It was barely legible, little more than a scribble carelessly scrawled on the bottom of an incomplete form. Thorsen could do little more than shake his head. He made little effort to hide the expressions of disgust and disappointment that had swept over the normally sanguine detective. He looked up to watch the manager's face grow red. The incomplete record keeping had become an embarrassment bordering on professional negligence. Rinadli then cleared his throat. "The client came from a very good referral," he blurted without warning. "We acted on that discretion."

"And where did the sudden deposit come from?"

"I've already told you everything I can."

Thorsen casually reached into his coat pocket, letting the first loop of a pair of handcuffs dangle from it. "Like I told you this morning, withholding information is a crime. At the minimum you could be facing a Failure-to-Supervise charge and disregard of the Know-Your-Customer rule. Do you want to reconsider your last response?" he asked, watching Rinaldi grimace.

"It was a private transaction."

"I don't care if it was from a Girl Scout cookie sale. Who sent it?"

"It was an international wire transfer."

"It had to come from somewhere."

"It came from our office."

"That's not good enough," said Thorsen walking closer. "I want you to freeze this account immediately."

"On what grounds?"

"Use your discretion. What's the amount of the deposit?"

"Three-hundred-thousand *euros*. About $250,000 US."

"I'm wondering if anyone would have noticed this if I hadn't showed up."

"You are very forceful Detective."

"You have no idea. I'll fly to Switzerland to nail this."

"Detective, please, be advised that in my country should a banker provide account information without the client's permission, immediate prosecution is begun by the Swiss public attorney. I could get up to six months in prison and fined 50,000 francs."

"If you cooperate you'll be excused because there's evidence that this deposit may be linked to criminal activity and I'll support you should there be an investigation. If you refuse I'll personally arrest you and you'll never work in banking again, probably lose your pension, most likely get some jail time. I urge you to use your discretion."

"You have no right," Rinaldi began. "We have been banking like this for hundreds of years. Our clients are paramount."

"Would you like me to read you your rights before I cuff you or after?"

Rinaldi paused, took a deep breath and began nervously flipping through an address book before quickly scribbling down a few bits of information onto a piece of note paper. He then tore the sheet from the pad and put it directly into Thorsen's hand.

"You don't have to fly to Switzerland," he said. "And you didn't get that from me."

"I see," said Thorsen looking at the note. It was a New York City office building address for Paxton Goode. It was very close to where he'd be returning after his meeting with Rinaldi. "I'll be taking this file with me. *Merci.*"

As Thorsen turned to leave Rinaldi called out to him.

"Detective Thorsen," he called.

"Yes," he said, not bothering to turn around. Thorsen had his hand on the office door knob and was ready to leave.

"Please be sure to put in your report that the bank acted lawfully and that I fully cooperated."

"I hope I don't have to come back here," was all the normally loquacious detective could say.

"Detective," Rinaldi once again called.

"What is it this time?"

"We do not aid criminal activity."

"Neither do I. You're going to have to do better than that. Now freeze that account and let me know if there's any attempt of further activity with it, like another deposit or a request to transfer funds. Otherwise I'll be back with a warrant."

"Yes Sir."

Thorsen then left the office, leaving the door open behind him. When he went back to his car he immediately called St. Charles.

"We may have made some progress today," said Thorsen as soon as St. Charles came to the phone.

"Go ahead."

Thorsen then reviewed that day's activity, concluding by telling the Sergeant that he was on his way to try to learn about who may have found the victim's handheld. In return St. Charles let him know that Krupcheski had successfully delivered the motion and that he expected Andy LaBroom to come to headquarters for questioning as well as the bite test within 24 hours.

"I'm going to order fingerprinting and DNA testing on the handheld," said St. Charles. "We'll see if a chip is still inside it."

"We'll let the chips fall where they may," Thorsen said with a laugh. "I'll have this machine out there by tonight, ideally after I get some information from Carlita Melendez. Then I'm looking forward to putting some heat on this international jet-setter."

"The noose is starting to tighten," said St. Charles. "And all of the suspects are trying to wiggle out of it before it's too late."

"Make sure the right LaBroom shows up," Thorsen said in response. "If a woman claiming to be the wife of a dead guy can use his Social Security number to open a Swiss bank account anything can happen."

CHAPTER 32

Harvesting Truth Amid the Vines

Maria Lambrusco parked her rental car outside the vineyard's office building and then carried her bag into the reception area.

"Maria," said the surprised Cindy looking out from the office. "I had no idea you were coming today."

Maria looked into the office from the reception area. Cindy had been in Maria's father's office and it was apparent she had been working at his desk instead of at the receptionist's area, which was in disarray with miscellaneous boxes and papers strewn about. There was a sour smell in the air. The waste baskets contained half-empty take-out food cartons and opened bottles of wine.

"When did you get in?"

"Early this morning. I got your note about the Brix and wanted to be here for the harvest. It looks like I missed the party."

"Great. It's so good to see you. I'll just get my things out of the way."

Maria watched Cindy haphazardly gather her papers and move to the reception-area desk.

"Nobody is supposed to be in here," Maria said. "You know that."

"Yes, I'm sorry," said Cindy. "It's just that last night we had a demonstration with a new bottle supplier. And the printer dropped off the new labels. They're in those smaller boxes. They sort of took over the reception area. And I needed to make some calls this morning. Andy and the workers were going in and out. I needed a quiet place. You know with the harvest so close there's so much to do and you haven't let me hire any new help so it's just Andy and me doing practically everything."

Maria surveyed the scene. There were some cartons from a prospective bottle supplier in the reception area and samples on Cindy's desk but Maria felt her claims about clutter were an exaggerated excuse for something she was not disclosing.

"I appreciate your help but tell the supplier we're not changing bottles," said Maria. "First problem solved. Feel better?"

"But Maria, these new bottle designs are more efficient. They'll fill faster. They're lighter. They'll save you time and money on shipping."

Maria took one of the bottles on her desk, holding it up by the neck to watch the way the sunlight shone through it. Maria tapped the glass with her fingertip and listened to the weak-sounding ping. The flat-bottomed bottle was made from a thinner, inferior grade of glass than her father had been using, material typically used for marketing a poorer wine. She also knew the vineyard-supply industry had its share of kickbacks and "special offers" for purchasing managers. And Cindy did not have authority to make such purchases.

"Like I said, call the supplier," she said to Cindy who then broke into a quick smile as if expecting a change in direction from Maria. "They'll break faster too. Return the samples today. Cheap bottles hold cheap wine. That's not our product. It's not our image or market. We have a reputation to maintain now more than ever. And speaking of Andy, please let him know I want to meet with him this morning to begin planning the crush. Also ask him to bring some grape samples. I'd like an updated Brix reading. Please make sure the lab is cleaned and ready." Cindy sighed and nodded. "Anything else?" asked Maria.

"I want to remind you that I'm going to the Food and Beverage Hospitality Show this weekend in Boston. Your father approved it. I wasn't sure if you knew but I won't be able to be here this weekend. I have his approval on this memo," Cindy said while taking a sheet of paper from a folder for Maria to see. "Everything's been reserved and paid for, hotel, train, seminar and exhibition tickets." While Maria did not know about Cindy's upcoming business trip or her father's approval to pay for it, she couldn't care about it at this time. Maria was not comfortable around Cindy and not having her at the winery for a weekend would come as a slight relief to her.

"Not a problem," said Maria without looking at the memo. "Any other winery personnel going with you?"

"Your father only approved me to go," continued Cindy. "I hope you don't mind. It's all been paid for. It's too late to cancel. We paid in advance. It would be a shame for me not to go."

"How are you getting to Boston?" asked Maria.

"I'm taking the ferry to New London, Connecticut. There's an Amtrak station on the other side. From there the train ride to Boston is just a little more than an hour."

Cindy's reference to "the other side," meant a roughly 90-minute ferry ride from North Fork Harbor across Long Island Sound to New London. From there one could make connections to numerous trains, buses and ferries that travel to a variety of locations to New England to the north and southern Connecticut and the New York City area to the south. It was a vital means for getting on and off Long Island's relatively isolated eastern end.

"When are you leaving?"

"I'm here all day, 'til five. Then I'm going back to my apartment to finish packing. I'm booked on the last ferry out tonight. I should get to my hotel by about midnight."

"You'll be back here Monday morning?"

"No, Tuesday. I hope that's okay. That was the arrangement. It's all here," Cindy said, again pointing to the memo. "Your father approved it but if you need me here I can change my plans. It's just that I'm booked for a seminar Monday. It's paid for and at this point I won't be able to get a refund."

"That's all right," said Maria. "I'm glad you told me so I can be sure we have enough staff for Monday. I would've come in Monday expecting to see you here."

"I took care of that," said Cindy. "The workers' schedules are set. A temp's coming in Monday to answer the phones and handle the basic office work. Sorry for the late notice, it's just been so crazy around here lately."

"This temp knows her way around the office?"

"Yes. She's been here before. Louise LaBroom. She's Andy's mom. Just be sure to call her Mrs. LaBroom and everything will be fine."

"Okay then," said Maria. "See you Tuesday."

After she exited Maria closed the office door and sat at her father's desk. She was becoming overwhelmed by the feeling that she was starting to lose control of the enterprise to which her father had dedicated much of his life. Maria still had responsibilities in California but she could not easily let go of what her father had built, not without first fulfilling his mission.

She then sat behind her father's desk, resting her arms on the sides of his chair while wondering who had possession of the data that was in his handheld. His security codes, not very sophisticated to begin with, were probably compromised by now. How would his information be used? Would they ever be caught? And who actually killed her father?

What to do next she thought. The ripening grapes would not wait indefinitely on the vine. There were people in the area capable of running the winery but who would share her vision? Who could she trust? Maria then remembered her promise to invite Vin Gusto to the crush. She also wanted to know the progress of his magazine article. Maria dialed Shanin's telephone number to let them know she had returned, asking them to get in touch with her. As she had no friends in the area Vin and Shanin offered some refuge. Maybe they'd be free for dinner she wondered. The crush would take place in a few days she was sure, judging by the information Cindy had sent but she was far from comfortable working with the crew her father left behind. Maria left a message on Shanin's phone before sliding back on her father's chair and shutting her eyes.

///

When Detective Thorsen returned to the office building to look for Carlita Melendez he noticed the address Christian Rinaldi had given him was to the building next door. Looking up to check the address, he saw that the two buildings were joined by a skywalk. Inside the lobby he was greeted by the security guard who was there earlier that day. Thorsen was carrying a brown paper bag which contained the handheld.

"Hello Detective," the guard said.

"Cleaning crew arrive?"

"A few of them are downstairs. Help yourself," the guard said gesturing towards the door that opened to a stairway.

"Know this name?" Thorsen asked the guard, showing him the slip of paper Rinaldi had given him.

"No," said the guard. "That address is for our sister building. But I can check their directory if you like."

"Why don't you do that?"

Thorsen watched the guard punch a few buttons on his computer screen. After a few seconds he pointed to a listing.

"This looks like him. He's with HCG," the guard said.

"How do I get there?" asked Thorsen.

"You can walk outside and go through the lobby next door or take the elevator here to the 15th floor, go across on the skywalk and then get on another elevator to the 29th floor."

"Before I do that can you tell if he's in?" asked Thorsen pointing towards the screen.

"According to this he was not in the building today. He wasn't in yesterday either. Maybe he's on vacation."

"What's HCG?"

"Highland Consortium Group," said the guard. "You've probably seen their ads, 'The Biggest Company You Never Heard of'."

"I can't say I know 'em," said Thorsen. "What do they do?"

"A little bit of everything, I guess."

"I'll check them out later," said Thorsen. "I'm going to head downstairs to look for Ms. Melendez. Thanks again for your help. You're the nicest person I've met today."

"You bet," said the guard who winked when he responded.

Thorsen then took the stairwell to the building's lower lobby level. In stark contrast to the opulent lobby the lower level was characterized by cinder block walls painted white, a black-tiled floor and bare light bulbs hanging from metallic fixtures screwed into the ceiling. Thorsen heard voices speaking what he thought was Spanish coming from the end of the hallway and walked in that direction. There was a room off the end of the hallway from where Thorsen could hear several Spanish-speaking female voices. On the wall outside of the room were a wire rack stacked with cards and a time clock. Thorsen stopped and read the names of the workers on the cards which were in slots on the rack in alphabetical order. As he did so he noticed the talking in the adjacent room came to a stop. From the corner of his eye he could see three Hispanic women watching him in silence. Thorsen noticed that a "C. Melendez" had checked-in for that evening's shift. Thorsen then entered the room as each of the women continued to silently stare at him. They were not used to an outsider interrupting their pre-work assembly.

"*Buenos noches*," he said, nodding at the women as he deliberately stood in the doorway to discourage any sudden exits. The women said nothing but continued to stare at him.

"Carlita?" he then asked. "Carlita Melendez?" He continued receiving blank stares.

Thorsen then glanced at his watch. It would soon be time for the women to begin their shifts. "Carlita Melendez?" he repeated, this time pointing his index finger individually at the women, each of whom shook their head. Thorsen then reached across a counter and took a napkin from a pile. He then reached into the brown bag he had been carrying and using the napkin removed the handheld. He smiled while he held it up before the women.

"Who find?" he asked while continuing to smile. "No trouble." Thorsen then reached into his other pocket and put a ten-dollar bill on the counter.

The women looked at each other. "Ah, Carlotta. I Carlotta. No Carlita," said one woman slightly raising her hand.

Thorsen then stepped aside and gestured for the other women to leave the room, which they did. He then closed the door, gestured for Carlotta to sit, sliding the bill towards her before showing her his badge. She nodded when he showed her his police badge but did not touch the money. "I find," she said. "I no steal. I find in basket," she pleaded pointing to a trash receptacle in the room as she pushed the bill across the counter back towards Thorsen. "I no take nothing," she said.

Thinking he could get more information from her by avoiding conflict Thorsen quietly took back the bill and folded it into his shirt pocket.

"Okay," he said. "*Por polizia, importante.*" Thorsen emphatically pointed towards the handheld which was now on the counter. Realizing foreigners are often apprehensive with authority personnel, he tried to gain the woman's trust. "You," he said, then pointing at Carlotta. "Take me," he continued, then pointing at himself. "Where you find, okay? *No problema. No polizia. Amicos, okay?*" he asked in a polite mix of rudimentary Spanish and English.

Not sure if she was in trouble or not Carlotta nodded. Thorsen then rose, put his badge in his pocket and returned the computer to the bag before extending his hand which Carlotta shook. He then opened the door and silently followed her to the service elevator. Thorsen followed her to the 15th floor where they exited the elevator. Taking the skywalk they then entered the sister building. They walked down another hallway before taking another elevator to the 29th floor. Most of the employees had now left the building but they were able to gain access to each of the floors and elevators with Carlotta's pass. If any remaining employees had seen the two of them walking together they'd likely think he was her supervisor. They walked until they reached a pair of thick, heavily varnished, wooden doors protecting a seemingly large office behind them. The gold-lettered name on the door read: Paxton Goode, Vice President, Americas. Carlotta tried the gold-colored knob but the doors were locked. Carlotta then turned and looked at the detective.

"I no go here," she said.

"*llave?*" asked Thorsen.

"No," she said.

Thorsen reached around her and tried the door himself. "You find here?" he then asked, pointing at the door. Carlotta nodded. "About one week ago?" he continued. Carlotta shrugged her shoulders. Seeing she did not understand what he said Thorsen decided to end the encounter. "*Gracias,*" he said, again extending his hand with the ten-dollar bill in it. This time Carlotta took it. Without saying anything she turned and left. Thorsen then stepped back and looked at the door and the name on it. He removed a handkerchief from his pocket and covering the knob tried it again but it would not budge. Thorsen then went to examine a desk a few feet away from the locked office. Theorizing it may belong to a secretary of Goode's he scanned the top of the desk where a calendar was opened. In two days time he saw the notation: PG back. Next to the calendar was a thick file marked "travel." Thorsen flipped open the cover and found an itinerary for Paxton Goode at the top of a pile of papers. Goode was scheduled to return from Argentina in two days after a connection in Panama. At the end of the desk was a tray containing what appeared to be the secretary's business cards: Cynthia LaBarone, Executive Assistant, Americas, HCG Corp. He put one of the business cards into his shirt pocket. It was time to go to headquarters, submit Dr. Lambrusco's handheld computer for fingerprints and DNA testing and then wait for the bite-test results and whatever new information St. Charles might obtain after speaking with LaBroom. Thorsen was not good at waiting. He liked cases that were quickly resolved. They had made progress but not yet nearly enough to make an arrest. Thorsen could feel the all-too-familiar sting of frustration that comes from working without substantial results swelling up within him. But as the detective left Manhattan via the Queens Midtown Tunnel he could not stop wondering how a cleaning woman came to find the computer of a world-renown winemaker in the waste basket of an international businessman's New York City office. To relieve his mind of the frustration he made a call to his collaborator on the case, Sgt. Henry St. Charles.

///

"Are you still in the office honey?" asked the sardonic Thorsen when St. Charles answered the phone. "I'm on my way home but I thought I'd give you a call. What's for dinner?"

"I'm waiting for our guest, Andy LaBroom. Dr. D's going to be joining the party as well. It should be a fun-filled night. We'll miss you."

"I'd love to join you boys but I've got a computer to drop off at headquarters that was allegedly found in the office of big-shot businessman Paxton Goode by a barely literate cleaning lady who plucked it from the waste basket and sold it to some computer-salvage place, probably for grocery money."

"Paxton who?" asked St. Charles.

"Don't you read The Wall Street Journal? See what you can find on Paxton Goode, vice president of the Americas for HCG," asked Thorsen. "Looks like he's got an office the size of a football field. Right now he might be in Argentina or Panama but should be back in New York in a couple of days, providing nobody tips him off. He's a dual citizen. US and Switzerland."

St. Charles took notes as Thorsen spoke.

"I don't think we should notify the Feds to have this guy held at the airport," continued Thorsen.

"No," said St. Charles. "We've got nothing on him. We don't know if the cleaning lady's telling the truth. If we spook him and he hides behind his Swiss passport it will only complicate things. Then we'll have to get the Feds and the internationals involved. Do you think this private banker will tip him off?"

"Doubtful. He doesn't know much about the case. He can't have a lot to say plus he's got too much to lose if this thing goes down the way it might. We'll do it your way," said Thorsen in a rare moment of agreement. "Now that you mention it, I say it's best if we keep quiet and let him return on his own free will for three reasons."

"And what are they?"

"The first is once the Feds swoop in and an arrest is made they'll take all the credit and I guarantee they'll have the papers there. After doing all the grunt work we'll be reduced to some country-cops sideshow. The second, I'm dying to hear his alibi. These guys have a way of believing their own fantasies. And the third is if he decides not to return we can always involve the Feds later. Let them do the international grunt work only if it ever actually needs to be done. Until then, this is our trophy and it's going to be a big one."

St. Charles sighed as he thought over Thorsen's comments. They may not have had the killer's full motivation but it was clear what Thorsen wanted. "We'll see what we can find out tonight," he said moving the discussion forward.

"How long are you going to wait for LaBroom to show?"

"As long as it takes. Anything else?"

"I'm going to send you my notes later but you might like to know $250,000 suddenly appeared in the Swiss account of the dead LaBroom today. Coincidentally they discovered it when I left the bank for lunch. I had them freeze the account."

"How'd you manage that?"

"I used my powers of persuasion. They almost always work."

"How does this fit into your control-freak theory?"

"Let me think about it while I'm driving home tonight."

"A big-shot businessman is not likely to commit murder," said St. Charles. "Cash is his currency, not blood."

"We may be hunting two different types of animals," said Thorsen. "One's a control freak. The other sees this strictly as the cost of doing business. Some of these guys think everything's for sale. If that's the case it'll be the control freak to crack first. The other guy's too cool. In his mind he's got no blood on his hands. Give my regards to Dr. D. and remember the deal the three of us made."

"What's that?"

"Once we crack this case we're going out for dinner, preferably to a Greek joint that's got good food, good wine and great belly dancers."

"I can hardly wait" said St. Charles. "Maybe we'll bring Stimmel along for laughs."

"Stimmel and laughs do not go together. You're prematurely ruining my appetite. Even I can't tolerate Stimmel for more than five minutes. Let's count him out. Good night Sergeant. You're a hell of a cop."

"Thanks," said St. Charles, not sure of the detective's sincerity but impressed with his ability to create psychological profiles and theorize motives. "You too," he added. "But I always feel like there's more I can do."

"That's because there always is. We'll talk tomorrow."

"I'm looking forward to it."

Thorsen hung up the phone and St. Charles shook his head. Could it be that he was actually starting to get along with Thorsen? In any event, he'd have Krupcheski begin tracking down Paxton Goode as he had to prepare with Dr. Dionasis for their possible meeting with LaBroom. Just then there was a knock at his door. It was Dionasis. He was carrying a large, black leather briefcase and was uncharacteristically casually dressed.

"When's the guest of honor getting here?" asked Dr. Dionasis extending his hand. St. Charles rose to greet him.

"No suit tonight? You're out of uniform," he said. Dionasis was wearing khaki pants, brown leather loafers, a short-sleeve, white oxford shirt and no tie.

"I want the suspect to feel comfortable around me so I dressed casually."

"I'm willing to give him 24 hours Doc," said St. Charles. "You're welcome to wait or you can show me how to give the bite test and head home."

"I'd like to administer the test," he said. "But remember what I told you, no bite test is infallible."

"I understand but if it's positive it'll bring us one step closer towards getting a subpoena if I have to do so."

"Let's see how it goes. One can never tell how these things will turn out," said Dionasis. "I'll wait for a while. Maybe the two of us can get some late dinner and should he arrive, you can be called."

"Good idea," said St. Charles. "It's amazing how hungry you can get sitting behind a desk. Grab your coat. I'll drive. I know a little seafood place you'll like. We can get a booth and talk where we won't be noticed too much."

"As long as they've got a decent wine list I'll be happy."

"The place I have in mind serves wine but I don't know how happy it'll make you. The food's good. A lot of the local cops eat there."

"As always, I trust your judgment."

St. Charles left word with the desk clerk after sending an e-mail to Krupcheski ordering him to immediately begin a criminal-history check on Paxton Goode. The doctor and the sergeant then left the police station.

Although Officer Krupcheski performed a thorough criminal—and public-records search of Paxton Goode, the businessman came through clean. He had no criminal record, no civil complaints against him, did not own a firearm and regularly paid his taxes on time. Krupcheski did discover however, that earlier in his career, Goode was a registered commodities broker. The firm that employed him mostly traded agricultural products. It also meant that at one time, Goode had to have been fingerprinted by the Commodities Futures Trading Commission (CFTC) which might still have his prints on file. Krupcheski entered a request with the CFTC's investigative unit for a copy of the fingerprints of former commodities broker Paxton Goode. Krupcheski also discovered one more thing while searching through various data bases for information on Paxton Gode that night. He owned a vacation home on nearby Shelter Island.

CHAPTER 33

Reading the Grape Leaves

Maria Lambrusco was puzzled when she tested the grape samples brought in from the field. The Brix readings were substantially below those previously supplied by Cindy a few days earlier, prompting Maria to make her trip east. To be sure, Maria went to the fields herself and personally took additional samples from grapes located at various spots in the vineyard but especially those in the spots that received more sunlight. She selected grapes from the outside of the bunch as these generally received the most sunshine and subsequently could be relied upon to provide the highest sugar content. But nothing matched the levels that had been supplied by Cindy. Maria checked and double-checked but regularly came forth with the same results. She thought about this as she reviewed her calculations in the lab. Did Cindy make a mistake in providing the data? She was not comfortable and decided not to speak with Cindy about the discrepancies of the results. Instead Maria stored her calculations in her laptop computer and decided to deal with the issue later. If her results were correct, which she was sure they were after double—and triple-checking them, she might have to extend her stay on North Fork Harbor and wait for the crop to peak. If she ordered the grapes to be picked early they would produce an inferior wine. But why the erroneous reading?

It was late in the day when Maria checked her e-mail. Shanin had responded to her message. She and Vin agreed to meet her for dinner that night. Shanin suggested the same restaurant she and Vin had tried to eat in a few nights earlier, when they abruptly decided to change their dinner to take-out. Maria agreed to meet them at the restaurant and then deleted the message. She then went to her father's apartment to shower and dress for dinner.

///

Vin Gusto and Shanin Blanc were seated in a corner booth discussing the events of the past few days while waiting for Maria Lambrusco to arrive when a familiar figure entered the restaurant.

"Don't look now," said Shanin. "But our favorite police officer and a friend just walked in." Vin quickly looked over his shoulder while Shanin peered into her menu, hoping not to be noticed in the busy restaurant.

"Don't tell me it's St. Charles."

"And he's with the county medical examiner."

"That's an interesting dinner combination. Can you imagine their conversation? Crooks and stiffs. Think we can slip out the back before they notice us?" asked Vin.

"Don't jump into your panic mode," said Shanin. "It's probably just a coincidence. There aren't that many restaurants in North Fork Harbor. They're probably just on dinner break. Besides, you're not in any trouble. Your assignment's nearly done. The heat's off as far as you're concerned. Plus we're waiting for Maria."

"I knew it was a mistake to get here too early."

"There's no escape in this town. You should know that by now," Shanin said. "Just try to relax. We'll get an update from Maria, you'll submit your assignment and in a few days you'll be on to the next job, the next town."

"The next stop for me is probably in the Bronx," Vin unenthusiastically said. "Why don't you give Maria a call? Maybe we can get out of here before they take our order and meet her someplace else."

Shanin tried Maria's number. "There's no answer. She's probably on her way here. Just keep calm. Why don't we order some wine?"

"Good idea," said Vin. "Whatever you like."

Shanin signaled for the waitress and when she arrived ordered a bottle of locally made Chardonnay. A few minutes later the waitress returned, holding the chilled bottle in such a way that they were able to read the label.

"Are you ready to order?" she asked.

"Not yet," said Shanin. "We're waiting for a friend but we'll start with the wine."

The waitress poured a tasting sample into a glass and gestured for Vin to try it. He politely declined, deferring to Shanin. "I trust your judgment," he said to her with a smile. Shanin then tasted the sample. After she nodded the waitress poured them each a full glass. "I'll be back when your friend arrives," she said before exiting.

"I don't like this," said Vin putting down his wine glass.

"What's wrong with it? The wine's perfectly fine."

"Not the wine, the situation," he answered. "Maria's not here. The cops are. This is not starting out right."

"Calm down," Shanin said. "Have another sip of wine. With any luck it'll soothe your nerves."

Vin took a deep breath and did as Shanin advised, all the while trying to discreetly watch the movements of St. Charles from his seat.

"What do you think you're going to have?" asked Shanin.

"I don't know. I'm too nervous to order. Why don't you order a dish-for-two? Something we can split."

"Whatever you say boss but as soon as Maria gets here, I'm ordering another bottle of wine."

About one-half hour had passed. Vin and Shanin had finished the first bottle of wine yet no sign of Maria Lambrusco.

"I'm getting worried," said Vin.

"You were born worried," said Shanin.

"I don't like this."

"There's not much you do like. In fact, I'm wondering if I like spending so much time with you."

"We can argue later. I'd feel a lot better if I knew where Maria was."

"So would I but I'm not having a heart attack over it. She's a big girl. It's a busy time of year for her. She's probably just running late."

"Give me your car keys," said Vin rising from the table.

"Why?"

"Stay here and wait for Maria. I'm going to the vineyard to check on her. Keep your cell phone handy."

Shanin sighed as she reached into her bag for the keys. "I'm still ordering that second bottle of wine," she said as he took the keys.

"Do you have your spare camera?"

"In my bag, at-the-ready as always."

"Give it to me," said Vin.

Shanin again reached into her bag and handed Vin a small, bright yellow, rectangular device that featured a slew of buttons.

"New camera?" asked Vin. It easily fit in the palm of his hand.

"It is," said Shanin. "I got it with a new subscription to Travel & Pleasure."

"Why would you buy a subscription to Travel & Pleasure? We're writing for the competition."

"My old spare was wearing out and this came for free with the subscription. Plus it's got a flashlight and a panic-alarm button," she said, pointing to a red button on the camera's side. "A girl's got to take care of herself."

Vin briefly hit the light switch. A bright beam, almost as strong as a photo flash quickly shot out in Shanin's direction. "Not bad," he said while sliding the compact camera/flashlight into the front pocket of his faded blue jeans.

"Does it do anything else, like make coffee?"

"It's got a GPS, a global-positioning system. Now I'll always know where I am plus a calculator that does currency exchanges, so I'll always know how much to tip and whether I'm getting the right rate or not. If I ever have a reason to panic, well, there's a button for that too."

"Figuring out tips is easy and on North Fork Harbor one can only go east and west. And currency exchange, really now?"

"Maybe with this I'll know where I'm going for the first time in my life. It'll help me see in the dark, plan a budget, give directions and take a picture of my happy memories, of which I plan to have many."

"Pictures?"

"No, happy memories. They're usually connected."

"Okay. I get it. So much for my dream of settling down to become a country-news reporter," Vin said. "Hopefully I'll be right back." He then began to exit the restaurant but not first without having to pass the booth where St. Charles and Dr. Dionasis were seated. As he approached, St. Charles suddenly leaned out from the booth in Vin's path, looking straight at the hustling reporter.

"Going off to write the great American novel?" St. Charles asked.

"I'm a reporter, not a novelist," said Vin stopping to respond. "I write facts, not fiction. One day you'll learn the difference."

"Why don't you and your lady friend join us for a drink? We can catch up. It's not polite to leave a lady alone at the table."

"When did you start being polite?"

"What's the hurry Scoop?" he asked, ignoring Vin's last remark.

"You'll have to read my article if you want to know."

"You have a big deadline to meet?"

"Don't use the word 'dead' around me right now. I've got to go gentlemen. Keep an eye on my 'lady friend.' Be sure no one hassles her. With any luck I'll be right back."

Vin then exited the restaurant, got into Shanin's car and headed directly to North Fork Harbor Vineyards.

///

When Maria Lambrusco had finished dressing, she checked herself in the mirror one last time. Before leaving the winery she needed to stop in the office. She had not set the security system for the evening.

Maria took a quick walk through the office, checking to be sure everything was in order before setting the security system, the same one that was in place the night her father was killed but now with different codes. Walking through the office, lab and tasting room she sometimes thought she felt her father's presence. She stopped to look at some of the grapes she had been testing earlier that day. They were on a dish next to a microscope. Maria was still puzzled about the differences in the Brix readings she and Cindy had noted plus the fact that Andy LaBroom failed to meet with her. The feeling of losing control was returning.

Maria put one of the grapes in her mouth. Even while chewing it, she could tell the fruit did not release the level of sugar needed to meet their wine-making specifications but still believed it was best to keep her observations to herself until she could get a clearer understanding of the dynamics around the winery. Maria then returned to the office to set the security system. She was looking forward to having dinner with Vin and Shanin. Maria badly needed the distraction as she had no friends in the area and without her father there any longer, quickly began feeling the effects of loneliness. Perhaps after the harvest was completed and the wine was made it might be better if she sold the business and returned to California. There she had friends and would not be faced with regularly seeing the spot where her father died. She could continue his work from there she was thinking when her thoughts were interrupted by a noise. Someone had opened the front door and entered the reception area. Maria stood behind the door, held her breath and listened to the sound of the approaching footsteps. She then quickly but quietly closed the office door, locked it, shut the lights and reached for her cell phone. The footsteps stopped only to be followed by a loud knock which she approximated to be from the reception area.

"Hello," the voice called. "Anyone home?"

Maria thought she recognized the voice.

"It's Vin Gusto," the voice continued. "Maria. Are you here?"

Maria breathed a sigh of relief and opened the door to greet him.

"Vin. Nice to see you," she said, extending her hand as she walked towards him. "Did you come to check on me?"

"Yeah, sort of," said Vin removing Shanin's camera from his pocket and placing it on the reception desk.

"What's that?" asked Maria?

"It's Shanin's spare camera."

"It's so small."

"Shanin's in love with it. It's also a flashlight, panic alarm, popcorn maker, secret decoder, you name it," he said. "It's like carrying a nuclear reactor in your pocket." He put the camera on the reception desk and then patted down his pocket. If you're ready then let's go," Vin continued. "I left Shanin at the restaurant. She's probably started a second bottle of wine by now."

"Okay," Maria said. "Wait for me outside. I've just got to grab my jacket and set the alarm."

"Let's take my, I mean Shanin's car," said Vin. "We'll drive you back later."

On the ride to the restaurant Vin informed Maria that Sgt. St. Charles was at the same restaurant where they'd be going. "Maybe we should pick another place," he suggested.

Maria waited a moment before answering. "No," she said. "It might be good if he sees us together."

"Why?"

"It'll let him know we haven't given up. It could pressure him to solve the case."

"I'm out of my element here. I'm still not so sure how this police department works but St. Charles doesn't strike me as the type to sit still and let a case as big as this slip through his fingers," said Vin. "But if you think it might help then I'm willing to eat there. That being said, has there been any progress in the investigation?"

"None that I know of. I'm hoping to speak with St. Charles soon. Maybe he'll have some news," said Maria. "You no longer have to worry for me. I think whoever did this got what they were after," she continued. "I don't think they'll be back. Besides, I'm actually considering selling the vineyard after this year's harvest. There are too many reminders for me here. I can continue with my father's work in California. But please keep that to yourself. For now, should anyone ask, the property's not for sale. None of this information is for publication. I'm only letting you know because you've been very helpful so I want to be honest with you."

"You've been very helpful to me too. This article could not have come at a better time for me. I won't say a word," said Vin. "For people who are supposed to spread the news it's amazing how many secrets journalists are asked to keep."

"It sounds like an interesting line of work."

"It can be. Has anyone approached you about selling the business?" Vin continued. "I would think that what your father built would have a lot of value in the wine world."

"It does but no one's approached me. Not yet, it's still too early. But I would not be surprised if someone does in the not-too-distant future. Cindy and Andy might be toying with the idea. They're trying to run it already without me but I doubt if either of them can get the money, or make the wine. Running a vineyard, raising grapes, making high-quality wine and turning a profit is a lot more difficult than it looks. How's your article coming?"

"Nearly done, so if anything big breaks over the next few days, be sure to let me know. Once I turn it in there won't be much time to make any changes."

"I will and thank you for checking on me. It was very thoughtful."

"No problem," said Vin. "I've always had somewhat of a protective nature."

"That's a very good quality to have," she said. "Your girlfriend should be very happy to have someone like you."

"She should be," said Vin. "That doesn't mean she is."

"I disagree," she said, managing a small smile.

/ / /

They had driven about halfway to the restaurant when Vin realized he had left Shanin's camera on the reception desk at the winery office. Remembering how fond Shanin was of it he decided to return and get the camera.

"Wait here," Maria said as Vin parked the car in the winery lot. "I'll just need to enter the code and then I can go into the office and get the camera. It'll only take a minute."

Vin shut the motor and waited in the car. It was a clear, quiet night. The only noise was a slight breeze rustling through the thick maple trees that lined the driveway. Looking up, Vin could see a nighttime sky full of stars and a bright, yellow moon casting it's golden glow across the broad leaves that filled the vineyard, their dark green canopy shielding a seemingly endless amount of grapes. Grapes are grown all over the world he thought. What it was about these grapes that compelled someone to murder Dr. Lambrusco and would they ever discover who committed the crime? Who was after the data in his computer and why did they stuff his mouth full of grapes? Vin then slightly opened the car window. He heard the far-away hoot of what he thought must be an owl perched in a distant tree before leaning back and shutting his eyes in the calm North Fork Harbor night.

Maria supplied the entry code into the alarm system to gain access to the winery office. She left the door slightly open behind her as she entered the reception area. When the security system was in operation, the front door would now remain open for 45 seconds before automatically closing and re-locking itself. Although the room was illuminated only by the moonlight temporarily shining through the door opening she was able to make her way to the reception desk to get Shanin's camera. Exactly where Vin had left it, she was able to spot the bright yellow camera in the semi-darkness of the room. Maria picked it up and was about to leave when she thought she heard a noise coming from the adjoining room. It had come from the vicinity of her father's office she thought. Maria remained motionless, squeezing the camera, continuing to listen in the silence. She began breathing slowly and quietly through her mouth and became aware of her quickening heart beat. Was it a noise or her imagination? She remained still, physically frozen as several thoughts simultaneously raced through her mind. Maria thought about entering the office to investigate the source of the noise. It was probably her imagination she then thought with maybe a small dose of her late father's paranoia exerting itself. Maria had left her cell phone in the car but there was a telephone on the reception desk if she needed to call for help plus Vin was waiting in the driveway. Perhaps what she'd heard was a rodent scurrying about the office, lured by the grapes she'd left there for testing. It could be a rat or raccoon. Such a creature could do a lot of damage in one night. Maria moved forward and slowly opened the office door. She was now engulfed in total darkness except for the blinking green light given off by the security system.

In the winery driveway Vin was awoken by the ringing of a cell phone. Maria had left her bag on the seat next to Vin. Her phone was on top of her bag. He recognized the caller's number as Shanin's so he answered the phone.

"Did you two decide to make your own wine to bring to the restaurant?"

"No," said Vin, slightly startled.

"What's taking you so long? I'm halfway through the second bottle of wine."

"I'm still at the winery. Are the police still there?"

"Yes but they look like they might be finishing."

"Good," said Vin. "I accidentally left your super, hi-tech camera in the office so we came back to get it. Maria's inside the office looking for it." Vin then checked the time on the phone. Maria had said she'd only be a minute but five minutes had passed. "I'm going to see what's keeping her. She's probably still looking for your camera. It looks like it's pretty dark in there. I'm sure I left it on the desk in the reception area. If you don't hear back from me in five minutes call this number again. If there's no answer get over here right away."

"I won't be able to do that Vin," said Shanin. "You have my car."

But Vin did not hear Shanin's last sentence. He had already ended the call and was walking towards the winery office.

///

Maria slowly entered the room, scanning its perimeter with the camera/ flashlight. The dish holding the grapes appeared to be untouched. Then, for a split second, Maria thought she saw the silhouette of a familiar figure. She returned the light to the area but saw nothing.

Then, from behind her there was a strong tug. A hand wrapped in rubber then came over her mouth and another around her throat. Maria struggled. The only light went out as she dropped the camera. The hand that was around her throat had come off but she was being pulled back and downward, arching her back and exposing her chest. Maria was starting to feel a pinch on the center of her chest when she managed to sharply jab an elbow into her attacker's rib cage, forcing him back and loosening his grip. Maria then spun herself free and turned to face her attacker. As she stood there breathing deeply she thought she heard footsteps in the darkness.

Her attacker was a slightly built person completely dressed in black, including a black ski mask. He took another step towards Maria. Stepping backwards her heels bumped against the cement vat. She could go no further. As her assailant approached she could see that his right hand held a small, shiny object. It was a hypodermic needle pointed in her direction.

"Who are you?" Maria asked between short, quick breaths, her left hand running over the rim of the vat as she tried to ascertain exactly where she was and how she might escape.

The assailant did not answer.

"Who are you?" she repeated. "Who killed my father? Who put grapes in his mouth?"

Just then there was a loud knock on the front door.

"Maria, are you there?" the voice called from outside. "We've got to get to the restaurant. Shanin's drinking all the wine."

Maria turned her head, about to call to Vin for help when the assailant lunged at her, aiming the hypodermic squarely at her chest. Seeing him out of the corner of her eye and with nowhere else to go, Maria instinctively leapt straight up. As she did, her knees collided with the charging assailant. The force from the collision pushed Maria backwards into the vat and knocked the needle from the assailant's hands. Maria was on her back but quickly pulled herself up from the shallow bottom of the vat. Standing knee-deep in wine she managed to regain her balance. By lunging forward and missing the target the assailant had hit his head on the vat's cement wall and was now facedown, lying still on the floor. Maria then stepped out of the vat and ran to open the front door.

///

Vin and Maria stood together in the dark doorway. Maria, overcome with fear, visibly shaking, breathing heavily but unable to speak, could only point in the direction of the other room. Her clothes and hair were dripping wet. Vin could smell the wine all around her.

"What happened?" was all Vin could ask.

With one hand over her mouth, Maria pointed in the direction of the other rooms as her body continued shaking. "Get in the car," said Vin. He put one of his hands on each of Maria's shoulders, turned her about, gently pushed her out the doorway and walked behind her until she entered the car. Opening the door on the passenger side, he sat her down. "Wait here," he said. "Don't leave the car until I get back." Vin then locked the car doors and took the keys with him. Maria, frozen but still shaking, silently stared straight ahead.

In the winery offices Vin slapped his open palms against the walls until he found a light switch. Once he was able to turn on a light he entered the tasting room. Looking over the vat Vin gasped when he saw the body of what appeared to be Maria's attacker lying face down on the floor.

"Hello," called Vin.

There was no answer.

Before he went closer, Vin pulled an empty wine bottle from one of the cartons in the office. Holding the bottle by its neck he slowly approached the motionless body. Vin stopped about three feet from the body and stared down at it. He could not detect any movement. Vin then reached out with his left foot, nudging the body at its side. There was no response. Vin then knelt down on one knee. In his right hand he held the wine bottle, cocked above his head should he have to strike. He then placed the palm of his left hand over the assailant's chest. Vin did not feel a beat.

"Oh no," mumbled Vin. A small pool of blood had appeared from beneath the assailant's head, dripping in Vin's direction. A hypodermic needle lay about three feet from the assailant's outstretched hand. Vin was sure to sidestep it.

Vin knew he was not to touch a body in a crime scene but before he would step back, he reached down. Placing the bottle on the floor Vin rolled the thin, black ski mask partially up to reveal the ashen face of Andy LaBroom.

///

CHAPTER 34

The True Color of Wine

Vin stepped back while continuing to stare at the body. A reporter at more crime scenes than he cared to remember, he could never get used to being close to a corpse. Further, he had tampered with the body, a crime, by nudging it with his foot and lifting the ski mask. He carefully rolled the mask back down over LaBroom's face before gradually stepping backwards, away from the corpse and turning off the lights. He wiped the empty bottle he'd been holding with his shirt tail and then slowly exited the building. When he reached the car Maria was sitting where he had left her.

"It was LaBroom," Vin said as he entered and sat on the driver's side.

"I think I saw someone leave the building," said Maria. There was still a tremble in her voice and due to the slight case of shock from which she was suffering did not outwardly acknowledge Vin's admission of the perpetrator's identity.

"Besides me?" Vin asked.

"Someone else."

"Impossible," said Vin. "There was no one else there. You're still shaken up. So am I. We're not thinking clearly. It's time to call the police."

No sooner had Vin said that when in the rearview mirror he saw headlights coming down the winery driveway. With his eyes transfixed on the mirror he continued watching the approaching vehicle. "It is the police," he said. "Did you call them?" Maria just shook her head and continued staring in the direction of the winery. Her lips and fingertips continued trembling. As they reached the end of the driveway the driver suddenly turned the vehicle sideways, preventing any other vehicles from leaving or entering the premises. The doors then opened. Sgt. Henry St. Charles emerged from the driver's side while Dr. Dionasis stepped out from the passenger side. A third, smaller figure then stepped out of one of the rear doors. It was Shanin. Vin stepped out of the car to meet her.

"You didn't answer the phone so I did like you said, I got here."

"And you brought an escort," said Vin.

"They were leaving the restaurant and I was worried for you so I asked them to bring me here."

"Hi there Scoop," said St. Charles. "Who's in the car with you?"

"Maria Lambrusco," said Vin.

"Everything okay?" asked St. Charles.

"Maria was attacked."

"Is she hurt?"

"I'm not sure. She's barely talking but she walked out of the building on her own."

"The Doc can look at her. What happened?"

"I just told you."

"You haven't told me anything. Who did it? Where are they?"

"Look inside Sergeant."

"Were you involved?"

"No. I was in the car the whole time," he lied.

"Anyone still inside?"

"I don't know," he again lied.

St. Charles nodded and then looked inside the car, directing Maria to roll down the window. "You okay Maria?" he asked.

She barely opened the window, slightly nodded but did not speak, continuing to stare straight ahead. St. Charles could see Maria was wet and smelled of wine. Then, turning towards Dionasis he said, "Take a look at Ms. Lambrusco Doc. I'm going to get the blanket from the trunk of the car. Then come inside with me. You two stay here," he then said turning towards Shanin and Vin. "I'm going to need some statements." St. Charles went to get the blanket while Dionasis tried to learn what had happened to Maria Lambrusco.

"How is she Doc?" St. Charles asked while passing the blanket through the opened car window.

"A slight case of trauma, mild shock. There are some marks as if she was grabbed around the throat. Not talking. She may need a mild sedative but they can decide that at the hospital," he said. "The most important thing now is to keep her warm and to have her examined as soon as possible."

"She may be the only one who knows what happened," said St. Charles. "The writer says he was in the car the whole time."

"You may be able to get a statement from her later in the hospital, after she's been fully examined and has had a chance to rest. I recommend she be seen by a woman physician. I'm going to call for an ambulance."

After Dionasis called for the ambulance St. Charles approached the winery building with the doctor following him. He had his hand on his pistol with the holster opened. When the two were out of earshot Vin turned and quickly told Shanin what had happened. When he finished he asked her to sit in the car with Maria. "I think she's okay, probably just in a slight case of shock," he said. "I'm sure she'd rather be in the presence of a woman. Her clothes are soaked. Turn on the motor and run the heater. The keys are in the car."

///

St. Charles walked to the front of the building and tried the door but the security system had re-set and he could not gain entrance. He sharply knocked on the door with his night stick. "Police," he called. "Anyone here?" There was no answer.

"Hey Gusto," he called. "See if you can get the entry code from Maria."

Vin went to the car and asked Shanin to ask Maria for the code. Maria complied and Shanin wrote it down on a scrap of paper. It was the second time Maria had verbally communicated since she was attacked and was a good sign. Vin delivered the slip of paper to St. Charles.

Before entering the code St. Charles again rapped on the door with his nightstick.

"Police," he called. "Anyone inside?"

He then entered the code and the door opened. Inside he repeated the call. "Police. Anyone here?" Silence continued to greet him. Using his flashlight, St. Charles and Dr. Dionasis walked through until they reached the large room with the cement vat.

"Here we are again," St. Charles said to Dr. Dionasis. "Look familiar?"

"Just once I'd like to come here on pleasant circumstances," said the doctor.

"Keep dreaming," said St. Charles. "Pretty soon it'll probably feel like déjà vu all over again." A few seconds later the two men stood still as the flashlight beam passed over a body on the floor. St. Charles cautiously approached it. After studying it for a few seconds from several feet away and not detecting any movement, St. Charles knelt on one knee alongside the body. Using the tip of a pen, he partially rolled up the ski mask, exposing a good amount of the victim's face. The blood that had earlier dripped from the back of his head had congealed into a dry pool on the cement floor and in strands of his hair.

"Andy?" was all St. Charles could say. He then put his hand on Andy's chest but felt no heart beat. "I think he's dead Doc. You'd better have a look."

"I wouldn't have believed it if I hadn't seen it with my own eyes," said Dionasis kneeling next to St. Charles. "It's too much of a coincidence, a terrible coincidence."

"I couldn't agree more."

Dionasis then put on a pair of latex gloves before placing one hand on LaBroom's chest. He then felt for a pulse on his wrist before running his fingers around his throat and examining his eyes. Dionasis then put his fingers behind the back of the victim's head, feeling the wound there. Dionasis shook his own head as he rose.

"The boy's dead," he confirmed.

"For how long?" asked St. Charles.

"Twenty, thirty minutes."

"Cause of death?"

"To be determined."

"What do we have here?" asked St. Charles while pointing to a hypodermic needle that was on the floor against the edge of the vat, not far from LaBroom's outstretched hand.

"However that got there it didn't kill this boy," said Dionasis. "The plunger's exposed. The cartridge is full. That needle's not been used. We don't know what's in it."

"No but I'm sure someone intended to use it," said St. Charles. "Maybe on Maria Lambrusco. Like you said, too many coincidences. It's almost like someone's following the same script."

"Possibly," said Dionasis.

"Stay here Doc," said St. Charles. "This trail is still warm. I'm going to go to the car, call this in, get the camera, print kit, evidence bag and anything else I can think of. We're going to have to drain that vat again too."

The two men then stared down at the lifeless body of Andy LaBroom.

"Check his chest please Doc," St. Charles requested.

St. Charles remained standing as Dionasis knelt back down and lifted the victim's shirt from beneath his pants. He then stretched his arm under the victim's shirt, exploring the chest with his gloved fingers. After a few seconds Dionasis stopped moving his hands and with a pointed middle finger carefully felt around the center of the victim's chest. He then withdrew his hands and lifted the shirt up to the victim's chin before closely examining the center of his chest.

"Anything?" asked St. Charles.

"He was injected," said Dionasis.

"Like Lambrusco?"

"Exactly," said Dionasis. "But not with the needle on the floor."

"No," answered St. Charles. "There's got to be another one. There's got to be someone else."

St. Charles leaned in for a closer look. He studied the slightly elevated, pinkish abrasion, similar to that of an insect bite, almost perfectly in the center of LaBroom's chest.

"I don't believe it," muttered St. Charles.

"I became suspicious," continued Dionasis, "when I felt the wound on the back of his head. Despite the blood it wasn't too bad. Head wounds tend to look worse than they are. The human skull's pretty durable. He suffered a strong blow, one that could've killed an older person. It was possible but I had my doubts as to whether it was enough to kill a younger man. It may however, have knocked him unconscious or weakened him enough."

"Weakened him enough for someone else to administer a lethal injection," said St. Charles completing the doctor's theory.

Dionasis nodded.

St. Charles ran his gloved fingers over the victim's body. Pressing on one of the pants pockets he heard the crackily sound of paper. Reaching in, he withdrew a small, folded slip of white paper. He unfolded the paper. It was a five-word note printed from a computer: *I killed Tugboat for Anthony.*

St. Charles and Dionasis stared at the note. It featured nothing else beyond its macabre message. There was neither a signature nor date. Similarly, the body search found no other items on LaBroom's person besides the note and clothing he was wearing.

"Stay here Doc. I'm going to call headquarters. We've got to get blocks on the roads leading in and out of North Fork Harbor. We've got to get personnel to the train station and ferry terminal. There's a couple of people I'm going to want to see right away. Give him the bite test if you still can."

CHAPTER 35

No Wine Before It's Time

After Sgt. Henry St. Charles had phoned in the news of the death of Andy LaBroom from the patrol car he remained inside the vehicle and thought about everything that had taken place and what his next move would be in order to push the investigation forward.

There were some suspects to speak with right away such as the winery personnel and LaBroom's friend, Larson the fiery mechanic. Cindy, his former girlfriend may know something as well. But what if an outsider had committed the crime? As he and Thorsen had earlier theorized, there were signs that this was the work of a professional killer, who after using a little known but reliable method, flees the scene with barely a trace, leaving only an unseemly corpse with a small abrasion on its chest and a perverse message as his gruesome calling cards. But how did the killer twice gain access to the secured winery? How did he know when his victim would be present and how best to attack? If it was an outsider, someone had provided the information necessary to commit the crime. There would have to have been an accessory.

Nothing was known to have been stolen this time but like the first murderer who left a message by stuffing the victim's mouth with grapes, this perpetrator left a message in the form of a terse note. The only other things that were certain were that Andy LaBroom had taken part in his last harvest and that someone did not want Maria Lambrusco in their way but that part of their plan had been thwarted by her quick thinking and athleticism.

Why kill LaBroom? What could Maria Lambrusco tell him? Why attack and possibly attempt to murder Maria? Why confess to the Tucker murder? Was it a legitimate confession or was it someone trying to blame LaBroom for it? Was the note an authentic confession or was it planted by someone else to blame LaBroom for Tucker's death? It was now highly doubtful that this was the work of one perpetrator acting alone. St. Charles had been thinking that he and Thorsen had made real progress and now suddenly the case had gone way beyond his control. St. Charles began collecting his thoughts. Two men had been killed the exact same way in the same location by an unknown assailant or assailants using a very discreet, barely traceable but highly effective method as well as leaving a pair of outrageous messages. It did not help that the second victim had been their prime suspect. The big differences between the two murders were that in the second, nothing was stolen from the winery. In the first murder, the handheld computer had been taken and the mouth of the victim had been stuffed with grapes. The second victim had been spared a similar humiliation as only a brief note had been left behind, linking LaBroom to the Tucker murder. Plus there was the attack on and attempted murder of Maria Lambrusco. Whoever planned the potential murder of Maria, St. Charles theorized, was not acting alone. Andy LaBroom was prepared to commit a crime and was dressed for the part. He had very likely been in possession of the unused hypodermic needle they'd found on the winery floor. A fingerprint test and an examination of the needle's contents would shortly determine that. Dr. Dionasis's examination which discovered the injection to LaBroom's chest, also gave credence to the theory that there had to be at least one other perpetrator behind the completion of the second crime. Perhaps now they were chasing two murderers, the second possibly copying the technique of the first to murder LaBroom who may or may not have been adequately motivated to avenge his brother's death. While some of the facts were certain, many others remained unclear.

In a few minutes police officers would begin dusting the winery offices for prints and other clues, examining the premises and interviewing suspects as they had after the first murder but would they get any closer to solving the case? Did the presence of the note confessing to the Tucker murder prove Thorsen's earlier theory that whoever did this would one day want recognition for their deeds? Did LaBroom setttle an old score by killing him? Was LaBroom actually behind the Tucker murder? While St. Charles believed LaBroom may have been capable of murdering Tucker, he was suspicious about the authenticity of the note. In any event, he stopped wondering briefly enough to call Det. Thorsen.

"Are you ready for Round Two?" St. Charles asked Throsen who despite the hour answered his phone before the first ring had finished.

"Sure," he said. "When you're as sleep-deprived as I am you'll say you're up for anything."

"Andy LaBroom's been murdered."

"What?"

"We found him tonight in the same room, killed the same way as Dr. Lambrusco. We think he first attacked Maria Lambrusco. She somehow fought him off, escaped. When we got there LaBroom was dead on the floor. Dr. D. determined the cause was a lethal injection to the chest."

"Anything else?"

"In one of LaBroom's pockets we found a brief note."

"What did it say?"

"I killed Tugboat for Anthony," St. Charles repeated from memory.

"The motorcycle guy?"

"Yes."

"And Anthony is the dead Anthony LaBroom?"

"Most likely."

Thorsen then went silent, absorbing and processing the facts in an attempt to advance their theory. "Sounds like a third-party's involved. Someone who is extremely motivated, possibly used LaBroom and then wanted him out of the way," he said. "You've got to get to Maria as soon as possible. See what she knows."

"She's suffering from a slight case of shock and has been taken to the hospital. I'm going to interview her as soon as I can. In the meantime I'm going to talk with a few of LaBroom's friends, if he's got any left. We're sealing off the roads and transit hubs. When can you get out here?"

"I'll see you in about an hour. Think the note is for real?"

"I'm not sure. It's not much in terms of a confession. I'm not comfortable taking it at face value."

"Think it was the hot-headed mechanic?" asked Thorsen.

"I won't rule out anyone but I don't think it's Larson. If it was him there probably would've been signs of violence. This job was clean. He's certainly physically capable of taking out almost anyone but I can't see what he's got to gain with something like this."

"He's famous for his temper, isn't he?"

"Yes and he's pretty smart too but Lambrusco was his customer. Business people generally don't murder their customers but I'm still going to talk to him, ideally tonight."

"Then maybe it is a pro, an outsider," Thorsen suggested.

"Why would a pro come back?" asked St. Charles. "They got the handheld. They got the data and probably paid a fair amount for it. Why try to murder Maria Lambrusco? I don't see the rationale. For a pro, I would bet that a second murder without a clear incentive is too much risk for too little reward."

"It may not be clear to us but it may make perfect sense to someone else. There could be a big price on her head," countered Thorsen. "This may come as a shock to you but not everyone is interested in grape data. Someone wants something else and Maria may have been an obstacle."

"We've got too many questions. Let's put our theories on hold until we finish scouring this place and run the second round of interviews," said St. Charles. "By then we'll probably be in a better position to move forward."

"We should be hearing about the handheld today plus Paxton Goode is due back in the States soon," said Thorsen. "We've got to get to him before any of this leaks."

"You take care of Goode," ordered St. Charles. "I'll find Larson and Cindy Murphy. And no talking to anyone until this is solved."

"Will do," said Thorsen.

"Thanks," said St. Charles, hanging up the phone. Thorsen may have had an ingratiating personality but it was hard to match his determination, energy and acumen. He was holding fast to his theory of identifying the motivating factor as the key to solving the Lambrusco and LaBroom murders. St. Charles couldn't agree more.

Dr. Dionasis had walked in the direction of where St. Charles was, stopping far enough so as not to hear his phone conversation with Thorsen. When he finished the call Dionasis approached.

"What's up Doc?"

"I was able to administer the bite test."

"And?"

"Remember, the bite test is not infallible and some time has passed since Dr. Lambrusco was killed. It's just a step that can bring us closer but according to my results, it's a match."

/ / /

Officer Nick Krupcheski and another junior officer were assigned the task of inspecting passengers about to board the ferry to New London. Krupcheski and his partner stood along either side of the guard booth, dutifully checking passengers before they proceeded through the gate and to the boarding area. They checked drivers' licenses and passenger identification before ordering people to open the trunk of their vehicles. With large flashlights the duo took turns regularly searching inside trunks and behind seats. But Krupcheski's mechanical rhythm came to an abrupt stop when he suddenly found himself peering into the car of Cindy Murphy.

"Where are you headin' on the midnight ferry?" asked Krupcheski with a grin. Cindy's sudden appearance was a surprise, causing the young officer to momentarily forget the seriousness of his mission. "You got a secret boyfriend on the other side?" he asked while shining the light onto Cindy's face.

"Hi Nick, what's going on?"

"Pull over there," Krupcheski said, a serious expression overtaking his face. He gestured for Cindy to drive her car to a gravel-covered parking area off the entranceway reserved for walk-on passengers. He followed her by foot and when she parked the car, entered through the passenger side. Like with Andy LaBroom, Krupcheski and Cindy had known each other for nearly their entire lives so it was with a degree of familiarity that he entered her small car.

"I barely got room to breathe in here," said Krupcheski as he wiggled into the small passenger seat.

"Maybe you should think about a diet," Cindy suggested.

"Seriously, what are you doing here?" Krupcheski asked.

"I'm going up to Boston. I got a winery business trip up there," she said. "A hospitality seminar. I booked it a while ago." She opened her bag to show Nick her itinerary. He glanced at the papers she handed to him, writing the name of the hotel she'd be staying at in his notebook before returning them to her.

"What happened Nick?"

"You don't know do you?" he asked.

"Know what?"

"Cindy, I'm sorry to have to tell you."

"Tell me what?"

Krupcheski looked down at his black uniform shoes while tapping his fingers on the door handle. They were scuffed with brown traces of mud from working the ferry parking area.

"What's the matter Nick?" Cindy pressed. Krupcheski looked directly at her as he prepared to deliver the news.

"Andy's dead."

"What?"

Krupcheski waited a few seconds before repeating what he had told her. "Something happened at the winery tonight," he said. "Andy was found dead."

Cindy stared at Krupcheski.

"This isn't some sick joke, is it?"

"No, I'm afraid it isn't," said Krupcheski.

"Was it an accident?"

"I don't think so." Krupcheski could see the tears begin to swell in Cindy's eyes as he reached across the seat to hold her. "I'm so sorry Cindy." He put his hand behind the back of her head which began shaking as she sobbed onto his shoulder. After a few seconds he could feel the moisture from her tears seeping through the fabric of his uniform. She then began breathing erratically, her head and chest heaving up and down in an irregular motion. "Stay in the car until you can pull yourself together. Maybe it's not such a good idea if you go to Boston," he said. "I've got to get back to searching vehicles. I'll come back and check on you in a little bit."

Cindy nodded. Krupcheski handed her a crumpled napkin from his pocket which she used to dry her eyes.

"Thanks Nick," she said. "I don't know if you know this but in his own way Andy considered you a friend."

"I liked Andy too. Lots of memories," he said. "And I know he liked you. He may have had a funny way of showing it."

"I can't believe everything's that's happened lately," said Cindy. "First Dr. Frank. He was such a gentle man. And now Andy. This is terrible. What's going on Nick?"

"Is there any place you can stay tonight? It might not be a good idea for you to be alone," Krupcheski advised as Cindy remained silent. "Go in the ticket office and get a cup of coffee from the machine. It's not bad," he said, trying to comfort her with a small smile.

"They're going to want to talk to me about this, right?"

"Yeah. I'm sure you'll be a person of interest."

"Okay. I'll do what I can."

"As of now I have no reason to hold you," said Nick. "We can always reach you in Boston."

"Unless I jump off the boat," she said, her spontaneous and irreverent remark shocking herself as well as Krupcheski.

"Don't kid around. For a second I thought you were serious. Three dead bodies is more than enough for this town. It's probably more than we've had in a hundred years. I guess all this is making me a little tense. You were kidding, right?"

"Yeah, of course. I guess I'm in a slight state of shock."

"I'll check on you as soon as I get a break." Cindy nodded as Krupcheski left her car to resume the inspection of passengers. The search by Krupcheski and his partner turned up no leads in the LaBroom case and as soon as the ferry's steel boarding gates closed Krupcheski entered the ticket office to look for Cindy.

When he did not see her in the ticket office he went to the parking area, thinking she had remained in or returned to her car. When he found the car unoccupied Krupcheski was about to return to the ticket office, thinking Cindy must have been in the ladies room. His search however was abruptly ended when he received a call from Sgt. St. Charles ordering him to come to the winery. St. Charles was on his way to the hospital to try to interview Maria Lambrusco and was putting Krupcheski in charge of overseeing the initial winery investigation in his absence.

"Find anything?" St. Charles asked. "See anyone of interest?"

"Yes. Cindy Murphy, Lambrusco's secretary boarded the last boat to New London."

"What?"

"She had reservations for a business trip to Boston. She showed me the papers. I had no reason to hold her."

"Did she know about LaBroom?"

"No Sir. I told her. She took it hard."

"She took it hard but got on the boat," said St. Charles.

"Actually, I'm not sure about that Sir."

"What do you mean?"

"She was crying and everything so I told her to wait for me in the ticket office. I didn't think she should be driving to Boston in that condition. She said she would but when we finished checking passengers I went to look for her and she wasn't around."

"She left the scene?"

"Her car was there."

"So she got on the boat."

"That's the nearest I can figure."

"Okay," said St. Charles, processing the information. "Before you leave, check with the ferry office. Be sure she boarded the boat. You can never tell what someone might do in these circumstances. The next ferry's not leaving until tomorrow morning," he said, changing the course of the conversation. "Once you get that information, get the pump and the other gear, get a helper and then get to the winery. Supervise draining the vat. You've got experience at this location so unless I'm present you're in charge. Consider this a battle-field promotion."

"Yes Sir," said Krupcheski but St. Charles had already ended the call. Krupcheski then immediately checked with the office manager who confirmed that Cindy had boarded the evening's last ferry to New London. He and the other junior officer then entered the patrol car and prepared to head to North Fork Harbor Vineyards.

/ / /

As she had planned and despite Krupcheski's warning, Cindy Murphy had walked in a nearly trance-like state from the ticket office and silently boarded the ferry. She was carrying a medium-sized bag and after handing her ticket to the attendant, boarded the ferry with the other walk-on passengers. Cindy then went to the boat's upper level and as Nick Krupcheski had advised, ordered a cup of coffee at the snack bar. She had never planned on driving to Boston and scheduled her arrival to coincide with a train that would be waiting on the other side of the New London wharf, a brief walk across the ferry terminal grounds. Perhaps she had not felt the effect of what Krupcheski had told her just a few minutes earlier but as she held the warm cup of coffee in her hand, Cindy stared out the ferry's large deck window. Beyond the few lights leading out of the channel, Long Island Sound was enveloped in near total darkness. All that could be heard was the hum of the ferry's gigantic engine and the thump of small waves far beneath her lapping against the sides of the boat. Cindy blankly stared into the darkness, all the while thinking of Andy LaBroom.

Cindy had loved Andy or tried to love him but his erratic and sometimes uncontrollable nature made it impossible for their relationship to move forward. Andy, Cindy learned long ago, was very intelligent, had an almost irrepressible energy level, was quick-tempered and deceptively strong—a volatile combination. Growing up with him in the tiny hamlet of North Fork Harbor Cindy remembered Andy as a quiet, almost shy boy but as he became a young man a hostility that could suddenly show itself without warning emerged from within him. As a teen he was frequently in fights, often with adversaries who were bigger than he was. Cindy coud not remember Andy ever losing a fight. What he lacked in size he made up for in speed, hidden strength and sheer will power. Andy spent an

inordinate amount of hours in the cramped training room beneath the high
school gymnasium, regularly lifting weights long after most of his classmates
had gone home. A promising but brief tenure as a running back on the school
football team abruptly ended when he yelled threatening remarks at his coach
for removing him after a failed play in a close game against a local rival. When
the head coach subsequently threatened to permanently dismiss him from the
team unless he apologized and changed his behavior Andy had to be physically
restrained by some of the other coaches and players from attacking him. Shortly
after that outburst he was permanently removed from the team and any hopes of
playing football in college vanished.

As a teenager Cindy often found Andy passing the time by throwing empty
beer bottles against the rocks that formed the jetties lining the numerous small
beaches around their town's perimeter. The beaches were the few areas in their
small town where young people could freely congregate but even there police were
often called to disperse them, leaving them very few places in the small village to
call their own. While his sudden hostility would often scare Cindy as well as others,
for a long time she also found herself attracted to him. As a young woman growing
up in a small, isolated farming and fishing town Cindy found it exciting to be
around Andy and the potential for trouble that regularly accompanied him.

Like Andy, Cindy was bright but came from a poor, uneducated family.
They survived on whatever money her father received from performing various
odd jobs, often at the summer homes of wealthy outsiders and her mother's
supermarket-cashier's salary. As a girl her favorite story was that of Heidi, the Girl
of the Alps. Growing up Cindy often fantasized about life in a bucolic land of
castles nestled amid snow-covered mountains. She read the story countless times
when she was home alone, dreaming that one day she would marry and raise her
family in the Swiss Alps.

As neither Cindy nor Andy was very popular at school, it was only a matter
of time before the two kindred spirits were drawn together. Not having the
inclination, guidance or financial resources to attend college, on the advice of a
family friend, Cindy, who at the time was seriously considering dropping out of
high school, managed to remain in school long enough to pass basic business and
secretarial courses and graduate on time. Andy, about who Cindy liked to remark
that she never saw carrying a book throughout four years of high school, was
bright enough to pass the final examinations on his wits. Despite missing enough
class to be expelled, the high school administrators were glad to see him graduate.
Cindy and Andy graduated together, each entering futures that were similar in
their uncertainty.

Facing a life of limited opportunity, Cindy at first found excitement with Andy.
While her job managing Dr. Frank's office enabled her to keep an apartment and
a small, used car, financially it was difficult for her to move any further forward.
Good opportunities were rare for a woman with limited education in an isolated

economy based on agriculture and seasonal tourism. She knew this also bothered Andy and the two shared a common frustration. Unlike him however, Cindy had no anger or resentment towards others and remained hopeful she and Andy might build a future together.

As they matured into young adults Andy's explosive personality worsened, becoming a great cause of anxiety for Cindy who had become mature enough to hold her job at the winery, maintain a car and keep an apartment which she furnished with second-hand pieces purchased at local yard sales. She remembered that Dr. Frank thought highly of Andy, often saying he was a very bright young man with great potential if only he could control his energy. It was obvious to Cindy that Andy never fully recovered emotionally from losing his brother Anthony, who enjoyed racing cars and motorcycles late at night down the isolated North Fork Harbor roads. Andy also resented the bankers who forced his parents to sell the farm that had been in their family for generations after talking them into borrowing against it. As a result, he could not get away to pursue his own life because his parents, despite selling the farm, were financially dependent on him. That dependence grew after the death of his brother.

For a young man who had trouble dealing with events that were beyond his control, life in a town without much opportunity only furthered his frustration. In Cindy's view, Andy either could not or would not put these issues behind him. They were the forces that drove his hostility and aggression and combined with his sudden outbursts, proved to be too much of a strain on their relationship. She had hoped that like the wine he helped to produce, Andy would mellow with age. As they grew older however, some of the same traits that had attracted her to him as a young woman had started to drive her away from him. There had been times when Andy truly frightened Cindy and she began to wonder if his combative nature was his way of communicating to her that he did not want their relationship to go forward but was unable to tell her so or was it a sign of something more serious? When they were alone, Andy often spoke of the events in his life that angered him. When he did so, Cindy noticed a coldness to his voice, a detachment and distance that grew as he became older and which she found frightening. She was not sure if he wanted justice or revenge but came to believe that his rants were not idle talk. He could not let go of the past and one day she was certain, Andy would act. She found this to be the most frightening prospect of all but because she still had feelings for him, never told anyone, not even Nick Krupcheski.

Consumed by her thoughts, the ferry ride across Long Island Sound passed quickly for Cindy. She knew what Krupcheski had told her was true but hearing it from him gave a chilling sense of validity to Andy's death. But as she was beginning to become gripped by the all-too-familiar feeling of anxiety that often accompanied much of the time she spent with Andy, she also felt for the first time in a long while a bit of serenity as she disembarked from the ferry and made the short walk across the New London wharf to the train station. It was there that she realized that she would no longer have to be frightened by Andy's sudden outbursts and unexpected rants. Cindy would no longer have to concern herself with the troubled young man who had been a steady presence for nearly her entire life, who threatened to follow and find her if she ever left him, as she boarded the train to New York City.

CHAPTER 36

Old Wine . . . New Bottles

Sgt. Henry St. Charles went directly from the winery to confront Scott Larson. In the absence of Cindy Murphy, Larson was the closest person to the mercurial LaBroom. There was another reason, Larson was the only area mechanic who made repairs in the field. Larson did not have a repair shop. When he wasn't driving across North Fork Harbor in his truck, he could usually be found on his boat, a small commercial-fishing craft he purchased very inexpensively some time ago. Larson was able to obtain the boat cheaply because it did not have a motor. Scouring salvage yards he found a diesel motor that like the boat, was destined for the scrap heap. He purchased the inoperable motor and brought it with his truck to the marine yard. With used parts he was able to scavenge he eventually restored the motor, sometimes with the help of Andy LaBroom, and installed it himself in the boat. Although he paid a dockage fee, usually in cash in exchange for a small discount, the marina also provided showers and restroom facilities. By living on his boat Larson was able to avoid paying rent or real estate taxes. Virtually his entire life was contained in his boat and truck. And although Larson did not have a commercial fishing license, he frequently supplemented his mechanic's income by selling his catch to some of the local restaurants. A shrewd businessperson, Larson knew the importance of keeping his expenses low. Were it not for his temper, his profile would have been equally low and that was the reason behind the unexpected visit by Sgt. Henry St. Charles.

St. Charles drove into the marina parking lot with the lights off on the police car. From where he parked he could see that Larson's boat was in its regular slip. The cabin light was on and there was a hint of diesel-fuel exhaust in the air, indicating that the mechanic/fisherman was probably onboard the vessel. St. Charles walked directly but quietly to the boat slip, stopping when he reached the boat's stern. Larson was sitting on a bench in the boat's cockpit, studying a small electrical motor which he held in his hands. An assortment of hand tools, scraps of wire and electrical tape were scattered around him on the boat floor.

"What are you doing there?" asked St. Charles.

"I already told ya. I don't know nuthin' 'bout nuthin'," said Larson without looking up from the equipment he was holding.

"You talk to everyone like that? Without the courtesy of looking them in the eye?"

"It don't matter how I talk. It matters what I say and I ain't got nuthin' to say that'll help you," he said, still without looking at St. Charles.

"What are you working on?"

"A winch motor," said Larson. "The mechanic here threw it out. Replaced it with a new one for some rich customer. They don't care. I pulled it from the dumpster. I'll make it run and sell it for half the price of a new one. That's how I spend my time Sergeant, workin'. Trouble with the folks you gotta deal with is they don't like workin'. They want to live high without the sacrifice. Like the Doc who got iced."

"Lambrusco?"

"The man worked hard his whole life, seen a lot of sufferin' but never gave up. That's why I worked for him."

"What do you mean?"

"I don't work for no one I don't respect."

"Then why'd you argue with him so much?"

"We was never arguin'. It wasn't personal. We was exchangin' views. Ain't nuthin' wrong with that. We respected each other."

"So who murdered him?"

"Wish I knew."

St. Charles thought Larson's response over. He had never seriously suspected the mechanic of being involved in the first murder but felt he may have knowledge of the workings behind it. "Speaking of respect, a lot of people respect you around here because you're a good mechanic. There's something I got to ask you."

"If it's about boats or motors go ahead. Otherwise I can't help you."

"Do you know where Andy LaBroom is tonight?"

"No."

"If you had to guess what might you say?"

"Probably with Cindy or maybe racin' his car up and down the back road."

St. Charles silently waited before responding.

"Andy's dead," he then plainly said.

"Dead?" repeated Larson who then turned, took a deep breath and looked out at the dark water. "It was only a matter of time. Car crash I bet." He then returned his attention to the motor he'd been repairing.

"Never mind. Where were you tonght? You were his best friend. Don't give me any of this mindin' my own business stuff."

"I ain't his best friend."

"What?"

"I just come in from fishin' Sergeant. About an hour before you got here. Look," he said. Larson lifted the cover to the ship's hole. Inside was a healthy pile of fish, mostly striped bass and some blue fish. "Feel 'em," Larson offered. "They're still fresh and the boat motor's still warm," he said as he turned to lift the cover off the motor. "I was on the water all night 'til about an hour ago."

St. Charles poked a few of the fish with his middle finger. Loosely covered in ice, they moved when he touched them. He then placed his open palm near the motor and felt its heat. Everything was as Larson described. "What did you mean by, 'only a matter of time'?"

"The boy had a death wish. It was so obvious a blind man could see it."

"It wasn't a crash," said St. Charles. "Andy was injected at the winery. Same as the Doc. Same location, same method, probably same poison. The only thing we don't know is if it was the same person. Now tell me what you know."

Larson turned and faced St. Charles, looking directly into his eyes, his large arms hanging at his sides. "Look Henry," he said. "You come bustin' on my boat in the middle of the night fixin' to take me in. I don't know nuthin' 'bout no murder. It ain't my fault. I ain't your man."

"Maybe not but you know plenty about LaBroom. Did he have anything against Lambrusco?"

"Andy hated the world," said Larson. "He used to get terrible pissed off. Blamed the banks for makin' his parents lose the farm. Blamed Tugboat for killin' his brother. Anthony was a damn fool, hot doggin' on motor bikes with no helmet. What'd he think was gonna happen? I told Andy that one night and he got real mad. Threatened to sink my boat when I was sleepin' on it."

"What else?" asked St. Charles.

"After that I told him I don't want him comin' around no more."

"What about Cindy?"

"Cindy couldn't handle Andy. Nobody could. She used to come here sometimes cryin' over him. I used to tell her to leave him. Get out of town. Cindy's a smart girl. She could get a good secretary job, a nice apartment in Boston or New York, but she was too afraid."

"Afraid of what?"

"Afraid he'd come after her."

Larson then stopped talking and again looked out at the water. The moonlight was casting a soft glow on the calm waters of the creek where the boat was docked for the night.

"Did she love him?"

"I guess. What else could make a person act like that?"

"You think Andy wanted the Doc dead?"

"I don't know. Some days yes, others no. Andy was unpredictable. Was he capable? Sure. Would he do it? I don't know. He made lots of threats. Hardly none of 'em came to be."

"What if I told you the bite marks found on Lambrusco matched with Andy?"

"I don't know," Larson said, shaking his head.

"Andy's dead. Now's no time to hold anything back."

If Larson was involved in any way with the Lambrusco or Tucker murders St. Charles was offering him a way out. The murders could now easily be blamed on Andy LaBroom but Larson did not provide a definitive answer.

"Tell me what else you know," pressed St. Charles.

"There ain't nuthin' else Sergeant. That's all there is."

///

Vin and Shanin followed the ambulance that was taking Maria to the hospital. While Shanin was driving a small beep came from her cell phone.

"Vin grab my phone. That's an e-mail coming in. Could be an assignment."

Vin took hold of her small phone. He had difficulty manipulating the tiny keys with his fingers. "I hate these miniature buttons," he said.

"I didn't ask you to pilot the Space Shuttle. Just tap on the picture of the envelope and read me the message," said Shanin.

"It's not for you. It's for me," said Vin. "It's Nadia from the magazine."

"Is it another assignment?"

"No. She wants to know when she'll get the rest of the first story," said Vin. "I can't finish the story until the story finishes. We got a new murder and an attempted murder on our hands. I can't submit until we know what happened. I can't believe she's working this late."

"It must be crazy there like she said. You remember how deadline's can be," said Shanin.

"She's worried about a deadline. We're worried about dead bodies,"said Vin.

"There is a difference," agreed Shanin.

"Do you think we can raise our fee?" asked Vin. "We are giving her more murders than when we took the assignment. She only paid for one murder. Now she's getting three if we include Tugboat. It would have been four if Maria hadn't gotten away."

"I don't know if I should laugh or cry."

"I'm going to call. Leave her a message." Vin dialed the number that was on the bottom of the e-mail. "Nadia," he said, surprised that she answered her phone at that hour. "Why are you in the office so late?"

"Because I have no life. Because we're trying to fill a huge hole in a magazine. The publisher's breathing down my neck. The printer's screaming over the schedule. I'm about to have a heart attack. Where's the story Vin?"

"The story's not finished," he said.

"I'm sticking my neck out for you. The least you can do is tell me something I don't know."

"What I mean is there's been a development, several actually."

"They'd better be good developments."

"One of the winery workers was found dead and Maria Lambrusco was attacked, nearly murdered as well. We're on our way to the hospital. I need about 48 more hours."

"What's happeneing? It sounds like everyone's gone crazy out there."

"Weren't you the one who said nothing's happened in North Fork Harbor for about 200 years? I guess they're making up for it now."

"What am I supposed to do on this end?"

"Run some interference."

"As long as we're still getting the exclusive I'll try to find some more time for you but I can't stop the calendar."

"These events are beyond my control. They're beyond everyone's control. I'll call you as soon as I have a clearer idea of what's happened."

"I need a good story, not a crazy one."

"What are you saying?"

"I've only got one neck Vin. Just get me the story before someone here gets murdered."

"Okay," said Vin as he ended the call. Then, turning to Shanin he said, "Everything's under control."

"You expect me to believe that? I've known you for too long."

"We've got to get to the bottom of this if we want to keep the assignment."

"Just when we think we're done someone else gets it," said Shanin. "It's not our fault we fell right in the middle of a small-town murder spree. What are we supposed to do, ask everyone to stop killing each other so you can finish your article? This is one time you cannot rush to meet the deadline. Stay calm Vin. It's going to end soon. Just be glad no one's taken a shot at us. That in itself is an improvement."

"As long as we're not on the wrong end of a needle I'm willing to wait a bit but eventually we've got to get something to Nadia or risk losing the job."

"Don't worry. Nadia's a businessperson."

"What's that supposed to mean?"

"She's willing to wait for a killer story because she knows it will sell magazines."

"Did you have to say, 'killer story'?"

"Sorry, poor word choice. That's why you write and I shoot."

"There you go again."

///

When Krupcheski stopped at the police station to get the pump before going to the vineyard he noticed a detective's unmarked car in the parking area. Once inside he was handed a large envelope from the officer managing the overnight desk. It was from the Commodities Futures Trading Commission. Stepping to the side of the desk Krupcheski opened the envelope, carefully removing its contents. It was the fingerprints of Paxton Goode.

"What do you got there?" the overnight officer asked Krupcheski.

"It's a little present for St. Charles. Can I leave this on his desk?"

"You can see him yourself. He's in his office wth some detective and the ME."

Krupcheski walked to St. Charles's office. He knew who the detective would be. The office door was closed and he could hear men's voices from inside. He knocked.

"Who's that, a girl scout with insomnia selling cookies?"

Krupcheski recognized the voice as that of Det. Thorsen. "It's Krupcheski, I've got prints."

The door swung open. Det. Thorsen was standing in the doorway with his hand out while Dr. Dionasis and Sgt. St. Charles stared at Krupcheski who instantly felt the unmistakable tone of tension in the air.

"I'll take that Nicholas," said Thorsen. "Anything else?"

Krupcheski was surprised that Thorsen called him by his first name as he handed him the envelope. "Nice work," said Thorsen, taking the thick envelope from the junior officer. Krupcheski noticed a handheld computer on St. Charles's desk.

"Cindy Murphy boarded the last boat to New London," Krupcheski said.

"You were able to confirm that?" asked St. Charles.

"Yes. Now I'm going to get the pump and go to the vineyard to drain the vat."

"Very good," said St. Charles, giving Krupcheski a brief salute to signal that their conversation had ended. "In a few hours double-check and make sure Cindy Murphy got to her hotel," he added.

"Yes Sir. Anything else?"

"Please shut the door on your way out." Krupchski turned and left, being sure to close the door as ordered. He was glad not to have to spend any more time than necessary in the room with the three men.

The police lab had found plenty of fingerprints on Dr. Lambrusco's handheld computer but none of them belonged to Paxton Goode or any of the key persons-of-interest in the case. Police lab personnel had also been able to cross-reference the CFTC prints and came back with a negative for Paxton Goode. They also discovered that the memory chip, which would have contained all of Dr. Lambrusco's data, had been removed from the computer. St. Charles, who had a background in fingerprint-checking from his New York City police days, then personally reviewed the handheld against the prints of Andy LaBroom which Dr. Dionasis had taken earlier that night at the winery. He came away without a match from the handheld but was able to confirm LaBroom's prints on the discarded hypodermic they found on the winery floor next to him.

Thorsen was the first to speak. "For all we know maybe Goode put the hit on LaBroom. Had it done while he's out of the country."

"Not likely," said St. Charles. "We've got nothing on this guy, just a theory. This whole thing is hanging on a statement from a cleaning lady who barely understands English. She may have been lying or mistaken. Any first-year law student could beat this case in about fifteen minutes."

"And what have you got?" countered Thorsen, anger rising in his voice. "A few dead guys and a note-writing psycho. You can't even get the first victim's daughter to cooperate."

"Maybe if you hadn't scared her in the hotel room we wouldn't have that problem."

The men then paused. Their frustration from not having made any meaningful progress in the case had been steadily mounting and was beginning to make itself felt.

"This much is true," resumed St. Charles, taking a deep breath while tyring to stay calm. "LaBroom was after Maria. His prints on the unused needle certify that. But then someone decided to have LaBroom exit the drama. The same way someone murdered Lambrusco. Probably thought LaBroom was too big of a security risk, if he knew anything at all."

"Or he was copying the first Lambrusco killing which someone else avenged when they had the chance," offered Thorsen.

"Attempting to copy the first killing," corrected Dionasis. "He failed and therefore someone quickly decided that he needed to be removed. As you say, LaBroom was either considered too big of a risk or someone killed him out of revenge, using the same method Lambrusco was killed in some perverse form of poetic justice as soon as they saw their chance."

"So maybe it is a psycho-killer?" Thorsen wondered out loud.

"I'll bet there are two murderers," said St. Charles. "The first wanted Lambrusco's data at virtually any cost, including if it meant taking the man's life, which someone did but viewed it as strictly business. Since Lambrusco wouldn't cooperate with the big conglomerates they wanted him out of their way. Since they got what they wanted there's no good reason for them to want Maria Lambrusco killed. It would only draw more attention to the first murder and intensify the investigation. LaBroom had an uncontrollable temper, a lot of anger. A bright guy, he may have been too consumed by anger. It may have caused him to temporarily lose his ability to think rationally. LaBroom may have become obsessed with wanting Maria off the land that used to be his family's farm and tried what he thought was a foolproof method. In his mind, it worked before."

"But then something went wrong," added Thorsen. "It's difficult to get away with one murder but trying to get away with two is virtually impossible, unless it is more than one murderer."

"So far, whoever it is, is succeeding," said St. Charles. "The only solid thing we have is a weak confession to the Tucker murder. What's your psychological profile now?"

"In light of the latest murder, LaBroom may have been behind the Tucker accident," said Thorsen. "But I don't think he wrote the note. I think the note was planted by whoever it was who killed him."

"Why?" asked Dr. Dionasis.

"Doesn't add up, psychologically."

"Why not?"

"When Lambrusco got killed, whoever did it made a dramatic statement by putting the grapes in the Doc's mouth. When Tucker had his fatal crash it was made to look like an accident in the middle of the night. It was two different killing styles. No one wanted to claim responsibility for Tucker's death, directly or indirectly. Now, suddenly, a note appears claiming responsibility. LaBroom may have been behind it but I doubt the authenticity of the note."

"Still think whoever did this subconsciously wants to be caught?" asked St. Charles.

"If he wants to be caught he couldn't make it much more difficult for us to find him. But he wants something," answered Thorsen. "If we're dealing with two murderers, the first one was probably somewhat sociopathic, wanted attention and at the end, didn't care how he got it. This second one, if there is one, wants to get away."

"So why the note about Tucker?" asked St. Charles.

"In a twisted way, leaving the note behind about Tucker was a bit of a conscience-cleaning exercise. Someone felt badly about what happened and wanted the rest of us to know it. In a perverse way they wanted to provide closure. I call it Murderer's Guilt."

"The note does not match the first murder for drama either," said Thorsen. "No signature. No prints on it. It came straight off a computer. Nearly impossible to trace but I'm almost certain it didn't come from LaBroom. The grapes were a cryptic message, no one's too sure what they mean. The note is simple, direct. It does the job but doesn't match the grapes for drama."

"Tucker was a local kid, people liked him," said St. Charles. "People feel he didn't deserve what he got. But why not a note about who killed Dr. Lambrusco?"

"But the Doc was a reclusive outsider with a secret formula who didn't welcome visitors," said Thorsen. "That's why he got the grapes in the mouth."

"That doesn't mean he should be murdered," said Dionasis.

"Of course not but there's not much sympathy for him beyond his immediate and very small circle."

"So someone's trying to tell us something without coming forward," said St. Charles.

"Coming forward would make them a suspect," said Thorsen with a characteristic grin. "Too risky. Maybe they felt he's gotten enough attention or they don't know who killed Lambrusco. It wasn't just about money although that probably played a role."

"Money may have set the entire scheme in motion, helping to unlock some suppressed desire or frustration," said Dionasis.

"The Lambrusco murder started off as a cold business deal," theorized St. Charles. "But at some point emotion and passion took over."

"We're not dealing with a logical mind or minds, so don't look for logical answers," said Dionasis.

"Goode's due back tomorrow," said Thorsen. "I plan on greeting him at the airport. I'd like a photo of the handheld to take with me in case his memory needs some prodding." Thorsen then removed his cellphone and photographed the handheld computer which was still on the desk in front of them.

"If you come away with nothing else get something from which we can get a DNA sample," ordered St. Charles. "I'm not convinced that we're done with that handheld but now I've got to get to the hospital to try to speak with Maria Lambrusco. Anything else?"

"I hate to dampen the mood at this happy little gathering but unfortunately there is something else to report," said Thorsen. "Since we're all here, I want to let you know I saw our esteemed Chief Stimmel earlier today. He got your report. To say he's unhappy is an understatement. He says if we don't make progress soon he's handing the case to the Feds."

"The Feds have enough to do. They won't be too anxious to handle some clueless case in the country," said St. Charles. "And speaking of reports, we've still got an out-of-town reporter on our hands. Plus there's the question of a Swiss bank account opened with a dead man's Social Security number and his mysterious wife."

Each man paused and looked at the other as they thought over what had just transpired.

After the meeting ended Det. Thorsen stopped at police headquarters. There he learned from a Port Authority Police Department (PAPD) report that the flight returning Paxton Goode to US soil was scheduled to land late the following morning at New York's John F. Kennedy International Airport.

CHAPTER 37

Scraping the Barrel Bottom

At the hospital St. Charles first met with the attending physician who informed him that Maria had suffered a slight case of shock brought on by physical and then emotional trauma but was relatively stable. She suffered no serious physical injuries, including no abrasions in the chest area. Maria, who was in a private room, had been given a mild sedative but was otherwise in stable condition. Maria would be observed during the night and if she remained stable, would probably be released some time the next day, pending the results of a meeting she was scheduled to have with a counselor specializing in trauma-victim diagnosis. The physician advised St. Charles that she permitted Shanin Blanc to stay with Maria that night in the hospital as she had no friends or family members in the area and the presence of another woman would probably help with her stabilization. The physician also said that if Maria felt she was capable, it would be permissible for St. Charles to interview her that night in the hospital.

When St. Charles entered Maria's room she was sitting up in bed talking with Shanin. A half-finished cup of tea was on the nightstand and her personal belongings were in a hospital-issued plastic shopping bag at her bedside.

"Good evening ladies," St. Charles said, knocking on the side of the half-opened door to Maria's room. "Can I come in?"

Maria and Shanin looked in St. Charles's direction and then looked back at each other.

"You may come in Sergeant," said Maria.

"How are you feeling?" he asked as he walked closer.

"Could be better," she said.

St. Charles, who had been carrying his hat in one of his hands, placed it on the nightstand. "If you don't mind, I'd like to ask you about what took place tonight."

"Okay," answered Maria.

"Miss," said St. Charles turning to Shanin. "You'll have to leave us alone for a few minutes."

"I understand," said Shanin who then rose to leave.

"Don't go too far," said St. Charles. "I'd be grateful if you can get your boyfriend here. I'd like to speak with him when I'm done."

"Yes Sergeant," said Shanin exiting the room.

"Now," said St. Charles, taking a seat and turning towards Maria. "The first question is how are you feeling?"

"Not bad," said Maria. "A little groggy from the drug they gave me but that should wear off by morning. I don't seem to be seriously hurt."

"Are you frightened?" he asked.

"A little."

"Before I leave I'm going to have a guard posted here until you're discharged."

"Thank you Sergeant."

"Maria, I need you to tell me everything you can about what happened tonight."

Maria took a breath and looked around the room. St. Charles waited without saying anything further.

"It all happened so quickly," she began. "I went back to the winery to look for Shanin's camera. It was dark. I was grabbed from behind. I got free, fell in the vat and ran out of there. That's really all there is to it."

"Do you remember feeling any pain in your chest area, like a scratching?"

"You mean like what happened to my father?"

St. Charles nodded.

"No."

"Could you identify your attacker?"

"I don't know."

"Was anyone else there?"

"Vin, the reporter, was outside waiting for me."

"Anyone else?"

"When I was in the car I thought I saw someone leave the winery but I wasn't sure. Vin said he didn't see anyone."

"You thought you saw someone leave the winery?"

"Yes."

"Can you describe that person? Man? Woman? Tall? Short? Anything?"

"It was only for a second. It was dark. Whover it was had on dark clothing. I'm not really sure. Not too big. Average size I guess. They moved fast. It was a dark blur."

"What did Vin do?"

"He helped get me in the car, called the police. Then an ambulance came and took me here," she said before pausing. "Do you know who tried to kill me Sergeant?"

"We think we may have a pretty good idea but need to chase down a few more things."

Maria's possible sighting of another person might help build their case that a third party was involved but St. Charles would need more evidence. Maria was under extreme stress at the time and admitted she was not sure if she did indeed see anyone leave the winery in the darkness. Nevertheless, it added further credence to the theory that a third party may have been at the scene of the LaBroom murder. Seeing that Maria was weak from the evening's events and the effects of the sedative she'd been given, St. Charles decided not to ask her any more questions.

"Thank you Ms. Lambrusco," he said. "You've been very helpful. I'm going to leave soon and hope the next time I see you it will be under more pleasant circumstances."

He then extended his hand and Maria shook it.

"Sergeant," she called.

"Yes?"

"What about my father's case?"

"We're doing everything we can Maria. We're trying to figure how his case and yours may be related."

"Are we any closer?"

"We might be," said St. Charles who then leaned closer to her. "I'm not supposed to tell you this but considering the circumstances, I thought you'd like to know we recovered his computer."

"So you are getting closer," she said as a slight smile formed on her face.

"I can't say. Now do what you need to in order to get well. I'm going to see about getting a guard here. There is one more thing Ms. Lambrusco."

"What is it Sergeant?"

"I realize you had a problem with one of our detectives. I want you to know I'm sorry about that. He's embarrassd about what happened and is working very hard on the case. It would best for each of us if we could be friends and work together."

"Okay Sergeant," she said, closing her eyes.

As St. Charles turned to leave, his cell phone buzzed. Looking at the display he saw it was a call from Krupcheski. Closing the door behind him he moved to the hallway to take the call.

"What's up Nick?"

"Cindy Murphy did not go to Boston."

"What?"

"I called the hotel. She hadn't checked-in so I called her cell phone. When she didn't answer I called the New London train station ticket office. Cindy exchanged her Boston ticket for one to New York City."

St. Charles paced rapidly across the hallway. "Call the Port Authority Police right away," he ordered. "Request that we be notified if a Cindy Murphy books any flights and that she be detained at any transit stations, including railways, buses and rental cars. Then call Thorsen and update him. He's going to New York in the morning. Then start calling around. Try to find out if she's got any friends in New York or at any of the stops between New London and New York that she may visit. And call the hotel back. See if she transferred her reservation to another hotel."

"Yes sir."

"Did you finish pumping out the vat for the second time?"

"Yes. We recovered what appears to be a couple of clothing fibers and hair strands. I've already sent them to the lab for analysis and identification."

"Good. There's a chance we get a DNA marking from one of them."

"And I asked the hotel if she transferred her reservation. It's a negative."

"Double-check on that later. There's a chance she'll do so if she suddenly realizes she needs a place to stay, wherever she is."

"Will do Sergeant."

"Any of the other roadblocks come up with anything?"

"Negative Sir."

"Is that all for now?"

"Yes Sir."

"Talk to whoever's on the desk tonight and tell him to get a guard outside of Maria Lambrusco's room until she's discharged."

"Yes Sir."

St. Charles then abruptly ended the call. He decided not to tell Maria Lambrusco about Cindy's movements as he did not want to further upset her and possibly impede her recovery because he would probably need to talk with her in the near future. As he turned he saw Vin and Shanin walking in his direction.

"Do you want to talk to me officer?" Vin politely asked.

"Yes," said St. Charles who noticed an empty room on the opposite side of the hallway. "Let's go in here for a few minutes," he said, gesturing towards the room. "I don't need to speak with you Miss," he said to Shanin. "Vin will meet you in the lobby when we're done."

Shanin nodded as St. Charles held the door open, closing it behind him after he followed Vin into the room. Vin stood by the window while St. Charles sat on the single chair, facing him in the sparse room. St. Charles remained silent as he collected his thoughts. Talking to a reporter, despite the fact that he may be a witness to a crime, was a risk but not trying to learn what Vin might know would be an even greater risk. It was Vin who spoke first.

"Sergeant, you don't have to worry about me," said Vin. "I'm happy to help and would not knowingly do anything that might impede your investigation."

"That's your civic duty," said St. Charles. "This conversation is not for print," said St. Charles. "If I find out you're wearing a wire, have some other recording device or plan on writing about this conversation, I'll charge you."

"No Sir," said Vin. "Search me if you like," he said, holding up his arms. St. Charles declined. He then leaned back and took in Vin's unexpected opening line of cooperation before asking questions. "Okay," he then said. "You're a reporter. Tell me everything you know, from beginning to end, about what happened tonight at the winery."

Vin's description of the evening's events was very consistent with that of Maria's with the exception of one very important admission. Staying true to his pledge, he told the officer how he entered the winery after Maria was attacked and rolled back LaBroom's mask.

"That's quite a thing to say" said St. Charles. "Do you know the seriousness of what you just told me?"

"Yes," said Vin. "But I told you I'd be completely truthful and I was."

"I'll have to take that under consideration," said St. Charles. "You know what you did is against the law, plus you did not tell me this when we spoke earlier at the winery. You can be charged with interfering with an investigation, withholding information. It could even make you a suspect."

"I guess I forgot," said Vin.

"Doubtful," said St. Charles.

"I wanted to protect Maria."

"That's two different reasons. Should we go for a third? You're inconsistent. Never mind, I'll tell you why. You were looking for the story," said St. Charles. "But you were too aggressive this time. It was the same rap on you in the city. You're trying to solve this crime before we do and sell the story. Except now you've admitted that you've interfered with an investigation. Tresspassed onto a crime scene and tampered with a body."

"That's not it," pleaded Vin. "I want to help."

"Listen Gusto," said St. Charles, not looking up from his notebook. "This kind of behavior can cause you to lose a lot of integrity, not to mention get you in a lot of legal trouble. I would think in your profession those are two things you'd rather not have happen."

"No Sir," said Vin.

"I'm not sure what I'm going to do with this information," said St. Charles. "You've interfered with an investigation. For the next few days I want you to stay where we can reach you. And stop sticking your nose in our business. Agreed?"

"Yes Sir."

St. Charles then stood and without saying anything further left Vin alone in the room. Another officer was already standing guard outside of Maria's room and the door behind him remained closed. St. Charles said a few words to the officer and then turned and left the hospital. When Vin exited the room he looked across the hall at the new officer standing guard. When the young officer noticed Vin he simply shook his head in his direction. Vin then went straight to the hospital lobby where Shanin was waiting.

They went directly to Shanin's car where once inside, Vin told her what had transpired with St. Charles.

"You're under virtual house arrest," said Shanin after Vin finished recounting the exchange. "He doesn't want you to leave town but you're not charged with anything."

"Not yet. He strongly requested that I stay nearby."

"Then you can leave town if you like."

"I can and he can still get me for investigation interference. But I think it's something more serious than that."

"What could be more serious than investigation interference?"

"St. Charles may have something else in mind. Can you just take me to the hotel? I'll call Nadia and leave her a message."

"What do you mean?"

"I've got to tell her I can't complete the assignment. It's the right thing to do."

Neither of them said anything further during the ride back to the hotel. When Shanin stopped the car to let Vin exit he remained in his seat.

"We're at the hotel," she said.

"There's something I've got to tell you too."

"What is it?"

"I know the assignment didn't work out the way we wanted but it was nice spending time with you again. It was kind of like the old days, only in a prettier location. Whether it's in a fancy winery or the trunk of a car, I guess a stiff's a stiff," he joked.

"Seriously, what are your plans?"

"Head back to the Bronx and wait for the phone to ring."

"And me?"

Vin paused before answering.

"Maybe you'd like to come with me," he said.

For a moment they stared into each other's eyes. Vin then reached across the seat to take Shanin's hand but she pulled back. She had thought about a future with Vin as well but didn't feel like he did.

"Having you here was great," she said. "I couldn't have asked for a better assignment. I'm glad you thought of me. It was a lot of fun. But as far as you and me together, I'm not sure Vin. It didn't work for us before. I'm not sure we can make it together for the long term."

Vin slid back in his seat. It was not what he expected to hear. "Shanin," he said. "There's not a perfect relationship on earth but if we each want it we can make it work."

"No Vin. Not now," she said, shaking her head. "It's too late. I'm not the same person I was when we worked in the city. I'm sorry Vin."

Without saying anything further Vin stepped out of the car, slammed the door shut and walked ino the hotel without looking back. Shanin watched him until he disappeared through the lobby door. Then, with her eyes becoming watery, drove into the dark North Fork Harbor night.

/ / /

Despite the long hours and growing frustration, Det. Thorsen was actually excited when he left his Long Island home early the next morning for JFK International Airport. The night before Thorsen had called the Port Authority Police Dept., and arranged to have Goode detained once he presented his identification to customs personnel. The upcoming surprise meeting filled him with a feeling of optimistic anticipation. It might lead to a new chapter in the investigation, moving it forward when it seemed that all doors to further progress were closed.

As he neared the airport Thorsen began squinting in reaction to the sun's early rays reflecting off his rearview mirror. The rising sun was warming the car's interior and he could feel the measure of its heat increasing on his back. Thorsen drove directly to the security-personnel parking area, presented his credentials and was granted permission to enter. He then took the shuttle bus reserved for security personnel to the terminal where the flight carrying Goode would land, checked-in with the Port Authority Police officers on duty and took a seat in a small room reserved for security observations. The room was adjacent to the US Customs receiving area and was outfitted with a special security window which allowed for arriving passengers to be secretly observed. It also contained a small table, a few chairs, a pushbutton landline telephone, water cooler and a few plastic cups. Before making himself comfortable Thorsen double-checked to be sure an alert was posted on passenger Paxton Goode. A dual-national, interrogating Goode might present some legal isseus. If Goode checked-in with his US passport he'd be afforded all protections of US citizens. If he used his Swiss passport Thorsen would have greater ability to interrogate him as a foreign national potentially involved in a serious crime. As St. Charles had noted the night before, their theory behind the winery murders was weak but depending on what he could learn from Goode, their case could gain much needed information and possibly additional evidence. Right now, much of it depended on what Thorsen might gain from speaking with Goode.

A well-educated, widely traveled and wealthy man, Thorsen wondered if Goode truly was involved in the North Fork Harbor murders. Customs personnel had given Thorsen a copy of Goode's US passport photo. He looked to be a man entering middle age. He had sandy-colored hair, starting to thin and light-brown eyes. What would motivate a person of his caliber to be involved in such dirty business? But Thorsen also knew that when it came to the criminal mind, motives were limitlesss and often led to the formation of strange partnerships, many of which self-destructed after the crime was committed, allowing clues to randomly fall like leaves across a landscape. Therefore, in the eyes of investigators, all persons of interest were considered to be equally suspect until proven otherwise. Revealing admissions frequently came from the most unlikely of sources, which is why in any successful investigation each lead had to be meticulously pursued, even if it meant interviewing wealthy, international businesspeople returning from a foreign country and who would seemingly have nothing to do with something as depraved as the violent murder of a reclusive winemaker.

These were the thoughts that consumed Det. Thorsen as he settled in with a cup of weak coffee from a pot the officers shared in their small kitchen and waited for the arrival of passenger Paxton Goode. A US Customs Agent would escort Goode into the small room once they examined his passport. It would be the first meeting between the two. The customs agent offered in advance to remain for the interview but thinking Goode would feel more comfortable with just the two of them in the room, Thorsen chose to work alone. But Thorsen was not to entertain these thoughts for long. As he peered through the security window into the still empty customs area Thorsen received a text on his cell phone. It was from Christian Rinaldi. A "Mrs. LaBroom" might be coming to the bank.

Chapter 38

Sniffing for Answers

Thorsen immediately called Rinaldi from the observation area.

"What do you mean, 'might' be coming to the bank?" he asked when the bank officer came to the phone.

"I received the briefest of messages. Barely legible. It was on a tiny slip of paper someone dropped on my desk last night or very early this morning," said Rinaldi. "I didn't personally speak with whoever this may be."

"Read me exactly what you have," ordered Thorsen.

"Ms. C. L-A-B," said Rinaldi, trying to convery to Thorsen how poorly the message was written. "Coming in," he read.

"That's it?"

"Yes."

"Does it say when? Who took the message?"

"There's nothing more. I assume the message was taken by one of our overnight staffers. They're currency traders. They have to work with different time zones. It's a separate department with whch I have nothing to do. I'm lucky I got the message at all. I called the number back but there was no answer."

"What's the number?" asked Thorsen.

Rinaldi read it to him and he wrote it in his notebook. It had a New York City-based area code.

"At what time was the call made?"

"I do not have that information. I'm sorry but there's nothing more I can do for you on this matter Detective."

"Yes there is," countered Thorsen.

"Detective, before you go any further be advised I spoke with one of the bank's lawyers after our last meeting. I'm under no legal obligation to cooperate."

"I trust you're a man of conscience Rinaldi. Be advised I'm not too far from your office. I'm going into a meeting in a little while. As soon as this mystery client appears, tell your staff to send her to your office. Once that happens, you immediately call this number and leave me the following message: 'Lunch is on.' I can be at your office in about 20 minutes."

"What if she's in a hurry? Won't stay?"

"Talk to her about special investment opportunities. Maybe she can buy a chalet in Switzerland. I don't care if you fill her with cappuccino until it pours from her ears. Hang 'Out-of-Order' signs on the elevators. Find some way to hold her until I get there."

"Detective, I just told you what our lawyer said."

"That's funny *Signor* Rinaldi. I should tell you that after our last meeting I spoke with someone in our Financial Crimes Unit," Thorsen lied. "In this country the courtesy is to give someone under arrest one telephone call. But it's only a courtesy. We're under no legal obligation to extend it. You can either protect your client or you can protect yourself and your bank. *S'il vous plaît?*"

Thorsen's last order was followed by silence. He was fairly certain Rinaldi's greater loyalty would lie with himself and the bank rather than his shadowy client. But if Rinaldi did not cooperate, Thorsen would have to decide whether to remain at the airport for Goode or go to the bank's office and wait there himself for the mystery client. While he indirectly threatened Rinaldi with arrest he did not want to actually charge him. Any moves made against Rinaldi at this point would be weak ones and more importantly, he was not who they were after. Rinaldi was potentially much more valuable to the investigation as someone who may be able to lead them to the architect of the crimes. Nor could Thorsen risk missing his meeting with Goode, who was nearly guaranteed to shortly arrive unlike the bank's anonymous client. It took Rinaldi a few seconds to respond. Thorsen quietly waited for his answer.

"*Oui Monsieur Inspecteur,*" he reluctantly said.

Thorsen turned from the receiver to breathe his own slight sigh of relief.

"*Merci Monsieur,*" Thorsen then replied in probably one of the worst French accents Rinaldi had heard since he'd been living in New York. "And you never know," the detective continued. "We may actually have lunch one day." Thorsen remembered the French restaurant recommendation he had earlier received and would not be opposed to trying it, even if it meant having the stodgy Rinaldi as his dining companion.

"If she arrives I will contact you about lunch," said Rinaldi.

"There's going to be a lot of public interest when I crack this case," Thorsen said only half-jokingly. "I may get a book deal. And then I'll need a place to put all my money. You could even get a small part in the movie."

"I wish you the best of luck in your crime-fighting and artistic endeavors but must go now. Please understand I'm expecting a very busy day. As I said, I'll let you know about lunch. You have my word." Each then hung up their phone and Thorsen resumed his watch from the security window while wondering how reliable the "word" of a private banker, someone who regularly deals in secrecy, might be.

Thorsen dialed the number from Rinaldi's message. After a few rings he received an automated message informing him that the call was made from a New York City-based pay telephone. Rinadli could have told him that had he stayed on the phone long enough to receive the message. Despite the wide rise in cell phones, hundreds of pay telephones remained scattered across New York City. They largely served those without enough credit or income to qualify for a cell phone account of their own while inadvertently enabling anonymous calls to continue being made.

Thorsen used his cell phone to call the North Fork Harbor Police Station. Speaking with Nicholas Krupcheski he gave the younger officer the telephone number Rinaldi had supplied, asking him to immediately find whatever he could on it. Depending on the time and location from where the call was made, there was a chance the caller's image may have been captured on a security camera, of which there were thousands in New York City. They might also be able to obtain a fingerprint or another piece of evidence from the location.

While the detective from Long Island was anxiously turning his attention to waiting for the jet carrying Paxton Goode to arrive in New York City he thumbed through his case file and came across a business card he had acquired earlier in his investigation. He studied the name as he rubbed the stiff edge of the card between his thumb and index finger. For that moment he could not help but stare at the name that was printed on the card's upper right corner in a bold, black font: Cynthia LaBarone. He then looked up at the arrival chart in the customs room through the window. The flight delivering Paxton Goode had landed.

/ / /

As Nicholas Krupcheski tried to find information on the source of the telephone number as ordered by Det. Thorsen, Sgt. Henry St. Charles was approaching the investigation from a different angle. When Krupcheski passed the Sergeant's office he could see he was taking something apart. Wearing surgical gloves he carefully placed various parts onto numbered sheets of white paper he had placed across his otherwise cleared desk. Looking into the office, Krupcheski recognized the shell of Dr. Lambrusco's handheld computer. Not satisfied with the "negative" report that had come from the police lab, St. Charles decided he had nothing to lose by personally dissecting the computer. He was looking for a stray fingerprint, piece of hair or any other small sample of biological evidence that might be used to identify who else handled what he still hoped would prove to be a key piece of evidence with a DNA match.

"How's it going Sarge?" Krupcheski asked, leaning further into his superior officer's cramped office.

"Nicholas, you may have entered during my moment of discovery," said St. Charles. In one of his gloved hands he was squeezing an oversized pair of tweezers.

In the end was an object so small Krupcheski could not identify it from where he stood. "C'mon in," he said.

St. Charles held the end of the tweezers close to Krupcheski's soft face.

"Know what I have here?"

The younger officer still had no idea what it was that had so excited his Sergeant.

"No Sir," he said.

"I think I may have found a fingernail fragment," said St. Charles who for the first time during the course of the investigation revealed a small smile. Between the blades of the tweezer St. Charles held a tiny, almost clear object. "Call the lab," he directed the younger officer. "Tell them we need a rush DNA analysis on some possible biological evidence. They need to see if it matches the Doc's DNA, or maybe someone else's," he said, once again extending a small smile.

Krupcheski looked again at the alleged evidence, wondering if it indeed held any promise or was it another blind lead? He then looked at the various parts St. Charles had meticulously removed from the computer and laid across the paper on his desk. The younger officer stole a glance at his superior's face and into his eyes. St. Charles, while letting forth two rare smiles during their brief conversation looked very tired. There were deep, dark circles beneath his eyes. He needed to shave. His ordinarily thick, dark hair looked like it had become more gray than he remembered and was uncharacteristically dirty and unkept while his uniform was severely wrinkled. Krupcheski wondered if he'd been working too hard or was suffering from some other form of stress. Nor could he remember ever seeing the usually serious St. Charles smile twice in the same conversation. Krupcheski then took a small, glassine evidence-envelope which was on a corner of his desk and held it open for the Sergeant.

Did St. Charles have a legitimate reason to be pleased with his discovery wondered Krupcheski or were the long hours with almost no real progress and pressure from headquarters starting to take their toll? Was he having trouble at home? Not feeling well? He'd been working a lot of overtime as a result of the Lambrusco case and with the fall tourist season approaching, demands on the small force St. Charles directed would only grow.

"You think you got something Sarge?" he asked with a forced grin.

"I might," St. Charles said, letting out a deep breath.

"Slip it in here. I'll get it to the lab right away, even if I have to take it there myself."

"Good man," responded St. Charles, who still using the tweezers, placed the fragment into the special envelope. The younger officer then completed a label, stuck it onto the envelope and began to leave the office. Before leaving he turned in the doorway to again check on his Sergeant. St. Charles engrossed in his work, did not notice the younger officer watching him. Krupcheski was about to suggest to St. Charles that he get some rest but could see that he had already resumed his work, combing through the computer's insides in search of more evidence.

"I also lost something," St Charles called out to Krupcheski.

"Excuse me Sir."

"The chip's missing."

"What's that Sir?"

"This computer's got no chip in it. You know, the thing that stores its memory. Whoever got to this computer removed the chip."

"I'll make a note of it Sarge."

"A couple of more things for you," said St. Charles. "Get Cindy Murphy's cell phone number and have headquarters request a satellite trace on it. We may be able to locate her that way. And then get back to the ferry parking lot and see if her car's still there. If it's not, find out where it is. Who has it? Okay?"

"Yes Sir." Krupcheski then shook his head and left the office.

/ / /

Thorsen watched from the security window as passengers lined up in the customs area. Eventually, Goode appeared and quietly stood in line with the other passengers. There was nothing unusual about Goode's appearance. Thorsen judged him to be barely six-feet tall. He appeared fit, tanned and wearing a well-fitted, probably custom-made, business suit. Goode carried only a slim, brown, leather briefcase. When he handed his passport to the customs official on the other side of the security window, Thorsen noticed the light briefly sparkle off one of the jewels on Goode's wristwatch.

Thorsen intently watched the exchange as the customs official double-checked Goode's passport. He then saw him gesture for Goode to step to the side of the line. When he did, a door opened and two other customs officials appeared. They then politely but seriously asked Goode to come with them. The two officers escorted Goode to the room in which Thorsen was waiting. After the first officer opened the door, the second gestured for Goode to proceed. Thorsen stood when they entered the room.

"Which passport?" Thorsen asked the officers.

"Swiss," answered one of them.

Thorsen nodded before thanking and then dismissing the two customs officers. "That will be all," he said. "I'll take it from here." He waited until the door was closed before sitting back down.

"Have a seat Mr. Goode," said Thorsen.

"What's this about?" Goode politely asked while he remained standing. "Who are you?"

"I'm Detective Conrad Thorsen, Suffolk County," he said, showing Goode his badge and handing him one of his business cards. "You're familiar with Suffolk County, Long Island, aren't you?"

"Yes. I own a home on Shelter Island."

"It's very pretty there. Do you get out that way much?"

"Not as much as I'd like but I hope to be there this weekend. What's wrong Detective?"

"You're not subpoenaed or under arrest or forced to talk with me in any way right now Mr. Goode," Thorsen calmly said. "You are a person-of-interest in a very important case. A lot of us would appreciate if you'd cooperate."

"I'll do what I can."

"Thank you," said Thorsen who then removed the photo of Dr. Lambrusco's handheld computer from his case file and placed it on the small table. "Recognize this?" he asked.

"No," said Goode, shaking his head.

"Do you know what it is?"

"A photo of a computer or some kind of electronic device. Maybe a scanner. I'm not very technical. Why?"

"I'll get to that in a minute. How about this photo? Recognize this guy?"

Thorsen then produced a photo of the body of Dr. Lambrusco when he was found on the winery floor. He hoped the shock value of the photo would propel Goode into cooperating.

"I'll get back to this later. Your guess about the first photo was right. It's a computer. It was stolen from a dead man in Suffolk County, North Fork Harbor to be exact. Someone told us they found it in the wastebasket in your office. Let's start by you telling me what you know about that."

"My office? I haven't been in my office for two weeks."

"We know where you've been Mr. Goode. Argentina, agricultural conference. Buenos Aires."

"Yes."

"Nice city? I've never been there."

"Yes. It's a very European-style city."

"Do you tango?"

"No Detective."

"I didn't think so. Now what about this computer?"

"I don't know anything about it."

"Let me give you a little background. We got a call from a national database about this computer, which was reported stolen. It was later sold to a clerk in a secondhand shop in New York City. We found the person who brought it to the shop. It was a cleaning lady who works in your office building. When we asked her where she found it she led us to your office wastebasket."

"That's what this is about?" asked Goode, growing angry. "A stolen computer some cleaning lady claims to have found in my office wastebasket. How do you know if she's telling the truth? How do I know if you're telling the truth?"

Goode's response was almost exactly what Thorsen and St. Charles had said at their last meeting. Goode was free to walk out of the room but remained there and Thorsen was not obligated to remind him any further of his status.

"That's not your problem," the detective persevered.

"Detective, I make a very good living. Why would I steal someone's old computer?"

"That's what we're trying to find out. Let me ask you another question Mr. Goode. What does the name Dr. Frank Lambrusco mean to you?"

"Nothing," he blankly said.

"He's a fairly famous winemaker. Also a scientist. Knows a lot about grape genetics. Your company's a big player in the world agriculture business and you don't know of him? He ran the North Fork Harbor Vineyard. Right in your neighborhood."

"I know the winery. I drive past it on my way to my home there. Their wine's supposed to be very good but hard to come by. I'm sorry if something happened to the winemaker."

"He's dead. That's him in the second photo I showed you. Maybe you heard about it while you were in Argentina. In fact, I think the Doc was scheduled to speak at the same conference."

The two men stared at each other as Thorsen studied his subject.

"Is there anything further Detective?'

"Yes. Would you like a cup of coffee Mr. Goode?"

"No thank you."

The suggestion for coffee was meant to slightly distract Goode and also enable him to see Thorsen's considerate, human side, ideally to provide some small bit of relief. On the technical side, it would also help him to obtain a DNA sample. "That's a good decision," he said with a small smile. "This stuff's barely drinkable."

Instead of leaving, Goode made himself more comfortable. Thorsen was intrigued and encouraged. Did he feel a need to cooperate? Thorsen rose and without saying anything, drew Goode a cup of water from the cooler, automatically placing it in front of him. Sensing an opening, Thorsen decided to accelerate the pace of the interview. He leaned across the small table and looked straight into Goode's eyes.

"We had a mutual friend," said Thorsen.

"We did? Who?" asked Goode, intrigued by Thorsen's statement.

"Andy LaBroom," said Thorsen. "And don't tell me you don't know him because it was you who recommended that naïve country boy to a private Swiss bank where someone opened an account with his dead brother's Social Security number and where a deposit inexplicitly arrived the other morning from Buenos Aires, Argentina."

Goode took a deep breath before speaking. Thorsen had blindsided him with the sudden barrage. "Detective," he began. "Andy LaBroom did some landscaping work for me on my Shelter Island home. We got into a conversation one morning and he asked me what I did for a living. We started to talk about money. He then told me his family had received an insurance settlement from the death of his brother, died in an accident I think, and wanted advice on where to put the money. He said his parents couldn't handle large sums of money and he never deposited the check because he was afraid of the government looking into his business. Andy seemed a little confused, apprehensive. When I told him the government would know because insurance companies report their payouts, he became angry. Andy didn't want people to know. He didn't trust the people in the local bank. He asked me if I knew of an offshore bank. I referred him to my banker."

"Rinaldi?"

"Yes, you know him?"

"We've met."

"He's a good man, a very good man. We've known each other for years."

"About how much money was LaBroom looking to deposit?"

"I'm not sure, maybe about $100,000. It was a lot for him."

"Don't you think it's odd that a kid who's hardly been out of his home county, barely graduated high school, would know enough to ask about offshore banks?"

"Someone could have mentioned it to him. He could've overheard a conversation," countered Goode. "They've been very much in the news lately. He could've seen an article in a financial publication or a television program."

"Or you could've suggested it," said Thorsen. "Did you advise him on any other matters?" he asked without giving Goode a chance to respond to his previous remark.

"No."

"Anything else about your relationship with Andy LaBroom?" he asked.

"That's the whole story concerning LaBroom and me. It's true I was just in Buenos Aires, you can see my passport. Even you'll admit that does not mean I took part in a crime."

"I don't have to admit anything. I'm the detective."

"Of course. But I know nothing about an account opened with a deceased person's Social Security number or illicit wire transfers. I used to work on Wall St."

"Right, agricultural commodities broker," Thorsen interrupted.

"Yes. Thousands of international money transfers take place each day, the vast majority of which are completely legal. And I'm sure thousands of computers are stolen each year, along with televisions, cameras, automobiles and anything else people can get their hands on."

"How did you come to hire LaBroom?"

"I'm not sure. There may have been a flyer put in my mailbox or I saw a newspaper ad. I needed some work done on the property and he was there."

Thorsen then thought he saw Goode glance at the cup of water he placed on the table in front of him but he made no move to take it.

"Okay Detective," said Goode. "I know I'm free to leave but before I do I'd like to be sure that this was our first and last meeting. If there is anything else that you'd like from me please let me know now. Otherwise I'd like to get out of here and on with my day. I hope you appreciate my cooperation."

"Maybe we'll see each other on Shelter Island," said Thorsen.

"Let me know, because if we do I probably will bring my lawyer."

The threat to call a lawyer had no effect on Thorsen, he had heard it hundreds of times during interrogations. Nor did he believe Goode's elaborate alibi. He doubted the sincerity of his answers about as much as he disliked his coolness and arrogance. Thorsen nevertheless remained convinced of Goode's involvement but was not sure how deep it was. During their investigation an insurance policy for Anthony LaBroom was never mentioned. Nor was the amount quoted by Goode the same as what Rinaldi had told him. Could Goode actually have been the catalyst that set the entire scheme in motion by encouraging it with a reward? Was he simply after the data and the Lambrusco murder was an unfortunate mishap, killed like an innocent bystander at the scene of an accident?

"LaBroom also worked for Lambrusco," said Thorsen.

"Did he? I had no idea."

"Andy LaBroom is dead," said Thorsen.

"Really?" said Goode, seeming sincerely surprised. "That's terrible. First his brother and now him. The poor family. How'd it happen? What's going on out there?"

"Winery accident. Somehow he got too close to some chemicals."

"I'm very sorry to hear that. He was a nice young man." Thorsen watched Goode look around the room.

"Who is Cynthia LaBarone?" he asked.

"She's my assistant."

"For how long has she worked for you?"

"About eight years."

"How much do you trust her?"

"I trust her within reason. She's never given me a reason not to trust her."

"Does she help with yor personal affairs?"

"Occasionally she'll make the personal phone call for me, get theatre tickets, things like that. Nothing too personal."

"Does she go to the bank for you? Handle any financial errands?"

"No," answered Goode.

"Is she married?"

"No."

"Are you?"

"No."

"Why'd you hire her?"

"She came with the office. What I mean is when I took the position she'd been the assistant to my predecessor, who retired. Since I was new to the company she was able to help with the transition."

"Got a wine cellar in your Shelter Island house?"

"Yes."

"Anything from North Fork Harbor Vineyards in it?

"I once bought a bottle at a charity auction. I've yet to open it."

"A lot of people bid on it?"

"There was some competition."

"There's plenty of wine on the market. Why do people bid on wine at auctions?"

"Sometimes it's one of the few ways to get a rare bottle but in the case of the North Fork bottle it was also to help a good cause. It can be exciting."

"A lot of other hard-to-find wines in your cellar?"

"I have some nice pieces, nothing too rare. What else can I do for you Detective?"

"That depends," answered Thorsen. "You can start by telling me with which you'd prefer to be charged, larceny or murder?"

Goode paused before answering. He was taken aback by the last question and looked quizzingly at Thorsen.

"That's a bit presumptuous Detective, don't you think?"

"Are you asking me? If you are you're out of order."

"I understand you're frustrated having to come all the way to JFK from Suffolk County for nothing but don't try to scare me Detective. I did nothing wrong and more importantly, I know my rights."

"That's hard to believe considering you checked-in under your Swiss passport. By doing so you've reduced your rights of protection which would have been greater had you used your US passport."

"Thanks for the legal advice. I might've done that if I'd known you were waiting for me. But you began this meeting by saying you needed my help. I told you everything I know about this affair. I hardly think I should be threatened for cooperating with the police."

"If you feel threatened you can call your lawyer right now. Here's a phone," he said, pushing the ancient-looking landline telephone across the table towards Goode. At that moment Thorsen's own phone beeped. It was the text from Rinaldi. "No lunch today," was the message. Trying to remain expressionless, Thorsen slipped the phone into his coat pocket.

"No thank you," Goode said as he rose to leave the room. "There's a car waiting for me."

"Thank you for your time," said Thorsen from his chair as he watched Paxton Goode exit. As the door quickly closed behind Goode, Thorsen could only wish that his trip to JFK, while not a complete loss, had been more productive. Although he did obtain some insight into who he believed remained a key suspect, as well as proof of a relationship between Goode and Andy LaBroom, he failed to get the DNA sample or meet with the alleged Mrs. LaBroom. It was going to be a long ride to North Fork Harbor.

CHAPTER 39

A Wine Most Foul

"What do you mean, 'no lunch'?" an aggravated Detective Thorsen barked into his phone at Christian Rinaldi as he entered his car and prepared to leave the JFK parking lot for the lengthy ride on the Long Island Expressway where he'd undoubtedly obsess over his plan which brought him far less than what he had hoped.

"I can't make her come to the office," he pleaded. "Besides, even if she came you made me freeze the account. How would I explain that? Under what pretense? That someone thinks she's involved in a crime. After all, it is her money."

"We'll see about that," argued Thorsen

"I remain at your disposal," offered Rinaldi.

"What about Goode?" continued Thorsen. "What's he do with his money?"

"What do you mean?"

"Does he do a lot of wheeling and dealing? Derivatives? Precious metals? Exotic stuff like that? Is he a very active client?"

"I'm not sure what you mean by that but Mr. Goode is a very basic investor, falling on the cautious/conservative side. He's got some foreign currency exposure, mostly euro-backed bonds and some gold but mostly cash. I haven't seen Goode make any big mistakes. Not a lot of account acitivity. Financially speaking, he keeps a low profile."

Rinaldi's financial description of Goode was consistent with the impression he gave Thorsen during their interview. Goode, Thorsen estimated, was not the type to take big risks, he preferred discretion and probably favored letting someone else do the actual work while he'd gladly settle for a lesser reward, quietly putting his money to work elsewhere.

"What's he worth?"

"About $2 million of which I know. Like I said, he's mostly in cash and easily marketable securities. He may have other hard assets of which we're not aware, real estate, antiques, artwork. "

"A wine collection."

"Yes but it's hard to place a value on those types of items."

"But they are bought and sold."

"Yes, there's frequently a collectors' marketplace, auction houses, special agents."

"Does a lot of cash change hands in those kinds of transactions?"

"It can but in many cases we truly don't know. Obsession can be a very powerful force."

"Does Goode have any obsessions?"

"He's very controlled but if he's got one, it's wine. We once went to a particular restaurant and he talked with the sommelier like he was Dom Perignon himself. In that same conversation I referred him to a colleague who later sold him a special insurance policy to exclusively cover his collection for everything from theft to lightning strikes."

Thorsen considered Rinaldi's latest admission, which he classified as completely circumstantial, before saying anything.

"Here's what I want you to do," Thorsen then commanded, changing course. "Get that Mrs. LaBroom in your office."

"And how will I do that? She's a client. I can't order her to do anything."

"Since you hold the keys to the vault, she'll call you."

"I've never met her. How can I possibly know what she wants or likes? I don't even have a means of getting in touch with her. She calls from pay phones. She sounds like one of those rich eccentrics. She's unreliable, unpredictable."

"Eccentric or not almost everyone wants money," said Thorsen. "You've frozen the account. You think she's unpredictable now? Wait until she finds she can't withdraw any money. I predict you'll be the first one she calls."

"I can guarantee that when that happens she will not be in a pleasant mood."

"People are passionate about their money," argued Thorsen. "Those who don't have any need it. People who have it want more. That's why you have a job. Try to set up something for Monday. Think of how good you'll look when I note your cooperation in my report."

"You're making my job impossible Detective."

"Tell her there was a clerical error and you need her to come to your office for a signature check. Then entice her with talk of some exclusive opportunity," said Thorsen. "You're the private banker. You know what someone like her might want, as you say, financially speaking, and offer it. If she won't come to the bank, offer to meet her someplace nice for breakfast or lunch."

Rinaldi, who had relied on careful discretion to quietly build his career in the aloof world of private banking, was not fond of the idea of appearing in any kind of law-enforcement report. While it certainly was better than being noted for unfavorable activity, he'd have preferred not being mentioned.

"That won't be necessary Detective. I'm happy to help from behind the scenes," he lied.

"Once the meeting's arranged send me the particulars."

"Are you planning on joining us Detective?"

"Not exactly," Thorsen said. "I'll talk to you Monday. You have my number in case you need me over the weekend."

"Yes," gulped Rinaldi. Dealing with Thorsen during business hours was bad enough. To talk with him over the weekend was a thought Rinaldi preferred not to entertain. "Good day Detetctive," he said, hanging up the phone. But it was too late. Thorsen had already dialed St. Charles's number.

"I struck out," said Thorsen as soon as St. Charles came to the phone. "I got no DNA and no meeting with the mysterious Mrs. LaBroom. She vanished."

"I found something that may be a fingernail fragment inside the handheld," said St. Charles. "It's being analyzed as we speak but it'll be useless if we've got nothing to compare it against."

"Goode, that gigantic egomaniac, is going to be at his Shelter Island home this weekend. Maybe we can all get together for a glass of wine from his exquisite collection, watch the boats on the bay from the veranda," said Thorsen, not making even the slightest effort to disguise his sarcasm. "What's our next move?"

St. Charles hesitated before answering. "It's no longer 'our' next move," he said. "There's something I have to tell you."

"What do you mean?"

"Stimmel called this morning. You're being removed from the case."

"What?"

"We've spent too many resources on it according to him. It's going to officially be moved to the 'Inactive File,' Monday. I can still pursue it but it will no longer be a priority. With the fall season coming we've got to reprioritize."

"Then where are they sending me?"

"Out to sea."

"What?"

"There's an environmental case, some New Jersey-registered commercial fishermen are allegedly taking clams from New York State waters without permits. You're going to be on a boat, investigating, maybe making arrests."

"I'm being moved from murder to clam poaching? Tell me you're kidding."

"That's what the Chief said."

"I hate that guy."

"You're to get me your notes and anything else you have on the Lambrusco case by end-of-day today Conrad. That's all I have. Chief Stimmel has everything for your next assignment. Cheer up. You can probably take the weekend off. Rest and prepare for the next job."

"Yeah, the Great Clam Robbery."

"I've got to start getting things in order for the fall season. See if we need to have parking tickets printed. Get the holding cells cleaned."

"Okay Henry," said Thorsen, with tones of resignation and frustration in his voice. "I'll update my notes from today and send everything to you as soon as I get back."

"Thanks Conrad. One more thing."

"What's that?"

"I know you weren't thrilled about working on this case but your efforts are appreciated. You definitely made a contribution. It was good working with you."

"Yeah. We can see how much that's worth."

St. Charles then hung up the phone. He did not want to lose Thorsen or see the case become "inactive" but was powerless against Stimmel who had the seemingly impossible job of balancing finite resources against virtually unlimited demands.

"We do the best with what we have," Stimmel told St. Charles earlier that day when he gave him the news about the case. "I'm constantly forced to do more with less and so is everyone else."

"But we're so close," pleaded St. Charles.

"Not according to what I see," countered Stimmel. "I've got to examine the evidence too and not enough progress has been made to justify keeping this case active. Face it, you were outmatched Sergeant. I've never seen anything like this. You've got more stiffs than legitimate suspects. Now it's time to cut your lines. I saw in the paper that North Fork Harbor is hosting the annual bluefish tournament. You'll need to be at full strength."

"Yes Sir," said St. Charles, hanging up the phone. He wasn't ready to close the Lambrusco case and did not like the sting from Stimmel's remarks but what could he do? He had to admit, at least to himself, that he was running out of leads. While there actually were more dead bodies than reliable clues, St. Charles could not accept the fact that three murders were committed in North Fork Harbor without one person being brought to justice.

Not being able to think of anything else at the time, St. Charles sat at his desk, took a sheet of paper and drew a vertical line down its center. On the left side he listed everything that went wrong with the Lambrusco investigation. On the right side he wrote the few positive things it produced. The positive list was admittedly short and played into Stimmel's decision. But in the space beneath it he began to note the elements of the case he did not fully understand, the questions that were not answered, people he came across in the course of the investigation and other miscellaneous items. One of those was Vin Gusto. Why was he still in North Fork Harbor? What might he know? How could he help? In his last conversation with the reporter he had alluded to charging him with investigation interference and advised him not to leave town any time soon. Could the threat of the charge against the writer be used to get him to help with the investigation?

Thorsen had just described Goode as an "egomaniac" with an "exquisite" wine collection. He also said Goode was going to be on Shelter Island this weekend, a 15-minute ferry ride from North Fork Harbor. St. Charles then recalled that the North Fork Harbor Reporter frequently published profiles of the area's more prominent summer residents in a special section, "People of Note." He wondered if Paxton Goode would agree to be interviewed by special reporter Vin Gusto. Maybe he'd like to discuss how he came to acquire his rare wine collection. St. Charles put a call into publisher Howard Gallant.

Remembering how their last meeting went St. Charles was a bit hesitant about again seeking the publisher's cooperation and was surprised when Gallant answered the phone in a friendly tone.

"Henry," Gallant said, opening the conversation. "I'm glad you called. I've had you on my mind after our last meeting. I want to apologize. I should have cooperated. I guess I just wasn't expecting to hear what I heard."

"I understand."

"We've deliberately covered the murders as minimally as possible," said Gallant. "It's against my better judgment but we're trying to keep the profile low for the sake of the business community."

"That's very nice of you," said St. Charles, clearly pleased with Gallant's cooperation and offer to mend their relationship. "I'm afraid I still need your help. I have a similar proposition with which you can redeem yourself."

"I'm listening," said Gallant.

"This is confidential, off-the-record, as the reporters say."

"Go ahead. You have my word."

"I'd like you to send Vin Gusto on a special assignment to interview a prominent businessperson and summer resident. We need your paper to provide the cover for this. You don't have to offer him a regular job at the paper. It'll only be for this one assignment. I don't want the reporter or suspect to know this is really for the police department. You'll have to set it up with the writer. In return, I'll owe you a favor."

"Like what?"

"How about I give you advance notice the next time the governor's wife comes through town on her way to the Hamptons? You know how stiff she can be."

Gallant slightly laughed at St. Charles's idea of a favor.

"I've got an idea," said Gallant. "Gusto, I hear, is dating one of our photographers, Shanin something."

"That's right," said St. Charles.

"Who's the suspect? I mean subject."

"Paxton Goode."

"Never heard of him."

"Neither has almost anyone else. He keeps a low profile. That's exactly why he'd make a good subject. Never been interviewed before."

"So now you know what makes a good interview," said Gallant only half-jokingly.

"He used to be a commodities broker," St. Charles continued. "A bachelor, he dabbles in some aspect of the international wine business. He's going to be unwinding at his Shelter Island home this weekend."

"Sounds like he shuns the spotlight. Why would he talk to us?"

"Because I have from a very good source that he's a huge egomaniac with a special wine collection. And I'll bet he reads the North Fork Harbor Reporter whenever he's out this way."

"What makes you think Gusto will take the assignment? We don't pay much and he's a city-crime writer."

"Once you make the offer to Shanin, I'll take care of Gusto," said St. Charles. "Do we have a deal?"

Gallant thought about St. Charles's offer for a moment. He did not want to remain at odds with the sergeant.

"Sure," he then said. "I'll have Emma call each of the parties and try to schedule an appointment. I'll let you know if we can make it happen for this weekend. It's very short notice. If Goode agrees, I'll call Shanin to assign her as photographer and tell her I need a good writer, someone new. I'm sure she'll suggest Gusto."

"Let me know what happens after you talk with Shanin."

"Will do."

"Thanks," said St. Charles as he hung up the phone. If Gusto could meet with Goode at his home for an interview it could be their best chance of getting a DNA sample. If it matched the fingernail fragment in the handheld computer St. Charles could move the case forward. If nothing else, it would prove that Goode had lied to Thorsen about not recognizing the handheld and erode the integrity of any information he previously provided, possibly getting him subpoenaed.

But until then, St. Charles could only wait to see if Gallant could get everything in place as they agreed he would. If he did so, he'd then tell Gusto about the need for the DNA sample, possibly using the leverage of the investigation-interference charge to further motivate the writer. And if this desperate plan didn't come together, St. Charles would have no choice but to follow Stimmel's order and effectively close the case.

/ / /

Vin Gusto was in his hotel room proofreading the final version of his Travelzonia magazine article that had been sent by special messenger to the hotel for his final review. Shanin's photographs expertly illustrated the open-ended story which left the murders unsolved. The article had been thoroughly edited by the magazine's staff—a practice writers generally don't like. Someone had noted in one of the margins that it "lacks direction" and that "readers are entitled to a conclusion." In about two weeks the issue would be on newsstands and in people's homes. Vin wondered if the murders would be solved by then, making his story even more irrelevant. Maria Lambrusco had called him earlier that day as well, inviting Vin and Shanin to the crush which would be starting in a few days. He thanked her but declined to attend, saying his work was now finished and that he needed to return home to start new assignments.

While it was good to have worked with Shanin, he wondered if he'd ever see their names together in the future. Would this be the last time he'd see her? He'd be going home to the Bronx some time the next day. He offered Shanin what he thought they each wanted earlier in the car. Maybe they were too distracted by the assignment and needed some time apart. The roundtrip train ticket he bought at Penn Station when his journey began was still in his bag and his stay at the hotel was coming to an end. Vin then took a break from proofreading to glance out the hotel window at the boats in the harbor. He had come a long way from delivering papers but wasn't satisfied, neither with his career nor his life. The North Fork Harbor assignment had taken some extraordinary twists and turns. It could have been a big opportunity for him but it did not turn out at all as he had expected. There'd be more assignments he told himself, and maybe another woman in his life one day too.

Once he was done proofreading, he'd go to the lobby and call his mom Gloria from the payphone to let her know he'd be coming back the next day. He'd take her to dinner and tell her as best he could as to what took place in North Fork Harbor. And Shanin would resume her life as well he thought. Their relationship, like his article, was without direction. People were entitled to a conclusion. Earlier that night in the car Shanin had provided the conclusion to their relationship. Vin tried to push these thoughts from his mind as he continued to proofread the article but was interrupted by the ringing of his hotel room phone.

"Hi Vin. It's me," said the voice as soon as he brought the receiver to his ear.

"Shanin? Are you okay?"

"I just got an assignment from the local paper. They need me tomorrow morning on Shelter Island to photograph some businessperson. They need a writer too. I told them I thought you could do it since you'll still be here for a few more hours. Can you?"

"Yeah, I guess, as long as I can make my train. You know how it is in North Fork Harbor, one train in and one out. I check-out tomorrow morning. I can interview him here, then write the story after I get home and e-mail it in."

"That should work."

"Okay then. Who are we interviewing?"

"Some business guy, Paxton Goode. It's for some notable-summer-residents section, a total puff piece. Maybe you can do some internet-research on him before we go. Howard, the publisher called me for this, not the editor. He said he couldn't give me any information on him but has to have it done this weekend."

"He didn't say anything about the subject? That's how this whole thing started, a rush assignment from someone named Goode."

"Howard was in a hurry. It's all very last minute. Maybe he'll e-mail me something. I'll pick you up about eight and we'll get the ferry. The paper's covering the fare and they'll mail you a check when the story runs."

Just then there was a knock on Vin's door. Vin moved the receiver from his ear and looked in that direction.

"Vin, Vin, are you there?" he could hear Shanin's voice coming from the receiver.

"Yeah. Sorry I was just double-checking the train schedule. Eight would be great." There was a second series of knocks. "Let me finish proofing this article. By the way, your photos really make the piece look great," he said.

"Bring the proofs with you tomorrow. I'd love to see them."

"Will do. I'll see you tomorrow morning. Thanks," Vin said. He then hung up the phone and went towards the door.

"Gusto," the voice called from the other side of the door. "If you're inside open the door. It's Sergeant St. Charles."

Vin recognized the voice and partly opened the door.

"What's this about?" asked Vin, not allowing St. Charles to enter the room. "You'll be pleased to know I'm leaving tomorrow. My assignment here is done."

"That's not why I'm here. Now are you going to let me in or what?"

"As soon as you tell me what you want."

"It's not what you think," said St. Charles.

Vin fully opened the door and stepped aside. He watched St. Charles cross the room and stand by the window overlooking the harbor. Vin collected the large proof sheets for his article which were hanging over the sides of the small desk and placed them in his bag.

"This isn't such a bad place," St. Charles said with his back to Vin, admiring the harbor's evening view.

"You're not here to discuss the accommodations," said Vin. "You told me to lay low and I have. I'm not showing you the article if that's what you want. It's the magazine's property now."

"That's not why I'm here."

"Then what is it?"

"I thought you might be able to help us."

"That depends."

"On what?"

"On whether you're going to try to send me to jail."

"Have you been charged?"

"Is that why you're here?"

"Gusto," said St. Charles, taking a deep breath and facing Vin. "We each want the same thing."

"My job's done Sergeant. Once I return the proofs to my editor the magazine will be sent to the printer. I'll be on the train to New York City tomorrow."

"What about your lady friend?"

"That's over too," sighed Vin. "Every story comes to an end."

"I don't believe you," said St. Charles. "You want to know who's behind these murders. You don't want to leave your lady friend. You could've left days ago but you didn't."

"You told me not to go too far Sergeant."

"Now I'm here to offer you a choice Gusto. You can leave or you can listen."

Like a good reporter, Vin nodded as he sat on the edge of the bed, his gaze fixed on St. Charles.

CHAPTER 40

The Wine Before the Storm

"I understand you and your lady friend have an assignment tomorrow morning on Shelter Island," said St. Charles. "What I'm about to say does not leave this room under any circumstances. We tell no one. Agreed?"

"Okay Sergeant. I trust you," he lied.

St. Charles took a breath and standing with his hands on his hips, faced Gusto. "You're going to interview Paxton Goode tomorrow," he said.

Vin nodded.

"What do you know about him?"

"Nothing. I was going to try to research him on the internet tonight. Why?"

"I don't care what you do or how you do it but I need you to get a sample of Goode's DNA tomorrow."

Vin continued to stare at St. Charles. It was an outrageous proposition.

"You're not serious are you?"

St. Charles silently nodded while returning Vin's stare. He knew then that St. Charles was serious.

"And what about the investigation-interference charge?" Vin continued.

"All you have to do is get something with biological evidence."

"What?"

"If he's eating or drinking you can take the utensil or cup. If there's mail ready to go out, offer to drop it at the post office. Go into the bathroom, get a toothbrush, scrap of used dental floss. Search the hamper for soiled underwear or a dirty sock. Find a comb or brush with some hair stuck in it."

"I'm a reporter, not some DNA thief."

"We're each trying to finish the same story."

"You didn't answer my question about the interference charge."

"I never intended to charge you. I thought it would be a good excuse for you to stay in North Fork Harbor and spend more time with your lady friend."

Vin rose from the edge of the bed and paced back and forth across the room. He had difficulty believing St. Charles's last few statements. "This is one of the most unbelievable conversations I've ever had," he said with his back to St. Charles.

"Too bad you swore never to repeat it," St. Charles said with a small smile.

"How do you know you can trust me?"

"I don't, just like you don't know if you can trust me. What if I come back later with a warrant after I said I wouldn't?"

"You like cornering people, don't you?"

"I hate unfinished business but I like bringing criminals to justice. They usually need to be cornered before that can happen. A DNA sample would let us know for sure if Goode's involved in the Lambrusco murders."

"I was originally assigned this story by an editor named Patricia Goode. Any connection?"

"Probably just a coincidence," said St. Charles. "You were free to leave North Fork Harbor despite what I said. I wasn't going to charge you although I could have, still can. Someone's literally getting away with murder. If you have the ability to help solve a crime, help justice be served, than you're morally obligated to do so. I'd appreciate if you'd return the favor."

Vin had always had an uneasy relationship with law-enforcement officials. Growing up in the Bronx enabled him to see the regularly shifting alliances that frequently took place between the guilty and those charged with pursuing them.

"A minute ago I accepted your word. Now you accept mine," continued St. Charles who still was not sure if Vin would help him.

"You realize this is a totally outrageous offer," said Vin as he approached St. Charles.

"That's right but that's still my offer," he added. "We've had some pretty outrageous crimes here. Now what's your answer?"

Vin took a deep breath while staring at St. Charles. Working with the police made him uncomfortable—it compromised his journalistic sense of honor. But like St. Charles, he did not like the idea of someone getting away with murder. He thought of Maria Lambrusco and her right to justice. He thought of the good-natured Vincent Tucker and the LaBroom family. Vin thought of his own family and when he lost his father while he was still a boy delivering newspapers.

"You'll have your DNA tomorrow. Have someone meet me on the North Fork Harbor side of the dock when I get off the ferry."

"It'll be Officer Jeffrey Jonah. You can't miss him. He's our six-footer."

"I know who he is. He spied on us at a restaurant one night."

St. Charles smiled again.

"He'll be dressed as a tourist reading the North Fork Harbor Reporter on a bench near the dock. Whatever you come back with hand to him and keep walking."

"After that I'm going straight to the train and heading home."

"You're a confident young man."

"It's all a question of motivation," he said.

"You might've made a good cop."

"Maybe but I prefer delivering the news. If you ever solve this give me a call."

"Better yet, I'll come to the city and take you to dinner."

"No thanks. This is risky enough. I can't afford to be seen socializing with a police officer. It can hurt my integrity. A call will do."

"Fair enough. Any questions?"

"There's no chance Shanin can get hurt tomorrow. She has no idea about any of this, does she? She won't be in any danger, will she?"

"No. Goode's not the type to soil his hands. He can afford to pay others to do the dirty work. You won't have to worry about anything like that," said St. Charles. "Don't forget to ask about his wine collection. That should get the conversation started."

They shook hands one more time and as Vin closed and locked the door behind St. Charles he could not help but wonder if he made the right decision. He then looked around his hotel room. Vin had not brought much with him so there was very little to pack. Although the conversation with St. Charles had left him exhausted, he began an internet search on his next subject but like when he tried to find information on Dr. Lambrusco, Vin came back with very little. He found a small photo on Goode's employer's website plus some brief notes on his education and professional background, not much upon which to build a compelling story. But what was his priority—to interview the subject or steal a DNA sample? At this point he could not be sure. Vin then decided to finish checking the proofs the next day on the train back to New York City before taking a shower and falling into bed.

/ / /

It was early the next morning when Officer Nick Krupcheski received a telephone call from Sergeant Henry St. Charles.

"Nicholas," the Sergeant called. "Don't act like you're sleeping. Fishermen are early risers."

"Hi Sarge. I ain't a fisherman. I'm a cop, remember? What's up?" he groaned, still in bed.

"What are you doing today?"

"I'm stamping permits for the Potato Festival."

"No you're not."

"I ain't?"

"We're going fishing today."

"What?"

"Don't wear your uniform. Come in fishing clothes with a hat, sunglasses and binoculars. Pack your police gear in a separate bag. I've got the bait and tackle. Meet me at the public docks at 7. I'll be at the far end of the dock in a small open boat."

"Sarge, I drove past the ferry terminal before. Cindy's car was gone. Then I went past her apartment but the car wasn't there."

"I'll have Jonah start searching around town for her. Anything else?"

"Are you bringing lunch?"

St. Charles did not answer Krupcheski's last question. He had already hung up the phone. Nicholas looked at the clock. It was 6:15. He'd have to hurry.

St. Charles kept a small, open boat and outboard motor on a trailer behind his home. He chose to take this instead of the police boat because he and Krupcheski would be on an undercover operation. They would be anchored in Peconic Bay, about 100 hundred yards off Goode's back lawn while Vin and Shanin conducted their interview. When they'd reach their position, the Shelter Island Ferry Terminal would be to their west and Goode's home would be to their east. St. Charles would explain the purpose of their assignment to Krupcheski while they pretended to be fishing.

/ / /

Vin had gotten to the lobby a few minutes early the next morning to call his mother and let her know he planned to be coming home that evening.

"That'll be great. I've missed you," she said. "How did the trip go?"

"Pretty unbelievable Mom. Nothing like what I expected. I'm looking forward to seeing you too. I can't talk long now. I'm waiting for a ride."

"One thing before you go."

"Sure."

"Those grapes I found outside your apartment. Ever get any idea on where they might have come from?"

"Never heard another thing about them. You?"

"No. Nothing. The super thinks someone dropped them but they were weird-looking, so small and dark. Not like any grapes you'd see in the supermarket."

"You didn't eat any, did you?"

"No. You know I won't touch anything that hits that floor. I'll see you tonight. And Vinnie, be careful by the water."

She was the only one who called him Vinnie. He gently smiled when she did so.

"Bye Mom. See you later," he said, hanging up the phone. He looked at the clock over the lobby counter. It was exactly eight o'clock. He turned to see Shanin stop her car in front of the Crashing Sea Gull Inn. Vin went to join her through the lobby door. He was carrying the same worn duffel bag he had when he first came to North Fork Harbor. Before entering the car he looked towards the sky. Dark clouds were forming over the western edge of the bay.

"This turn of events must've come as a surprise?" remarked Shanin as Vin entered the car. "Guess you were hoping you could sleep late this morning."

"You have no idea," he said.

"Look Vin, this may be the last time we work together. Let's make it a good one."

"We'll keep it professional," he said. "As always."

"Get any information on this guy?" asked Shanin as she began driving towards the ferry terminal.

"Very little," said Vin. "I poked around on the internet but just got basic bio and business background. He's a wine collector."

"How'd you know that?" asked Shanin.

"I don't know," shrugged Vin, trying to cover his slip.

"Was it listed under hobbies or something?"

"I don't remember. Too much has happened on this trip," said Vin. "I hope he's not a difficult interview. How long 'til the ferry terminal?"

"Vin," said Shanin. "The whole town's only a few miles wide. It never takes more than 15 minutes to get anywhere around here."

"How long's the ferry ride?"

"Again, only about 15 minutes to cross the channel, depending on the currents, tide, wind speed etc. I heard it's a little rough out there today."

Shanin was wearing her photographer's jacket with the oversized patch pockets and the shirttails which hung over her faded jeans. Vin had not seen her in that since their New York City days.

"That jacket you're wearing brings back memories."

"It's still too big for me but it works with the kind of wind we're having today."

"For a guy who can barely swim I'm certainly spending a lot of time around water."

"You grew up in the shadows of the Throgs Neck Bridge. You okay?"

"Didn't sleep well. Want to be sure I get my train, that's all. I checked-out of the hotel."

"You'll be fine. The station's right down the road. You can walk to it from the terminal once we get back. But you already knew that. It's the station you came in on. Before you know it you'll be back in the city, 24-hour diners, calls to cover big stories in the middle of the night, the rush to meet the morning-edition deadline."

Vin remained quiet despite Shanin's exciting description of city life. While it offered action, returning to the city also meant a cramped apartment, erratic assignments, unreliable pay and life without Shanin. When they reached the terminal she steered her car on line behind the few other vehicles planning to board the vessel for the 15-minute ride across the narrow Peconic Bay channel separating North Fork Harbor from Shelter Island. Vin then reached into his bag and removed the article proof sheets he had been reviewing the previous night.

"You can see your photos on the proofs," he said to Shanin. He then spread the sheets across the car's small dashboard and they reviewed them together for the duration of the ride across the channel with Vin periodically looking out the car window, watching the westerly wind create haphazard patterns as it whipped across the water's surface. Unlike the first time they visited Shelter Island, the waters were not calm and they could feel the waves banging sharply against the sides of the ferry.

"It's a shame we don't know who's behind this," said Shanin as they came to the end of the ferry ride.

"Be careful what you wish for," said Vin as he folded the sheets and returned them to his bag. "I'll finish the proofreading on the train ride back. I should have more than enough time then." Vin could not concentrate during the ferry ride. All the while he was thinking how to get a DNA sample for St. Charles.

Shanin had no trouble finding the home of Paxton Goode and in less than 15 minutes they were at the edge of his long driveway, overlooking a summer home that was more like a small mansion.

"What's this guy do again? asked Shanin.

"I'm not sure," said Vin. "But whatever it is he must do it well. Let's try to start before a security guard or some other household help hassles us. Why don't you walk around the perimeter? Take some exterior shots and then join me inside."

Shanin nodded and parked the car at the end of the long driveway. The house had a large front lawn ringed by gigantic rose bushes, a few sporting faded blossoms, a sure sign that the end of summer was approaching. Vin watched the thick rose bushes wave back and forth as the wind was blowing hard on the Shelter Island side of the channel. Holding his hand above his eyes and squinting, Vin could see that a floating wooden dock was connected with rope lines to a long, wooden ramp that led to a bulkhead rimming the other end of the property which did not end until it met the pristine waters of Peconic Bay.

"Crushed clamshell," Shanin said when they stepped out of the car.

"What?"

"That's what we're standing on. This driveway's covered with crushed clam shells. They used to commercially harvest and process clams and oysters here. They used the shells for stuff like lining driveways."

"Thanks for the tip. I'll try to work it into my notes," said Vin. "I'm surprised no one's come to greet us."

"Maybe the help's off for the weekend," said Shanin. "Doesn't matter. I'm sure we're on camera."

"I'm going to try the front door," said Vin.

"If no one's going to escort us around the premises I'm going to start my shooting down by the dock. The light there's perfect now. See you in a bit."

"Wait for me," said Vin. "You shouldn't go down there alone with this wind. There may be a storm coming. You can wind up in the bay."

"I've been around this bay nearly my whole life," said Shanin waving Vin off. "I can handle myself. Try to locate Goode. You're the one with the train to catch."

Shanin then turned and walked towards the bay-side of the property while Vin walked up the steps and across the wide front porch before knocking on the door. He waited but there was no answer. He knocked again but still received no response. Vin stepped back and looked around. The wooden porch was long and wrapped around the entire front of the house. The property was very clean and meticuously maintained. He walked to each end of the porch but saw no one. Vin looked out onto the bay. Two fishermen were in a small, open boat anchored not far off Goode's property. Not a good day to be on the water in a small boat with this wind thought Vin who then wondered if he and Shanin got their appointment time right before deciding to knock on the front door one more time. When no one answered he put his hand on the door knob, gently turning it. The heavy, wooden door easily swung open, revealing a huge living room complete with ornate, period furnishings such as overstuffed chairs and couches, a plush red carpet, a gigantic chandelier and shelves filled with various antiques and wine paraphernalia, such as gigantic bottles, decorated goblets, oversized glasses stuffed with flowers and posters promoting French, Spanish and Italian wines. Vin stood in the entranceway, the front door still open behind him.

"Hello," he called. "Anyone home?"

When there was no response he repeated the call. Again he received no response. Vin then took one step into the room while continuing to survey the surroundings in silence. He scanned the perimeter of the room. On the opposite end, between large windows that provided an unobstructed view of Peconic Bay, was an opened doorway. Without taking another step further Vin peered into the open doorway. "Hello," he called in the direction of the doorway. Vin then looked down. The red carpet ended at the same entranceway. He could see at that point that the floor turned to wood. When he looked further he saw what he thought to be the underside of a man's shoe pointing upwards. Vin peered further and thought he saw another shoe pointing in the same direction. "Oh no," he said. Vin approached the entranceway and looked down into the next room. He then noticed something else, so forceful it caused Vin to lean back and blink at what he saw. He could not believe his eyes. Lying on his back was a man Vin thought he recognized from the small photo he found on his computer screen the night before. It was the seemingly lifeless body of Paxton Goode. Vin took a deep breath before crouching down on one knee. Next to the body he placed his palm on Goode's motionlesss chest. But as he did so, Vin could not help but stare at the victim's face. His mouth was stuffed with grapes.

Remembering what had happened at the winery, Vin did not want to further touch the body and stepped back from it. But even while looking down, he could see that the vicitm's skin still retained some color, indicating Goode was probably not dead for very long. Vin needed a telephone and was breathing heavily as he stepped out of the room to call Sgt. St. Charles.

Chapter 41

Red Like Wine

Vin scrambled across the living room until he found a telephone. Picking up the receiver he dialed 9-1-1. Before his call could be answered he heard a woman scream. Looking out one of the oversized windows he could see Shanin struggling on the dock. Held from behind by someone wearing a ski mask, their arm was around Shanin's throat. Her camera was lying on the dock. Vin dropped the receiver, ran out the front door and around the house in the direction of the dock. Without stopping he continued across the lawn and down the wooden ramp that led to the long dock that extended out over the deep waters of the bay. But Vin had to come to a sudden stop at the end of the ramp. It had become separated from the floating dock, leaving about a five-foot chasm. Only one thin line that somehow had not been removed, was keeping the dock and everything on it from being swept into the bay. In between was nothing but water. As he stopped, a few bits of dirt fell into the bay and were instantly swept eastward by the steady current. Only by wildly waving his arms and twisting his body was Vin able to keep himself from falling into the water.

"Stay where you are!" yelled the person who was holding Shanin.

Vin took a step backwards and instinctively raised his hands, plams turned outwards. "What do you want?" he asked.

"I want you out of here! Out of North Fork!"

Vin thought he recognized the female voice.

"Let her go!" Vin yelled in response. He then knelt down to pull on the remaining line holding the dock. "Let her go or I'm coming to get her!"

"Drop the line. Not a step further," she commanded. She then revealed her free hand. In it was a hypodermic syringe, the needle's clean, steel tip shimmering in the sharp sunlight.

"Do what she says Vin," yelled Shanin. "This stuff's got a five-minute kill time."

Vin stopped and again raised his palms into the air, trying to buy time for Shanin. The sudden roar of an outboard motor then ripped through the wind. Shanin's attacker turned to see the small open fishing boat that Vin had earlier spotted bouncing over the waves and headed in their direction. Before she could turn back Vin quickly reached down and yanked the thin line that was keeping the dock from drifting into the bay. The line snapped. In just seconds Shanin and her attacker would be drifting into the bay. Vin took a few steps back. He then ran and leapt onto the dock. Vin fell forward, his impact combined with the increasing waves and wind, violently shook the dock. Taking advantage of the chaos, Shanin twisted her waist and shoved a sharp elbow into the underside of her attacker's rib cage. She then spun to her side and horizontally extended her free arm, delivering a blow to the attacker's opposite side. Then, using two hands, Shanin grabbed her attacker by the wrist which still held the hypodermic and twisted it. Vin, who had gotten to his feet, then grabbed Shanin's camera and quickly slipped the strap around the attacker's neck, pulling and twisting it until she fell to her knees, dropping the hypodermic which began bouncing towards the edge of the dock.

"Get that!" Vin yelled to Shanin who dove across the dock to save the syringe from falling overboard. A large wave then crashed into the dock, knocking Shanin over its side and into the bay. The same wave knocked Vin and the assailant to their knees but Vin held onto the camera strap with one hand, still increasing the pressure, further weakening her and forcing her to gasp for air. With his free hand he tossed the line to Shanin but the wind blew it far out of her reach. She had no lifevest and the current was quickly taking her eastward towards a rock pile that extended out from the shoreline. The fishing boat was approaching with St. Charles now standing in its bow displaying his police badge in one hand and a small grappling anchor in the other. Krupcheski was in the stern, expertly working the outboard motor to manuever the light boat against the wind and waves in an attempt to reach the drifting dock. Vin knew from when he was a boy sailing boats around the treacherous Bronx waters that the current and wind would not permit the light police boat to safely navigate around the sharp rocks that Shanin was quickly approaching. Vin then let go of the camera strap and jumped into the water in pursuit of Shanin who was struggling to fight the wind, waves and current, each of which had seemingly combined to violently sweep her into the rock pile.

St. Charles then boarded the unrestrained dock which was quickly heading into the choppy bay waters. "Don't move," he ordered. "You're under arrest." St. Charles then secured the line to a cleat before tossing the small anchor into the bay. As he had been ordered, Krupcheski then aimed the boat in the direction of Vin and Shanin, leaving St. Charles alone to subdue the still-masked attacker who had retreated to the dock's opposite corner. Neither had secure footing on the still wobbling dock.

"You're under arrest," said St. Charles. "Cooperate. There's no place to go. Don't make things worse for yourself."

As the attacker's hands were raised in an apparent surrender, St. Charles moved forward with the handcuffs. As St. Charles extended the handcuffs and began reciting the Miranda rights, the suspect suddenly extended a foot, pressing a sharp heel into St. Charles calf, stinging his lower leg and causing him to lose balance. The attacker then reached towards his waist, pushing him down before climbing over his chest, trying to wrestle his gun from its holster. St. Charles however, was able to overpower the attacker, freeing himself. The attacker however rose first to lunge again at St. Charles who this time, quickly stepped to the side before turning and delivering a strong blow that landed between the shoulder blades. St. Charles then grabbed one slim wrist and twisting it behind the attacker's back, slapped a handcuff over it in one seemingly quick and singular motion. He then grabbed the other and did the same. "Take a seat," he then ordered, and with one hand on each shoulder and a foot discretly placed behind an ankle, forced his now bound attacker to the deck.

Further east Vin was struggling to stay afloat as he strained to reach Shanin. The waves were now pounding his chest, arms and legs. Vin felt the cold saltwater rush over his face and enter his mouth and nose, briefly but repeatedly knocking him below its surface. He continuously fought back, wildly swinging his arms to reemerge in what had become a race to reach Shanin before she hit the rocks. In the distance he could see her now limp body twisting over and under the waves. Then, with the force of a wave that suddenly rose behind him, Vin was thrust forward. He closed his eyes and extending his arms outward, a few seconds later felt something soft on his fingertips. He reached further and grabbed Shanin by her loose jacket, pulling her weakened body towards him. They were now in dangerously shallow water, only a few yards from the rock pile, just ahead of the waves' breaking point. Shanin was barely conscious as Vin, who was now able to stand, turned her onto her back. Two lifevests then splashed onto the water next to them. They had been shot from a special airgun by Krupcheski who was piloting the open boat about 100 yards behind them. One of the vests had a line attached to it. Vin slipped it around Shanin's arms and neck before securing it by closing the snaps. He slipped the other one over his own neck but kept it undone. Then with the back of her head resting in the palm of his hand, Vin lightly pinched Shanin's nose closed with his fingertips and breathed into her mouth. She did not respond. Vin took another deep breath and tried again. Still no response. Vin removed his hand from the back of her head. There were spots on his fingers and palm. They were red like wine. Vin rubbed the back of her head again and then looked at his hand. Shanin was bleeding from the back of her head. He again ran the palm of his hand around the back of her skull. There was a slight bump on the base of her head. Vin then slipped the palm of his other hand under the lifevest, placing it onto her chest but could not feel anything. He then breathed one more deep breath into Shanin's mouth. When he finished he lifted his head back and watched for a reaction, any reaction. "C'mon Shanin. You can do this," he said. Then with one hand supporting her back he sharply pressed the palm of his other into the center of her abdomen. "C'mon Shanin," he again cried. In a few seconds she spit out a mouthful of water. Still gasping, Shanin's eyes then slightly opened and she started to steadily breathe. Vin then signaled to Krupcheski who began towing in the line with Shanin at its end. A few minutes later Krupcheski pulled Shanin into the boat, helping her to lie down amid a pile of lifevests and covering her with a blanket before giving Vin a "thumbs up" signal. Vin then climbed onto one of the rocks in the pile and began walking across them towards the shore but not without first stopping to look out to the dock. There he saw that St. Charles had subdued Shanin's attacker. With hands cuffed and ski mask removed, the suspect was kneeling at the foot of the dock which had finally stopped drifting eastward in the rough sea thanks to the anchor. Vin had to squint before he could recognize the somber face of Cindy Murphy. Vin then turned and watch Krupcheski pilot the boat to the dock and toss a line to his Sergeant. Once the line was secured and the anchor hoisted, Krupcheski, despite being stunned by the attacker's identity himself, dutifully towed the dock carrying his Sergeant, their key suspect and an injured photographer back to Goode's bulkhead.

When they reached Goode's property they were met by a handful of North Fork Harbor police and emergency personnel who had responded to Vin's 9-1-1 call. Tracing the call to Goode's residence they were ready to assist. Cindy was immediately escorted into the back of a police car and taken to a holding cell where she would later be interrogated and charged. Shanin, who was now conscious, received treatment for mild injuries and was going to be taken to a hospital for observation. Vin walked up to the back of the ambulance where she was lying on a stretcher.

"Never thought I'd see you on one of these," said Vin, trying to smile. "Want me to take your picture?"

"No thanks," she said, slightly smiling at Vin while extending her fingertips towards him as her arms were strapped onto the stretcher. She had bandages on the back of her skull and forehead. Purple bruises dotted her face and neck. Vin loosely held her fingers in his hand.

"Vin," she said, nodding downward with her chin. "Cover your hand with something and carefully go into the pocket by my waist. Go slow. Be very careful."

Vin covered his hand with a spare cloth he found on the side of the ambulance and slowly reached into her jacket pocket.

"You got it," he said removing the hypodermic needle Cindy had dropped on the dock. He was holding it between his thumb and index finger. "I don't believe it."

"I was so focused on getting the needle I fell into the bay."

"But you got it. You're amazing," said Vin before tearing a page from his notebook and wrapping the needle in it.

"So are you," she said. "For a guy who can barely swim you probably saved my life."

"If it wasn't for me you wouldn't have fallen into the bay."

"If it wasn't for me you wouldn't have come to North Fork Harbor."

Shanin may have sustained a slight concussion remarked one of the EMS workers who was now standing next to Vin while looking down at Shanin who was in otherwise stable condition.

"Can I give him this? It's not a good idea to bring personal stuff to the hospital," the EMS worker asked Shanin. She nodded and he handed her bag to Vin.

"Say goodbye 'cause we've got to get to the hospital," the EMS worker then said.

"How's she doing?" asked Vin.

"Pretty stable," the EMS worker replied. "They'll probably keep her overnight."

Vin leaned over and kissed Shanin on her bandaged forehead.

"I'll see you later," Vin said as the EMS worker loaded the stretcher into the back of the ambulance before slamming its rear doors closed. Vin watched the ambulance wind its way down Paxton Goode's long, crushed-clamshell driveway. The perimeter of his large house had been sealed with yellow police tape. Various police personnel were scurrying about, photographing, dusting and taking notes of the surroundings. Vin then saw St. Charles who was standing next to one of the police cars talking with Krupcheski.

"I've got something for you," said Vin as he approached the two officers. He placed the folded sheet of paper on the hood of the police car. "Be careful opening it," he advised.

The two officers watched closely as St. Charles unfolded the paper.

"Where'd this come from?" asked St. Charles.

"The photographer recovered it," he said. "Chasing that needle probably caused her to fall into the bay. She gave it to me just before she left in the ambulance."

St. Charles slid his hand under the sheet of paper and carefully gave it to Krupcheski. "Get this in the evidence file," he said. "Thanks," he then said, turning towards Vin.

"Think you got your suspect?" asked Vin.

"Why don't you check with me in the morning?" asked St. Charles, nodding his head in the direction behind Vin. Two men in suits were approaching. Vin took this as a sign to make his exit.

"The first thing I did," said Dionasis when he and Thorsen reached St. Charles, "was to reach under the victim's shirt. I felt with my fingertip and knew right away that it was the same as the others. It was a slight bump, a small reddish abrasion about the size of a mosquito bite, almost perfectly in the center of the victim's chest. Then I swabbed the inside of his cheek. I estimate Goode was dead for a little better than an hour so I was able to take a DNA sample. It's on its way to the lab for a rush analysis."

"It's a different killer," said St. Charles.

"How do you know?"

"This time the grapes were plastic."

Krupcheski then returned and the four men became quiet as each surveyed the scene that had just taken place around them. After a few seconds, Thorsen broke the silence.

"That woman you just had taken into custody is probably going to need some time before she's ready to talk."

"What are you saying?" asked St. Charles.

"I smell a Greek dinner," said Thorsen.

"There's a Hellenic place almost on the tip of the North Fork I've been meaning to try," added Dionasis. "I've heard from a trusted source they make a good *tiropita lamia.*"

"A good what?" asked St. Charles.

"It's a traditional dish of feta cheese, scallions and bacon."

"Bacon?" repeated Krupcheski.

"Nick's earned a seat at the table," said St. Charles, nodding in the younger officer's direction. "Will they take customers dressed as fishermen?"

"Sure. I know the *maitre'd.* He's my best friend's nephew."

"You're practically family," said Thorsen.

"Okay then, who's driving?" asked St. Charles.

"I am," said Thorsen. "I took a mini-van that belongs to one of my ex-wives. I had to hurry when the Doc phoned to tell me about the 9-1-1 call. We can all fit, plus she filled the tank last night. She must've gotten my check."

"How many ex-wives do you have?" asked Krupcheski.

"Nicholas, is that important?"

"I don't know Detective. I was just asking."

"Police officers just don't ask. A key part of any successful interrogation is to know which are the important questions. And never admit to a suspect that you don't know something. It's all part of an elaborate cat-and-mouse mind game. But if you're finding this to be a difficult exercise, take leave of us now, go to the station and interview the suspect," said Thorsen, placing his hand on the younger officer's shoulder. "But if you want to be like me, and not everyone can, I mean be a hugely successful detective, let some basic criminal psychology do the groundwork for you."

"I'm afraid I don't understand Sir."

"Only the lucky few can," said Thorsen with a wink towards St. Charles. "Most likely our suspect is going to be hostile and confused for a bit. We've worked hard on this case. Our Sergeant made a very daring arrest in which you played a supporting role. Why subject ourselves to the unpleasantness of what very likely will be a difficult witness? It's best if we first let her come to terms with the shock of being arrested. An hour or so in a holding cell should soften her, help her come to her senses, be more cooperable. In the meantime, while the other officers take care of the more mundane, housekeeping-type details around here, we'll enjoy a nice Greek dinner and return refreshed, ready to complete a successful interrogation. My advice to you is to follow the example set by your superior officers and don't ask any more questions unless they concern a menu item."

"Now I see Sir," he said with a smile.

"You're catching on. There's hope for you yet," said Thorsen. "Get in the car. With any luck our night's just beginning."

EPILOGUE

And Let There Be Wine

Vin watched St. Charles and the others leave soon after the ambulance left to take Shanin to the hospital. If he was going to complete his assignment for the North Fork Harbor Reporter as well as Travelzonia it would be helpful to get a quote from St. Charles, the arresting officer and lead official on the case. But that could wait he thought. There was other, more pressing business.

Vin sifted through Shanin's bag and finding her cell phone, first called Maria Lambrusco to tell her an arrest had been made. She was pleased to hear the news but Vin could also hear her slightly crying over the phone. Maria reiterated her invitation for Vin to come to the winery and promised to send him a case of that year's wine. It looked like it was going to be one of which her father would have been proud and collectors' were sending orders she said. Vin asked that Maria send it to his mother's house. Maria again thanked Vin and the two promised to stay in touch.

His next call was to Nadia Rivera.

"There's been an arrest," Vin said when Nadia came to the phone. "The story's got new life. We've got a real ending now."

"Vin you're killing me," was all she said.

"Be careful with your word choice."

"This has got to be the end. Changes at this point cost a lot of money. We'd better make up for them with sales."

"Don't worry. You'll have it tomorrow and it's going to be big," he said.

Vin made his last call for the night to his mother.

"Hi Mom. I've got to reschedule dinner."

"Are you okay Vinnie?"

"I'm fine but the photographer I was working with had a little accident. She's in the hospital."

"What happened?"

"She's going to be fine. A lot's happened on this trip."

"Some good things I hope."

"Yes, and this photographer, she's more than a photographer. I want to bring her to dinner."

"So she's someone special."

"Yeah Mom. She is. I want the two of you to meet."

"That's great Vinnie. A new Cuban place opened where McFarley's used to be. It's very pretty, lots of flowers, bright colors. My friend Darlene's the seating hostess. She'll get us a good deal. Would that be okay?"

"That sounds fine. We'll set the particulars tomorrow. I've got to go now, I'm on a deadline. Goodnight Mom."

Vin now held the keys to Shanin's car and to the small house she rented. Once the ferry returned to North Fork Harbor he made the short drive to the hospital. It was the same hospital from where he had tried to find information on Dr. Lambrusco. Vin parked Shanin's car and walked through the Emergency Room entrance. He recognized the security guard on duty.

"Hi Jimmy," he said approaching the desk.

The guard just looked at Vin from his chair. That day's edition of The New York Tattler was opened on the desk.

"Any word on Shanin Blanc? She was admitted a little while ago."

Jimmy checked the computer screen.

"You the husband?" he asked.

Vin nodded.

"Go to the second floor," he said, pointing his thumb over his shoulder in the direction of the elevator bank. "Ask at the nurses' station for the room number."

"Thanks," said Vin who then followed Jimmy's directions. Once on the second floor Vin avoided the nurses' station and instead walked the perimeter, checking names outside of doorways and peeking into rooms. Outside of one room Vin thought he heard a woman mention a newspsaper article. He looked in the doorway and recognized the nurse from the first night he had been at the hospital. She was talking to an aide. Vin looked further and saw Shanin sleeping. He remained in the doorway and waited for the nurse to finish talking. Vin then lightly tapped on the opened door.

"May I help you?" asked the nurse who turned to face him.

"Hi," said Vin softly. "I just wanted to know how she's doing."

"She's doing pretty well," said the nurse approaching Vin and ushering him into the hallway. "She's suffered a slight concussion but her vitals, pulse rate, blood pressure, temperature are okay. There was a small amount of water in the lungs. She's had a mild sedative so she should sleep through the night. There's a note here, it says no abrasions on chest. How'd this happen?"

"Boating accident," was all Vin said.

"You've got to be so careful," said the nurse, rubbing her hands together. "Your best bet would be to come back late tomorrow morning. She should be awake by then."

"Will she be discharged then?"

"Probably, after the doctor sees her and if everything's okay."

"If she wakes before I get here please tell her I came by tonight."

"I will," said the nurse smiling. "We all need someone to take care of us."

Vin watched the nurse and aide enter the next room. He then looked at Shanin from the doorway. As she was sleeping soundly he thought it would be a good time to go to her home, finish his articles and try to get a quote from St. Charles in the morning. He'd then submit the revised articles and if all else went well, take Shanin and his Mom to dinner.

///

When St. Charles returned to the police station he instructed Officer Jeffrey Jonah to bring Cindy Murphy into an interrogation room where he and Krupcheski would be waiting. Earlier she had provided her basic personal information before being fingerprinted, photographed and having the inside of her mouth swabbed for a DNA sample. Her criminal background check was negative. When Cindy arrived St. Charles instructed Jonah to remove the handcuffs and exit the room before gesturing for Cindy to take a seat on the opposite side of the small table, across from the two officers. St. Charles then reached into his briefcase which he had on the floor beneath the table and produced the handheld computer which he placed on the table. It was wrapped in a clear plastic bag with a numbered tag attached to it.

"Recognize that?" he asked Cindy.

"Yes," she said, not looking at the two men. "It was Doctor Lambrusco's."

"Something's still missing," said St. Charles. "The chip with the data."

"It's in my car," said Cindy. "In the glove box in an envelope."

"What?" asked the stunned St. Charles.

"Where's your car?"

"It's behind the church, in the parking lot. The keys are in my bag." Cindy was starting to cry.

St. Charles reached for the telephone. He called Officer Jonah and ordered him to take the keys from Cindy's bag and bring her car to the police station.

St. Charles then produced several photographs of Dr. Lambrusco taken after he was found dead in the winery. St. Charles did not say anything about them, allowing their sudden appearance to impact Cindy. He then produced photos taken at the accident/crime scene that claimed Vincent Tucker, again without saying anything.

Cindy shook her head as more tears ran down her cheeks. "Poor Tugboat," was all she could say, her face in her hands. "He didn't deserve that." Krupcheski handed her a tissue which she used to dry her face.

St. Charles then displayed several photos from when Andy LaBroom was found dead. St. Charles's subtle plan had worked. The tension was too much for Cindy to bear. Her head dropped to the table and she began to uncontrollably sob.

"Nicholas," said St. Charles, rising from his seat. "I'm going to get some water for the three of us. "Why don't you talk to Cindy?" St. Charles then left the room.

St. Charles had not given Krupcheski any instructions before the interrogation and was actually surprised the senior officer invited him to participate. Now he sensed why. St. Charles wanted to see if Krupcheski could go from small-town police officer to professional interrogator. Did he truly deserve a seat at the table with men like St. Charles, Thorsen and Dionasis or would he prefer to spend the rest of his career directing back-to-school night traffic? Krupcheski looked at Cindy who was staring at him with her large brown eyes, which had now become dry. He had known her, as well as Andy and Tugboat for nearly his entire life. Cindy was leaning across the table, continuing to stare at him. Krupcheski leaned back and took a deep breath.

"Why don't you tell me what happened?" he asked, leaning across the table.

"I took the computer chip to keep the data from those crooks," she said.

"Which crooks?"

"Goode and his corporation."

"What?"

"Last year Goode started to come by the winery. I sat outside the office. I heard their conversations. He wanted to buy the rights to the genetic code. Dr. Lambrusco refused. He tried a few times. He used to say things like: 'You're old. Why are you holding out?' One day Dr. Lambrusco asked Goode: 'When was the last time you were hungry?' They both started yelling. Goode called him crazy and stormed out of the office. I saved Dr. Lambrusco's work."

"Then what happened?"

"Goode approached Andy and offered him money for the code which was only in the handheld. Andy wanted to buy back his family's farm. It was a matter of honor for him."

"So he killed the Doc?"

"Andy hated being poor. He was so smart but unhappy his whole life. He was humiliated when his family lost the farm. His ancestors and brother are buried there."

"So why kill an old man and stuff his mouth with grapes?"

"I don't know Nick," Cindy said, shaking her head. "I told him it wasn't Dr. Lambrusco's fault. He bought the farm from the bank. I didn't know until later that Andy killed Dr. Lambrusco."

"When?"

"After Tugboat died Andy told me he was going to have a lot of money and we could get married and move to Switzerland."

"Like in the story books? And the money came from Goode?"

Cindy nodded before continuing.

"He said that's why I had to go to a Swiss bank's office in New York City. Someone there said Andy was a friend of Mr. Goode's and that I was his wife. Everything had to be secret if I wanted to be happy."

"And what about Tugboat?"

"Andy took the oil from the reporter's girlfriend's car to make it look like Tugboat had an accident."

"Was Larson involved?"

"No. Andy used to say he did his best work alone. He blamed Tugboat for his brother's death. And he dropped the grapes outside the reporter's apartment. He wanted to scare them into leaving town. That's when I knew something had to be done about Andy."

"So you killed Andy?"

Cindy nodded.

"Why didn't you come to me Cindy? Four people are dead."

"Nick," said Cindy leaning across the table. "There's $250,000 in a Swiss account."

"Is that why you went to New York when you said you were going to Boston? Where'd you stay? We were looking for you."

"I was going to go to Boston. Then I remembered the money. Thought about what to do. I went to New York but found that the account was frozen so I went to see Goode."

"And what happened?"

"He said the deal was off and was going to have the money removed from the account. I said I had the chip. He said he wouldn't give me a penny and if I didn't give him the chip was going to report everything. He didn't care that Andy, Tugboat and Dr. Lambrusco were dead. He stayed on his couch and talked to me like I was a servant. Wasn't even polite enough to look at me when he talked, ordering and threatening me. Called me a small-town tramp."

Cindy suddenly stopped talking.

"And then what?"

"I started to leave the house. I didn't know what to do. Then I thought of Dr. Lambrusco and how he wanted to help people. And I thought of how Goode took advantage of Andy and that this was all Goode's fault. And then I remembered the needle."

Cindy again stopped talking as her eyes glazed over. She appeared to enter a dream-like state. Krupcheski slipped a pen across the table in her direction. Still in a trance-like state Cindy took it between her index and middle fingers, pressing her thumb on its top.

"What about the needle?"

"I took it from my bag, went behind him and stuck him in the chest. When I went to leave I saw the fake fruit on a table. I put the grapes in his mouth."

"Why?"

"For Dr. Lambrusco."

The two childhood friends then stared at each other.

"What have I done Nick?" asked a distraught Cindy.

Not knowing what to say, Krupcheski rose and sat next to Cindy. She turned to him and placing her head on his shoulder began to sob. St. Charles then returned holding a plastic water pitcher and three paper cups. Krupcheski rose when he entered and took Cindy by the arm.

"I got it," he said to St. Charles who watched silently as Nick returned Cindy to the holding cell.

///

Vin rose early the next morning, his last day in North Fork Harbor. He spent most of the previous night trying to work on his articles but had trouble concentrating as Vin found himself mostly thinking about Shanin. He had left a message with St. Charles asking for a brief interview before submitting the final version to Nadia who had convinced the publisher to hold the presses one more time. He was staring at the computer screen which he had set up on Shanin's kitchen table when he saw a car stop in front of the house. Vin watched as an out-of-uniform St. Charles stepped from the car carrying a small brown bag.

"Hey Scoop," St. Charles said when Vin opened the front door. "I figured with your girlfriend in the hospital you could use some bad coffee." St. Charles then removed two cups of coffee in take-out cartons and handed one to Vin.

"I could use information more than coffee," said Vin, taking out his pen and notepad as the two sat at the small kitchen table.

"Cindy confessed to murdering Andy LaBroom and Paxton Goode who paid Andy to get the genetic code Dr. Lambrusco developed. Andy killed the Doc and Tugboat."

Vin shook his head, allowing himself to absorb the news.

"I got something else for you." St. Charles reached into his shirt pocket. He handed Vin a copy of Cindy Murphy's booking photograph. "It's an extra. Thought you might want it for your article."

"Thanks," said Vin.

"I don't expect any more murders in North Fork Harbor so I guess we won't be seeing you around here any longer," said St. Charles, rising from the table. "Except when you visit your girlfriend. Excuse me," he suddenly said, correcting himself. "You told me that story ended. Sorry."

"That's okay," said Vin noticing St. Charles's wedding ring. "How long have you been married Sergeant?"

"About 25 years."

"You recommend it?"

"It's not for everyone but when it works it's a beautiful thing."

The two men then shook hands and St. Charles exited. Vin began working on the revision when the phone rang. It was the call for which he'd been waiting.

"Hi Vin, it's me."

Vin was happy to hear Shanin's voice.

"How are you doing?"

"The doctor told me to take things easy so I guess I won't be going on assignment for a while," she said. "I took a few stitches in the back of my head, otherwise I'm fine. I should be checked-out by noon."

"Great," said Vin. "I can pick you up."

"Okay and thanks for coming by yesterday. Have you finished the articles?"

"I just met with St. Charles. He gave me what I needed."

"Maybe you can fill me in later."

"I've been thinking about our last conversation," said Vin before briefly pausing. "We're more than a photographer and writer. The only time our lives have direction is when we're together."

"We've got a lot to talk about," she said.

"Let's have dinner tonight. A new Cuban place opened in the Bronx. I'd like to take you there."

"All the way to the Bronx for dinner?"

"There's another reason. I want you to meet my mom."

"That would be great Vin. I'd love to."

"I'll get you about noon," said Vin. "We can go whenever you're ready."

"Okay Vin," said Shanin. "A nurse just came in. I'll see you later."

Vin then put down the receiver and returned to his work. He gave the articles one last read, took a deep breath and hit the "send" button. He then called his home answering machine to check for messages. There was a call from Patricia Goode. She'd been "let go," from Travel & Pleasure and did not understand why. Hadn't been given a reason she said but added that she was sorry about canceling his assignment and would still like to have lunch with him. Smiling, Vin shook his head and deleted the message.

Vin had come to North Fork Harbor to interview a winemaker and write a "happy" travel piece. Instead he found himself writing about four violent murders but was also able to resurrect his career and reunite with Shanin. From the small kitchen window he could see the sun's rays glistening over sparkling Peconic Bay. For the first time in a long while Vin did not concern himself with what lie ahead. He had no upcoming assignments and did not know from where his next check would come but for some reason Vin liked his odds.

The End

ABOUT THE AUTHOR

J oseph Finora, a New York City native, lives on Long Island's North Fork with his family. A fulltime writer, he's written thousands of articles, numerous speeches and one off-off-Broadway play. He is a graduate of Fordham University and Hunter College. Also an amateur winemaker and grape grower, this is his first mystery.

CPSIA information can be obtained at www.ICGtesting.com
Printed in the USA
LVOW06*1446110514

385311LV00002B/4/P